Alena

Also by Rachel Pastan

Lady of the Snakes

This Side of Married

Riverhead Books
a member of Penguin Group (USA)
New York
2014

Alena

RACHEL PASTAN

RIVERHEAD BOOKS
Published by the Penguin Group
Penguin Group (USA) LLC
375 Hudson Street
New York, New York 10014

USA • Canada • UK • Ireland • Australia
New Zealand • India • South Africa • China

penguin.com
A Penguin Random House Company

Library of Congress Cataloging-in-Publication Data

Pastan, Rachel.
Alena : a novel / Rachel Pastan.
p. cm.
ISBN 978-1-59463-247-1
1. Art museum curators—Fiction. 2. Women—Fiction. 3. Cape Cod (Mass.)—Fiction.
4. Psychological fiction. I. Du Maurier, Daphne, 1907–1989. Rebecca. II. Title.
PS3616.A865A43 2014 2013030316
813'.6—dc23

Printed in the United States of America
1 3 5 7 9 10 8 6 4 2

Book design by Meighan Cavanaugh

For Anna and Bess

It was as though she who had arranged this room had said: "This I will have, and this, and this," taking piece by piece from the treasures in Manderley each object that pleased her best, ignoring the second-rate, the mediocre, laying her hand with sure and certain instinct only upon the best.

—Daphne du Maurier, *Rebecca*

Dying
Is an art, like everything else.

—Sylvia Plath, "Lady Lazarus"

1.

Last night I dreamed of Nauquasset again. It was dusk. Somewhere beyond the scrubby hills, full of brambles and beach plums and pine trees bent and twisted by the sea wind like old men, the sun was going down over the bay. From where I stood on the sandy shoulder of the two-lane highway I couldn't see it, but I could feel the damp chill take hold of the afternoon. The light faded from clear gold to misty gray, the way everything fades there: the shingled houses, and the wooden docks, and the leathery skin of the Cape Cod women who live their lives in an abrasive broth of salt and sun. Whose brows furrow early from so much squinting against the light.

There I stood on the edge of the road, blue-black asphalt holding the heat. I could smell the tar melting, smell the pines and the brine of the sea, the restless, pungent, ever-present sea, primordial source of life and cause of so much death: floods and riptides, shipwrecks and suicides. Suddenly the gates began to swing from the two great weathered posts, the lovely gates by Simeon Wexler that Bernard commissioned right at the beginning. Each plank of silvery wood was carved with reliefs of animals, stratum by stratum: starfish and conch along the bottom, fish in the row above, deer and foxes, cats and porcupines at chest level, and along the top, six feet up, the birds of the local woods and seashore, ospreys, finches, swallows, and sandpipers, along with many other species I didn't recognize. I was never much of a naturalist, having early on turned my eye to art. (Though this has changed in recent years, along with so much else, so that today I can follow a path up a Napa hillside and turn to note a swallowtail butterfly or a red-shafted flicker, and even Bernard can be persuaded to admire a hummingbird balanced in midair above the swaying bee balm in his own small garden.)

Those gates were the first thing I loved about Nauquasset, the first night Bernard brought me there, and in the dream I was jubilant at seeing them again. I put out my hand, half to run my fingers along the contours of an alert field mouse carved into the wood and half to push open the gate. But as I touched it, I saw that the shadows had tricked me. The gate sagged, splintered and defaced, from weary posts held together with iron chains. I cried out in sorrow even as—it being a dream—I passed like water through the barrier and found myself on the other side, walking, as I had so many times, up the rutted lane.

The first quarter mile or so was paved, though the color of the old asphalt had faded to a pale gray. Cracks and potholes fragmented the surface so that it looked in the gathering dusk like a road of rippled water cutting through the pale scrub and dune grass and poison ivy, like a mockery of the bright path moonlight makes on the bay. Then abruptly the shattered pavement ended and the lane changed to crushed shell glinting white against the dull beige of the sand. Even when the Nauk was at its peak, the lane, rising and falling among the dunes, was kept primitive and rough like most of the roads leading out to the bay. When it rained, huge muddy puddles gaped, and visitors in BMWs skirted them gamely—or else wished they'd thought to take their Range Rovers instead. Even in fine weather the pricey underbellies bumped and scraped, and sand got into the upholstery. Repeat visitors learned to leave their cars in the dirt lot by the road and walk. The way rose and fell, rose and fell. After the second rise you could hear the sea. It poured itself onto the breast of the shore and then drew back—gave itself and drew back. It would not stay, and it would not keep away, so that the unhappy shore could never possess, could never forget. Or maybe it was the shore's pale indifference that drove the sea wild, so that every so often she whipped herself into a hurricane or a nor'easter, wreaking her vengeance indiscriminately. Just so, an artist, ignored too long by a callous world, may break into brilliance, or flame up into cynical stuntsmanship, or drop herself like a stone down the dark well of despair.

Once contained by gardeners and muscled maintenance men, the scrub was growing wild. Long arms of bayberry reached in every direction, and the thick trunks of the low pines were as wide around as a man could reach. The sprawling, spreading brush encroached on the road, and the arrowwood and the rugosa roses had grown in my absence to a monstrous size, massing in two high walls of dense foliage. The restless wind rattled the dry leaves, and the crickets sang their elegy to summer. On I walked, my feet slipping in the sand, the grass that grew along the central hump in the lane tickling my bare legs, the sound and smell of the sea leading me on. Pinpricks of stars broke out suddenly in the sky, then were covered over by scudding clouds and strange shadows that might have been night birds or just-awakened bats. And then I rounded a bend and ascended the final rise, and there was the Nauk before me: the long shingled building with its great windows facing the sea. For half a moment time seemed to coil inward like a spring, present and past, dream and reality coming together so that I felt I was seeing the place for the first time again: its serene yet lively beauty, its strange angular shapes made almost natural by the vernacular shingle, the copper weathervane in the shape of a mermaid with a spoon and fork for arms and pert triangular breasts, pointing steadily out to sea.

Then the moon sailed out from behind the tattered clouds, and I saw that the place was abandoned. The roof was stove in, the glass shattered, even the walls blown away in places, revealing the studs and beams. The building looked like a wrecked ship sitting high up on that long dune, a rich merchant vessel perhaps, whose cargo of spices or gold had been doomed from the start.

Of course, Nauquasset has been lost to me for a long time now, if it was ever mine. It has been years since I stood looking up at its silvered shingles, its sloped roof, the blue bay and the paler blue sky beyond extending the picture, framing it, so that on a sunny day or a quiet, moonlit night you felt there could be no more peaceful place in the world.

These days Bernard and I run a little gallery in Russian Hill: estate work mostly, with a focus on the Bay Area Figurative School. Not for us any longer the drama of the living artist with her hopes and dreams, her anxieties and insecurities and unpredictable demands. We deal exclusively in the work of the dead. You can buy a moody Elmer Bischoff from us, or a tender Diebenkorn, or a bold Joan Brown. I live in a small apartment with a view of this very different bay, and Bernard has a bungalow in Sausalito. Even after all that happened, he likes to take the ferry to work. He has recovered his fondness for boats.

In the mornings I stop at the French bakery halfway up the hill and pick up café au lait and rolls, and we have breakfast together in the office before the gallery opens. Bernard has grown stouter. His head is completely silver now, and he has acquired a moustache. His resemblance to a walrus is striking, but he seems happy enough. As am I: happy enough. Happier, perhaps, than I have ever been.

If Bernard has lovers, he keeps it to himself. As for me, I have a man I see from time to time. He travels a great deal for his job, but when he's in town, he calls and I make him dinner, which we eat on my little Pacific-facing balcony, and then we go to bed. As love affairs go, it's not remarkable, but it suits me. I'm always happy when his name pops up on my caller ID, but I'm equally glad to wave good-bye in the morning and head up the hill, where Bernard will be cursing at his email. I'll look over the papers and read out to him any item of interest from the *Chronicle* or the *Times*. We particularly enjoy reading about the bad behavior of our colleagues: suspected of trafficking in suspiciously acquired art, or carrying on too public an affair with the wife of a famous painter. An article about tax fraud can cheer us for a whole morning. For ours is a world of sharks and scorpions, and we are a pair of dull, ethical fools who—everyone says so—could make a lot more money than we do. Which is no doubt true. But what would we do with more money? Bernard, after all, spent most of his life practically drowning in wealth, and I have everything I want. Truly I do. I have escaped that naïve, idealistic, anxious young woman, my former self, neurotically devoted to Art like a novice nun to God. Debasement and ambition are two sides of the same heavy coin, but I have changed currencies. I have shed my chrysalis and become—not a butterfly, but a happy moth, fluttering my brown wings peacefully through the dusk. And here is Bernard with me, though too heavy to be a fellow moth, perhaps. Make him a possum then, ambling along under the yellow moon while I flit just above his ear. It's a peaceful, pleasant, predictable life, as long as we avoid the hypnotic dazzle of the freeway lights.

And, of course, we both follow the auction prices. We keep a special eye out for those names who used to show at Nauquasset, some of which now belong to superstars within the hermetic, looking-glass world of contemporary art. And then at ten, Scarlet jangles open the door, music leaking from her earbuds, wearing something outrageous we can tut over admiringly: a low-cut sheath of fuchsia lamé, a high-necked vintage dress of patched and faded lace, a form-fitting asymmetrical jumpsuit studded with safety pins and chains. I used to think she frequented secret midnight boutiques and underground seamstresses, but now I know she buys it all on the internet. Every month or two, as well, she radically rethinks her hair, altering its color and its shape, still young enough to believe a person can actually change. Or maybe she's just enjoying herself.

Best of all is when she has a new tattoo to show us, an addition to the bright menagerie spreading across her back. We cluck and scold at the irrevocability of what she's doing to her young, beautiful body—as though that weren't exactly the point—but we always admire the work. She has a fetching, bright-faced monkey on her shoulder blade that made me take the name and number of her tattooist—tattoo artist, she says—but of course I never called. Scarlet keeps us entertained. She makes us laugh. In return, we pet her and fuss over her and give her advice to which she pretends not to listen. She's wonderful with the customers. What does she think of us, two eccentrics growing slowly older in a business better suited to the young? Does she suspect we might have once done things, wanted things—things for which we were willing to risk everything? How does she describe us to her friends, those hipster graffiti artists, vegans, performance poets, and app designers with whom she texts all day?

Probably she doesn't talk about us at all.

2.

FOR A LONG TIME when I was growing up, I thought I could do anything I wanted. I was a bright child, good at school, and my parents—well-meaning people, a farmer and a former schoolteacher—encouraged me in the belief that if I only set my mind to a goal, I could achieve it. Passion and hard work were the stars I was taught to steer by. When, in college, I announced my intention to study art history, they just nodded. My father, who had done some watercolor painting when he was young, was pleased that I was interested in art. My family assumed I would marry and be supported by my husband, so it didn't matter how much money I would make. What mattered was that I find something I loved and, of course, the right man. In this way my happiness would be assured.

Certainly I loved art history. It amazed me that sitting in a darkened room looking at slides of Madonnas and Venuses and bowls of oranges counted as work. I loved the colors, and the way forms floated in perfect balance in the picture plane. I loved the way you could trace the evolution of perspective, how it was perfected in southern Europe over centuries, and then stretched and tested and discarded over more centuries until it became a quaint anachronism, like a whalebone corset or a doublet and hose. There was no law against a man wearing hose, but you didn't catch anyone doing it. And although I was taught they didn't matter, I loved the stories of the artists: Michelangelo on his back under the Sistine Chapel ceiling, Gauguin running away to his island and dying of syphilis in self-imposed exile. Their passion sparked my passion, their imagination my imagination, their labor my labor. Because it wasn't all dreaming away in dim lecture halls, of course. I spent most of my time at my small Midwestern college in the library, and when after four years I emerged, blinking, into the light, I had a magna cum laude degree and a place in a Ph.D. program at NYU. In my whole life, I'd never been to a city larger than Milwaukee.

I decided to head out to New York early, in the middle of June. I had waitressed every summer since I was sixteen and figured I wouldn't have much trouble finding a job. A girl I knew from college, a year ahead of me, was living in Hell's Kitchen and needed a roommate. All the pieces were falling into place as though the hand of destiny were arranging them. So on a cool June day I boarded a Greyhound bus with one suitcase and a shoulder bag and three hundred dollars in twenties in a zipped pouch around my neck. Twenty-four hours later I emerged blinking once again, only this time it was into the noisy spectacle of Manhattan. How bright and alive the city looked! It was as though my whole life up until then had been one long half-dream in which thoughtful but disembodied voices had drifted through the dimness as colored images flashed by in slow succession. In that classroom—my early life—all was order, reason, gentle instruction. Even the crazed visions and terrible poverty and cultural rejection of the artists I'd studied had been tempered and mediated by time into something acceptable, digestible, dignified.

New York City was none of those things. I arrived on the first day of summer, the city in the middle of a heat wave. Sweat soaked my cotton blouse and hand-knit cardigan as I dragged my suitcase up Eighth Avenue amid the blare of cars and the rush of trains under the pavement and the jostling impatience of the crowds surging up and down the sidewalks. I passed half-naked teenaged girls with caramel skin chewing gum and laughing, wrinkled Chinese women pushing metal carts, blind men with canes, black policemen in uniforms as stiff as armor, and muscled men in skimpy nylon shorts crooning to small dogs on leashes. The air smelled of urine and of burning. A fizzing started up inside me like bubbles rising in a beer bottle when you prise off the cap. It wasn't fear. Or rather, it wasn't only fear. It was amazed delight, excitement, glee, and a thrilled, horrified prickling as though my skin were being scoured off, leaving me raw and new. The world was so much bigger and stranger than I had suspected! It made me feel that I could be bigger and stranger too.

That summer I worked at a coffee shop on Sixty-third Street, breakfast and lunch, wearing a white apron stitched with someone else's name. I took orders and poured coffee and carried trays of eggs and meatball heroes. I got bawled out by the manager and hit on by the sleazy line cook. But I didn't care. At three o'clock the apron came off and I slid away into the streets.

Art was everywhere in that blazing, blaring city. On Fifth Avenue, venerable institutions stood shoulder to shoulder, each one overflowing with beauty and strangeness from every era and culture and corner of the globe, each one a gigantic mouth swallowing entire afternoons. Again and again in those tall chambers I encountered paintings I had learned about in school—paintings about which I had written papers and exams. Each one was a surprise, a shock, full of unsuspected depth and the vibrating brashness of life, so that it was as if I'd never seen it before at all.

More extraordinary still were the encounters with the kinds of things I hadn't learned about in school, which included pretty much all art made after 1965. Some of these were paintings—vibrant and violent scribbles on gray canvases, tightly controlled boxes of color, shimmering grids, people with strange faces picnicking on beaches, photographs of lawn mowers and of tables heaped with sand—while others were three-dimensional boxes, leaning boards of colored fiberglass, neon phrases, webbed tangles of melting resin, stones hung on strings. And that was just at the museums! Galleries abounded uptown and down, common as pizza parlors. Each one had its own gravity, bright things glittering inside like fishing lures, so abundant Manhattan couldn't contain them all and they spilled out raggedly into Brooklyn and Queens. One broiling Saturday, I took the 7 train to Long Island City, where Alanna Heiss had famously transformed an old public school building into an expansive aviary of new art: rubber flowers blooming out of chaotic canvases, videos of bodies moving like shadows against white walls, typed pages of partly redacted text surrounded with pictures like contemporary illuminated manuscripts, rough sculptures of road barriers and traffic signs, orchestrated oratorios of light. I attended late-night dance performances at the Kitchen, where women in red blazed and flickered, never moving their feet, and poetry readings where words, bypassing sense, sang to me in pure sound. If what I'd seen in Elvers Hall had awakened me, these new visions took that awakened self and shook it up, seduced it, scared it, made it laugh out loud. This art unzipped me and turned me inside out. Like a snake, I shed the old rag that had been my skin.

September rolled around, but I never registered for classes. My roommate moved out but I stayed in the apartment, got another roommate. She had just moved to New York from Boston to get a master's in curatorial studies.

"Curatorial studies—what's that?"

Sadie was tall, her long blond hair very dark at the roots, a small tattoo of a sunburst on her ankle. "As in curating," she said. "The people who organize shows?"

Of course I knew what a curator was. It just hadn't occurred to me that you could go to school to become one, like becoming a doctor or an accountant. And, in fact, the idea of such a degree was fairly new. In the past, curators usually had degrees in art history but chose museum work instead of the academy. Many still do. It's possible that I might have become a curator eventually even if I hadn't met Sadie. But she certainly sped it all up for me. Six months later, I entered her program. Two years after that, I got my master's. I had hoped to stay in New York, but all of us from the program applied for the same few jobs. I didn't get one of the desirable positions in town, but I was offered a curatorial assistantship at a decent museum in the Midwest. It was a start.

My job, at what I will call the Midwestern Museum of Art, was in the contemporary department. It was not a department to which the museum gave much priority. There was a curator, a woman named Louise Haynes, who was occasionally permitted to organize an exhibition, and even less occasionally to acquire art for the permanent collection. There was a wing in the museum called the Haynes Wing, which presumably had something to do with her presence, though no one ever quite said so. I was never sure why she was given a curatorial assistant, since there wasn't much work to do. Maybe it was just that she had made a fuss and they were hoping to quiet her down. She had a loud, strident voice and a louder braying laugh and a very un-Midwestern habit of putting her hand on your arm or shoulder when speaking, holding you in place. She wasn't old, maybe fifty, but she had the look of someone held together by cosmetics and control-top panty hose, like a blowsy flower collared in a narrow vase. Not having much work to do, she spent prodigious amounts of time on the telephone doing what she called "cultivation," meaning that she spoke to wealthy art collectors who might lend to a show if a show ever materialized, or who might possibly leave their collections to the museum. "Rich people are so fragile," Louise liked to say. "They need constant attention or they wither up and die." I guess she felt that part of her job was to keep them unwithered. I could never work out how much money she had herself—a fair amount certainly, but maybe not as much as the prospects she cultivated? Certainly she was comfortable in their world. I got the feeling she didn't have to work. I suppose you could say that it was admirable she chose to. Or at least that it was interesting.

In a way, my job was to give her the attention she craved—to keep *her* from withering.

Louise had a wide and shifting circle of acquaintances who were more or less in the art world. Rich women, staff from the municipal and science museums, couples who ran fancy art galleries featuring oil paintings of the blue Mississippi. She chattered away with these people daily, gossiping and making lunch dates. I did a little filing, had slides copied, or went over to the library to xerox articles about artists she thought we might show. Every so often she drove to Chicago for a few days to look at art, and occasionally she flew out to New York. But the highlight of Louise's life was the Venice Biennale, to which the museum did not send her but which they encouraged her to attend—on her own dime—no doubt in part because it was restful having her away from the office. I started working at the museum in October, and the following spring Louise announced that she had a treat for me. She invited me into her crepuscular office, thickly hung with framed exhibition posters from her shows, and pinned-up invitations to openings, and dusty shawls, and a special rack where she kept several pairs of expensive shoes, and she announced that she was taking me with her to the Biennale.

"You've been to Venice? No? To Italy? Heavens, and you an art history major! What a crime—never to have seen the Giottos."

I felt such contradictory feelings—the thrill of the idea of Venice (Italy, travel, glamour, the Biennale) and the sting of her false sympathy that was really scorn. Dismay at all the time I would be forced to spend with Louise, dread of the obligation I would be put under, shame that I didn't have anything decent to wear. But mostly the thrill. I was twenty-five years old and I had never been on an airplane! I would have to get a passport. I would step into a gondola in the golden light and watch the fabled façades drift by. I would dazzle my eyes with the riches of St. Mark's and stroll down narrow byways overhung with flowers where a handsome Italian with a cigarette would follow me with his smoldering eyes.

And so I found myself, in the last week of June, in a small room adjoining Louise's large one in the Hotel da Silva in Venice—crowded, hot, smelly, bedazzling Venice, city of water and glass. We spent the first days of that trip in a whirlwind of parties and pavilions. Never having been to Venice—never having been anywhere—I would have liked to spend a day in St. Mark's Basilica, to visit the Accademia and the Peggy Guggenheim Collection. But of course, we were here to see the Biennale, which, along with the other exhibitions, programs, and special events that spring up in its shade every odd-numbered year, spreads its tentacles out from the Giardini and holds the city tight in the grip of glitter and celebrity.

Nothing could have prepared me for the way all of Venice was possessed by the passion for art, for the new, for the most outrageous. I had seen a lot of strange, disturbing art in New York, of course, but in Venice the work seemed bigger and stranger: giant insectlike forms hulking in marble rooms, heavy canvases thickly smeared with what looked like bloody footprints, video projections showing images of glaciers cut with bodies crowded into hovels, crystalline constructions shattering the dazzling light, monoliths made of counterfeit money, collages of naked superheroes tumbling through space. There was no quiet art in sight—no understated painting, no delicate sculpture of spun thread, no place the eye could find rest. Or maybe it was partly the crowds, the echoing cries as people greeted one another, the constant jockeying and air kissing and insincere murmuring and sizing up.

Louise knew everybody, though the compliment wasn't always returned. It wouldn't be fair to say she didn't look at the art at all, but it seemed to me she looked at it only in order to have something to say about it later. I half expected her to ask me to make the rounds of the pavilions and then type up a report to save her the effort. That would have been preferable, actually, to what she did want, which was for me to stick by her side every moment as a kind of lady-in-waiting. "This is my assistant," she'd say. "It's her first Biennale. Her first time in Italy, actually, if you can believe that! I've half a mind to send her off to Florence this very minute!"

But she never did send me. Instead, I stood in her shadow and took in what I could: names, faces, titles, styles. We went to parties with fantastic chandeliers like glowing palaces and marble buffets offering pale goblets of champagne like women's breasts and great piles of Russian caviar shining like black pearls. We spent considerably more time at parties than looking at art.

Sometimes Louise would send me off to get her another glass—not in my job description, but I was happy to go. Away from her sharp eye and her possessive talons for a few minutes, I could gawk more freely at the golden gowns with emerald ruffles that made their wearers look like great lizards, and the tiny black dresses that made their wearers look like lingerie models, and the shoes that seemed designed more for trussing pigeons or scooping eggs from their poaching baths than for moving from place to place. But if I lingered too long, I might pay when I returned, especially if the wealthy collector or museum director to whom she had attempted to attach herself like a barnacle had managed to escape.

"Lose your way?"

"There was a line."

"Having brought you all this distance, I don't think it's too much to ask you not to disappear for half an hour at a time."

"I'm sorry. It wasn't half an hour."

"It's a great opportunity I'm giving you, after all."

"It is. I'm very grateful."

"No, no, no—a great opportunity! Do you understand?" Glaring, she took the glass and sipped, her purplish lipstick staining the rim. "I would have thought a girl like you, from your background, would be thrilled to be here. Absolutely thrilled!"

It was hard to keep repeating the same assurances of gratitude. Sometimes it was better, with Louise, to change the subject.

"Who's that? The one by the pillar with the enormous—"

"Don't point." (I wasn't pointing.) "Surely even you know who that is!"

I shook my head. "Please tell me."

"Heiress to the largest railroad company in Europe. Gigantic collector! She had a long affair with the director of the Guggenheim Foundation, now they can't be invited to the same parties. And the woman in the cape, that's Gisella Bonaventuri. Oh! And that's Bernard Augustin, the one who— You must have heard that story?"

"Story?"

"He started that museum on Cape Cod, that one where the curator disappeared. The Nauquasset Contemporary Museum. Very small, a sort of vanity museum, like the Vista in Taos, or the Brant. He funds it with his own money and shows what he wants. People come from Boston, from New York. From the Hamptons and Provincetown in the summer. It was all due to her, of course—Alena. She had the eye."

"And she disappeared?"

"She was supposed to meet him right here, at the Biennale, two years ago. But she never showed up. It turned out she'd never even gotten on the plane!"

"What happened to her?"

"Nobody knows for sure. There was a tremendous search, but it turned up nothing. The presumption was that she died. She liked to swim at night, apparently. Alone. And they have terrible currents out there. The body never washed up, so nothing could ever be proved, but what else could have happened? A tragic accident!"

I couldn't help staring at Bernard Augustin, tall in his winking tuxedo, his grizzled hair razored close to his head, dark smudges, glowing faintly green like the inside of mussel shells, under his eyes. He was listening politely to a younger man with a surfer's flop of blond hair who had a hand on his arm, but at the same time I had a sense of him standing apart, as though he were alone in that crowded, noisy hall with its Carrara marble floors and dazzling chandeliers, their pendants shattering the light. "Maybe she committed suicide," I said dreamily. It seemed a more interesting and tragic scenario, swimming out with no intention of ever coming back, like the woman in *The Awakening* or James Mason at the end of *A Star Is Born*.

"What a horrible idea! There was no suggestion of that. After all, she had everything to live for." Louise goggled in Bernard's direction. "Poor man, doesn't he have a tragic look? They were very close. Friends since childhood, he and Alena. Of course, it was a bigger shock to him than to anyone. They say he's never gotten over it. Perhaps I'll just go say hello." She handed me her empty glass. "You stay right here—I don't want you disappearing again." And off she went, cutting her way through the crowd like a boat through water in her cherry-red suit that, despite having been designed by Chanel, somehow managed on her to look Midwestern. Without waiting for the blond man to finish speaking, she claimed Bernard Augustin's attention with a hand on his other arm. I could hear her voice, as loud as a tornado siren, as she said, "Bernard? Bernard Augustin—is it you! We met at the Lowensteins', but you won't remember. Louise Haynes, from the Midwestern Museum of Art. We had a long chat about Donald Judd and Smithson, and why so many artists are drawn to desert landscapes. I remember you compared the desert to the sea!"

The blond man had vanished. Bernard Augustin turned toward Louise, over whom he towered, his head bent and his brow furrowed as though he were genuinely trying to remember. "Was it Manhattan, or up in Maine . . . ?"

"Manhattan! Such a lovely home. And, of course, the collection! Yet it doesn't feel artificial, does it, the way she's arranged it? You always feel you're in a home, not a gallery."

"Mmm."

"And that magnificent Twombly in the dining room—not everyone would have the strength of character to eat in the presence of that! But Elaine always had nerves of steel."

"I'm afraid I don't know them well. You obviously—"

"No, not *well*," Louise interrupted. "I wouldn't say *that*." And on she chattered, like a squirrel on a fencepost, occasionally throwing back her head to release that braying donkey's laugh. Despite my direct orders, I moved farther into the crowd for a respite from the sound of her voice. I felt ashamed on behalf of my native soil that Louise was its representative here in Venice. I had fled the infinity of cornfields and the tyranny of five o'clock dinners as soon as I could, but there was a part of me that still loved the Midwest. The smell of thawing earth in spring, and the vastness of the sky at noon, and the faint Norwegian lilt caught in people's voices as though their Viking-blooded ancestors still ghosted inside them, playing the filaments of their vocal cords like harps.

3.

On the third day, at breakfast in the hotel restaurant, Louise complained of a migraine aura and took a pill. The starched cloths on the tables hurt her eyes, and the penetrating smell of the spotted orange lilies in their vases made her turn her head away. Still, nothing would prevent her from keeping her appointment to meet friends at the German pavilion. She sat stoically on the vaporetto, her hands pressed together in her lap as we growled down the wide green waterway. It was hot, the crown of the sun blazing in the aching sky, and the sour smells of rot and muck threaded up from the water and the slimy stones and the dark, dank corners of the luminous city. How odd it seemed, the façades of the palaces there before my eyes but entirely remote, so that it was almost as though I were still sitting in a darkened classroom looking at slides projected on a screen. Were there people in there? Sleeping, eating, bathing, talking? It was impossible to imagine; it was unreal. Reality was Louise pressing her hands to her head and saying, "I don't know why I didn't bring my Oscar de la Renta. Oh, if only it weren't so humid!" while the stink of diesel fumes curled around us, and the boat rocked up and down. Nearby a fat American couple argued about tipping, and farther away a thin couple argued in Italian about who knew what. "Did you remember that bottle of water?" Louise asked.

It was the first I'd heard of a bottle of water. "I can go buy one."

"Oh, never mind!"

Stepping onto dry land, Louise sighed as though she'd been holding her breath. The Giardini was already buzzing, people ducking in and out of pavilions looking dissatisfied. The rank smell of the boat clung to us as we walked slowly toward the German pavilion under the heavy blue sky.

Inside, the light was muted. Away from the sun and dust, Louise seemed to revive. Presumably there was art on the walls, or perhaps on plinths and in vitrines scattered across the echoing floor, but with the crush of people talking in a dozen languages, calling out to one another, admiring one another's clothes, criticizing Venetian disorganization, making scathing comments about certain artists and obsequious ones about others, it was hard to be absolutely sure. Dark glasses firmly in place, Louise pushed me through the buzzing crowd looking for April and Sarabeth. *"Scusi, scusi!"* she bleated. *"Mi dispiace!"* We found them at last in an alcove with a starburst chandelier studded with paper money—dollars and mark notes and pounds—amid which pfennigs and pennies spun on threads of translucent fishing line.

"It's always like this," said Sarabeth, a tall, redheaded ostrich of a woman in a black Armani suit. They were all three wearing black, in fact, like three witches—but then so was everybody else. "I always swear to come later in the summer when the crowds die down! But then for some reason I don't."

"There's practically no point even being here," said April. "They'll want to know what I saw, and I'll have to say I saw Ellsworth Dietz slip his hand down Margy Donovan's waistband as they were waiting for the vaporetto!" "They" were her clients, agribusiness magnates mostly.

"I heard she paid just over a million for that Hockney," Louise said, meaning Margy Donovan. "The smudgy one."

"No, not a Hockney, it was a Chetwith."

"No, it wasn't."

"Oh, Chetwith!" April said. "I heard his show at Gagosian bombed, they hardly sold anything."

"No, no," said Sarabeth. "Bernard Augustin bought up the whole show. Betsy Green told me, and she should know."

"Not the *whole* show—not of Chetwith!" April was appalled.

"Those chain-link pieces that sort of sag on the wall. He thinks Chetwith is the new Damien Hirst."

"But why is he buying at all?" April asked. "I heard he shut up the whole museum. The Nauk. After . . . you know."

"Can't he still *buy*?" Louise demanded. "For his own *pleasure*?"

"Drowning his sorrows in art," Sarabeth said. "Art therapy."

"I don't understand," April said. "I thought he was gay."

Louise fanned her hand in front of her face. "Yes, he's *gay*, of course. Just look at his ties. But they were close. They were like brother and sister!"

"He couldn't run the place without her," Sarabeth said. "It was all her, the Nauk. Her taste. He just wrote the checks."

"I heard he warned her against swimming alone," Louise said. "But she was a free spirit!"

"Look," Sarabeth said suddenly. She was taller than the rest of us and could see, a bit, over the crowd. "There he is."

We swiveled our heads in the direction hers, periscope-like, pointed. For a moment I saw the big head with the cropped salt-and-pepper hair floating like a grim moon over that surging sea of well-dressed humanity. He looked like a man who had lost his way and found himself in a rank jungle full of monkeys and mosquitoes.

"I don't feel . . ." Louise said. She leaned heavily against me, so that I teetered and almost fell against April.

"Let's get her some air," Sarabeth commanded.

I took one arm and Sarabeth took the other, and somehow we half guided, half dragged Louise, who was sweating and greenish, out into the dusty heat. She threw a hand across her face to shield her eyes, already behind dark glasses, from the glare. "If I could just lie down for a moment," she said, alarming us with her apparent intention of depositing herself on the dusty Giardini path.

April spied a bench behind us in the blazing sun. "Let's just get you over there," she said.

Louise nodded. She took a step and stumbled over nothing. Her solid, black-clad body slumped sideways like a blunt needle on an instrument dial slipping suddenly to zero. Then she was on the ground. We knelt around her.

"Louise!" April cupped her shoulder.

"She's fainted," Sarabeth said. "Go get help!" She was looking at me.

"How?" I cried. Oh, what were we doing in a city without cars! What did they do in emergencies? Did amphibious vehicles roll up out of the murky water? Did uniformed men appear bearing litters? I looked around for a policeman, a guard, someone in uniform, but there were only well-dressed citizens of the world buzzing from pavilion to pavilion like flies.

"There must be an office! A guard booth. Go and see!"

I stood up and looked wildly around. Which way to go? Should I run back down to the busy vaporetto landing? Into the pavilion? I was just turning toward the steps when Bernard Augustin stepped out the door into the white hot day.

"Mr. Augustin!" I said, but he didn't hear me. He was walking fast in our direction, his eyes fixed vacantly on nothing that I could see.

Sarabeth and April rose. Louise lay slumped, a black humped shape like a seal. Bernard noticed her in stages—you could see him register first an obstacle, and then an anomaly, and finally the fact of a body on the ground. He stopped, staring fiercely into our faces. "What happened?" he demanded.

"She fainted," Sarabeth murmured, suddenly demure.

Bernard knelt beside Louise, then rose again and began calling out loudly in Italian, the knees of his expensive suit soiled. Louise made a sound and opened her eyes. Suddenly everyone was looking at us, moving toward us. We had been invisible, and Bernard had materialized us. Two officials in black brass-buttoned jackets and stiff hats were suddenly present, making a fuss, producing bottles of water, talking into cell phones. Apparently Bernard had materialized them too.

Louise sat up. She looked dazed but not displeased to find herself at the center of this little fuss. *"Grazie, grazie, mille grazie,"* she sighed. *"Non è niente."*

"Which hotel is she staying at?" Bernard asked Sarabeth.

Sarabeth looked at me.

"We're staying at the da Silva," I said.

"You're with her?" Bernard turned his face to me like a searchlight. It was my first close look at him: gray-white skin, handsome nose, dark, darting, impatient eyes with those mussel-shell shadows. He seemed angry, formal, almost electric, as though if you came too close you would get a shock. He seemed to take up a great deal of space. He looked me up and down: my blue knit dress, my frightened face, my bare smudged knees. "Come on, then!" he commanded.

Five minutes later the three of us were in a water taxi, skimming back up the canal. "What happened?" Louise asked me groggily, but I wasn't sure. Time seemed to be passing very oddly. Suddenly we were stepping off the boat, which disappeared without anyone seeming to have paid for it, and then we were walking slowly up the hot street, Bernard Augustin on one side of Louise and me on the other, and then abruptly we were inside the hotel, and he was speaking to the man behind the counter who dispensed the keys. Fragments of phrases kept escaping Louise's lips: "You shouldn't have," "I'm very," "No reason," "Now and then," none of which our escort responded to with anything more than a hum. And then we were getting out of the dark, groaning elevator, just the two of us—Louise and I—and as the doors closed she leaned against me and asked, "Did you tip the elevator boy?"

Had she mistaken Bernard Augustin for an elevator boy?

In her room, Louise asked me to call room service for tea, lemons, ice. "Please shut the blinds," she moaned, sitting heavily on the bed.

"They're shut."

"Tighter." She laid her head on the pillow, the thick strands of hair making me think of leeches in the pond on my grandparents' farm. She let her shoes slip off, and her scrunched skirt rode up her pale thighs. I felt bad for her, but I also thought now I would have some time to myself. Maybe I could wander over to San Marco while she lay in bed with the blinds tightly shut. When room service came, I poured the tea.

"Just leave it on the table," she said.

"All right." I moved toward the connecting door.

"I'll call if I need anything."

Hmm. What were the chances of that? "If I'm not there, I'm just down having an espresso in the bar."

"You should have ordered one when you called room service," she said.

"I didn't think of it."

She was feeling well enough to give me a look.

"Sugar?" I asked.

"Yes. No. Do they have Splenda?"

"I don't see any."

"God, the Italians! How do they stay so thin?"

I went into my adjoining room and sat on the bed. It was a single bed with a white spread and small blue decorative pillows. A child's bed, a virgin's. In hotels in America you never saw a single bed, did you? I didn't know, I hadn't stayed in many hotels.

What should I do? Would she call? Could I—should I—sneak away? I might not be in Venice again for years, or ever. Didn't I owe a debt to Art larger than the one I owed to Louise? And anyway, she had taken another pill, she could sleep for hours. Why should I stay like a nanny to watch over her? It was ridiculous. It was wrong. She just wanted to stop me from enjoying myself.

I stood up and walked softly to the connecting door, turned the knob as carefully as a thief in a movie, peered into the darkened room. If she was awake, I could say I just wanted to check on her—which was true. But she wasn't awake. She lay as I had left her, a loose, lumpy package on top of the spread, snoring in light, congested bursts like a little dog.

Outside, the sky had changed, gone smoky flat and white. As I crossed the street, a few drops of rain spotted the pavement and chilled my arms, giving me goose bumps. Armed with my Fodor's and unnecessary sunglasses, I wormed past a family of American tourists, some noisy Germans, and a school group with matching T-shirts, my heart thumping as I breathed in the smells of rain, ancient grime, dank stone, coffee. I was in Venice! I turned to look back at the shuttered handsome face of the Hotel da Silva to see if it reproached me. I counted up to the fourth floor, remembering to start at zero. If Louise had awakened and come to the window, she would see me escaping—or rather, she would see me hesitating, standing like a fool in the rain, which was falling a little harder now, making umbrellas flower all over the narrow street. Somewhere someone was singing in Italian. The clear, aching sound drifted over the wet flagstones as it might have a hundred years before—two hundred years—a thousand years. What was my life or Louise's life in those terms? A wink, a cough, a single note in a long symphony. I turned my head up into the rain, caught a sour drop on my tongue, and fled toward San Marco.

By the time I reached the piazza, the rain was coming down harder. The water puddled in hollows, spreading out across the stones. Rivulets formed, connecting puddle to puddle, and soon a network of little streams gurgled and hissed across the slippery, gritty pavement, where dark huddled pigeons shifted like living shadows. A long line of people hugged the columned arcade, crowding under umbrellas or shielding their heads with sweatshirts and newspapers. Above them rose the froth of marble, the glistening arches and cupolas running with rain, the gray, glowering sky. A line! Of course there would be a line—of course the ordinary tourist hordes were here in Venice with their knapsacks and their cameras, their sneakers and guidebooks and baseball caps. What if I went to the front and explained that I was a curator (curatorial assistant) on her first trip to Italy, that I had only a couple of hours? Would they let me in?

In the piazza, rail-thin African men draped plastic sheets over their key chains and snow globes, squatting on the stones with their shoulders hunched to wait out the rain as they had waited out, no doubt, worse things in whatever countries they had left behind. The water slipped down my back in chilly streams, dripped from my hair. Oh, well! Nothing was stopping me from looking at the domes, was it? At the busy, bright façade? I walked toward the building, my eye sliding over the elegant clusters of columns, the glowing stone, the mosaics in the

Romanesque archways. What was the word for those arched spaces tiled into image? Lunettes—the term drifted back to me from the twilit lecture room in Elvers Hall. My heart rose. Were those angels up there with their wet, golden wings? A solemn winged lion represented Saint Mark himself: noble, patient, gleaming dully in the rain against a backdrop of painted stars, a book clinging improbably to one paw.

And then, quite suddenly, the rain ceased. Or anyway, it ceased falling on me, though the sound of water rattling onto the piazza was as loud as ever. Someone had come up next to me holding an enormous umbrella. I jumped sideways and looked up. It was Bernard Augustin.

"You're the girl from the Giardini," he said. He stepped toward me so that I was again under the umbrella, politely declining to notice my suspicious fright. "How's your friend?"

"Resting," I said, though Louise wasn't my friend, and I wasn't a girl—I was twenty-five. I hoped it was true, at least, that Louise was resting. Possibly this very instant she was opening the connecting door and calling my name.

"Have you been inside?" He nodded toward the basilica.

I shook my head. "I didn't realize the line would be so long," I said, as though I had expected any line at all. I tried to picture a line at the Midwestern Museum of Art, snaking down the shallow steps and across the asphalt turn-around, under the mimosa trees. Never in a million years, not if we were giving the art away!

"It's worse than Disney World," Bernard Augustin said. "Which is strange. Because I don't think most people enjoy it, once they get inside, as much as they enjoy Disney World." He was dressed in a dark blue belted raincoat and black tasseled loafers, a handsome dark gray hat on his head. The big black umbrella he held over us had silver stars on the inside, faintly glowing like foam on the ocean at night.

I looked at the ragged line snaking across the piazza, the tourists wet and dogged, their expressions unreadable. German, Japanese, Chinese, Australian, Russian, Hungarian, American: all of them determined to see those tiles set in place the better part of a millennium ago. "It's nice to see people lined up for art."

"I would agree with you, if art was what they were lined up for. But it's not."

"What, then?"

"To check the box. Three days in Venice: The Rialto? Check. Gondola ride? Hmm, pricey. But—check. San Marco? Let's see: long line, raining, but what the hell, might as well get it over with."

I was offended, as though he were talking about me. "Maybe they'll love it. Maybe they've been dreaming about coming to Venice for years!"

He laughed. "Maybe."

"Or maybe they *are* just coming because Fodor's told them to, but once they're inside and see it—maybe it will open their eyes, open them up." Wasn't that what had happened to me? And not even in San Marco in Venice, but in a stuffy basement auditorium. Hadn't my whole life been changed by that sustained encounter with Beauty? I thought Bernard Augustin would laugh, but I didn't care. This was my credo—the power of art to transform what I could only call the soul, although even I wouldn't have said that word aloud. Not to Bernard Augustin, anyway. But he didn't laugh. Instead he looked out to where the rain was falling lightly, slantwise, in thin gray needles, and began to spin the umbrella so that the stars went around. "It's slowing down," he said.

We strolled across the wet, slippery stones. Bernard took my arm. It was a gesture I'd read about in books, seen shimmering in black and silver on movie screens and television screens. His big hand braced my forearm, and, although I didn't lean into it, I felt its steady presence as an unlooked-for comfort, like a stuffed toy belonging to a child who has more or less outgrown it. Our steps aligned. I could smell the damp cloth of his coat, the sour smell of the rain and the canals, and a faint, bitter, aromatic smell, like orange peels and brine, that I would later know was his cologne. We stopped on the far right-hand side of San Marco and looked up at the first lunette, a half-moon niche of mosaic supported by frothy columns. On one side of the picture, some people wrestled with a bundle, while in the middle, men in robes and turbans seemed anxious about something.

"The transport of the body of Saint Mark from Alexandria," Bernard said. "You know the story, of course?"

I shook my head. Louise, if she had been there, might have spoken the same words, using them to mean the opposite of what they said. Bernard's tone of benign, bland politeness put me at ease. I didn't know why he was being so nice to me, but I was grateful.

"Saint Mark was buried in Alexandria," Bernard said. "His body lay at rest there until the ninth century, when two Venetian merchants stole it and smuggled it to Venice. They did this by hiding the corpse—I suppose it was only bones by then—in slabs of bacon."

I laughed.

Bernard smiled. His eyes lightened a shade from near black to deep brown, and clusters of starfish lines appeared on his temples. "You think I'm kidding, but I'm not. Muslims can't touch pork, so the customs officials in Alexandria had no way of discovering the body."

"That's terrible," I said. "It sounds like something that would happen today."

He made no comment. We walked along the façade to the second lunette, in which the men with white turbans had been replaced by different men in black hats. "That was in 828 AD. Or CE, if you prefer. After they smuggled the bones out of Alexandria, they brought them back to Venice." The long body of the saint, covered in a blue cloth, dominated the foreground of the third lunette, a glowing halo circling his head. "The doge and the people receiving the body," Bernard said.

You could see his head—the dead saint's head—lifting toward the man in white and gold whom I guessed was the doge. "He doesn't look dead. Maybe saints don't decompose? Maybe that's one of the benefits?"

"I'd think that was more likely to be true of devils."

I felt faintly disappointed. Not that the mosaics weren't lovely, gold and pinkish red and clear blue shining down from under the white-veined marble. But somehow I wasn't transported. Maybe it was just because the pictures were so high up and difficult to see. I strained my eyes toward the image of Saint Mark under his blue cloth, willing myself to feel something.

"After that, they lost the body for a while. They hid it away for safekeeping, so no one could steal it while they built the basilica. But of course that took a couple of hundred years, and when they were done they couldn't remember where they had put it. Calamity! Disaster! Just imagine—all those priests and cardinals rushing through the city, peering into vaults and storage sheds and hidey-holes all over Venice. That was in 1063. A couple of decades went by, and still no Saint Mark. So, what do you think they did?" He looked at me with a kind of patience behind which I sensed something else—a weight, a sadness. I remembered what Louise had said—*He never got over it*. Was he thinking of his friend, then, who had disappeared? Who had never made it to Venice? I wanted to distract him, to amuse him. To make that shadow of sadness disappear.

"I'd manufacture one," I said. "Out of clay, maybe. Or just find some other old bones. Like when a kid's guinea pig dies and the parents get a new one and secretly make a switch."

"I never had a guinea pig," Bernard Augustin said.

We were silent. The rain fell. The pigeons rose in waves and settled again farther away. The damp line of tourists snaked slowly forward. I thought how strange to me he was, this man: rich, cultured, educated. He was a man who had made a mark on the world, who had suffered a grave and mysterious loss, yet was kind to Louise, kind to me. I wasn't falling in love with him, exactly. I knew he was gay, and he must have been twenty years older than I was. But perhaps I was falling in love with him inexactly. With him, or with the life he represented. It was hard, then, to tell them apart.

"Anyway," I said shyly. "I hope the cardinals didn't do that. Perpetrate a fraud. Maybe they prayed. Isn't that what they're supposed to be good at?"

"They did better than that," Bernard said. "They organized the whole city to pray. All of Venice got down on its knees and prayed for the recovery of the bones! All over the city, from the palazzos and the hovels, the canals and the *calli*, prayers rose up in clouds past the chimneys into the sky! After three days, they reached the ear of God. Down in the city, a column burst open, and there it was—Saint Mark's body, like a rabbit emerging from a hat. Just think how much it must have scared the guy who found him." His voice changed, went low and thin. "Just because you've been praying for a corpse doesn't mean you like it when you find it."

We walked toward the fourth and final lunette, Bernard's arm still forming a platform for mine, the rain lightening to a drizzle and the sky brightening. "So, at last, the Venetians transferred Saint Mark to his final resting place, the Basilica of San Marco, where he could stretch out in style after all those centuries walled up in the pillar."

Why should it be final? I wondered. It seemed to me that a body exhumed, stolen, hidden, lost, and found again by way of a miracle might well have some life in it still. "Maybe it's not finished," I said.

"Maybe the body is just resting, getting ready for more adventures." I smiled up at Bernard, but his face went blank, like one of the old stones. My little joke had fallen flat. Embarrassed, I looked up at the last mosaic, and everything else fell away.

The fourth lunette was different from the others. Gold ringed a towering building with floating domes that I saw was San Marco itself: dark domes, white Istrian stone, and figures in gold and green and blue standing in the foreground in groups—standing, in fact, just where we were standing. Some of them carried staffs, and some had hoods, and their feet peeked serenely out from under the robes as if to signal that they were of the earth rather than of heaven. Something lifted in my chest, and a spark of energy spread through me as though along a golden fuse. I felt alive, awake, and my vision seemed to grow clearer, so that I could take in every part at once—detail and architecture, line and hue, composition and expression. "Oh!" I said. "I love this one!"

The rain had stopped. Bernard shut up his umbrella. Over our heads the domes of the basilica glowed in the wet, and inside the lunette the miniature basilica glowed too, and the ancient citizens of Venice rejoiced. In the piazza, the African peddlers uncovered their wares. I looked and looked, losing myself in the picture, until at last Bernard said, "This is the only lunette that survives from the thirteenth century. The others are seventeenth- and eighteenth-century restorations."

"That's why, then! This one is . . ." What was the word for what it was? There were no words. The feeling had to be expressed in tiles of gold and clay and glass.

After a while, Bernard said, "I'm going to have a drink. Would you like to join me?"

I blinked at him. I had no idea how much time had passed. The sky was bright blue with a few long strands of cloud, and suddenly I thought of Louise, her long strands of hair across the pillow. "I have to go!" It was like the time I was sixteen and fell asleep in the backseat of Tommy Starankovic's car, parked beside a potato field in summer. It was the only infraction my parents ever spanked me for, though I was far too old for spanking by then. Never mind that we were only kissing, never mind that I only missed curfew by twenty minutes. Never mind that it was the first time—both for kissing and for being late.

And what if I *had* slept with Tommy Starankovic? What if I had gotten pregnant, dropped out of school, married him, or someone? I might have three children by now and live in a little house a stone's throw from where that car had been parked—less than a mile from my parents. Wouldn't that have been a better outcome, from their point of view, after all?

~

When I stepped, breathless, into my room, Louise was sitting on my bed wearing a violet silk kimono patterned with yellow lotuses. She looked groggy, her disheveled hair clipped back. There was a faint whiff of sulfur in the air—no doubt from the canals—making it seem that she was smoldering. No way of knowing if she had been planted there for a minute or an hour.

"I was calling you," she accused.

"I'm so sorry, Louise. I just ran down for a . . . What can I do for you? How are you feeling?" I took a step closer, but she raised her hand like a policeman and shut her eyes.

"Please speak softly," she enjoined me. I stood on the rug and waited. Her head bobbed, and the wrinkled stem of her neck sagged, and she put her hand to her eyes. Then she peered up at me. "I get these migraines. I have pills. There isn't anything else to do."

"I'm sorry."

"Please, just *listen* to me. I'm asking you to help me. Just listen, all right?"

I nodded.

"I can't make the party on San Giorgio tonight. Obviously. I need you to call and tell them we won't be there. All right? Can you do that? Make sure you explain that I'm ill, I don't want Alonso to think I just didn't . . . I need you to make sure he gets the message. Make sure you speak to Wendy. That's his assistant. And make sure she *tells* him, how's that? Say Louise said she sends a thousand apologies—*mille scusi*—how's that?"

"Yes," I said, but she held up her hand again.

"Don't. Just, please, help me." Her eyes glowed angrily in the dim room, and her voice was full of pain. "The ice has all melted, and the tea is cold. Could you please just see if they can send up some soup? I don't want them to knock. Have them send it up to you, and then you bring it in. Don't knock, just bring it in. Can you do that?"

I nodded.

"*Can* you?"

"Yes," I said, keeping my voice low.

"My God, I should think so." She rose from the bed and shuffled across to the connecting door, stopping suddenly with a hand on the knob.

"Where were you, anyway?" she asked. "You look damp."

"I just thought I'd get a breath of fresh air."

"In the *rain*?"

"It's such a beautiful city," I said, "even in the rain. It's just a wonderful opportunity for me, being here in Venice."

4.

THE NEXT DAY, Louise was still ill. Or rather, she was differently ill—sitting up against her pillows, makeup gleaming, wearing a bed jacket. I had never seen a bed jacket in real life, and I looked at it with interest. It was robin's-egg blue and trimmed with lace, tied loosely over a pearly nightie through which Louise's heavy breasts were just visible, like the shadowy shapes of fish in a murky pool. "There you are," she said when I came in, summoned by the bright blare of the telephone. "My head—I can't go out! The sun would flay me. The best thing is rest, my doctor says, and even in Venice one must obey the doctor's orders."

"You're looking better," I said. Her face was animated, her glance sharp, her voice no longer tense and shrill.

"No, no," she said irritably. "I feel terrible."

What did she want from me? "Should I send down for coffee?"

"Cappuccino and rolls. No, not rolls, a *cornetto*. They can send it right up."

I picked up her phone to place the order: *"Due cappuccino, e due cornetto."* Should I have said *cornetti*? I was glad she hadn't wanted rolls, I didn't know the word.

"Some people will be stopping by," she said, rearranging herself on the balustrade of pillows.

People?

"In a little while. Of all the terrible luck—to not be able even to set *foot* in the Arsenale!"

The coffee arrived. I took the tray from the young woman and carried it to the bed, where Louise settled the plate of *cornetti* onto her lap. "Nothing for you?" she said.

I had expected April and Sarabeth, maybe another middle-aged woman or two, but somehow Louise had organized, from her sick-bed, a party. Around noon fists began rapping on the door, bottles emerged from purses and plastic bags—prosecco, gin, Campari, sparkling rosé—and Louise sent me down to the hotel breakfast room for glasses, for ice, for bottles of San Pellegrino and slices of lemon. A bald man in a beige suit sat on the bed and took Louise's freckled hand in his, calling her *cara*. A plump man in a fedora had brought a secret ingredient in an unmarked bottle and was mixing drinks he called "Biennales." Sarabeth took out her cell phone and started dialing: "I know it's early for a party," she said to everyone she reached. "That's the beauty of it!" With the heavy blinds shut and the soft lamps draped with scarves, it was possible to imagine that it was night rather than early afternoon. I stood by a window with a glass of San Pellegrino as the room filled up, trying not to look miserable. Although the blinds were drawn, a few dim wavelets of watery light slipped in around the edges, poignant emissaries from the world outside.

"Open the door," Louise said.

I thought she meant that someone needed to be let in, but when I checked, there was no one in the hall.

"The *door*." She had a way of pronouncing perfectly innocent words as though they were aspersions. "The connecting door. Please!"

"But that's my room," I said stupidly.

"Yes. And we need the *space*."

I stood still, squeezed between a woman in green speaking German and a man holding a full glass in one hand and an empty one in the other, waiting for my mind to work out what to do.

Louise groaned, a groan of exasperation rather than of illness. She seemed to have made a full recovery there on the bed, leaning like a sultaness against her berm of pillows, a drink sweating on the bedside table, the rim of the glass smeared with that purplish red. "Please," she said. "Please just do it, how about that?"

I moved blindly toward the connecting door, glad the crowd would make it hard for her to see my face. I turned the knob and the party surged through, though the narrow space of my little room couldn't hold many of them. A man with a cowlick sat on my bed and lit a cigarette. "I'm Miguel," he said. "I came with Meredith. Great Biennale, isn't it?"

"It's my first, actually. I don't have anything to compare it to."

"Did you see that field of umbrellas made of snakeskins?" he asked. "That was something."

"No. Which pavilion was that?"

"Portugal. Portugal is always wonderful! Countries emerging from fascism always produce great art."

Someone had brought a small CD player and a burst of music rose over the din. The admirer of postfascist art stood up and began swiveling his hips, his cigarette between his lips, ash floating to the rug. He grabbed my hands and pulled me toward him in an energetic two-step.

Louise was calling. Her voice snaked its way through the laughter and the marimbas. I pulled myself free of my dance partner and pushed back into the other room. Half a dozen people were lounged across Louise's bed, one couple kissing, their hands in each other's hair.

Louise's eyes were bright. "Ice," she said. "Would you please?" She held the metal ice bucket aloft, causing the loose bed jacket to fall open. Her hair brushed her shoulders, and she sat up very straight, looking vaguely like the Statue of Liberty with an ice bucket instead of a torch. Her flushed face glowed in the veiled light, and her gaze was hotly imperious. The man lounging next to her stared through his black-rimmed glasses at her breasts, quite visible through the skimpy nightie, his drink tilting, and Louise twitched her shoulders like a fisherman twitching a line, making the twin lures bounce.

I took the ice bucket and fled.

In the lobby, I dropped the bucket on the concierge desk. "More ice for the *signora* in room 402," I said, and then I pushed out the front door and onto the street.

The sun was out. The sky was a searing poignant blue overhead as I walked quickly toward the vaporetto stop, then rode the boat down the green canal. It was wonderful to be out in the open air. I began to wonder whether I could have dreamed the wild carnival that was Louise's party. What did it mean that a woman like her—stout, solid, staid, old—could become, in a Venetian hotel room, a wild sylph? Did everyone have that in them—that naked pagan under the clothes of their civilized persona? Even people, I wondered, like my upright, steadfast Wisconsin parents? Even me?

At the Arsenale, I wandered through the rooms in a daze not unlike the daze in which I'd wandered the streets of New York when I first arrived in that city. How long the handful of intervening years seemed to me, and how different I felt I was from that girl from LaFreniere, Wisconsin, who got off the bus knowing nothing and no one. But of course, I was hardly different at all.

I wandered from room to room, past giant photographs on walls and spills of objects on floors and large sculptural things set on plinths.

At first I couldn't focus, the art was an undifferentiated river of color and form rushing past me. But slowly my feet and my heart and my racing brain slowed down, and then it was more like being on a raft, or in a canoe, paddling slowly through vivid shifting landscapes. In one room, Polaroid snapshots, each of a single flower, were arranged in circles on the walls, making bright, intricate patterns that looked like flowers themselves. In another room, a small tree grew out of the floor, its graceful branches hung with feathers, a white tutu around its trunk like a ballerina. In a third, an antique writing desk lay sprawled on its side on a faded Oriental rug, a video projection of a fire in its open belly, the sound of crackling wood playing over speakers. Each of these installations, performing patiently, seemed as though it had been waiting for me. Each made my heart ache joyfully, made that slow flame thrill up the golden fuse of my body. The world—people—might be beyond understanding, but others too had wrestled with that searing, opaque mystery, had spun it into this. I knelt down before the faux fire, warming myself at its flames. I stayed there a long while, faintly aware of time passing—the earth spinning through space like a skater—people crossing back and forth behind me like shades. My nostrils caught a faint scent: oranges and brine. A large shape settled on the carpet beside me, and a voice said, "People are starting to think you're part of the work."

I shivered, dragging myself back from one world to the other like a swimmer hoisting herself out of a pool. Bernard Augustin crouched on the floor beside me in a mist-gray suit with a pale orange pocket square and a cravat. His pant legs were hiked up, and I could see his socks—oyster-gray silk, calf length. I'd never seen such beautiful socks in my life. I blushed and started to stand up, but he stopped me with a hand on my arm. His hand was big and rough-textured and powerful, like the paw of a well-bred lion. "Don't," he said. "I was just teasing." I could feel myself blushing harder—blushing because I couldn't stop myself from blushing. "Didn't you have brothers?" he asked.

I had two brothers, in fact, one now a successful agribusinessman, the other in real estate. They had teased me, yes, but with a stinging indifference as far from Bernard's tone as their heavy woolen socks were from his silk ones.

"They were older," I said.

"Were?"

"Are."

"Ah, you're the baby." He released my arm and sat heavily on the rug. Before us, the fire flickered and crackled, cradled by rather than consuming its wooden hearth. I began to be aware of people slowing as they wandered past, staring—not at the fireplace piece, but at us. "Who is that girl with Bernard Augustin?" they would be asking. I wondered if somehow Louise would hear.

"How about you?" I asked. "Brothers or sisters?" Then, as he paused before answering, I remembered what Louise had said and wanted to sink through the floor: *They were like brother and sister, he and Alena.*

"One," he said at last. The glowing shadows under his eyes seemed darker, like coals burning down. The ease he'd made for us had disappeared, unmade by my thoughtlessness.

"I should let you go," I said.

"Are you holding me here by force?"

I didn't know what to say. He sounded tired, as though his own responses wearied him beyond bearing. "I think you can do anything you want," I said. "You're Bernard Augustin."

He laughed shortly. "It's funny," he said, "because I never used to be."

"Who did you used to be?"

"Oh, nobody. I didn't much like it at the time, though. So, you like the fireplace? Or did you just happen to fall to your knees here?"

"I think it's wonderful."

"Why?" He spoke so casually, glancing around the room with that slow, sleepy gaze he had, as though his attention were elsewhere, that I didn't understand he was testing me.

I rattled on, confabulating: the evocation of the elemental, the paradoxical tension of the flame that could never consume, the antiquated cultural artifact of the wooden desk overturned but not destroyed, the sensual pleasure balanced with the intellectual statement, God knows what. My words seemed to gather momentum, spinning themselves into skeins, organizing themselves into sentences that fell shrilly on the air. This was the knack, the disembodied voice that lived like a twin inside me, that had helped me sail through school all my life, and at the same time isolated me, the subtle sentences a kind of sticky silk, cocooning me in a chrysalis of my own making. As I spoke, I felt myself grow cooler, as though the warmth of the faux fire were leaving me—the fizz of the burning fuse doused with the cold water of my own improvised erudition. I stopped in the middle of the sentence I was addressing to the middle distance and looked up at Bernard. "I felt something when I saw it. It's hard to describe. Sometimes, when I look at art, it just—does something to me."

He nodded, looking into the fire. "I've collected Gianna for a long time. She used to make these spiky flowers that were also lamps out of blown glass, white ones and pink ones. And burning bush sculptures from steel and LEDs. She just keeps keeping better."

I didn't know what to say. Hadn't I known he was a collector?

"Did you see anything else today that did something to you?" he asked.

I knew he was teasing me, but I thought I might as well say. I told him about the Jauss ballerina tree and the Kikumura Polaroids. "It sounds ridiculous," I said. *"I don't know much about art, but I know what I like."*

"You seem to know quite a lot about art, actually."

"No, I don't," I blurted. "Not really." Usually I was guarded, but something about Bernard disarmed me: his bruised eyes and his pocket square and his semi-ironic formality.

"I won't tell anyone," he said. "Certainly not that woman you work for. The fainting one. How is she, anyway?"

The thought of Louise made me itch and squirm. "She's made a stunning recovery."

"You like working for her?"

"I like working in contemporary art. I like getting to come to the Biennale."

"And in ten or twenty years? What do you see yourself doing then?"

"I'd like to be a real curator at a real contemporary art museum!" I didn't dare name one. It seemed too presumptuous to say MOCA or MCA Chicago or the Menil.

"Even though you don't know anything about art?" Teasing again.

"I think I have a mind for it," I said shyly.

Like a flash of lightning, the smile Bernard gave me made him look different, like a different person—bright and sly and boyish, almost happy. "I'll tell you a secret," he said. "I think I do too." He hoisted himself to his feet and held out his hand to help me up, and we walked together into the next room.

It was a small room, and dark, and it felt crowded although there were only a handful of people here. Against the wall, rows of glass shelves displayed a tightly organized collection of seashells—or rather, extremely realistic sculptures of seashells, also made of glass, clear and acid green and fuchsia and electric blue. We stood together in front of the installation. The more I looked at it, the less I liked it, it seemed so flashy and pleased with itself, self-consciously foregrounding its own contradictions. It made me think of another artist who also worked with shell forms, but in ceramic rather than glass, and in a different mood and color palette. Celia Cowry's sculptures, which I loved, were glazed in shades of beige and brown, ivory and brick. She used skin tones, human colors, and her shells made me think of people turned to clay by an eccentric sea witch.

Bernard stepped back, tilted his head, squinted, sighed. "These make me think of Celia Cowry," he said. "But they're completely different."

"I was thinking exactly the same thing!" We looked at each other, suddenly near hilarity. "I didn't think anyone but me had heard of her!" I said.

"I've known her for years. She's from my part of the world."

"Cape Cod." No wonder she was interested in shells. "Have you shown her at the Nauk?"

The moment I said the name, I knew it was a mistake. Without moving, Bernard withdrew. His eyes grew distant and his nose seemed to grow straighter, keen as a blade. He looked at his watch, feigned surprise. Or maybe he really was surprised, maybe he had stepped out of time and the squawked syllable from my lips had sent him tumbling back into it. "I'm sorry," he said. "I have to meet someone." Maybe he really did.

I went back to the Hotel da Silva.

As I went up in the cramped, clanking elevator, dazed and thrilled by what I had seen, and at my own daring at having seen it, dread sent butterflies fluttering up and down my veins. The fourth-floor hallway was quiet. I had trouble fitting my key into the lock, and my sweaty hand slipped on the small brass knob. Inside: silent chaos. My exhausted eyes took it in slowly, the rucked bedclothes, the crumbs and damp spots on the carpet, glasses everywhere, some with cigarette butts floating in dregs of wine and gin. The stink of smoke, the striped chair overturned, and—most disturbing—in the bathroom a ring around the tub, the tap dripping with the forlorn sound of superfluous water flowing back into the aquifer of a drowned city. The connecting door was ajar, but no sound came from Louise's room. I dared to hope she might be absent—or if not absent, at least sleeping, drunkenly or otherwise, after her day of debauchery. But when I peered through the crack, I saw she wasn't.

Even more than my own, Louise's room seemed to have been shaken like a snow globe by a giant hand. Furniture, bottles, glasses, shriveling lemon slices, stained and crumpled napkins, wine corks, the tops of gin bottles, a couple of scarves, a collapsed umbrella, damp towels, and bags of mostly melted ice lay in shadowy confusion all over the room. Only the bedside lamp, over which someone had thrown a red silk scarf, was turned on, and in its Martian glow I could see the erect figure in the middle of the ravaged bed. Tousled locks of hair twisted in every direction, and her eyes burned with drunken desolation.

"Do you have any idea what time it is?" she said in a raw, dull voice, and for a moment I felt I was back in LaFreniere on that stifling summer night, sneaking in the kitchen door after awakening in Tommy Starankovic's car beside the potato field. What was Louise going to do—spank me?

I looked at my watch. "Eight," I said brightly. "So—everyone left? Are you feeling better?" Absurd questions, but what could I have said that wouldn't have been absurd under the circumstances?

"Eight-thirty!" she seethed. "Do you know how long you've been gone? My God, without a *word*? Without a *hint*? Did you think I wouldn't notice? Or that I wouldn't care?"

I clutched the doorjamb harder, trying not to flinch. "I'm sorry. I didn't think you needed me."

"Needed you? No, no—listen! Listen. It's not a question of whether *I needed you*, it's a question of courtesy. Common politeness. Gratitude!"

I had known she would get around to gratitude before long.

"It's not that I'm not grateful," I said.

"Oh?" she said. "What is it, then?"

I thought about what I could say. Not any of the true things, the sentences floating like lucid dreams in my head: *It's that you're a controlling witch. It's that I despise you. I'm sick to death of gratitude!* I waited for words that could be uttered to come into my mouth, and then they did.

"I wanted to see the art," I said.

5.

THAT NIGHT I AWOKE several times to the sound of Louise vomiting in the bathroom adjoining mine. She didn't call for me, though, and I didn't go to her. I didn't even feel particularly sorry for her.

In the morning she was hungover, wrung out, her headache blazing. She lay weakly on the pillows with no thought of picking up the phone. "I think I have a virus," she said. "Or maybe food poisoning." The room still looked like a tornado had hit it. Mechanically I started cleaning up, gathering the glasses onto the desk, placing the empty bottles in a row by the door, throwing trash in the bin, folding pieces of clothing that had been left behind. "Thank you," Louise said. She sounded like she meant it. After a while she asked if I would bring her some tea. When I brought it, she lifted the cup to her face and let the steam slide over her. She pointed to a tie I had overlooked, an eggplant-colored length of silk slung over a chair. "Give me that," she said. I did, and she laid it across her lap and stroked it gently, as though it were a pet.

"Whose is it?"

"Johannes Roth's. He works at the Deichtorhallen." She paused, her hand slowly smoothing the tie from the wide end to the narrow.

I wondered if I had seen him. Was he the ogler in the black-framed glasses? Had he taken off more than his tie?

"I'm going to get up," Louise announced. "I can't spend another day in this room." She slid gingerly to the edge of the bed and arranged her feet on the floor, but when she tried balancing upright she wobbled and sat heavily down again, both hands pressed to her head. "Do you have any Tylenol?" she said. "Maybe just another hour in bed," she said. She looked awful, her face blotched and sallow, her eyes ringed with smudges.

I brought her two Tylenol and a glass of water. "Can I get you anything else?"

She grimaced, a wan, unhappy attempt at a smile that was more recognizably human than the cold, critical ones she usually displayed. "I'll be all right," she said. "You go ahead and see what you can. I'll meet you back here later."

I almost wished she wasn't acting suddenly so human. It made it harder to justify how much I despised her.

I went back into my room and shut the connecting door. I was almost dressed when the telephone rang with the long old-fashioned bell of a phone in a black-and-white movie. I let it ring for a long time—after all, I might have been in the shower—but my upbringing would not permit me to ignore it altogether.

"Oh, good!" I recognized Bernard's voice immediately—warm, thin, half abstracted—as though I'd known him all my life. "I'd almost given up on you. Did I wake you up?"

My heart thumped hard, alarming in its puppy-dog ardor. "No. I'm awake."

"I'm going to Padua," Bernard said. "For the day. Do you want to come?"

Padua! For the day! Was he serious? Once in Venice for the Biennale, how could you leave? It was as preposterous as Louise spending yesterday in bed. "But there's so much to see here," I said.

"There's also a lot to see in Padua."

I laughed from the sheer fizzy absurdity of it. Somehow I had slipped out of my life into a new, quixotic dimension where desire, sudden inspiration, and contingency ruled in place of logic, toil, consequence. I was Dorothy awakened after the cyclone into Technicolor, Alice stepping through the gauzy looking glass. I was Danaë ravished by a shower of gold.

Bernard met me in the lobby wearing a seersucker suit over a white open-necked shirt, a Panama hat set jauntily on his head. He looked as though he had just stepped out of a speakeasy, except that he seemed drawn and abstracted rather than lighthearted and boozy. He took my arm without a word, almost without seeming to see me, and drew me out the door and down the hot street to the canal, taking fast strides on his long legs so that I had to almost scramble to keep up. I felt like a chess piece being conveyed from square to square. My real life began to leak away.

"Beautiful morning," I said.

"Mm." He stopped abruptly at the corner as a crowd of slow tourists in red T-shirts blocked the narrow street. "Come on," he said, plunging into the stream of them, shouldering through.

"Are we late?"

No answer.

"Bernard?"

A large woman with a face as red as her T-shirt stopped to adjust her shoe, blocking our way. Bernard groaned audibly. I stumbled on the uneven pavement and he yanked me upright. "Careful," he warned.

After that, I concentrated on keeping up.

In the water taxi, he stood with one hand on his head to keep his hat on, the other braced against the boat for balance, his gaze directed toward the smoky line of the horizon. I thought of what I might have been doing in Venice, the pavilions and auxiliary shows and spin-offs I'd made lists of. I stood up from the seat where he had placed me and edged my way to his side. "Are we taking the water taxi all the way to Padua?" I called over the buzzing motor.

He blinked at me. "What?" he said. "Padua's not on the water." Then he turned away. And so we rode on through the brightening morning. The canal opened up into the Venetian Lagoon and the sun blazed golden, its reflection glittering and sparkling, a million brilliant shards on a mirror of water. Gulls soared and dove, squawking their shrill laments. Did Italian gulls speak a different language from American ones? They looked the same as the birds I'd seen at Coney Island, the same as the flocks on the shore all those summers we'd rented the cabin in Door County. I shut my eyes, the spray cooling my face, and felt the unsettling slippage of time: the cold, deep blue, white-capped waters of the inland sea that was Lake Michigan, where great clipper ships had once sunk in sudden storms, and the brilliant sapphire tongue of the Mediterranean licking since the beginning of time at the stone body of the city. Worlds apart, separated by every facet of culture, language, and tradition, yet both beribboned in the sharp, aching cry of the birds that, like ghosts, seemed at home everywhere and nowhere. One of the gulls flapped down and perched on the rail of the boat. Bernard took off his hat and shook it. "Scat!" he cried. The boat man began to scold in Italian. The gull, squawking, fluttered away, caught the breeze, circled back and settled again, and again Bernard chased it away.

"What do you have against the poor bird?" I cried.

He turned slowly toward me and lowered his sunglasses. "They're filthy," he said. "Garbage eaters. Corpse pickers."

"Corpse *what*?"

He straightened, his joints moving stiffly, clumsily. "They're like vultures or rats. Eating carrion, pecking at the dead."

"There aren't any corpses here." I gestured at the blue waves with their clean caps of foam, risking a little impatience with him. Risking the reference to drowning.

Bernard pushed his sunglasses back up his flared nose and looked skyward. "They found a body in the canal this morning," he said. Behind his head the sky seemed to pulse, shimmering around the edges. My heart felt odd and heavy, waterlogged.

"Whose?"

"A woman's. A prostitute's, probably. They haven't identified her yet." His lips pressed together, the color going out of them. I could feel him watching me from behind the smoky glass. "A city built on water," he said, his voice tight and cracked, a thin vessel crazed with fault lines. "It's lucky they found her at all! She might easily have drifted out to sea and disappeared."

I stared at him, cold in the hot sun. Was he thinking of Alena washed out to sea? Imagining her body desecrated by gulls? I stepped toward him and reached for his hand. He was trembling. *Alena*, I thought. *Alena*—afraid of accidentally saying the name aloud. I had never heard Bernard say it, but I began to understand that he never stopped thinking of her. She was the shadow in which he was always walking. Maybe he didn't want to be free.

Once we had retrieved the car, a pale green BMW convertible, from the island of parking, Bernard cheered up. Tucking his hat under the seat, he pressed the button to retract the roof, and the clean blue sky spread placidly above us, a few puffy clouds scattered picturesquely. Before long we were speeding down a shimmering narrow highway between black and yellow fields, and Bernard began to sing in Italian, something bold and melodic that I supposed was opera. He sped around a slow-moving Fiat with a great roar of the engine and a hot blast of wind. I laughed, holding my hair back with my hands. I felt safe, as though we were on a roller-coaster ride on a closed track, enjoying the thrill and the speed, knowing there was no real danger.

"Do you like to go fast?" he shouted over the noise of the car and the road.

I nodded. "Do you keep a car in every city?" I yelled back.

His bristly grizzled head gleamed silver and black in the sun. "It belongs to a friend of mine!" He passed a semi truck on the straightaway, and my heart, like a sun inside my chest, glowed. We sped past fields of waving grass, neat vineyards on a gentle hill, stands of tall frondy trees. I shut my eyes and gave myself up to the rush and the sun. It was too noisy to talk, and what was there to say anyway? I was happy, happy in a way that seemed, like a great painting, to make words superfluous. I didn't care if we never got to Padua.

But we did get there, after only about an hour. We strolled down the streets of little shops and old painted doors and flowered iron balconies. We walked slowly, arm in arm, pointing out merchandise in shop windows: a scarf, a glass, a pair of shoes. Bernard moved through the streets solidly, gracefully, like a man on horseback. The top of my head came up just to his shoulder, and I smelled the clean cloth of his jacket, the old stone of the buildings, smoke, earth, and, faintly, the briny orange of his cologne. I leaned closer, breathing it in.

We came to a restaurant, a long low room a few steps down from the street, where Paduans on their lunch hour ate plates of thinly sliced veal with anchovies. We ordered the same, and a carafe of wine, which we drank out of tumblers, talking of the summer weather, the Italian roads, the landscape. I told him I was surprised at how empty the fields had seemed: in Wisconsin the corn stretched right up to the highways. All the land was organized, improved, accounted for. You could measure the progress of summer by the height of the corn. How did you measure the season here, I wondered. Or did the Italians drift through time, marking centuries rather than months, permitting fields to grow their own crops of grasses and wildflowers?

"Where else have you been in Italy?" Bernard asked.

"Nowhere."

"Not to Florence? Not to Rome? No junior year abroad? No whirlwind art history class trip in college?"

I explained that at my college almost no one went abroad. I had begun to understand that this wasn't the norm in the kinds of colleges art-world people generally went to, but it didn't seem unreasonable to me. Wasn't the leap from the farm or the small town to the college campus enough cultural dislocation? Wasn't college education itself enough of a voyage? All around us, well-dressed people ate their veal, keeping their knives in their right hands, their lyrical, unintelligible speech rising and swirling like music. It was as though we were alone, Bernard and I, on a green island floating in the lapping sea. Leaning over the table to refill my glass, he touched a finger to my earlobe. "Look," he said. "You don't even have pierced ears."

Over coffee, Bernard told me about growing up on Cape Cod, where the land was always changing, literally reshaped year after year by storms and tides. "When I was twelve, my father had our house raised up and moved thirty yards back. It would have fallen into the ocean otherwise. Up till then we'd only spent summers in Nauquasset, but we moved there year-round that fall. He had retired early, because of his health, and he wanted to see the ocean every day."

"Was that hard for you? The move?"

"No. Nauquasset always felt like home to me. I loved it there. Have you been to the Cape?"

I shook my head.

"It's barely land at all. Just a curved ribbon unrolling into the blue—or smoky gray—Atlantic. The sky is so wide open, and everything is always in motion. The grass, the flags, the clouds. Even the land, shifting under you. It's a bleak landscape in some ways, especially in winter, but I've never been anywhere else I felt so alive." A vibrancy I hadn't seen before rinsed through him while he was speaking. His gray face flushed, his eyes softened, and his hunched spine straightened like a tree growing toward the light.

After lunch we strolled down arcaded streets and past green lawns dotted with neatly trimmed shrubs. There was a line at the modest brick building that was our destination—modest, anyway, compared with San Marco—but Bernard had tickets and strode unhurriedly to the front. "Are you ready?" he whispered in my ear. He held my hand as if I were a child.

"Ready for what?" I leaned into him, the soft ridges of the seersucker pressed into me as I stretched my mouth toward his ear.

"Ready to burn."

And so we went into the Scrovegni Chapel.

At first it was hard to take anything in but the sound of feet ringing against the tiles, the coolness of the narrow space. Then the blue arch of the roof pulled my eyes up, glinting with painted stars. The ribbon of portraits led my gaze along the barrel vault, and I began to take it in: the aching blue and the clear burnished pinks, the solid, graceful figures reaching, bending, kneeling, weeping, soaring (in the case of the angels), the way the scenes floated in space like visions, yet at the same time settled the space around them, making of them shimmering transparent windows into the divine.

In one panel, Joachim and Anna, haloed and passionate, met in a kiss, the arch of their leaning bodies echoing the arch of the Golden Gate. In another, a bearded Magus kissed the holy infant's feet while tall camels looked joyfully on and a fat orange star blazed overhead. In a third, a flock of angels, avatars of lamentation, filled the purple sky above the bone-white body of Christ in his grieving mother's arms. I had seen slides of these frescoes in school, I had answered exam questions about Giotto, I had memorized his dates and the names of his influences. I would have said, if anyone had asked, that I loved Giotto; but nothing in my life had prepared me for this. My skin tingled, flooded with warmth, and a sweet golden honey seemed to slide through me—molten sunshine—melting me and lifting me, making me stand up straighter, desire and delight mingled, the hot sweetness filling me like breath. My heart blazed like the golden star of Bethlehem in the painting of the Adoration.

A voice floated through the quiet. *"Ecco, ecco, è tempo,"* someone said. Around us, feet shuffled, the crowd shifted. I looked at Bernard.

"Time, it's time," the voice said in singsong English. A man in a black uniform decorated with gold braid stood in the middle of the room, repeating his line in three or four languages. Though we had just gotten in, he was motioning us out.

"They just give you fifteen minutes," Bernard whispered, "but don't worry." He went over to the guard and began to murmur, softly, surely. The guard interrupted with a blast of Italian. Bernard took a paper from an inner pocket and showed it to him. The man frowned at the paper. He picked it up and held it to the light, then tapped it with a sausagelike finger while Bernard murmured some more. By now, everyone had exited the chapel but us and, of course, the winged lamenters and the pale Christ and all the characters from those ancient stories who, struggling through their difficult lives, could have had no idea that they were shaping the history, hopes, terrors, habits, and morals of half the world.

Without artists, would this heritage have descended to us? Would the words and deeds—the revelation—have survived the arduous journey into the present without the painters, the mosaic workers, the storytellers, the stone carvers, the poets, the singers, the workers in stained glass? Wasn't it art, I thought—as I watched Bernard open a handsome black wallet and remove a handful of lire—that had been the carrier of the divine? Popes had understood that. The Emperor Constantine. Monks in damp Irish monasteries illuminating the Word. Bernard folded the lire and passed them to the guard. The man's eyebrows twitched as he tucked the packet of bright paper into the recesses of his uniform.

At our red-brick Methodist church in LaFreniere, everything—the pews, the altar, the garish windows, the hulking candlesticks, the leather hymnals—had been ugly. Why was that? What if the congregation had engaged real artists? Did such a thing happen anymore, anywhere in America? Why were artists considered heathen, dangerous, heretical, sly? Since when? Since Andy Warhol? Since Paul Gauguin? Since Manet and his *Olympia*—was it the fault of the French?

Another group of tourists filed in. Bernard came back to me and put his hand on my arm, its pressure conveying the thrill of the suave, illicit transaction. "We can stay as long as you like," he said.

I stood on my tiptoes and kissed his cheek with my burning lips.

6.

And here I was again, rising through the dark in the clanking elevator—my ungrateful heart, too, clanking—to face my benefactress. It was almost midnight. When we finally left the Scrovegni Chapel, we had walked through Padua, seen the cathedral and the university, the green parks and the Orto Botanico. We had dined at a small restaurant specializing in Venetian cuisine—risotto with peas, fish with olives, *baicoli* (from the local word for the sea bass these biscuits are shaped like), and zabaglione—then driven back to Venice in the soft black night. On the boat up the Grand Canal from the Tronchetto, the floating city shimmered like a city in the clouds, shifting and unreal.

In the fourth-floor corridor, however, reality returned. The hallway was dim and still, smelling of old carpet and cleaning fluid, the striped wallpaper faintly damp to the touch. In my room, the light on the phone was blinking. I had three messages, increasingly vexed, all from Louise. Well, she had the right. She had no doubt expected me back for dinner, though she hadn't actually said so. Still, I was indignant. Listening to her angry recorded squawk (so like my mother's scolding perorations), my body still reverberating with the thrill of the day, my fear of the consequences of my disappearance was tempered by the cold disdain that rose in my throat like bile. I stood at the connecting door, knocked, tried the knob. It turned.

The room had been neatened since the morning. The bottles and glasses had been cleared away, the floor vacuumed, the scattered clothes folded out of sight. A lamp on the desk cast a small circle of light by which I could make out a suitcase in the middle of the floor, half full, and also the shadowy shapes of three women huddled together like witches, the one lying in the tidied bed and the other two in chairs pulled close to either side of it.

"At last!" Sarabeth said.

"Where on earth?" April broke in.

"They found a body floating in the canal," Louise pronounced slowly, her voice hoarse. "It could have been you."

"No," I said loudly into the silence. "That was a prostitute."

"How do you know that?" Sarabeth demanded.

I thought. "I heard some people talking."

"I would have felt responsible!" Louise cried. "What would I have told your poor mother?" The other two nodded ritually.

"I'm sorry if I worried you," I said. "You said I should go out, so I went out. It never occurred to me—"

"She didn't think you'd be so *late*!" Sarabeth said.

"The least you could have done was *called*!" April said.

"It's not as though you have a lot of experience traveling," Louise remarked. "Anything might have happened."

It was as though my mother, about whom Louise claimed to be so concerned, had been split in three, each part with its own mouth and pair of thrilled, indignant eyes. I couldn't think of anything to say that wouldn't make me sound more childish, so I said nothing.

Louise put her hands to her head. She groaned.

"What is it?" Sarabeth asked, while April, still fixing me with her laser stare, noted aloud, "Louise is ill."

"I know," I said. "She told me."

"No, really ill. Feverish. She sees lights burning, like fires in the dark. She has to go home. She's had it before, her own doctor knows what to do."

I squinted at Louise through the gloom. It was true that she was pale, her eyes glittering and hollow, greasy strands of hair sticking to her forehead. Her chest rose and fell visibly, effortfully, with a kind of mechanized shudder like a machine running down. Still—didn't Italy have doctors? At first I was merely annoyed by her attitude, and then, as though a cold wave had washed over me, I apprehended what it meant. We would be going. We were supposed to stay till Tuesday, but we would be going now. The suitcase on the floor. The purple necktie she had stroked like a pet. I'd had no idea how much I counted on staying—it was only three more days, after all—but oh, how my life had altered in the last three! Italy, Venice, the Biennale, Giotto. The rich coffee and the green canals and the hot timeless piazzas. And Bernard. My heart stumbled at the thought of not seeing him again. What was it I felt? Not love exactly; not desire exactly. But a diffuse erotic longing twinkling like a sparkler. In LaFreniere on the Fourth of July we used to inscribe our names on the dark with sparklers, hurrying to finish before the spitting wands burned out, leaving us with a hot metal scrap smelling of sulfur. If I never saw Bernard again, I felt, my heart would be like that: a black, burned-out, foul-smelling stump. Maybe there was something else as well—some wiser, more sober seed of what I would become that recognized something in him that was recognizing me. A likeness, a kinship. I'd like to think so. But actually it was probably closer to a crush, the infatuation of a girl for a charismatic teacher. "When do we go?"

"Nine o'clock tomorrow morning. You'd better pack tonight. April changed the tickets. Since you were AWOL."

AWOL—that summed it up exactly. The senseless orders, the routine humiliations, the exaltation of rank: working for Louise was like being in an army of one commanded by a vain general whose uniform had been designed by Prada!

I excused myself and turned to go, feeling the building pressure of tears.

Louise's voice, rising out of the darkness, was thin and steely. "Where were you all day?"

Was it a trick? Did she have spies? "I was looking at art," I mumbled.

"Nobody saw you. Not anywhere. No one I spoke to."

I thought about saying I had gone to the smaller satellite projects, I had taken a walk and gotten lost, I had run into some people I knew from New York and gone to a party. But then I changed my mind. It wasn't that I thought I owed her the truth—I didn't. I wanted to see the look on her face when I said it. "Actually, I went to Padua with Bernard Augustin, to see the Giottos. He invited me." The words, as I spoke them, filled me with light. I felt I was glowing in that dim room, a bright moon in the midst of their darknesses. Louise's face went blank for a moment, and then she smiled icily.

"Funny," she said. "Very clever. Well, if you don't want to tell us, I can't make you."

For a moment my lived experience seemed to crack under the pressure of her disbelief.

"Better get packing," she advised. "Unless Jeff Koons is taking you to a disco."

I couldn't sleep that night. It was hot. I lay in the narrow bed with the windows open, hoping for a breeze. Outside, the sky was a cloudy, shifting black through which noises traveled obliquely, as though from no particular direction: a shout, a boat engine revving, a clatter of footsteps, distant music with a harsh, throbbing beat. Bernard had said he would call me tomorrow, but tomorrow I would be gone. He would dial the hotel and ask to be connected to the room. The phone bell would ring out four times, six times, how many jangling bleats shivering the silence before he gave up? Maybe he would think I'd stepped out or was in the shower, and so he would call again a little later, and then perhaps he would ask the front desk to take a message, and the clerk would glance at the register and say, *Sir, the young lady has checked out.* I would be gone—vanished, disappeared.

Earlier that night, toward the end of dinner, stuffed full and sleepy, brash with wine, I'd asked, "Why did you come to Venice?"

"For the Biennale, of course. Why did you?" Bernard smiled benignly, speaking to me as though to a child, a farm girl, a lamb. I didn't like it when he spoke to me like that.

"I came because I was invited," I said.

"Oh? And do you accept every invitation issued to you?"

The waiter cleared away our dessert plates and Bernard ordered two espressos.

"I would have thought—" I began. "It's just that, after what happened . . ."

His courtly, formal expression sagged. He knew what I meant. I should have stopped—I knew I should stop—but I couldn't. I was a rogue baby carriage rolling downhill. I was a heavy stone gathering moss. I was a runaway train.

"Is it true her body was never found?" I said in a hushed squawk. Words perched on my tongue like vultures, and his face seemed to recede from me down a tunnel of black feathers. I leaned forward, eager and abashed, gripping the edge of the table. "I heard she liked to swim alone, that there are currents . . . It must have been terrible for you, you were so close!"

"Stop!" He spat the word across the table.

I stopped. I was trembling with the dark euphoria of my transgression. He had been nothing but kind to me.

"You don't know what you're talking about," he said. "I came to Venice because I collect art. I love art! I love Venice. Why should I give that up? I decline to. I always come to Venice for the Biennale. I *always* stay at the Gritti. I *always* spend a day in Padua! Do you understand?"

The thrill of my wild questioning sank beneath the glassy surface of silence. I nodded. "I understand."

"No, you don't." The waiter brought the espressos. Bernard lifted his cup to his lips, then set it down again soundlessly. "You don't understand anything about it."

It was true—I didn't understand. But I wanted to. And not just because it was a thrilling story, though no doubt that played a role. I wanted to understand him—to understand Bernard. I felt connected to him by a bright thread, yet we could not have been more different. He was rich and I was poor. He knew everyone and everything, and I knew no one and nothing. What was I doing with him here in a restaurant in Padua? Why had he asked me? Was it pity? Whimsy? A game? What did he see when he looked at me? What did I look like? He could have chosen anyone. He'd had Alena. And now he had me.

~

After a long time the sky began to lighten: black fading to a gray that, after growing misty pink, suddenly revealed itself, like a handkerchief turned inside out, to be a clear pale blue. I got out of bed, put on my clothes, and took the elevator down. It was just before seven o'clock when I made my way through the quiet streets to the Hotel Gritti Palace, host to princes and divas, on the Grand Canal. Bernard had told me his room number, which happened to be the same as his birthday, so I went straight up in the elevator. But alone in the hallway, standing at the door, I lost my nerve. What right had I to wake him? No, better to leave a note of farewell and explanation, just so he knew what had happened, where I had gone. Perhaps I could append my phone number, my address, and someday if he happened to be passing through the city he might . . .

I pressed my cheek to the cool, hard wood and, my eyes aching with exhaustion and desire, sent a silent appeal through the door. I visualized the thread connecting us, spun out from my heart like spider's silk, navigating the whirling atoms of the door, arcing through the unknown space of the room to terminate just above the lapels of his pajamas. (I was picturing him clad for bed like a movie star from the forties—Clark Gable, perhaps, or Cary Grant.) Then, quite unexpectedly, I heard the sound of paper rustling, a stream of water, a window being thrust up. My heart flared. I knocked. Nothing happened. I knocked again, louder.

The door opened and there was Bernard, dressed not in ironed pajamas but in gray silk boxers with stars on them, his fish-white jaws rough with stubble, his hair spiky with sweat, his body big in the shoulders and chest like a swimmer's. It was a shock to see him like that, almost naked. He looked younger than I thought of him, more physically vigorous. He stepped into the hall. As he shut the door behind him, a flicker of movement inside the room caught my eye: a young man, perhaps my age, lounging on the rumpled bed. "What's wrong?" Bernard said as the door clicked shut.

"I came to say good-bye!" I said. "We're leaving, Louise isn't well. We're flying back today, and I wanted—I didn't want—" I tried to be calm, but my tears spilled over and my words caught in my throat. I was trembling.

Bernard frowned, putting a thoughtful finger to his lips. "Go downstairs," he said. "I'll meet you in the breakfast room. Order coffee."

"I don't have time!" I wailed. "We're leaving the hotel at nine!"

He smiled, the weary, patient smile I'd already come to know. "Better hurry, then," he said.

~

In the grand, hushed breakfast room, lush and intricately patterned carpets in blue and pink stretched luxuriously across the gleaming floors, and chandeliers of twisted, watery glass, suspended from the ceilings, caught the morning light and gave it back, honeyed and liquescent. Flowers bloomed in bowls on creamy tablecloths: frilly yellow peonies and carnal purple irises with green-white beards. The very air seemed golden, luscious, faintly narcotic. For a moment, stepping through the door, I forgot everything. So this was what wealth could do: transfigure a fragment of the world into beauty. For the first time a thin spine of envy pierced me. Not luxury, power, leisure: I didn't care about those. But beauty, every piece of the world made golden. How was it fair that I should be barred from it like the poor relation I was, my face pressed to the window? I sat down in a daze and ordered two cappuccinos from the gleaming waiter who shook the snowy swan in front of me into a napkin and laid it, a linen blessing, across my lap. I looked hard into his handsome, neutral face. Coffee eyes, inky lashes, hair the color of butter. Did they choose waiters here for beauty too? Did the waiters know they were cogs in the machine of the sublime? And if they did, did they care?

The cappuccinos arrived in pale green cups designed to look as though they were made of overlapping leaves. A moment later Bernard appeared, slipping through the liquid air, his hair wet, his face smooth, his skin hidden under scrupulous layers of buttoned cloth. "Now," he said, "what's all this about you going?"

I pulled the gilded air into my lungs for strength. "Louise is sick. She needs to go home. We're leaving in an hour."

The waiter materialized, perfect as a statue, though I imagined I saw the shadow of a smirk on his marble features as he took Bernard in, murmuring, *"Signore?"* Bernard ordered toast, fruit, yogurt. He looked at me but I shook my head. I was too grief-stricken to eat. When the waiter was gone, Bernard sipped his coffee. "But you don't want to go."

"Of course I don't! I've barely seen anything. I haven't even been in the Accademia, I haven't seen all the pavilions. I—"

"So don't go." He looked away from me, out the long windows toward where the green water slipped invisibly through the steep channels. "Don't go."

"But I can't *stay*! I'm not like you, I can't just do what I *want*!" So Bernard was just a rich person after all, I thought. A rich man with no notion of life.

"Cara," he said, finger to his lips. "Listen. You can stay if you want to. You could stay with me."

Stunned into silence, I waited for my brain to make sense of his words. "What do you mean?" My voice was like cardboard, stiff and pulpy.

"I'm offering you a job, *cara*," Bernard said. "At Nauquasset."

"A job?" Feeling like the butt of a joke I was too stupid to understand, I gaped at him. "What kind of a job?" Was he asking me to be his secretary? His—what—personal assistant?

"I need a curator."

"Don't tease me," I said.

"Tease you? My God, why would I do that?" His sharpness startled me. "It's not as exalted as it sounds. We're a small place, a small staff, everyone does everything. But I can't— I don't want— It's impossible for me."

The waiter appeared again, bowing over a silver tray, placing on the table all the things Bernard had said he wanted, and a few more besides. Bernard tucked a napkin into his collar, picked up a glinting knife, and began spreading honey on his golden toast. The room grew lighter as the day brightened. I didn't know what to say.

"Of course, I understand if you don't want to," Bernard said. "You hardly know me. Why would you throw your whole life over and go somewhere you've never seen with a man who . . ." He stopped, a dark note in his voice I hear clearly in memory, but which at the time was drowned out by the brilliant halo that seemed to be falling over us, a general glow like something out of one of those seasons-of-life paintings by Corot.

"But," I said, instinctively groping for a reason, though God knows I didn't want to. "I can't do a job like that. I don't know anything!"

"Are you listening to me?" Bernard said. "You see things. You look at a work of art and you know what it is. Do you know how rare that is? Do you think I want someone who's spent decades learning names and prices?"

I felt—how can I describe how I felt? Like a parched field drenched with rain. Like a plant the first time it bursts into flower.

Louise was already in the lobby when I stumbled in, panting, my hair a mess, my sweaty face flushed with joy and doubt. Already I feared I had invented the scene at the Gritti, that I would tell Louise I wasn't going back with her only to discover that what had happened with Bernard would turn out to be, if not a hallucination, then a crazy misunderstanding. What would I do then?

Louise was packed into a navy suit, and she wore a small navy hat pinned to her head. Her skin looked sallow and blotched, and one side of her face was swollen. She stood fuming under a framed poster of gondolas on the Grand Canal. "Don't talk!" she said. "I can't even *speak* to you."

"I'm not going," I said. "Thank you for everything."

She held up a warning finger. "Not a word! Not one word, do you understand me! If I were a different kind of person I would—you don't even want to *know* what I would do." She yanked the handle of her suitcase.

"I'm not going," I repeated a little louder. "I'm staying here. I've been offered a new job." The sound of the words reassured me—solid, plausible. I would be the curator of the Nauquasset Contemporary Museum! I would have an office with a window overlooking the sea! I would buy new dresses and be gracious to artists! *Ms. Sherman, so nice to see you, won't you come in?*

"Stop it," Louise said. She started for the door but halted when she saw I wasn't following. "Whatever it is," she sighed, "we can discuss it on the plane."

"I'm not getting on the plane," I said. "I'm staying in Venice. I've been offered a new job and I've accepted it. Bernard Augustin has hired me."

She laughed. "To be what? His beard?"

I was still innocent enough that I didn't know what she meant; I had never heard the term. "To be the curator," I said. "At the Nauk."

Louise blinked, her clumpy lashes leaving black stains in the hollows under her eyes. "Nonsense," she said.

"You'll miss your plane," I said.

"Nonsense! Did you sign a contract? Did you negotiate a salary? Did he put anything in writing at all?"

"There hasn't been time," I said. "It just happened." But my hot face grew hotter and a lump bloomed in my chest.

Louise smiled her timeless hag's smile. "Maybe he was joking," she suggested with a plausible wink.

"He wasn't joking."

"Sometimes it's hard to tell. With men like that."

"He wasn't joking."

"Maybe not." She shrugged. "Maybe he knows what he's doing. Maybe he wants someone as *unlike* Alena as possible! For that job. She was beautiful, you know." I knew. "Dynamic, brilliant. Impeccable taste. Clothes looked gorgeous on her, she could have been a model if she wanted. Fluent in three languages! She sailed, water-skied, swam like a fish. And so charming! She could charm the fur off a cat, that's what people said." A faint, whining buzz like a mosquito started up in my ears. Oh, when would she go! "Yes," she went on. "I suppose it makes sense. He wants someone who won't remind him of her in the slightest." She tilted her head and looked at me hard, a long look, up and down, as though I were a suit of clothes. I knew what she was doing—comparing every inch of me to Alena. She was giving me a preview of the way everyone would look at me from now on when Bernard introduced me or when I introduced myself. *How unlike Alena,* they would think. *Poor Bernard, what was he thinking?* How could he expect this waif to do? This sparrow, when he had had a falcon.

I did my best to stand up straight, but I could feel myself shrinking into myself, my flesh shriveling under the harsh beam of her gaze. Still, I wasn't a child. "He says I have an eye," I said in a fraying, defiant voice. "I see things, he says."

Louise let go of her suitcase and seized my arm in her claw. She leaned over and brushed a cold kiss against my cheek. "I hope you don't see ghosts," she hissed.

Then I was alone in the damp, cramped lobby with the concierge, who winked at me from under his cap.

7.

IT WAS EVENING by the time we reached Nauquasset, but so close to the solstice that the sky at that hour was still filled with light. The clear blue overhead fell away in streams of orange and salmon, ragged streaks of pink and scarlet and rose. I thought of all the real and painted skies I had seen in the past few weeks—the watery dome of Venice, the elegant roof of Paris, the billowing clouds of Rubens and Turner's luminous shifting fogs. We had spent another week at the Biennale, and then—because, as Bernard said, we were already practically there—a week each in Florence and Paris. "It's not much," he said. "Not in the scheme of things." But we saw a lot of art in those three weeks, and other things too: churches, gardens, monuments, galleries. Also promenades, boutiques, hotels, railroad stations, and cafés. Those were works of art too, weren't they? Made objects expressive of human thought and desire. The question of what art was—especially in the contemporary art world—was slippery enough. The leavings of a happening, the repeated eating of a tuna sandwich, an unmade bed littered with underpants: if such things were recognized as art, how not the Ponte Vecchio or the Luxembourg Gardens or the entire city of Paris at sunset? Art and life, life and art, had never bled into each other so freely as they seemed to during that late June at the beginning of a new century, as Bernard led me through dim rooms and brilliant streets, directing my eye there and there.

Back in America, everything looked strange. Through the airplane window, as we landed, the city of Boston seemed as provisional as a stage set, and once we were on the ground, the buildings and bridges had the jaunty brightness of hastily painted façades. Highways and tunnels spun away in all directions, looping and dividing, changing their names as they separated and joined up with one another, but Bernard threaded the big car expertly through the maze, whistling, his top button undone to reveal a clean undershirt and a graying tuft of hair. Gradually the city fell away, the towns grew sparser. Then we were crossing high over the canal, and I looked down on the toy boats with the abstract benign approval of a minor god. Speeding down the highway on the other side of the bridge, Bernard cracked his window. I smelled pine woods, flower gardens, diesel fumes, the sea. "Just another hour," he said.

On either side rough-barked pine trees and small gray houses edged the road. Before and behind us, cars were stuffed with suitcases and children, bicycles and kayaks clamped to their roofs, while rattling trailers bearing motorboats or sailboats clanked behind, jouncing on their hitches. "How long has it been since you were last here?" I asked.

Absorbed by the driving, perhaps, he didn't answer.

"Bernard?"

"Hmm?"

"How long since you were last here?"

He adjusted his sunglasses on the bridge of his big, handsome nose. "Oh, quite some time."

"This year?"

"I don't think so. No. Not this year."

In the humming silence I listened, trying to hear the ocean. My family used to go canoeing in the summers on Lake Michigan; sailing too in a little Sunfish rented by the hour. Oh, those timeless blue and golden afternoons that stretched out for days on end, unbroken by any event save the cool breeze swelling the belly of the sail! At noon the sun stood absolutely still in the sky as though it were painted there. The gnats swarmed like living veils. A week in the quaint, purgatorial cottage with its putty-colored pasteboard walls and curtains printed self-referentially with rows of curtained cottages felt like an eternity.

"Do you have a boat?" I asked.

"What?"

"A boat? You're right on the bay, aren't you? At the Nauk."

"Yes," he said. "But no boat."

"Really? I imagined you with one. A white sloop with a little cabin, maybe."

"I did have one," he said. "Two, actually. But I sold them."

"Oh? Why?"

"No reason. I lost interest." He rolled his window all the way down and rested his elbow on the frame. The wind from his open window flung my hair across my face, and I fished in my purse for an elastic, twisting it back into a knot. He glanced at me sharply. "What are you doing?"

"Doing?"

"With your hair."

"Just—tying it back. The wind."

"I wish you wouldn't. It makes you look . . ."

The wind was chilly on my bare shoulders. "What? How does it make me look?"

He glanced at me, glanced away again. "Old."

The car whizzed on, past the little huddle of stores—a hairdresser, a real estate agent, a garden center. I remembered the wind on the road to Padua, how I hadn't minded it then. I pulled the elastic out of my hair. And then we were back in the woods among the bent trees and the smell of sap and the blue-black shadows.

The closer we got to Nauquasset, the faster Bernard drove.

"Tell me again," I said. "Tell me about the Nauk." In Venice, and later in Florence and Paris, Bernard had painted the picture for me: the long museum building with its angular wings, its framed views of the blue rolling water. How, because the Cape curled out from the mainland like a beckoning arm, you could stand on the bluff and watch the sun setting in the west over the bay. And the shingled house in the lee of the cliff, with its gravel walkway, its daylilies, its fenced grassy yard for hanging laundry. The house that would be mine.

Bernard pressed his hand to his forehead, between his eyes, as though it ached. "You'll see it soon enough," he said.

A few miles farther along, the road forked and we veered left onto the narrower branch. For a while the trees grew thicker, the trunks more hunched and misshapen—nothing at all like the pine forests of Wisconsin with their tall straight trunks like groves of arrows. It was easy to imagine fantastic creatures lurking in the shadows—trolls or fauns peering out with yellow eyes—though I knew the real threats were the hungry, feckless, tick-infested deer. And then, quite suddenly, we shot out of the woods into the wide watery light of the fading day. Here were scrub roses, blooming pink and white among the thorny shrubs, the bayberry and beach plum, the thistle and poison ivy and Queen Anne's lace. On either side, the asphalt was edged with fine ribbons of sand above which rose the gentle hills, the pale salmon-colored clouds, the yellow twilit sky. Distant gulls, like something a child might draw, floated in the pink distance, while nearer by, other birds—swallows and sparrows—flicked their tails on telephone wires and chattered down at us.

"Look!" Bernard raised a finger but I turned my head too late; all I saw was a diving streak of sooty gray out of the corner of my eye.

"What? What was it?"

"A hawk. Catching a mouse, probably. Or trying to."

"Oh, I wish I'd seen it!"

"We have owls too. You can hear them at night. And foxes. Rumors of a coyote, but I've never seen it myself. Here we are." He swung the car into the mouth of a rutted lane, stopped, and got out, leaving the motor running. Before us, a pair of weathered wooden gates barred the way, covered with reliefs, like the baptistery doors we'd seen in Florence, only in long rows instead of square panels. A heavy padlock held them shut, and as Bernard fiddled with the combination, I stared at the rows of creatures crowding the surface: graceful starfish and spiny conch, turtles with patterned shells, little salamanders, statuesque foxes, brave rabbits, opossums sleeping with their naked tails across their noses. A peaceable wooden bestiary that made me forget for a moment how tired I was, and how scared. I leaned forward to see better, elbows on the dashboard, but Bernard had snapped open the lock and was already swinging the gates back.

Up we bumped along the narrow lane, Bernard steering carefully through the ruts as the drive dipped and rose. The wheels crunched over patches of shell and the bottom scraped twice, despite his care, against the high hump of packed sand in the middle of the lane. Light and color faded quickly from the rust-red sky, the swaying grasses on the dunes swimming in my vision. And then we could hear the sea.

How to describe the effect of that sound on a child of snowdrifts and searing summer skies? I knew Lake Michigan, as I have said, and I had been to Coney Island, and I'd recently made the acquaintance of the Venetian Lagoon. But none of that had prepared me for this: the hushed, monotonous sucking like the indrawn breath of a beast, and then the distending roar of the wave building, breaking, shattering against the sand. A pause, and then the beast drew another breath. A restless, endless, living sound. For a moment, as it filled my ears with its slow panting, I knew I had made a terrible mistake. And then we crested the second hill, and I could see the bay.

The deep azure expanse was flecked and crested with white, and long streaks of gauzy pink cloud floated across the blazing sun, which just touched the rim of the water. A golden road stretched straight across the deepening blue, the near end apparently just below the bluff we were approaching, so that it seemed as though, if we hurried, we could take a quick stroll across the glittering surface toward the sun before it dropped out of sight. My heart bloomed in my chest, beating hard against the lattice of bone, as it had bloomed in the hot Uffizi as we stood before Botticelli's Venus on her shell. And there, spread like a mantle across the shoulder of the bluff, the long silvered shape of the museum rose out of the sea of grass like the breaching back of a whale. Nauquasset.

Bernard stopped the car. The evening breeze chilled my bare arms and I shivered with exhaustion, awe, doubt, and a taut, ferocious joy. No wonder Bernard loved it! No wonder he couldn't stay away. But when I turned to him, I found neither pleasure nor relief in his face. Rather, a new, dark blankness was drawn like a shade over his eyes. He stood for a few seconds looking out over the restless, glittering sea, and then he turned back to the car and popped the trunk. "Let's go," he said, tugging my rolling suitcase down the path.

The small house where I was to live, nestled in the lee of a bluff where it was protected from the north wind, smelled of damp, of old wood smoke, and faintly of ammonia. The downstairs consisted of a kitchen and a living room with an elbow for a nonexistent dining table, while the upstairs boasted a bathroom and two bedrooms, the smaller one with a desk and a bookshelf and a narrow daybed covered with a plaid blanket. It was all very plain, very ordinary, the furniture solid and battered. In the glare and buzz of the fluorescent kitchen light, I could see the speckles of age on the walls and on the surface of the refrigerator. Crooked shelves held squat canisters for flour, sugar, coffee, rice. There was a ceiling fan with a chain to pull, and a ceramic sink, and in the corner a washing machine with a scratched glass porthole in its belly. No dryer. Suddenly the function of the little fenced yard with its clothesline, so picturesquely described by Bernard, hit home: I would have to actually hang my wet laundry there. My towels and sheets, my sweatpants and underpants, my heavy denim jeans.

Tugging open a drawer to cover my dismay, I confronted a stack of thin, frayed dishcloths. They looked damp. The whole house was damp—the woodwork, the lampshades, the sofa cushions and rag rugs. Well, we were by the ocean, after all—though you couldn't see it from the house, which was shrouded in the bluff and faced the wrong direction. Suddenly that seemed remarkably unfair.

"I thought there'd be a view," I said, looking up at Bernard. He seemed to sway slightly in my vision, as though he were standing on a boat.

"You'll be comfortable here," he said.

"I mean, it doesn't seem right," I said. "To live all the way at the edge of the world and not even be able to see the ocean!"

Bernard's jowls were blue with stubble after the long journey, his eyes shot through with red. He said: "You'll get plenty of the ocean."

I could feel a shift in the air, like a storm moving in, only instead of rain it would be tears gushing. I slammed the drawer shut. The old wood splintered, the sticky tarnished handle coming off in my hand. I looked up at Bernard. How had either of us believed I was equal to this?

"Roald will be out in the morning," he said faintly. "He'll fix it."

Who was Roald? And how could he fix our essential error? And why was Bernard speaking to me like a well-mannered zombie? "And she lived here?" I said. "Alena?"

He stared at me. "Here? No. What gave you that idea?"

What indeed? I had supposed that a house on the property, untenanted, would have been hers. Bernard dug his keys out of his pockets, ran a hand through his hair. He looked older than he had ever looked in Europe. "Well. I'll let you get to unpacking. Good night."

The door banged, the warm dark night swallowed him up. I heard the whine of the engine, the crunch of the tires, and then silence. I was quite alone.

8.

How well I remember my first night in that house. I had so little with me—just the suitcase I had packed less than a month before in my studio apartment a thousand miles away. Here was the cotton nightgown, knee length, white with blue forget-me-nots, that I had worn between the heavy ironed linens of the Ritz—the Baglioni, the Gritti—and before that, the more ordinary sheets of the Hotel da Silva in the little room adjoining Louise's, back in the dimness of my other life. Now, pulling back the candlewick bedspread on the sagging bed, switching on the light with its frayed cord, pressing my face to the window out which the wan moon rode low over the scrubby meadows, I wondered about Louise. Had she recovered from her illness? From my desertion? What version of my story was she telling in the museum, which would travel like wind through a cornfield across the Midwest? It wasn't that I wanted to be back there; I didn't. I had no false nostalgia. But lying in the damp, crooked room that was now mine, listening to the brigades of crickets chanting in the grass all around the house, the occasional car passing on the road at the end of the lane, a bullfrog croaking in a marshy pond somewhere, I began to shiver despite the warmth of the close night. My mind spun its wheels, trying to assimilate all that had happened to land me exactly here, and my pulse raced every time the house creaked, jolting me out of half-dreams. I tried to relax, to force myself to breathe, but my muscles twitched like the whiskers of a nervous cat, and my lungs seemed choked by the acrid smoke of the bridges I had burned.

It was a relief when the first gray light seeped through the curtains and I could give myself permission to get up.

Downstairs, the refrigerator was empty, but I found coffee and filters, and there was clumped sugar in one of the sticky canisters. I was wandering around the house looking everything over—the pedestal table, the skirted yellow couch, the begrimed paintings of fishing boats—when someone knocked. Assuming it was Bernard, I hurried to the door, eager to put last night's unpleasantness behind us. But when I swung it open, an unfamiliar man stood on the wooden step. Perhaps fifty-five, with broad shoulders and a weathered face and more than a bit of a gut, he wore a plaid flannel shirt untucked over his jeans, the laces of his paint-spattered work boots dangling. His thick silvery-brown hair was wet—I could see the comb marks—and his pale blue eyes, set deep under a sunburned brow, were spun with green, like a marble I'd had when I was a girl: a rare sea-glass swirlie. He held a brown paper grocery bag in one arm.

"You're the new curator?" I pulled the lapels of my robe together as his voice, all stretched vowels and missing *r*'s, drifted toward me, as thick as seaweed. It was the first real Cape Cod accent I'd heard: *Yoo-ah tha noo-ah kyoo-ray-tah?*

"Yes."

He held out the bag of groceries. "Brought you a few things. Tide you over till you can get to a store." *Tide yoo o-vah. Get to a sto-ah.*

Behind him the morning was turning from pink to blue. Birds

chattered in the bushes, and the smell of the sea freshened the air, though I could not see it. "Thank you," I said.

"I'm Roald Egeland," he said.

I waited for more, but there wasn't any, just the brown bag, a little crumpled, that he held out patiently, like a dog offering a ball. "I've made some coffee," I said. "Would you like some?"

"Wouldn't say no."

I held the door and he came in, looking around at the kitchen in silence as I poured coffee for him and more for myself, adding the milk he'd brought. The swirl of white descending through the dark liquid soothed me. "I hate to drink it black," I confessed.

"I'll take it any way I can get it. On the boat we drink it out of thermoses, three days old."

I put away the milk and bread, bacon and butter, bananas and cans of soup, and the sweating bag of mixed frozen vegetables he'd brought. Noticing the broken drawer, he crouched down and peered at the cracked wood. "What happened here?" *What happaned hee-ah?*

"I guess I pulled too hard."

He frowned, opening and shutting the other drawers. "I'll come back later and fix it. And anything else that needs. I'll take a look around. I can get you a dehumidifier for the damp, not that it'll do any good if you have the windows open. Can't dry out the whole Atlantic Ocean, can you?"

"I guess not," I said. "Sorry, you're a fisherman? A handyman?"

He stood up straighter, the green swirl in his eyes glowing almost fluorescent as his springy eyebrows lowered. "I'm the head preparator," he said. "I install the shows."

"Oh!" I said. "Bernard didn't— Head preparator, then. How nice of you to think of bringing . . . of fixing . . ." I couldn't seem to finish a sentence, they broke up or trailed away, leaving acid bubbles of anxiety floating in the damp air. I wished I was dressed at least, not wearing my old robe with its pattern of red hibiscus and yellow canaries, a Christmas gift from my aunt Bet in Green Bay.

"Bernard asked me to come by. He didn't say? Sometimes he forgets, he gets distracted. And he's impulsive. Well—I don't have to tell you!" He laughed, a bright clap of mirth that took me by surprise. "Who else would skedaddle off to Venice and come back with a new curator in tow?"

I flushed. It seemed crazier all the time—that he had chosen me, that I had come. One of these days I'd have to fly out and deal with my apartment and my things, but not yet. Not yet. I looked up shyly into Roald's broad face with its tracery of lines like the surface of fired clay. "I keep wondering about the last curator," I said. "The one who . . . Was this the beach she would have swum out from? Right here?"

Roald's face shut up like a clam and he looked away out the window where a bird twittered mindlessly in a bush. "Who knows? Probably. She often swam there." He drank his coffee. I stood very still, my bare feet cold on the gritty linoleum.

"And her body was never found?"

"They looked for a long time. Boats, nets, charts of the currents. At first it seemed just a matter of time until they found her. But time kept going by."

"So no one really knows if it was an accident or not?"

"What else could it have been?"

"I just thought—maybe she could have run away?" I didn't want to say that I wondered if she had killed herself.

Roald turned his blue and green marble eyes to me. "Sometimes," he said, "I try to convince myself of that. She was Russian, you know.

Her family. She came here when she was five, but she remembered things. The cold, the sky. The shimmering gold domes they have there, on their churches. She wanted to see the Ural Mountains, the Amber Room, Lake Baikal. She always said . . ."

I waited, trembling, for him to tell me what she always said. It was the first time, I think, I understood that she was real. Alena.

"What?"

"She said she was too big for this country. She said Russia was big enough, *free* enough." He laughed, more darkly this time. "Isn't that a joke? Russia, free!" He put his hands together and cracked his knuckles. His ring finger was missing on his left hand, a pinkish stump marking the place it should have been.

"What happened to your finger?"

"Accident," he said, and put his hands behind his back.

"You were close to her." I was sorry when I realized it. I had started to feel he was someone I could like.

"No," he said. "No. I wouldn't say that."

There were footsteps on the stoop, a perfunctory knock. The door swung open and there was Bernard, wearing an expression of weary, gray-faced geniality like a courteous ghost. He was dressed like Roald, except that his jeans and red plaid shirt looked stiffer, newer. "Good morning," he said. "Hello, Roald. Beautiful morning, isn't it? Thanks for coming over. Is that coffee you're drinking?"

"I'll make some more," I said. "It'll only take a minute." A false heartiness hung in the air like an oily gauze. I wanted to brush it away, to see the contours and corners of the world clearly, but instead I put another pot of coffee on and said I would go get dressed.

"Yes," Bernard said. "Let's get going. It's a busy day!"

Busy with what? I thought of Louise sitting in her office with her plump, taupe-stockinged legs crossed, talking on the phone, scanning the paper, stirring cream into her tea. Surely Alena hadn't spent her days like that! I hurried up the stairs. Behind me I heard Roald say, "How was Venice?"

"Crowded. Every year it gets more . . ."

More what?

My few clothes were crumpled and in need of washing. I'd have to find some time to run them through the washing machine and hang them out to dry. That was all right for summer, but what would it be like in February? Perhaps there was a laundromat in town. Well, but how would I get there? My thoughts chased each other in circles as I threw on the blue skirt that used to be my favorite, and a yellow blouse that wasn't too wrinkled but that, I suddenly remembered, Bernard had said made me look like I was ten. Still, it would have to do. I brushed my hair, put on lipstick, ran the mascara wand through my lashes. I slipped into my shoes, black slingbacks with a high wedge heel and an open toe. They were a little scuffed by now, but they made me taller.

At the top of the stairs I hesitated, suddenly wobbly. The air was thick with damp and salt so that it felt like inhaling a heavy broth through which oxygen trickled and burbled, paddling valiantly toward the thirsty lungs. What if I climbed back into bed? What if I pretended to be sick? What if I really was sick?

"Yes, very young." Bernard's voice echoed up the stairs, followed by a murmur I couldn't make out. "No, I don't think so . . . Obviously." More murmuring. "Well, it was Agnes's idea. I don't care one way or the other . . . Did she? Well, she'll just have to—"

I clattered down, making as much noise as I could. It was obvious they were talking about me: Bernard didn't think something about me, Agnes would have to do something-or-other about me. It was I, without a doubt, who was very young.

And what was Roald saying in his quiet, *r*-less voice? I was pretty sure I didn't want to know.

When I came into the room, all sound ceased except for the buzzing of the overhead light fixture.

"I'm ready!" I said.

Bernard looked me up and down, frowning slightly. "Are you really going to wear those shoes?" he said.

~

I saw what he meant as we walked up the sandy dirt path. The high slingbacks slipped, my feet nearly coming out of them. The day was bright with a strong breeze fluttering the beach grass. On the long back of the dune, the south wing of the Nauk glittered in the sun, just as in the pictures I'd seen. Where the wings came together in a shallow V, like a child's rendering of a soaring gull, there was a little grassy area mostly enclosed by tall square hedges. Here, out of the wind, roses bloomed on trellises, and benches on either side of the entryway invited sitting. Flanking the broad door, narrow strips of glass extended from the foundation to the roof, offering a glimpse—through the museum's tiled lobby—to the glass wall beyond, out which blue waves rolled in foam-capped ranks toward the invisible beach. Standing there, bracing myself to go in as though to dive into that cold blue water, I felt for the first time the strange tension I would later understand the spot was designed to evoke: the peaceful garden stasis of the green grass, the pink roses, the trimmed fragrant yew hedges blocking the wind, confounded by the haunted sound of the ocean waves behind the building. The restless, relentless roar and suck of the sea.

Bernard opened the door.

In the cool, airy lobby, the glittering ocean through the wall of glass surged and lolled, not blue from this vantage but gray: a gun-metal gray and dirty white prairie stretching away to the horizon. My breath caught like a fishbone in my throat. My ruined shoes leaked sand across the terra-cotta. I felt sure a whale would surface from the deep as I watched, or a proud luffing galleon glide into view from out of the frame, beyond which lay the sixteenth century, perhaps, or the beginning of time.

"It's beautiful," I breathed, dislodging the fishbone. Beautiful! The most banal and meaningless word in the language, catchall for everything from the decorative to the compellingly grotesque.

"It's an instructive view," Bernard said. "If the art doesn't make you feel something at least approaching that, what's the point?"

"And one day, of course, it will swallow us all."

I turned to see who had spoken. A woman I hadn't noticed stood near the reception desk. She was large, tall and overweight, wearing a black, low-cut, calf-length dress. Her hair, an unnatural, glassy, pink-streaked black, made her pale face look even paler than it was, pale as a fish belly, or a scrim of frost. How did she manage that, living here? Her lips and fingernails were painted crimson, and her lobeless ears were studded up and down with holes, most of them empty except for the two long curtains of red stones and gold filigree that rippled and swung whenever she moved her head. A gold chain hung around her neck, disappearing down the top of her dress to lodge invisibly between her breasts, which looked hard and potentially dangerous, like a pair of torpedoes.

"Hello, Agnes," Bernard said.

"Hello, Bernard. How nice to see you back at the Nauk." Her voice was cool and smooth, like the underside of a stone. Neither of them made a move to kiss or shake hands.

"It's good to be back," Bernard said.

"You look tan. Europe suits you."

"Nothing suits me like home."

She made no comment, instead turning her stone-gray eyes to me. She bowed her head, then tossed back her fine jet hair. "So you're the new boss." She paused, looking me over with a bright red frown, her eyes chilling me everywhere her gaze settled.

I tried to step forward and offer my hand, but I was frozen where I stood as though struck with a spell. Anyway, she would have seen it tremble.

"I'm Agnes," she said. "The bookkeeper." Something in the way she said it made me think that the words held concealed meaning, as though the entries she kept in her book were not, perhaps, merely financial.

"Agnes is the business manager," Bernard explained. "Office manager. Keeper of budgets and schedules. She has one of those minds, what do you call it, Agnes? A photographic memory?"

"Eidetic," Agnes said. "Eidetic memory."

"The Nauk couldn't run without Agnes," Bernard said. "She's been here since the beginning."

"I worked for Alena," Agnes said. Her eyes darkened like stones darkening with rain. "She brought me here when the museum opened, and I've been here ever since."

"They knew each other since they were kids," Bernard said.

Out the window, the waves gathered and broke, roaring and hissing. I knew I should say something—that my muteness was ridiculous, embarrassing to Bernard as well as to myself. "Well," I managed. "I look forward to working together."

She stretched her lips. "Won't it be nice."

Bernard looked at his watch. "Let's see the galleries, shall we? I have a meeting in Bourne at eleven."

"You'd better get going." Agnes lifted her head, making her earrings shimmer. "You won't believe the traffic. I'll take her through."

"Would you mind?" Bernard was already moving toward the door. "I'll be back this afternoon. And then there's dinner at my house at eight. I've invited a few people. Roald can drive you."

"People?"

"To meet you. No point waiting." He waved to me, frowning distractedly, and was gone.

I looked around for Roald, but he had vanished too. It was just Agnes and me in the chilly lobby, the waves annihilating themselves on the shore behind us, and motes of silvery dust swimming in the glare.

Agnes shifted her weight to one hip and narrowed her eyes. "I can't say you're what I was expecting."

"I guess not," I said.

"And you worked where before?"

I told her.

"You were a curator there?" She had a way of standing very still so that she seemed almost like a primitive sculpture, something Gauguin might have carved out of ebony.

"No."

There was no need to say more, to pin down my exact position like an insect on a pin. Curatorial assistant or coat-check girl, it amounted to the same thing.

"Well," she said, "Bernard's always been sentimental."

Starting to feel light-headed, I sucked the humidity-controlled museum air into my lungs and stood up straighter, trying not to wobble in my sandy heels. "Of course, this is all new to me," I said. "I'm sure I'll have a million questions."

She lifted her chin slightly, tilting her head like a large bird, possibly a swan. Like a swan, she had a surprisingly long and elegant neck and a haughty, inscrutable glare. "You're the boss," she said.

Passing the front desk, we slid through the empty galleries that opened off a long sunlit corridor she called the "colonnade." There were four galleries, with tall arched doorways between them, although there were no doors. The walls were white, the wooden floors a weathered silver. It wasn't an enormous space but it seemed to unfold endlessly, like a building in a dream. It was strange to me how empty it was, though of course I'd known it would be empty. The walls were blank, but at the same time they felt inhabited, as though the ghosts of the art that had hung there lingered, invisible but attendant, on the verge of shimmering into view. I hadn't done a lot of research—there hadn't been time—but I knew about the Nauk's famous show of Kimball Whiting, those enormous pale collages of cotton and pasteboard and bits of bone, and I'd seen the catalogue for the Denise Dolorian fish exhibition where the tanks she filled the galleries with held only water, while dead fish, nailed to the walls, decayed in real time. Visitors were given plastic pinchers for their noses, but the health department shut the show down after four days. The reviewer for *The New York Times* had declared, "Particularly in the last gallery, where hundreds of tiny sardines are pinned to the walls in the shape of a great, glittering, Hokusai-like wave, the beauty of the form, the rankness of the smell (against which the colorful nose plugs are inevitably, if not intentionally, insufficient), the moral indictment in regard to the emptying of the oceans, and the inescapable presence of the process of decay, give this exhibition an exciting and visceral complexity that almost compensates the viewer for the ordeal of being there."

"What an extraordinary space," I said. My voice echoed in the empty room, extending the platitude.

"People talk about this space as a train with a series of cars," Agnes said. "Something about the view of the ocean through the windows of the colonnade gives a sense of motion. Don't you think?"

I paused, trying to feel it. "Yes," I said. "I see what you mean."

Agnes smiled to show she knew I was lying. "Alena used to say she felt like she was on the railway from Moscow to Vladivostok. You know where that is?"

"I know where Moscow is."

"Vladivostok is clear at the other end of Russia, on the Pacific Ocean. The end of the world! We think America is big, but Russia is twelve time zones long. Can you imagine that?" She was looking at me hard with those fish-gray eyes. I felt there was another, larger question smoldering under the one she was ostensibly asking: not could I imagine a country with twelve time zones but, perhaps, did I have imaginative scope? Could I push my mind out to the edge of the world? Was I strong enough, daring enough? Was I—in the smallest way—like Alena?

"For someone who grew up in the Midwest, Nauquasset feels like the edge of the world," I said.

Agnes tilted her chin higher and looked around as though considering the empty gallery. "It's not a huge amount of space," she said. "Still, four rooms. To fill them just so, to control the flow from one to another, letting the story of the show unfold. Allowing for mystery, surprise, even shock. It's not as easy as you might think."

"But I suppose you can take the walls down? Make one big space?"

"Certainly. If that's what you want. Alena used to say that anyone could hang contemporary art in a warehouse." She waited, letting the words settle through me like splinters of ice. "Of course, you'll have your own ideas."

"Of course," I echoed.

The empty rooms stood patiently, a row of fallow fields waiting to be sown.

~

The offices were in the opposite wing, a few rooms opening off a central space with a couple of work stations and a waiting area with a couch and copies of *Artforum*, *Parkett*, and *BOMB*. The curator's office—my office—was large and airy, with a view of the bay. The desk was a drawerless, tapered, finlike sheet of polished steel jutting from the wall, the chair a nest of cushioned gray leather panels. There was a wall of books, an oval mirror, Robert Arno prints on the wall: a silver leaf, a golden bug, a rust-colored seed at the end of an emerald stalk. They were stunning prints, the lines full of tension, the colors shimmering, a sense of life caught by a pin even through Arno's stylization. But though I admired the work, I didn't like having it there. It was beautiful but cold, dark beneath the glowing color. Arno was famous for sometimes using his own blood to ink the plates, though some people said he only used chicken's blood. That was what I had always assumed, but looking at the prints now, I suddenly believed that the rusty red came from his veins. That he had left a piece of himself there on the paper, that pain had been part of the process of bringing this object to life.

Beyond the desk, a sitting area near the window contained a low square table, an iron-gray sofa, and beside the sofa, a paper Akari light sculpture rising sinuously from metal legs. A conch, a quahog, and a handful of slipper and jingle shells bisected the table, along with three flat gray stones with veins of white like lightning. I picked up the nearest stone and ran my fingers down the pale seam. Behind me, Agnes drew an audible breath, and suddenly I understood that the grouping was not just an arrangement; it was a work of art.

"Andy arranged those for Alena," Agnes said. "One day when he stopped by."

I glanced at her with minnow eyes that darted immediately away. Could she possibly mean Andy Goldsworthy? I put the stone down.

"Of course, if you don't like them there, I can have them moved."

"No, no. Thank you! They're fine."

"I don't know what arrangements you made with Bernard about redecorating."

"Oh," I said. "The office is fine. I wouldn't change anything." I gestured helplessly at the table, the prints, the books, the desk.

"That desk is by Vaarni. She had it sent from Finland."

"It's beautiful." It *was* beautiful—everything in the room was beautiful—but cold too, like something that belonged on the bottom of the ocean, or on the moon.

Agnes moved silently across the dark carpet and touched the sheet of steel. She ran her index finger along the cold surface tenderly, as though along a body. "Even Bernard was shocked when he saw the price. But she got her way." She glided out of the room again, leaving me to scurry after her.

In the outer area, a young woman who had not been there when we passed through before leaned against the edge of an ordinary wooden desk. Sylph-thin, pale-haired, clad in a tiny pink dress and tall white boots, she regarded me from within a cloud of bubble-gum-sweet perfume. Nearby stood a young man, the sleeves of his T-shirt cut off to better reveal the tattoos snaking up one arm, encircling his neck, and sliding down the other arm in a weave of roses, pirate flags, scrawny lions, and sword-wielding angels. Later, when I knew him better and had had more time to look, I would notice the three-headed rooster, the blooming saguaro cactus, and the constellation of brightly colored poison-dart frogs vying for space on his skin. He wore eyeliner, and eye shadow the color of a bruise, and his honey-colored hair lay in fat cornrows across his head. "This is Sloan," Agnes said, nodding toward the woman, "and that's Jake."

Sloan was a year or two younger than I was, Jake a few years older, but basically we were peers, or could have been in a different place under different circumstances. Here, though, I was their new boss, timid and jet-lagged and wearing a wrinkled butter-yellow blouse with a floppy collar. Still, if I had been able to summon something—some spark of warmth or authority—it might have been better later. As it was, they regarded me with hooded eyes as I asked awkwardly, "And what do you do at the Nauk?"

"I'm the AA," Sloan said. She had a thin, tinny voice and a way of holding her head forward on her long neck that made me think of a small giraffe. "Phone answering, mail sorting, appointment making. I'll keep your calendar, and I can sign your name if you want me to. I don't do spreadsheets."

"Okay," I said.

"Jake is the front desk," Agnes said.

"When we're open," Jake said. "When we're not, like now, I'm laid off. But, hey, I have my own art to do, so that's cool."

"You're an artist?" I asked politely.

"I can wield a blowtorch."

"Well, I hope we'll be open soon."

"Yeah, we all hope that," Jake said.

"Of course, things will take time. But I hope we can at least pick what the first new show will be this summer."

"But the next show's selected," Sloan said. "Right?"

I stared at her. With her pale face and her long neck, she looked oddly like a thin version of Agnes. She uncrossed her high white boots, her feet stamping lightly against the floor.

"It is." She looked at Agnes. "Right? Alena promised Morgan."

"I didn't know there were exhibition plans," I said. "But if promises were made . . ." If promises were made, what? Was I obliged to keep Alena's promises? Of course, if there were contracts, that would be something else.

"Morgan McManus." Sloan's face flushed the color of the inside of a conch shell. "His show was on the schedule. His first big show. Right, Aunt Agnes?"

Aunt Agnes! I looked from the young pink face to the older whiter one: the same sharp chin, the same thin nose, the same frown, though one mouth was painted pale rose and the other crimson.

"Sloan is my sister's oldest," Agnes said, her voice no more or less chilly than it had been before. "But you don't need to worry. She's an excellent AA."

"Sloan's the best," Jake put in.

"I'm not worried," I said. I was feeling more and more out of place, like a cow trying to negotiate a beach. "Who is Morgan McManus?"

"He's a wonderful artist," Sloan said in her tinny voice. "Brilliant and daring."

"He's a wild man," Jake added. "Gulf War vet. Lost a leg and an arm! But nothing stops him."

"What does he do?" I asked. "I mean, what kind of art does he make?"

"He shows how it happened, man," Jake said. "War. And he shows his prostheses. He makes them out of all kinds of materials: wood and plastic and steel."

I could feel my face go flat. Of course, I knew body art—the Viennese Actionists, Vito Acconci, Marina Abramović. But whether because

I still carried LaFreniere, Wisconsin, within me or for some other reason, I had never been drawn to it.

"He's a photographer," Sloan said. "He does nude self-portraits, with and without prostheses. And portraits of other wounded soldiers. Big. Bigger than life. Also video and installation work." She looked down and started fiddling with her phone.

"Political," I suggested. "Antiwar."

"No," Sloan said. "I don't think he is antiwar. It's more just personal with him." Her face flushed even pinker, like a strawberry ripening in the sun: a succulent fruit many men might hope to pluck.

Then Agnes said, her voice as cool as ever—not the stone, but the earth under the stone, "Lately he's doing re-creations. The battle of Fallujah. The battle of Najaf. The battle of Kandahar." In her mouth, the place names stretched out: *Nah-jaahf, Kahn-dah-hah . . .*

"For this show," Sloan said, "he's going to stage the scene where he lost his . . . where he was injured. Rubble, dead bodies, limbs in wax. Sound. And himself, all painted in blood and ash, lying in the middle. Six hours a day!" She held up the phone and I could see what looked like a photograph they might show on the news out of Iraq, only more graphic than anything I'd ever seen on the news: half a torso with its pink insides spilling out; a bright stream of blood flowing out of a gash in a leg; fragments of something—mercifully unidentifiable—in lime green, canary yellow, livid orange. An arm, neatly detached, lying in a puddle with its fist clenched. Oh, I prayed, let there not be contracts! Let my first task at the Nauk not be to coordinate the gaudy calculated restaging of death and dismemberment! I thought of the white galleries with their shining floors, their ever-shifting light, their glimpses of wild blue through the doorways and the colonnade, the rooms I was already falling in love with. Blood didn't belong there, nor screams, nor burned and blackened bodies. What did belong I couldn't say yet, but

I felt that if I stood still and waited—just me, alone in the Nauk—the thing that did would swim into view.

"Alena promised him," Sloan said again. "It'll take a while for you to organize something new, anyway, and it's wrong for the building to keep sitting empty."

"Plus, you know, nature abhors a vacuum," Jake said. "That's why you find ghosts in empty places."

"I hope there aren't any ghosts at the Nauk," I said.

"Oh, there are ghosts," Jake said. "Maybe not up here. But down on the beach where the bodies washed up." No one spoke. Agnes raised her chin, making her blood-red earrings sparkle, while Sloan looked at the floor. "From the wrecks, I mean," Jake explained uncomfortably. "You know. Old shipwrecks. Ships would blow up onto the sandbar in storms and break apart. People say you can see Maria Hallett walking the point on foggy days, scanning the horizon. Waiting for Black Sam to come back to her."

"Who's Maria Hallett?" I asked.

"It's a local myth," Sloan said. "Pirates and storms. Eighteenth century."

"It's not a myth," Jake said. "It's history. It really happened."

"Something happened," Sloan said. "A ship sank. Nothing else is particularly clear."

"A ship called the *Whydah* went down on April 26, 1717," Jake said. "An African slave ship filled with gold. Off these shores. A pirate captain named Black Sam Bellamy was sailing back to Cape Cod to meet the woman he loved, Maria Hallett, when a storm came up and the ship went down in sight of land. There wasn't anything anyone could do."

Agnes, who had been silent since the subject of ghosts came up, said suddenly, "Some people say Maria Hallett was a witch."

"Yes. The Witch of Wellfleet," Jake said. "They say that after the wreck, mad with grief, she lived in a little hut in the dunes, watching the sea, causing other ships to go down. Other men to die. Her hut is still there," he said, turning to me. "Or anyway, a hut people say is hers. Still today people blame her when engines stall and radios malfunction. They say she causes strange currents that pull people out to sea and drown them."

Another pause. Agnes had gone so still she might have been turned to stone. Then Sloan said bravely, "I go to the beach at night all the time! I've never seen a ghost."

Out the window, the ocean slid silently by, bright caps of white on navy peaks. A cloud passed in front of the sun, dimming the room.

9.

In the afternoon Bernard took me to meet his sister, who was chair of the Nauk's board of trustees. "You'll like Barbara," Bernard said, but it was becoming clear that Bernard had little idea who or what I would like. Why should he? We barely knew each other.

I could see now what a folly the whole escapade was—this new life. We had behaved like lunatics, or like children, or like lovers in a play. Like Romeo and Juliet, we had met at a masked ball and made a doomed choice. Oh well, I thought as we sped along the sun-drenched pavement under the pale blue crystalline bowl of the sky. The speed and the air were cheering me up. Oh well, at least I'd escaped Louise! I wondered what she was telling people: that I was ungrateful, unstable, disloyal, deranged. I had left her in the lurch, I had leaped before I looked. Well, it was true, all of it! The thought gave me courage. I glanced at Bernard, who was driving fast. He looked very handsome, his chin thrust up and his nostrils flaring like a racehorse catching a scent in the wind. What did I know about him? My mother had asked that when I'd called to tell my parents about my change of plan. (That's what I'd said: "I've had a change of plan.")

"It's not like I'm marrying him," I'd replied over the crackling waves of air. "I'm just taking a job."

"But is he . . . Has he . . . ?" my mother said. I could see what she was asking: Whether passion was involved, whether he had used desire as a lure to trick me onto his hook. It was, and he had, but not the way she meant.

"No, Mom," I said. "He's gay, actually."

But of course, that didn't make her feel any better.

What *did* I know about Bernard? Nothing, or practically nothing. He might have been a con man, or a cokehead, or even a murderer for all I knew; but I was sure in my heart that he was none of those things. He was a man who loved art—loved it the way I did, as though it were a plate of food when I was starving, a long cool draught when I was dying of thirst. He was a man who had looked at me and seen something no one else had ever seen. What more did I need to know than that?

And as it turned out, he was right about Barbara. I did like her. She wasn't anything like what I expected, which I suppose was a female version of her brother: tall and fashionable, swarthy and self-possessed. Barbara was noticeably older than Bernard for one thing, stout and blond and sunburned, with an enormous square-cut diamond on her finger and smaller hoops of diamonds in her ears. She and her husband, Tom, lived in a big white house on a big green lawn, fenced so her border collies had room to prance. She had two of them, Dolly and Major, old dogs, impeccably behaved, who followed her everywhere, looking up into her face with perfect devotion. "These are my loves," she said, introducing them to me in her big sunny living room full of couches and rugs and chiffoniers and bulging armchairs and ugly lamps, the flowered upholstery covered with dog hair and knitted afghans. Photographs in silver frames crowded onto tables and windowsills, revealing the existence of a clutch of blond children shown at a range of ages, riding horses, captaining sailboats, brandishing trophies, roughhousing with dogs. I found out later that Barbara had four children in all, the youngest in France on a college year abroad. Now, with her husband off at work, or sailing, or playing golf, her daily passion was directed at the dogs, who sat on either side of her, keeping a wary eye on me. When Bernard hugged his sister, they looked on resignedly, as though they would have liked to drive him away if it had been permitted.

We sat on a flagstone patio and a maid brought tea, cookies, tangerines, cheese and crackers. "Or would you prefer a drink?" Barbara asked. "Wine? Gin and tonic?"

"Campari and soda," Bernard said.

"Bernie. Don't be difficult on purpose."

"Vermouth, then."

"Marta," Barbara said to the maid, "please bring Mr. Augustin a glass of vermouth. And you, dear?"

"Tea is fine," I said. Had Alena sat here drinking tea with Bernard's sister on summer afternoons? Or had she preferred gin, vermouth, Campari and soda?

Barbara poured from a big green china pot in the shape of a cabbage. The creamer was a china shepherdess and the sugar bowl a woolly sheep. The cups, very delicate, were decorated with orange roses. Everything was obviously old and valuable, but extraordinarily ugly. Even the cushions of the wicker furniture were crowded with busy vines and scarlet blossoms and little pop-eyed bunnies peeking out from behind bushes.

But the house itself was a fine house, and the patio looked out over a wide pond, perhaps a mile across, with a little sailboat and a couple of kayaks bobbing by a gray dock. "We have swans," Barbara announced. "Not nice birds, but very beautiful."

"I remember when we were kids and that swan attacked you," Bernard said.

"That was a goose," Barbara said.

"It was white," Bernard said, "with a long neck."

"A white goose. It wanted my jelly sandwich."

"It wanted you," Bernard said, smiling. "You must have been five or six, just the size for a nice meal! I remember you were wearing a yellow two-piece bathing suit with polka dots. Hideous! It went right for your belly."

"Oh, how I screamed!" Barbara laughed. "It hurt like heck. I think we went to the emergency room."

"All the rest of the summer you went around pulling up your shirt to show people your scar."

"I don't remember that. But Mama must have hated it if I did." She leaned over to touch my knee. "Our mother was a very proper lady. Poor woman, neither Bernie nor I was the child she had envisioned! I was so plump and brash, and my hair was always a mess. And Bernie was so . . . artistic."

Bernard snorted.

Barbara's hand, warm against my knee, melted me. Suddenly I missed my mother. Barbara was big and rich and loud, and my mother was a farmer's wife; still, they were both mothers. "Tell me about yourself," she said. "I hope you won't mind my saying I pictured someone different. When Bernie said he'd found this woman in Venice who— I don't mean it the way it sounds. It's just that you're—*younger*. To be basically running a museum. Aren't you, dear?"

"Bernard runs it, though." I glanced at Bernard. He had finished his drink and was peeling a tangerine.

"Oh, but you can't count on Bernie! He's always flying off somewhere, or going out on his boat. But you sold your boats, didn't you,

Bernie?" she added. "I still can't understand why you'd do a thing like that."

Bernard, helping himself to the cheese, frowned at the dog that was following the morsel's trajectory with its damp, quivering snout. "I've lost interest in sailing." He denuded the tangerine, broke it open, and slipped a slice between his lips.

The wind rippled the surface of the pond. The sun turned the crests of the ripples golden. A high, sharp cry pierced the blue air. "That's our osprey," Barbara said as the dogs pricked up their ears. "We have a nesting pair on the pond. Sometimes, if you're lucky, you can see them dive for fish."

"Who would win a fight between an osprey and a swan?" Bernard wondered idly, picking up another tangerine. He stood and wandered down through the thick grass to the dock. In his khakis and faded pink oxford shirt and old sneakers, he looked like someone playing a part; but I was starting to understand that this was actually who he was.

Barbara watched him. "He always loved sailing," she said. "He won races when he was a boy, when he wasn't off at archery tournaments, and he and Alena were out on the water all the time. I used to try to get her to join the yacht club, but she never would. You don't have to like the people, I told her. It would have been good for the Nauk, all those wealthy businessmen. Of course, Bernard is a member, not that he ever goes. I'm sure he'll get another boat eventually. Life goes on." She paused, still looking worriedly across the lawn at her brother. What was I doing here with this frowsy, doggy woman and a man who had competed at archery?

Then she said, "You know what happened to her, of course?"

"Yes."

"It's been a terrible two years for poor Bernie. For a long time he was expecting her to be found—her body, you know. But no, nothing.

At first he was agitated, and then he was despondent, but at a certain point he realized she wasn't coming back. The whole thing has been absolutely devastating, but he's beginning to get over it. You're proof of that."

I couldn't bear to hear her say it, it felt so untrue to me. Bernard was throwing pebbles from the end of the dock, contemplating the ripples.

"We were delighted, Tom and I, to hear that Bernie had found someone. It's time the Nauk was open again. Long past time. Frankly, we didn't see why it had to close at all—the board didn't. And not everyone is sorry there'll be some new blood. A new vision. Some of the locals, even some of the board, didn't like that show with the fish. Or that other one where the artist lived in the gallery and you could watch him doing, you know, everything."

"I read about that," I said. "Percy Kronfield. The guy with the X-Acto knife."

She sighed. "Well, that was Alena. Always dramatic, always with the grand gesture! Not that she wasn't superb at her job. We took Bernie's word for that. What do Tom and I know about art? We're just on the board because Bernie asked us. I'm on a lot of boards. And Tom knows about money. Though it did seem to us that the shows had gotten stranger in recent years. Fewer paintings and more . . ." She trailed off, either unable or unwilling to put a name to the kind of thing there had been more of.

"What does the board do, exactly?"

"We meet a few times a year. Get told what the upcoming exhibitions are and nod sagely. Give money, of course. Cast our eyes over the financial statements. I organize the fundraising gala. I'm good at parties." It was very peaceful out there by the pond, but Barbara looked troubled, her broad brow rippled like the water. "I've arranged tonight's dinner, for instance. Not that it's much, just twelve people."

"Oh! Twelve . . . !"

She pointed her worried brow at me. "He didn't tell you? You'll get used to that. Bernie has a big heart, but things slip his mind. Well, not business things so much." She stopped.

"So, who will be at this dinner?" I tried to sound casual. For a panicked moment I considered asking to borrow something to wear, but I had a sudden image of blowsy roses on dinner gowns (surely people wouldn't wear *gowns*?). And of course we were nowhere near the same size.

"Tom and me. And the Hallorans, who live down the road and are big collectors. And Bernie's friend Chaz and his partner, Will, and the Steingartens, who bought that enormous place in Sandwich. Roald. And Chris Passoa, who we've known forever. Don't look like that, there's nothing to worry about. They'll love you."

I could picture it: a long oak table lit by a row of silver candlesticks with me at the far end in my yellow blouse and ruined shoes. And eleven pairs of eyes fixed on me, my farm-fresh face in their shocked vision superimposed—as in the famous nineteenth-century "spirit photographs" of William Mumler—with a shimmering, glamorous image of Alena.

The blue pond was placid after the restless ocean. Somewhere overhead the keening of the osprey inscribed the air, and something caught my eye, streaking downward. "Look!" Barbara cried. I saw the great bird rise, wings beating hard, from the sun-stippled water, something glinting and dripping in its feet. On the dock, Bernard stood motionless, the sun casting his long shadow across the riven, trembling pond.

10.

Bernard's house was an airy nineteenth-century shingled barn that had been cleverly converted with the help of a new wing of bedrooms along one side and a broad deck overlooking the bay. In the high white living room, Cindy Sherman film stills hung in a row over the fireplace. Glenn Ligon's smudged words dripped illegibly across a large canvas near the door, and the wall opposite the deck was penciled with the fine regular lines of a Sol LeWitt. In one corner, thousands of Félix Gonzáles-Torres candies in ice-blue wrappers lay twinkling in the light of the black glass Fred Wilson chandelier. Voices and laughter came from the deck, but I found myself going the other way, slipping through a door into a hall off which opened a powder room, a butler's pantry, a gleaming laundry, and a large tiled mudroom, crowded but neat. A row of plaid jackets and waterproof slickers hung on hooks, duck boots and rain boots were lined up on a shelf, and there were four or five fishing rods, several tackle boxes, two pairs of binoculars (one large, one pocket-sized), some tennis rackets, and three black unstrung crossbows standing in a corner like forgotten Giacomettis.

In the hallway itself, framed photographs hung on the wall, some old black-and-whites of long-ago brides and babies and family groups, others of Bernard at various ages, engaged in various vigorous outdoor activities: holding up an enormous fish; drawing a bow on an archery range; sailing. I was going down the row looking at them when Barbara bustled through, wearing not an evening gown but rather a plain blue skirt and sweater. "Hello!" she said.

"What amazing photographs," I said. What I meant was how startling it was to see Bernard so young, though it was true that they were good pictures.

She touched a finger to a photo of Bernard when he was probably barely a teenager, grinning and sunburned, a medal on a blue ribbon around his neck. He had been a skinny boy, his hair brown and shaggy, braces on his teeth. The field he stood in was so green—green as Easter grass—it looked like you could eat it. "I took that one," Barbara said. "At the state archery championships in Nenameseck. I used to take a lot of pictures."

I pointed to one of the sailing photographs, taken when Bernard must have been about twenty. Lean and brown, bare-chested, a blue captain's hat perched on his head, he squinted into the wind with the faraway look of a young Greek sailing off to Troy. "That's beautiful."

"That's not one of mine. Alena took the sailing ones. That was the first summer she spent here, after Bernie's freshman year at Middlebury. Well, and hers too, of course."

"That's where they met?"

"Yes."

I scanned down the row, a sudden clamminess palpable in the air. I could see now that the sailing pictures had a similar look, full of dramatic shadows and odd angles, so that the subject (Bernard) seemed magnetized in place on a shifting plane. The photographs captured him looking not directly into the camera, as in the picture Barbara had taken, but obliquely, his gaze suggesting a world beyond the frame, from which the viewer was excluded. "She was talented," I said.

"Yes. At a lot of things. Sailing, swimming. She studied ballet. She used to do these performance things down on the beach, very strange, but Bernie said they were good." We stood together, listening to the laughter from the deck that drifted toward us like the laughter from some ghostly ship away over the water, and to the waves rolling, and then to the crunch of a car approaching along the oyster-shell drive, some last guest arriving. Or perhaps—the thought irradiated me—perhaps it was Alena herself arriving! Perhaps she had had enough of the company of the dead and was returning to claim her place, was putting in a surprise appearance like a guest star gracing the set of a plodding comedy. Perhaps, as I had half suspected, she had never died at all! Mad as it was, it seemed to me that Barbara had the same apprehension. She froze, listening, as the car came to a halt and the engine quieted. The door slammed with a metallic shudder, and then a man's voice called, "Hey! Where'dya want the ice?"

Barbara turned up the wattage on her hostess's smile. "And you?" she asked brightly. "What are your hobbies?"

~

Dinner was served on the deck at an oval table arrayed with plain white plates, heavy silverware, dishes of seasoned almonds, votive candles. It was an informal party. In the sleeveless black shift I had worn to every occasion in Europe I was overdressed and, despite the discreet heaters that warmed the air as the temperature dropped, chilly. The sun hung, red as a Joan Miró sun, on the horizon, laced by ragged salmon clouds that pinkened and thinned as the flushed disc slid downward.

Overhead, the dome of the sky lit up almost turquoise, then faded to lavender, topaz, violet-gray. A plump, balding man in cranberry trousers—Barbara's husband, Tom—stood near me as the dark sea took its first bite of the blushing orb. "Watch," he said. "Watch for the green flash."

"Flash?"

"A flash of green light. Just when the sun disappears."

"Have you seen it?"

"No. But it's a proven astronomical fact."

Obediently I watched as the crown of light was swallowed, sublimely, by the hungry sea. All the guests watched, standing at ceremonial attention with their champagne flutes lifted as the final sliver was devoured, the encrimsoned clouds sagging and shredding, as though it were a performance prepared for their pleasure by a necromancing impresario.

"Did you see it?" Barbara's husband demanded. "Did you see the flash?"

"No. Did you?"

"No. Well, the atmospheric conditions here aren't ideal."

"Too much moisture in the air." This pronouncement was made by a big, bullet-headed man in a black pullover, his blond-white hair shorn as close as an astronaut's. "It's easier to see in a drier climate."

"Hello, Chris," Barbara's husband said. "Have you met the Nauk's new curator?" We shook hands. "Chris is a good person to know," Tom advised. "He's the local chief of police."

"Oh! How impressive!" I was starting to feel the champagne, the golden bubbles shimmying through me, leavening my mood, loosening my limbs.

"Of a miniature police force," the chief said mildly.

"I think I had one of those when I was a child. It came with a miniature police station you could fold up and carry around by a handle."

"Very convenient," Chris Passoa said. "Especially if you could inflate them in a moment of need."

"By dropping them in water, perhaps," I suggested. "Like sea monkeys." Maybe because we had police chiefs in LaFreniere, Chris Passoa, unlike the other guests, seemed like someone it was possible to talk to.

"The first time I ever saw a sea monkey was at Bernard's house. I remember pouring the instant-life eggs into the tank and watching the creatures appear. It was tremendously disappointing. Living on the Cape, we knew a shrimp when we saw one."

Bernard drifted over, refilling glasses. "Hello, Tom," he said. "Hello, Chris."

"Come fishing tomorrow," the police chief said. "It's my day off."

"Sorry." Bernard placed his hand on my bare shoulder. "I have a curator to look after."

"Bernard is a fish magnet," Chris Passoa explained. "Put him in a boat and the fish are drawn right to him."

Bernard laughed. "You make me sound like a piece of squid."

"You have fish pheromones is what it is. Larry says the bass are running." He called across the deck to a stocky man of medium height with an alert terrier's face and hair that seemed to have been frozen in place in the moment of blowing back in the wind. "Right, Larry?"

"I caught three this morning off Willet's Landing," Larry said. "And I was barely trying."

"Maybe the Plunge. That'd be quick. Leave at six, back at nine. No problem."

"Excuse me," Bernard said. "I just—" Like an apparition, he melted away into the house, leaving behind a cold place on my shoulder where his hand had been.

"Do you fish?" the man with frozen hair asked me.

"Only in lakes."

"Get Bernard to take you. The Plunge is a great spot, a mile out, straight off the beach in front of the Nauk. It's a sort of deep pit in the ocean floor, left behind by the glaciers after the last ice age." Feeling a lecture on local geology coming on, I excused myself to fetch the sweater I hadn't thought to bring. Once in the house, I poked my head into all the rooms I dared, looking for Bernard, but found only a gaggle of caterers clattering pans in the kitchen, a den with a breathtaking violet-and-puce Warhol Jackie silkscreen across from a wall of bookshelves crammed with fat glossy art books, and a blond woman with the pointy nose and beady eyes of an opossum smoking a cigarette in the back hall.

Dinner was green gazpacho, followed by grilled swordfish, couscous with raisins, and haricots verts, with raspberry mousse for dessert. Seated between Roald, who barely spoke, and Larry, the man with the hair, I had trouble eating. Larry spent the meal refilling his glass and demanding to know what I thought about various artists, then offering his own opinions.

"You should do an Ed Ruscha show! Anyone who can make gas stations look like that is worth showing. I could lend you some, if you decide to go in that direction."

I said I understood that it was the Nauk's policy to give artists who wouldn't otherwise have the chance a special opportunity to extend themselves in a new way. Ed Ruscha and his gas stations, meanwhile, were doing fine.

"Yes," he reflected, "Alena could always tell who was about to become famous just before they did. It was a gift she had. A kind of second sight."

"Remarkable," I said.

"She had a brilliant mind," he said. "A brilliant woman, beautiful clothes. Thin as a rail, and that black, black Russian hair! It comes from interbreeding with Tatars."

"Oh?"

"Absolutely. And, you know, the Mongolians." On my other side, Roald made a noise in his throat, then lifted his glass and drained it. He kept his left hand, the one with the missing finger, in his lap. "Which?" he said. "Tatars or Mongolians?"

"She said she was descended from Genghis Khan!" Larry said.

"She said a lot of things," Roald said.

Larry emptied the bottle of Pinot Grigio into his glass and set it down on the table, where it was spirited away by a discreet hand and replaced with a full one. "What about you?"

"Me?" I touched my own brown hair that came from nowhere in particular.

"Who are you thinking of showing? The first show after we've been closed for two years! That will be an event."

"I don't know yet. There'll be time to figure that out, I hope."

"Not much. Not if we're going to open Labor Day weekend!"

I stared at him, at his red face and his preternaturally wide eyes (maybe they were Botoxed?) and his stiff, silvery, wire-terrier hair. "Isn't that soon?"

"Bernard!" Larry called down the table. "Didn't anyone tell this young lady we're opening Labor Day weekend?"

Bernard, who was seated at the far end of the table next to his sister, looked around at the shadowy faces shifting in the candlelight. "Are we?"

"Certainly we are! When Barbara told us you were bringing back a curator, we decided. The Nauk has been closed too long. If we open Labor Day, while the tourists are still here, we'll make a splash. Otherwise, you might as well wait until May!"

"Larry's right," said the blond, opossum-nosed woman I'd seen smoking. "You know we pretty much let you do whatever you want, Bernard. But this time we're putting our foot down."

Bernard looked at me across the flickering lights. It was full dark now, with a river of stars overhead, the mild surf lapping. "That's not a lot of time to put together an exhibition," he said.

"Just a modest one," Larry said. "Just to show that the Nauk hasn't actually fallen into the sea! Wait another season and people will forget we ever existed. Your new curator seems smart enough. She's young and energetic." He turned to me with his bright terrier's face. "You're up to the challenge, aren't you, sweetheart?"

And then they were all looking at me: all those wealthy, casually well-dressed people with their expensive hair and their boats and their hard sparkling eyes. I sought out Chris Passoa's clear blue gaze, but he was no longer at the table.

11.

THE NEXT DAY I was up early, but I dawdled around the little house till close to nine. No one had told me what time to show up at the office. I had imagined that Bernard and I would be together here at the Nauk the way we had been in Europe, meeting for breakfast, spending the days together, sharing ideas, thoughts, perceptions as we worked—I think I had pictured us at facing desks—planning exhibitions and organizing the Nauk's brilliant future as easily as we had planned our daily itineraries. But the reality was quite different.

So I headed up the path alone, this time in flat sandals, arriving at the little enclosure of green by the front doors at exactly nine.

It was a sunny morning. The pink roses glowed against the white wooden trellises, and the soft rushing of the waves formed a steady backdrop to the bright twittering of songbirds. The green grass dazzled, its blades thick and blunt, some sturdy variety that could withstand the salt air. The doors, however, when I tried them, were locked. Inside—as well as I could tell, peering in through the long sidelights—all was dim and quiet. Through the foyer, the wall of glass on the far side framed the green swells. I sat down on the bench and looked up at the cloudless sky. I tried to imagine that sky unrolling across America: Massachusetts,

New York, Ohio, Illinois, Wisconsin. What were my parents doing now, eight a.m. their time, breakfast long over, the cows milked, the dishes washed, the beds made, the tractor halfway down the long field where the corn stood in neat, tall rows like a zombie army? Was it really the same sky, stretching from here to there, from me to them? I stared hard into the blue, which was milder, softer than the blue of my childhood, as though the paint on this part of the sky wasn't quite dry. There was a tempera quality to it, an opacity different from the flat, factual blue of home. My head ached. I shut my eyes and pressed my hands to them, wishing I could lie down on the bench with my arms over my head, but surely someone would come soon, and I didn't want to be seen like that.

Shortly after ten, the sound of an engine rumbled up the slope, and a car rolled into view, turning off the lane into a little grassy area bounded by a rail fence. Agnes and Sloan got out either side. Dark-haired and blond, fat and thin, middle-aged and young, they nonetheless moved with the same apparent indifference, both dangling their purses from their fists, both tossing their hair back with the same reflexive jerk of their long pale necks, so that they seemed for a moment like two characters played by a single actress appearing in the same frame by some cinematic trick. I stood up.

"Oh dear," Agnes said. "Are we late?"

"No, no," I said. "I'm afraid I was early."

"I hate to think of you waiting. If I had known when you wanted us, of course we would have been here."

"I didn't know when—what was usual."

"Well, *usually* we get in at ten or ten-thirty. But of course, you tell us what you think is best." She had her key out and was fitting it into the lock. She was dressed in black again, a long-sleeved cotton knit dress and black stockings, thick black eyeliner enlarging her cool gray eyes. "Didn't Bernard give you a key?"

"No."

"Really?" Agnes stood, plump hip cocked, black and pink hair lifting slightly. "I thought he did."

I shook my head. But had he? He had given me a key ring, that was true, with a key on it, the key to the house, and a little silver horseshoe charm on the ring. I had left it on the kitchen table, it had hardly seemed worth locking up just to come across the way. It wasn't as though I had anything to steal. "Unless the key to the house unlocks the museum too?"

"No," Agnes said. She was still looking at me as though waiting for me to acknowledge my mistake. Sloan, meanwhile, hadn't said a word.

Could there have been a second key on the ring? Was that the sort of thing a person could forget or be mistaken about? I concentrated, thinking of the silver horseshoe charm, the metal ring with its single key lying on the scarred Formica, and in my mind's eye the key began to shiver, splitting itself down the middle. Now there were two keys, I could see them clearly, lying in a rhombus of sunlight. Agnes opened the door to the cool tiled lobby and we went in. "I'm sorry," I said. "I must have made a mistake."

Agnes bent over an alarm system keypad on the wall and punched in numbers. "It doesn't matter. Like I said, if we had known what time you wanted to start, of course we would have been here. Alena never got into the office before eleven, but you'd get emails she'd sent at two in the morning. She was a night owl, that was her. Her nature. But Sloan and I will do whatever you like, just let us know."

By now we were upstairs. Sloan turned on the lights and sat at her desk in the outer office. "Would you like some coffee?" Agnes asked.

"Sloan can make some." Sloan was busily typing away at her computer, not paying any attention.

"No, thanks. I'm fine."

"Do you prefer tea? Sloan, would you boil some water, please."

Sloan pushed her chair back and stood up. She was wearing a chartreuse dress today, thigh length with a square neck and a back consisting of crisscrossed straps, the same white boots and bubblegum scent as yesterday.

"Please don't bother," I said. "I had coffee when I got up."

As though she hadn't heard me, Sloan continued on into the kitchenette and ran water into an old red kettle that she put on the stove.

"Really," I said. "I don't want any."

I could see Sloan's lips move, but her words were drowned out by the hiss of water boiling off the burner.

"I'm sorry?"

"It's for us," she repeated. "We always have tea in the morning. Alena drank it all day long."

Even today, after all that happened—safely landed on this cool balcony bright with flowers and swaddled in fog—that morning floats in my memory like a tar ball on the back of a wave. I couldn't do anything without help—help that was given so condescendingly, with such calibrated disdain, that I felt like an old lady asking for assistance using the toilet. How young I was! I believed, I suppose, that I should have been born knowing how to get onto the Nauk's computer network, how to jiggle the cord on the printer when it didn't work, where phone numbers were kept, and stamps, and notepads—or, if I hadn't breathed in this knowledge with my first breaths, that I should certainly have picked it up in graduate school. It was weeks, I believe, before I stumbled on the supply closet—or rather, on my way to the kitchenette, caught a glimpse behind the door Sloan was closing on the shelves of paper, tape, staples, and pens. Until then, when I needed something, I asked Sloan or Agnes, who procured the item seemingly by magic. I suppose I knew there must be a supply room somewhere. I should, of course, have simply asked—in fact, I believe I did ask once, stumblingly: *There must be someplace I can get pencils myself?* At which Agnes lifted her sharp chin and remarked relentlessly, "I'm always happy to bring you anything. If I'm not here, Sloan will do it. You don't need to get up. Alena would just buzz through on the intercom."

"Is there an intercom?"

"Of course. That blue button on the phone." Impatience leaked from her like water from an irrigation hose.

"Thank you, Agnes. I didn't realize."

"Don't thank me. It's my job."

I remember, a little later, pressing and re-pressing the blue button in the cold tank of my office and nothing happening. I didn't realize you had to press it *before* picking up the receiver rather than after. I couldn't bear admitting to Agnes that I couldn't make it work, so I sat a long time, still and silent, like a rabbit hiding in the grass.

The expensive desk by Vaarni had no drawers, no cubbyholes, no in-baskets or blotters. It was a smooth sheet of steel, cold to the touch, slippery, with a thin silver computer, a black phone by Bang & Olufsen, and a tall vase of mother-of-pearl pussy willows. When I wanted to make notes, I made them on pads of paper in my lap rather than disrupt the glittering surface. I took a few books from a shelf and piled them along the tops of other books to make a little space to store my pads and pens. When Agnes noticed, she said, "Would you like me to get rid of those books?"

"No, no. I just—wanted a little space."

"I can have them boxed up if they're in your way."

"Please don't bother."

"It's no bother. No doubt you have your own books," Agnes said, her gray eyes fixing me in place.

"Yes," I said with growing panic. "But I don't have them with me. It will be a while before they come."

"Still," she said. "We might as well be prepared." At that moment, Bernard happened to come in, wearing jeans and flip-flops, his checked shirt untucked, a big, greasy cardboard take-out box in his hand.

"Lunch," he said. "You like fried clams?" Then, seeing or sensing something—my panicked face, the electric chill in the air—he asked what was going on.

"I was just saying to Agnes that there's absolutely no need to pack up the books!" I blurted.

"What books?"

It wasn't that Agnes was warmer with Bernard, but that he never seemed to notice how she behaved. I wondered later whether she minded that. He treated her cordially, but no more so than he would have treated a humanoid automaton, so that the fact that she behaved a bit like one seemed, in his presence, more or less natural. When I was alone with Agnes, she always felt too large to me, too cold, but Bernard's presence—also large, but warmer and livelier—seemed to put her into acceptable proportion.

"Alena's books," Agnes said. "She wants the shelves."

"I don't!" I said. "Just half a shelf, a place to put my things. Pads and pencils and—"

"Why don't you put them on the desk?" Bernard asked impatiently. "Isn't that what it's for?" Then his eyes snagged on the rows of books, as though they had suddenly become visible: Tracey Warr's *The Artist's*

Body, Carolee Schneemann's *More Than Meat Joy*, a Vito Acconci catalogue. The handsome features that had inscribed themselves on my memory over the last weeks were sliced open in one blow, like a melon under a cleaver. "Yes," he said. "Box them up! I don't know why you haven't done it already."

"Right away," Agnes said.

"But it's not . . ." I said. "I mean, I don't see why. Not *all* of them!" But neither Bernard nor Agnes paid any attention.

12.

The days streamed by, rippling and skittering, drawing me along in their current. I had been thinking of the Nauk as a kind of Sleeping Beauty's castle (though with the princess herself mysteriously absent), an enchanted stillness fixing the very air so that nothing breathed, no dust gathered, no spider threaded a web across any sunny corner of the silent building protected by invisible thorns. But of course, that wasn't what it was like at all. While in the southern wing of the museum the galleries had stood empty, on the north side Agnes and Sloan and even sometimes Bernard had continued to work. The board of directors had to be dealt with, the building kept up, bills paid, and email answered. Even Jake and the public outreach coordinator, a tall, quiet, weathered man who wore his prematurely gray hair in a ponytail tied with a piece of string, came in from time to time, though what they found to fill the hours during those long, slow months wasn't exactly clear. Still, what had Louise done besides read the papers and talk on the telephone? Not much. And of course, during all that time—the time since Alena had disappeared—inquiries and proposals from artists kept coming in, and requests for images from past shows, and people wanting catalogues, and other people wanting to rent out the building for weddings, not to mention journalists wanting information about Alena and floating absurd and speculative stories, based on ghosts of rumors picked up from dubious and untraceable sources, about how she died. There was a theory that she'd been the victim of one of a series of shark attacks the authorities were hushing up, another about a pagan ritual, conducted at night on a driftwood raft, that had taken a tragic turn. There was an elaborate and persistent story about a secret party held on a yacht out in the bay—booze and drugs and naked partygoers, wasted off their gourds, with painted bodies and glitter-encrusted hair, leaping from masts into the black, churning ocean—all of them making it back aboard but one.

Whose yacht? Why painted bodies? How was it there were no witnesses to this glittering carnival? Nobody could say.

If only news of exhibitions traveled half as widely, or generated a quarter of the interest! It seemed clear to me—as Sarabeth had suggested in Venice—that by closing after Alena's disappearance the Nauk had wasted the kind of publicity that comes perhaps once in a lifetime, and which might have been leveraged to bring a small flood of first-time visitors through the door. Even if only one in ten actually took in the art, that would have been something! Of course, had I known it, we would have more than enough of that kind of curiosity before long.

In the mornings, the sun woke me early. The thin curtains were no match for the strong pink light that pooled on the floor shortly after five, then spread and shifted, pink going to apricot, to butter, then bleaching to dazzling bone. I would lie for a while on the lumpy mattress, my hand tracing the curves of the painted metal headboard, breathing in the smells of must and sun and salt. Mice scrabbled in the walls—I could hear them if I woke up in the night—and innumerable spiders, small, almost transparent, spun webs in every corner and were efficiently replaced by their relatives, or rivals, after every vacuuming.

Every morning I woke with the sour taste of anxiety on my tongue, dimly aware of chaotic, exhausting dreams. Before heading up to the chilly, humidity-controlled office of the Nauk, where Agnes would either be waiting for me, making a dumb show of her patience, or would shortly swim into view full of false, effusive apology, I climbed up through the sharp, whispering dune grass and stumbled down through the soft sand to the beach.

Bernard had left Nauquasset almost as soon as we arrived. He maintained, in addition to his large house on the Cape, an apartment in Manhattan, another one in Boston, and a lodge (that's what he called it) in Aspen for skiing. He spent at least half his time elsewhere, and he seemed surprised that I was surprised about this. As though I could have had any idea what a life like his was like!

Another thing that became clear almost at once was that, although Bernard was the Nauk's nominal director, and though Barbara had suggested that I would be in charge, it was Agnes who ran the place. All the strings for all the systems were held in her pale plump hands with their sharp crimson nails. She kept the accounts, created and tracked the budgets, processed payroll, paid the bills, supervised the staff, kept the contracts, and, of course, was the holder of the keys. There were a surprising number of locked doors at the Nauk, especially considering how small the staff was—how small the whole place was. I had seen inside some of them—one was a file room, one a storage room for cartons of Nauk publications, one held AV equipment, and one was a janitor's closet. When, occasionally, I asked about one or the other of the doors, Agnes would say, "Of course we can arrange for you to examine everything from top to bottom when you have the time." Or, "I can assure you, there's nothing remotely interesting in there, but of course, if you insist on seeing for yourself, you need only say so and I'll arrange for it immediately." But insisting was not something I was able to do.

Instead, I would nod, blush, and change the subject, as though I had done something to be ashamed of. Agnes had a great bouquet of keys on a length of green leather that she must have kept in her office somewhere. Every now and then she carried it looped around her wrist, and then she clanked as she walked, like a Victorian ghost.

~

Every morning the beach was made anew. The patterns of seaweed, of shells, of the dark damp sand of the lower beach and the paler, finer sand of the upper—of the gaping and shutting holes made by mole crabs, and the clusters of geometric tracks of little birds, and the ribbons of rounder, deeper tracks left by dogs—all these were different each day than they had been the day before. Looking out toward the horizon, I waited to see great whales breeching, spouts like giant geysers squirting white into the sky. I imagined wooden ships from the days of the explorers, their sails pregnant with wind.

Even as early as six I was seldom alone. Occasional joggers huffed along the shore, leaving dark tracks. Women in hooded sweatshirts, with bare brown legs and floppy hats, exercised ambling Labradors and trotting shih tzus, and the occasional surf caster, strong-armed and patient to the point of indifference, whipped his line again and again into the teeming white-laced waves, reeling in nothing but the wet salty air. Sometimes an old man—white hair blowing around his ravaged face, as thin as a blade of grass, in sweat-stained shirt and jeans the color of the sky—stood at a portable easel painting the scene: blue sea, pale sand, pink clouds, and the distant shimmer of land on the horizon as the arm of the Cape turned back on itself.

The beach was long and pale and striped at low tide, and black crinkled seaweed lay in dark ranks, the water glittering gold and navy blue.

I left my towel on the sand, waded into the cold water, and dove into a gathering wave. The clean chill washed through me. I could feel the sharp outline of my body as I moved through the water, arm over arm, out past the surf to where the swells rose and fell in gentle humps, my warming body strong and easy in the sunlit bay. I turned and swam along the shore, tingling with exertion, reminding myself not to swim too far in this direction. The powerful tide was with me now but would be against me when I turned back. The water turned green as the sandbar came up underneath me, then blue again as it fell away. I stopped to tread water, looking out to the horizon. Birds dove around the wreck of the *Lady Margaret*, its rusting iron hull a feeding ground for fish, the tops of its black chimneys just visible at dead low tide. And beyond that was the Plunge, the kettle hole in the ocean floor created, as I understood it, by a large chunk of stagnant ice that had lingered as the rest of the glacier had receded after the last ice age—exactly the process that had formed southern Wisconsin with its constellations of shining lakes.

One morning on my walk I ran into Chris Passoa. In an old gray T-shirt from which the message had faded, aqua swim trunks, and old black sneakers, he had apparently been running on the beach. Now, though, he was just walking, his tall shadow knifing across the sand. His pale hair caught and held the yellow light, and his legs were tan and muscled. I had just finished my swim, and my hair dripped onto my shoulders and down my back, the salt drying on my flushed skin.

"How's the water?" he asked as we stopped to say hello.

"A little warmer than yesterday. And yesterday was a little warmer than the day before. By Labor Day it should be almost pleasant."

He smiled. "And teeming with tourists as well."

I couldn't picture the beach as anything but mostly empty. "I love how easy it is to swim here. How the salt holds you up."

He held up a finger. "You have to be careful. Especially if you're not used to the currents."

Must every action—every word and thought—recall Alena? Swimming, currents, beaches, exhibitions, artists, parties. How long until my bodily presence had half the substance her absence did?

I told Chris Passoa about my Lake Michigan summers, how the great lake was as powerful and unpredictable as any ocean. He listened with an attentive skepticism in his sky-blue eyes, the sun setting the hairs on his brown arms alight. He reminded me of the men of my childhood, friends of my father and of my older brothers, who could split a cord of firewood in an easy afternoon, shoot a rabid skunk at dusk, chow down half a pork roast at supper, and whistlingly ease a cow through a hard labor at midnight, no effort or muck or animal stupidity or human failure ruffling their steady competence. There was a kind of uniform tranquillity, an ageless, timeless sufficiency about them—about him—that consoled me, though I had fled from it not so very long ago.

"I can't imagine a lake that big," he said.

"Don't tell me the stereotype of policemen having no imagination is true."

"Well. It's hard to compete with you creative types."

"I'm not a creative type. I'm an academic." I poked at the sand with my toe. Gritty at the surface, it was cool and fine underneath, almost silky. There were small stones buried in the sand, brown and beige and muddy white. "Of course, some people are both."

Bending, he picked a flat stone out of the sand, measured the waves, then skipped it out across the water: five, six, seven, *splash*. A wave ran up the beach as far as our feet, its white foam boiling then receding, sinking into the sand. A gull glided by on a current of air, its shrill lament tumbling down the sky. "They treating you well up there? Up at the Nauk?"

"Yes," I said politely. "Everyone's been wonderful."

"You getting along all right with Agnes?"

"Oh, yes."

"You know, she was very close to Alena." The syllables of her name, with their long open vowels, sounded like an incantation on the morning air.

"Oh?" I said. I wanted to know—I burned to know—but I would not let him see me burning.

He picked up another stone, also flat and perhaps five inches across, though when I looked at the beach all I could see, aside from broken slipper shells and eviscerated crabs, were large bumpy pebbles. Five, six, seven, eight, *splash*. "They grew up together. In Oregon somewhere. The story is that Alena helped Agnes out of a situation—an abusive boyfriend, maybe. Or it might have been something that happened when they were kids. A drunken father? An older cousin who . . . ? Something. And then, when Alena's father died, Agnes asked her parents to take her in, and they did. Otherwise she would have had to go back to Russia. Her mother had died long before, when Alena was very young. So, if Agnes is slow to warm up to a newcomer, you can understand why."

The sun edged higher in the sky, hotter. Terns circled and dove in the chop beyond the wreck. A noisy family with an enormous spotted dog was settling in for the day with blankets and deck chairs and insulated coolers. Was Chris Passoa asking me to feel sympathy for Agnes, with her stony eyes and her vampire style, her obstructive obsequiousness? To pity her, even? "I imagine she'll warm up to me sooner or later," I said doubtfully.

"Of course she will. Once you show her what you're made of."

And what was that?

He bent again, plucking a thin white stone with an elegant vein of dark gray out of the sand. "Your turn."

Our fingers grazed as I took the flat slab. Distractedly, I hurled it out over the chilly waves.

One, *splash*.

Although a general impression of those days stays with me—a mood, a muffled, foggy adumbration despite the fine weather—I remember very little of how I actually spent my time once I got into my office, which didn't feel like my office at all. Always when I went through the door in the morning, there was a moment when I had to force myself to remember that I wasn't trespassing, and it was always a relief to find the gray chair empty and to see the pool of cold sunshine on the floor and my little stack of notepads and pens on the empty shelf where I had left them, as though I half expected someone to have moved them in the night. But what I did when I sat behind that finlike desk I can neither remember nor quite imagine, though I know I must have sat there for hours at a time.

I do remember that from time to time I went to the exhibition wing to walk through the galleries—to stand in them, measuring the walls with my eyes, and to feel the way one space moved into the next: what the space itself suggested, accommodated, perhaps denied. I loved those galleries immediately—inordinately—and every day I came to love them more. I loved the way the outside light fell, by way of the colonnade—obliquely, delicately, creating a golden glow that invested the rooms, even when empty, with something of the vibrancy of art. Visiting at different times of day, sometimes staying a long while, I learned how that glow brightened over the course of the morning and into the afternoon; how different walls lightened and dimmed as the hours passed; where the shadows collected. I loved the way the sound of the waves cast a mood, varying as the weather varied, so that both sound and sight brought the landscape of the outer world into the galleries. Somehow, instead of the sensation of time standing still, which I had felt so often in the great museums of the world, here at the Nauk the movement of time was more present to me than it had ever been before, as though I could feel the earth turning slowly under my feet.

From the bright colonnade running the length of the galleries, one looked out and down not only on the surging ocean and the wide stretch of beach, but also onto the dunes themselves, where the pale green beach grass waved, interspersed with black patches of dried seaweed and large shells and the long swaths of weathered fencing intended to prevent erosion. Although the galleries were on the first floor, from this side—the back, ocean-facing side of the building—we seemed to be quite high up. As I began to understand that the Nauk was built into a hill, I wondered what was underneath the galleries. Storage rooms? A shop? Boilers and pipes and dehumidifying compressors? There must be stairs somewhere, I thought, leading down. And one day, perhaps my second week at the Nauk, I noticed for the first time a door at the far end of the colonnade. It was an odd sort of door, made to blend into the wall, with a C-shaped recessed handle instead of a knob. I went over to it and pulled, but, like so many other doors here, it was locked.

What a mix of emotions I felt at that moment surging and frothing through me the way the ocean surged and frothed on the beach below. What was I doing here in this place of empty rooms and locked doors? Why had Bernard brought me here only to strand me as though on a sandbar while he ran off in pursuit of money, or distraction, or sex, or whatever it was that kept him moving, as though he were a molecule of ocean water rather than a man? Why had I not been able to so much as get a front door key? Why couldn't I stand up to Agnes, or even to Sloan, to insist on a key, or a desk with drawers, or a detailed copy of the budget, or Alena's Rolodex, which had, according to Agnes, been temporarily misplaced? Something was wrong with me. I was the curator, it should have been simple. I shut my eyes against the tears that began to fall—more salt water in this watery world—angry at myself for crying but too despondent to stop, when I had the sudden, sickening conviction of being watched.

And when I opened my eyes, there was Agnes, standing at the far end of the colonnade.

She was dressed, as always, in black, her hem just brushing the tops of her boots. She had changed the pink streaks in her glossy hair for electric blue, and she stood fixing me with her stony eyes, her head cocked to one side like a giant crow. I blinked at her, determined not to show how much she had frightened me. I had no idea how long she had been there. "I was wondering where you were," she said. "You weren't in your office."

"I was looking at the galleries," I said. "It's so important to get to know the space." I sniffed hard and wiped my fist across my nose.

"It looks to me," Agnes observed, "like you were trying to open that door."

I turned back to the door, which stood blankly, blandly shut, like a wall of snow. "I just happened to see it," I said. "I never noticed it before, somehow, the way it's built into the wall."

She moved toward me, her high-heeled boots making surprisingly little noise on the hard floor. "Of course," she said, "it's designed not to be noticed, isn't it? The eye—most people's eyes—slips right over it. But you have sharp eyes, don't you? Eyes that have been trained to notice. That's what they teach you at curator school, isn't it?"

I nodded, though it wasn't. The curatorial studies programs were about art history, and theory, and individual research—presumably one knew how to see already. Not that skills didn't get honed there. Not that there weren't many kinds of seeing. "Of course, I only went to community college," Agnes said, stepping closer, "but I notice things too."

My mouth was dry. She continued toward me down the hall, growing larger, blocking out the light, her starburst of keys jangling on their leather strap.

"Do you want to know what's behind there?" she asked. She was so close that I could smell her: the burnt chemical odor of her hair, and the sweetness of incense, and the pungency of old cigarette smoke and cloves.

I shrugged. I didn't care what was behind the door, not anymore. I wanted to get away from her, but I knew I had to stay.

"Why don't I show you." Agnes drew nearer still. Heat radiated from her body in the cool hall. She was standing far too close to me. I took a step back and she took one forward, and now I was pressed up against the door. There was nowhere to go. She chose a key from her dangling bundle and shook the whole bunch at me until my slow brain understood that she wanted me to move aside.

The key turned silently in the lock. Agnes put her hand out and pushed the door inward, motioning for me to go first. When I hesitated, she smiled. "Don't be frightened," she said. "This is the way to Alena's rooms. You didn't know she had her own special rooms in the building, did you? In case she didn't want to go home. Or if there was someone she wanted to entertain privately. Or if she and Bernard wanted a quiet place, you know, to have a few drinks."

I moved through the door into the shadowy stairwell lit by dim LEDs on the walls, small square fixtures arranged in a cascade of staggered columns following the spiraling stairs down. The stairs themselves were steep and slippery. "Careful," Agnes said. "You don't want to fall."

Down we went. I could smell earth, and damp, and something else, an overripe odor I couldn't identify, like the smell of my mother's kitchen when she was making jam. At the bottom of the stairs, another door with another lock. I don't know how Agnes found the right key in the near dark. Maybe she knew them all by touch.

Beyond the door was a long low-ceilinged room. Old Oriental rugs in shades of garnet and pearl and sapphire stretched across the floors, some with patterns of gardens and others with spirals or paisleys. Low velvet couches sat plush, brushed, draped with scarves, and a square black-and-gold table supported cut-glass candy dishes and crystal vases and amber eggs and ivory figurines and malachite lamps with green silk shades. The walls were covered with what looked like tangles of seaweed, the thick, dark green, rubbery kind they call dead man's fingers. You would have thought it was the worst kind of décor for a room so close to the ocean, subject to damp and mildew, but the museum's climate control must have extended here too, for it was cool and dry, not even any cobwebs in the corners or dust on the crystal rims of the dishes or the smooth head of the plump jade monk. Crimson roses bloomed in a bowl, not a petal drooping, as though they had been arranged that very day. And along the wall that faced the bay, sliding glass doors, each like a living canvas, seemed carefully composed: pale green beach grass at the bottom, tossing in the strong breeze; then a wide strip of shifting blue-gray and green-gray that was the ocean; and above that, the robin's-egg blue of the sky stippled with clouds. The air was still, but the sound of the ocean was like a living thing in the room: the long, low gathering of the swell; then the pause, like a suspended breath; and at last, after the aching delay, the falling off, the tumbling, the heaving collapse of the mercurial wave, foaming white onto the steadfast shore.

"It's a beautiful room, isn't it?" Agnes said. Again she fixed me with those sharp eyes, standing lightly like a big black bird on the glowing carpet, swinging her galaxy of keys.

"Yes," I said. "It's beautiful."

Agnes began to glide around the room, her fingers drifting down to straighten a violet glass dish that didn't need straightening, to pluck a paling petal from a rose in the bowl, to graze the bald head of the jade monk with her fingertips. "Have you ever seen a room like this?" she asked. "Alena had extraordinary taste, didn't she? She'd walk through a market in Istanbul or Tangier, and she'd see the one thing worth having." She reached up and touched her own dangling earring, shards of ruby-colored pendants arrayed in tapering rows. "She brought these back from Malta for me," she said. "I used to fill my holes with studs and rusty safety pins. Then Alena said, 'Agnes, why do you want to wear all that junk? Aren't the holes themselves more beautiful than that fistful of cheap hardware?' And she gave me these. 'Better one perfect thing,' she would say, 'than a hundred ordinary ones!' And then she would laugh, because one perfect thing was never enough for her. She always wanted ten perfect things—a hundred—why not? When they called out to her the way they did, as though begging her to choose them. 'Aggie,' she used to say, 'it's like they have voices only I can hear. They cry out to me like lost souls. Who am I to turn them away?' It was the same when we were kids at Woolworth's and she'd come home with the best nail polish colors, the best lipsticks, hidden inside her shirt. 'They were calling out to me,' she'd say. 'I couldn't let them languish!' No one ever caught her. She was always special, even then. She had a kind of glow that made you want to be near her. People were always giving her gifts—men were. Even when she was twelve. Women too. Once we were walking down the street and a woman in a fur coat gave her a diamond clip. Out of the blue! *This will look pretty in your beautiful hair,* the woman said. And it did. Alena wore it for a few days and then, when she got tired of it, she gave it to me."

All the time she spoke, Agnes kept her eyes fixed on my face, but I couldn't tell if she was seeing me or not. Out the glass doors, the ocean rose and fell—the same ocean you could see from upstairs or outside, but it looked different here, darker and wilder, as though somehow Alena's spirit was touching everything, even the view, intensifying it, perfecting it—as though things themselves could be changed merely by being chosen.

"I guess you're wondering why I'm telling you this."

I shook my head. I knew why, even then, young as I was and afraid of her. I knew she was telling me because she had to tell me, showing me because she had to show someone. This room was her work as much as it was Alena's. Alena might have made the room, but Agnes had conserved it—exhaustively, painstakingly—with all the care, patience, attention, exertion at her disposal. It was a task literally without end. Did the room exist if no one saw it? And if it didn't exist, did Agnes?

"I remember the last time we were together in this room," Agnes said. "Just before Venice. She was looking forward to the trip. She loved to travel, loved to dress up, to see and be seen. It was extraordinary that she stayed in Nauquasset as long as she did. She could have gone anywhere: New York, London, Zurich. But she stayed. She used to say, *Where else could I have freedom like this? Where else could I answer to no one?* Of course, nominally she answered to Bernard, and to the board. But Bernard never said no, and the board did whatever he told them to. And she loved the ocean! She swam like a fish, she could have swum to the Vineyard and back if she wanted to. And she sailed all the time, she was a wonderful sailor. *Even the wind does my bidding, Aggie,* she used to say."

"Yes," I said. I could picture it: Alena perched like a Nereid on a white boat, sheet in one hand and rudder in the other, her long ivory limbs impervious to the sun.

"You can almost see her, can't you—here in these rooms?" Agnes said. "I can. I can see her sitting just there, on the sofa, her legs tucked under her, talking to me that last night. The night I was telling you about."

I could, I could see it too. Alena sitting there, just as Agnes described.

"It was very late. I had finished her packing for her, even though she wasn't leaving for another two days. I was taking a trip too, to visit my mother who was ill, and I had to leave before she did. But I always did her packing. It was good fortune that our trips overlapped, that if I had to be away, it would be mostly when she was too. I didn't have to worry she would need something and I wouldn't be there.

"Alena had just come back from a swim. She liked to swim at night off the beach here, she knew the tides and the currents. It's a quiet stretch, no one ever bothered her. And then she'd come back up to shower and dress. Sometimes she'd sleep here if she didn't feel like going home."

I wondered where home was, where Alena had lived, what had happened to her house. I wondered what had happened to Agnes's mother, whether she had gotten well.

"She sat right there," Agnes repeated. "Her hair was wet, a dark fountain, and her skin glowed. She was talking about Venice. 'Every year it gets duller, Aggie,' she said. 'The art world. More shiny and obvious. Oh, the artists are all so clever—they'd fuck with their brains if they could!' She liked to say that—*fuck with their brains*—it made her laugh. She'd had enough of the mind, it was the body that interested her. The art she loved—the artists she loved—were the artists of the body. Marina Abramović, Catherine Opie, Carolee Schneemann. Art should be felt in the gut, she said. Art should scare you. It should take your breath—literally—away."

I put my hand to my chest. My own breathing was coming and going, fast and shallow as though I had a fever. I thought of Marina Abramović lying still as a viewer cut her with a knife and licked the blood; of Catherine Opie inscribing her wish on her body in scars; of Carolee Schneemann choreographing a dance with naked bodies and raw meat. I was starting to feel uncomfortably warm. The room was crowded with objects: shiny, heavy, blind forms that seemed to me suddenly like living things turned to stone. I fanned my face with my hand, listening to the waves. Agnes was talking, her voice droning like a hornet. I could hear everything she said, but the words seemed to float into my mind from a great distance. "The last show had just closed," she said. "Dessa Michaels, the dissection pieces. It got a lot of attention, Alena should have been pleased. But she had decided it was too distanced. Too abstracted. *The thing itself was eclipsed,* she said. She said that a lot about art that didn't live up to her standards—*The thing itself is eclipsed!* She wanted to strip it bare, whatever it was. Like staring into the sun, or looking at the naked face of God! That was what she wanted—art so potent it would make the heart stop. *I wish I could die from art,* she used to say. Die from art! The ultimate consummation."

She paused. The room buzzed with her words, my ears rang with them. I needed to sit down.

"You look pale," Agnes said, watching from her height as I lowered myself onto the velvet sofa.

"I'm fine."

"Probably you're tired. You get faint, maybe you're anemic. You should make sure you get enough rest."

"It's nothing," I said. "Don't worry about me."

"Does talking about art like that upset you?"

"No. Of course not."

She sat down beside me. "Do you like it too, then? Might we see some shows about the body from you?" The derision in her voice was unmistakable.

"I like all kinds of art."

Heat shimmered off her in waves as if from pavement on a summer afternoon. "We sat right here," she said. "She asked me to brush her hair. I always used to brush Alena's hair, and braid it or put it up, from when we were kids. She had beautiful hair, thick and black and slippery as obsidian. Volcanic glass. I could French braid it by touch in the dark. So I did. I brushed it out for her, and she said, 'Aggie, I don't even know why I'm going. Maybe I'll just change my mind and stay.'

"'Yes,' I said. 'Stay. Why should you go? What's there that's better than what you have here?' I meant it too. Art-world celebrities, super-rich collectors, jealous curators, everybody trying to look more successful than they were. Why did she need that? Why did she want it?

"But she always went, she was restless, that was part of who she was. But she always came back." The ocean was restless too, surging forward and falling back, always clamoring for the shore but unable to possess it, like a ghost lover whose arms drift through the body of the beloved.

Always came back, Agnes said. But not this time. Did Agnes decline to believe that? Did she refuse, like the mother of a soldier reported missing in action, to look death in the face? Was that why she kept the room like this, immaculate? Did she believe Alena would return any day—any hour—and the Nauk would be ready, waiting for her like a bridegroom? "It's been two years," I said, or thought I said, but my syllables, like motes of dust, floated away and disappeared.

Agnes leaned close. "I'm telling you this because you need to understand." Her words spiraled down through my ear, their tiny vibrations reverberating like thunder in the dark. "You're only temporary here."

13.

ONE MORNING I WOKE UP thinking of Celia Cowry, whose small ceramic sculptures Bernard and I had remembered at the same moment in Venice. An African-American artist, she often used the forms of seashells, glazed in the hues of skin: pinkish white, coffee brown, clay red, ochre, golden, ebony. Some of them were delicate, some cruder and heavier. Some glowed pristinely, while others seemed encrusted with barnacles and mud. She showed in New York, and her work had been included in group exhibitions in half a dozen contemporary art museums across the country, but as far as I knew, she'd never had a solo museum show. And she lived on the Cape, Bernard had said. Maybe she would be the right artist to relaunch the Nauk. The local connection would be useful, attracting press attention and a crowd at the opening: Cape buzz. She was unquestionably deserving of a larger audience. I remembered the insistent pull of her work, posed on square columns arrayed around a sunny upstairs room in a Chelsea gallery.

One piece in particular had stayed with me, a sculptural diptych of scallop shells side by side, one pink, the other a coppery brown, both of them speckled with tiny holes. The two shells were almost touching at the edges of their flared bases, and the narrow gap that separated them was tense and electric. They seemed to ache toward each other, fluted ridges leaning inward like the wake of two boats on convergent paths, so that you could imagine the rocking, heaving waves that would result when the two sets crossed. The piece was called *Parents*. The burn in my chest when I saw it stayed with me for a long time. It rekindled when I read a review of another show of hers in *Sculpture* magazine accompanied by a photo of five or six similar pairings—the vacant bellies of oysters, the private spirals of snails, the spiny and skull-like conchs. The work was about identity, which could help attract attention, but it was subtle and complicated. I wouldn't be choosing it because of its content, but I knew that content would provide a useful hook for reviewers. Finding her phone number in an old telephone directory in a kitchen drawer, I called her and arranged for a studio visit the next day.

Bernard was in New York, so I asked Roald to drive me. "How are you getting along?" he asked as we bumped through the silvery gates with their orderly menagerie and sped into the hot, florid morning. *Haow-ahh yoo gettin ah-lah-ng.*

"Fine," I said. "Thank you."

Roald's truck was old, with cracked vinyl seats, roll-down windows, a radio but no CD player. Sand had collected in the grooves of the rubber floor mats and formed pale drifts in the corners of the foot wells. It had a standard transmission, so he had to keep his left hand on the steering wheel much of the time; I tried not to look at the place where his finger wasn't. The cab smelled musty, but the breeze through the open windows was fresh. We passed a doughnut shop, an ice cream shop, a bait and tackle shop, their parking lots crowded with muddy pickups and simmering SUVs. "Are you finding things to be what you expected?"

"It was hard to know what to expect." He nodded as though what I had said meant something. "Everyone has been very helpful. Of course, it must be strange for them, having me here. No one could blame them for finding it an adjustment." I watched his face out of the corner of my sunglasses.

"There had to be a new curator sometime," he said. "They had to expect that."

Noo-ah kyoo-ray-toah.

"Well, but it was so sudden. And everyone was so used to Alena." I tried to say the name casually, naturally, but although I did not actually stumble over the syllables, they came out louder than the rest of the sentence: a blurt, a cough, like a pelican disgorging a fish.

Roald glanced over at me, a flash of those blue-green eyes with the cloudy swirl in them, a dark vein in a pure crystal. "It's good to have new blood," he said. "It's good the Nauk will open again. What's the point of an empty museum? The place should have reopened long before now."

We had entered the town, and Roald was forced to slow as we were caught in the web of high-summer tourist traffic, everyone wanting lunch or T-shirts or sunscreen or tequila. Rows of towheaded children dressed in pink trailing after their salon-blond mothers, athletic-looking men in flip-flops talking on cell phones, bronzed and wrinkled old women in T-shirt dresses whistling to dogs. "Do you think they'll ever find her body?" I asked.

In front of us, a yellow VW bug stopped short, the driver calling out the window to some teenagers on the opposite sidewalk, something about fishing, drinks, the marina. Roald pressed the heel of his hand to the horn. "How should I know," he said, and his thumb found the empty spot above his knuckle.

~

The small house stood at the end of a bumpy driveway. We were inland now, the ocean neither visible nor audible from this patch of lawn surrounded by orange daylilies, purple roses of Sharon, and a ragged clump of butterfly bush with actual butterflies on it: small yellow ones and delicate white ones and a few lavender blue ones—dozens of butterflies clinging to the slender branches and the purple flower clusters. Getting out of the truck, I moved softly across the lawn, not wanting to disturb them as they sat so quietly, some with their wings open and others with their wings pressed together like praying hands.

"Nice," Roald said loudly, seeing where I was looking, then reaching across the long seat to slam my door. It was only then, my heart set fluttering like a cloud of butterflies itself, although the creatures remained absolutely still, that I understand that this was art. "Thought they were real, didja?" Roald said.

"I guess she fooled me," I said.

"Guess she did. I'll be back at noon." Waving, he bounced the truck back down the driveway, leaving me alone.

The stoop was dark, damp, concrete, shaded by a corrugated plastic overhang festooned with egg-sac-studded cobwebs. I rang the bell and a minute passed, then another minute. Invisible sparrows twittered behind me in the hot grass. The butterfly bush with its false cloud of butterflies glowed hotly in the sunshine. I wondered what she had made them out of, those perfect replicas. Or perhaps they were preserved specimens she had caught, or bought, and affixed with wire or glue to her living bush. I rang again.

Unless the bush, too, was artificial.

Growing anxious, I held my thumb to the bell a long time. At last

I heard shuffling footsteps, the distant rattling of dishes, a cat meowing. The door rasped open.

Celia Cowry was a small, plumpish woman in a bright pink muumuu and green silk Chinese slippers. She had smooth toffee-colored skin, and her eyes glowed almost golden under her thin, arched, crow-black brows. "Come in," she said. "I was dreaming about this half the night! We had such a nice visit in my dream." She laughed as she led me into the musty hall. "In my dream you were taller, though. And your hair was darker."

I followed her into the studio, which was the main room of the house, what once would have been an open-plan living room/dining room. A shabby paint-spattered couch and kilim rug under a coffee table provided a sitting area, but the rest of the space was given over to a big worktable, a wheel, open shelves lined with jars of tools and tubes of glue and paint, with cleansers and brushes and labeled glazes, and with sculptures in every stage of making: damp cloths shrouding what I presumed were works in progress, shapes formed in clay waiting to be fired, as well as finished pieces. More finished pieces sat on a long table pushed up against the sliding glass door, shell sculptures mostly, peach and pink, coffee and cocoa, bone and ochre and terra-cotta red. A large sculpture of a horseshoe crab caught my eye. Brown and green and black, hunched as though exhausted, it looked like the last survivor of a dead planet. Beyond the glass doors, a big brick wood-fired kiln sprawled on the patchy grass. I moved toward the table of shells. "Are these new?"

She looked pleased. "Yes. I made these this winter." She touched one with her finger, a scallop, fluted and mottled, slightly asymmetrical, curled in on itself like a sleeping animal. "I love scallop shells, don't you?" she said.

"You've been making them for a long time," I observed.

"Well," she said, "but these are completely different." I smiled, taking the remark for a little joke, but then I saw that she wasn't joking. "I was so excited that you called now, just after the major breakthrough I had this winter!" There was something childlike about the unguarded way she spoke, her golden eyes glowing with affection as she moved through the room, pointing and describing, her Chinese slippers making shushing noises against the linoleum and her plump, blunt-fingered hands opening and shutting like bivalves in bursts of enthusiasm. She told me about the experiments she'd been doing with glazes, and how she'd come to understand that her earlier work had been too matte, the colors too dull, that the brushes she had been using were the wrong kind entirely. Also, she explained, the constancy of temperature while firing could not be overemphasized. As she talked, her fingertips caressed first one small sculpture and then another; she couldn't keep her hands off them. She'd pick one up, cupping it carefully, and offer it to me to touch. "See how smooth that is?" she asked of a long, pointed, cone-shaped shell, rather like an icicle. "Your finger glides over it like glass." Putting it down, she picked up a simple clamlike shell. "See how this one is just the slightest bit coarser? Smooth but also rough, the way silk is rough." She picked up a shell that looked like an icing flourish on a fancy cake. "This one's a periwinkle. It feels like polished quartz." Obediently I touched each one, running my finger across the surface, listening and nodding, trying to feel the differences. "Sometimes," she said, "I think I'd like to have a show where the room was pitch black, or where everyone was given blindfolds. Instead of looking, people could use their sense of touch."

"It would be a shame not to see the colors," I said.

"The world has had enough of color," she said. "No one has ever used color better than Giotto, and no one ever will. But to make art for the blind—now, that would be something!" Her eyes were as bright as a bird's, her head cocking, birdlike, to one side as she went on: "Before

I die, I want to make a glaze the exact texture of skin. Can you imagine that? But the technical challenges are mind-boggling."

Slowly we made our way around the room. In addition to the shell ceramics, there were a few large pieces resembling tree stumps that she had carved out of wood, very detailed. She explained which was which, the American beech with the smoothest bark, the oak furrowed with dark rings, the white pine patchy and scaly with broader rings reflecting its quick growth. The roots spread out across the floor like the tentacles of octopi. I liked them very much. I wandered among them, asking questions, touching, comparing. The longer I looked, the more human they seemed: the apple with a kind of maternal grace, the several oaks dark and handsome like the heroes of romance novels. I asked her how long she had been making them.

Her mouth pursed and her forehead furrowed (like an oak!), making her look older. "This is my memorial series," she said. "The lady who owned the land behind me died last year. Her sons sold it to a developer—five acres of mostly woods. They cut down the trees to build one of those places, you know. Oak Farms or Pine Estates or Cherry Tree Bower."

I said it must be a hazard of living on the Cape.

Her golden eyes glowed angrily. "I took pictures," she said. "I documented it! And I worked from those. These are portraits of corpses."

I looked at the wood pieces again, seeing more clearly their penumbral, desolate quality, dark smears and stains where the sap had been spilled—very different from the shells that pulsed with gossamer being—and what came into my mind was Morgan McManus. His photographs of exploded human bodies. His candy-colored viscera and dismembered limbs. What was the essential difference between them, the narrow but profound crevasse that made me like the one and reject the other? Was it that the subject of one was human and the other wasn't? That one was beautiful—aspired to beauty—and the other wasn't, and didn't? Did it have to do with the impulse of the artist?

But how could one ever pin down impulse, really? And how hopelessly outmoded even to try. "Have you shown these pieces?" I asked.

"I wouldn't show them," she said feelingly. "That would be like exhibiting the dead."

~

You never know quite how a studio visit will go. Generally I consider these sessions among a curator's greatest pleasures. The deep access. The invitation to step into the embodied mind of the artist. Some studios are messy, materials everywhere, the floor littered with old rags and dirty T-shirts and empty bottles and shriveled mouse droppings. Others are so clean and tidy it's hard to see how any work gets done in them at all—and indeed, sometimes I think very little does, that a blocked artist will spend her energy arranging and rearranging until the shelves of tools become a kind of sculpture, displacing the actual work. Some artists are preternaturally verbal, especially the ones who have recently emerged from art school, where talking about your work is almost as valued a skill as making it. Increasingly in the art world, artists must be their own interpreters and advocates. The work is not presumed to speak for itself; rather, the artist becomes a living extension of the work, a kind of conjoined twin whose function is to mediate between the art—which like an autistic sibling speaks only in codes and riddles—and the outer world of gallery owners, collectors, curators, writers, and, of course, the public. With artists like these, studio visits come to resemble graduate seminars or *Artforum* essays, and a great deal of alert tact is necessary to pry open cracks in the slick surface of the verbal assault and let something like substance leak out.

Celia Cowry was not an artist like that. While hardly inarticulate, and sometimes no more comprehensible than your average recent art school graduate, her words seemed to me more like occult objects than exegeses. She seemed almost to consider the pieces she had made as though she had dreamed them into existence, like a character in Borges, rather than to have actually made them with her hands. When I asked her about that first show of hers I had seen in New York, her answer shocked me.

"I threw that work away," she said. "It was all wrong."

A hard shiver washed through me. "You—what?"

"Threw it away! I smashed it first. Working in ceramic, you spend so much of your energy trying not to break things, trying to prevent them from breaking themselves. It's almost like spell-casting, as though if you concentrate hard enough you can summon a protective field around each object. But of course, it mostly doesn't work. Sometimes an object just *wants* to break, you know?"

I tried to look as though I knew.

"It's amazing to break something on purpose," she said. We were sitting by now on the shabby, sagging sofa in the corner, sipping the sun tea she steeped in jars on the concrete ledge outside the sliding glass door. "Especially something you've put so much time into. And not just you! Other people. And when that something has been on display, had a value placed on it, been carefully packed and even more carefully unpacked, dusted by a trained expert with a single feather or whatever they do. To pick up an object like that and hurl it against the wall!" She leaned toward me. Her face was alight and I could smell the patchouli oil she wore, and wet clay, and the pungency of chemicals, and the fustiness of the Cape damp, and the clean pines that stood around the house, surviving cousins of the trees whose massacre she had memorialized.

"I was so interested in those pieces," I said carefully. "I liked the pairings. The doublings. I thought—well, of course the forms were so extremely realistic, and then the colors were natural colors but not the colors the shells would naturally have been. Human colors. Skin tones—right? You said just now that you would like to make a sculpture with the exact texture of skin. Isn't that the next logical step after your exploration of skin's color?"

"No, no. Not at all!" She shook her head vehemently, her shoulders in the pink muumuu trembling with ardor, raised herself higher on the couch like a stretching cat, kicked off her slippers, and tucked her bare horny feet underneath her. "You're missing the point. Color is—" she began, then broke off. "While texture . . ." Her plump arms described expansive shapes in the air.

"What?" I asked urgently. "Color is what? Texture is what?"

"Texture is *universal*!" She plucked the word triumphantly out of the buzzing air.

I decided to go back and try again. "When I saw those pairings," I said carefully, endeavoring to pile my words into a solid edifice, "it was the subtlety I loved. The objects were beautiful, but you also found a way to bring in other things. Family, and race. The personal and the political."

"No, no, no," she said again. "That's not it. I made the shells some colors and not other colors, that's all. I put them in pairs because the vitrines were too big for one, too small for three."

I couldn't take that statement seriously. The vitrines would have been made to whatever size she and the curator worked out. "But," I said, "that one piece. *Parents*, it was called. And isn't it true that your mother was white and your father was black?" I was afraid she would be angry or offended, but she only sat back on her heels, leaning into the sprung sofa as though the invocation of her parents had softened her.

"The purpose of titles," she said, "is so you can refer to the works conveniently, without confusion. Otherwise you're reduced to pointing, like a caveman."

"Still," I persisted, "you could choose any name you wanted. You could have called that piece *Snow*, or *Kitty Cat*, or *Anarchy*, but instead you called it *Parents*."

She gave me a sly, sideways look. "What if I told you there was a typo on the label? That really the piece was called *Patents*, but the printer made a mistake?"

"*Patents?*" I echoed in confusion. "What kind of a title is that?"

"You're the curator," she said triumphantly. "You tell me."

14.

A FEW DAYS BEFORE Bernard was scheduled to get back, Barbara picked me up in her old Mercedes station wagon with the dogs in the backseat. We had an appointment in Provincetown to meet Willa Somerset, the first person other than Barbara whom Bernard had asked to serve on the museum's board. "She's old now, of course," Barbara said as we sped down the Mid-Cape Highway. Like her brother, she liked to drive fast. The dogs draped their muzzles ecstatically out the open windows, their ears careening like windmills. "And her mind isn't always quite . . . To us she seemed old even when we were children. She used to come by on her bicycle in her skirts and long socks to bring our mother cuttings from her garden. She's famous for her garden, and for her scrimshaw collection. She's a scrimshaw expert. And she knows a lot about Wampanoag culture. The Wampanoag hunted whales here, you know, long before the British came."

"Wam-pa-what?" I asked. I was nervous, unsure how I should speak to this great Cape lady.

"The native populations of the Cape. Nauquasset is a Wampanoag word. It means crown of the sea. Isn't that pretty?" I thought of the building we had left behind us, glittering on the brow of the dune. It was good to be away for a morning, to be borne along amid the smells of dog and old leather and Barbara's flowery perfume. "Of course, she doesn't ride her bicycle now. She's ninety-three and she's had two strokes. Trouble with her lungs. It was Willa, you know, who donated the land for the Nauk. Her family has lived on the Cape forever—since the eighteenth century, I think. They owned a lot of property. Now she owns it. She's the last one."

"What will happen when she dies?" I was thinking of Celia Cowry's neighbor's land, the trees cut down, the houses built. "Does she have children?"

"She never married. She's—you know. Like Bernie." At first I didn't understand what she meant, but then she went on, "I think she knew what he was before he knew himself. She used to bring him books, big books about art. Books about temples in Greece and Egyptian pyramids. There was one about Michelangelo, he used to drag it with him everywhere. He must have been about six! Oh, she always adored Bernie."

I tried to imagine Bernard as a boy: thin as a shadow, girlishly beautiful with those gray eyes and long lashes. Watchful, melancholy, passionate. Caressing with his gaze glossy pictures of the statue of David, the Vitruvian man inscribed in his circle, the erect finger of God igniting Adam into life. I remembered an old book my father had for some reason, of Dürer's engravings. As a child I used to make a game of finding the hidden animals in those tricky forests of etched lines. Even then I felt something: a stirring, a veiled mystery. The bright secret magic, sensed but not understood, that rose and fell beneath the surface of marks like breath.

Willa Somerset lived in a roomy shingled saltbox cottage set back from the road and enclosed in a riot of flowers. You entered the property through a latched gate, then ducked under a trellised archway smothered in white star-shaped clematis. Orange trumpet vine grew up the south wall of the house, tiger lilies and white and pink hollyhocks gave way to foxgloves and dark purple columbine. Fragrant tobacco flowers filled the space under the magnolia tree, and golden nasturtiums spilled their round leaves down the sides of broad terracotta pots. In the corner, beside the spent peonies, tall fringed orange spikes, like something in a surrealist painting, flamed out of clumps of feathery bluish foliage.

The door was opened by a broad-faced nurse in a white uniform, including the sort of winged cap I had otherwise seen only in old movies. Through the hall, in the long dim room, an old lady was arranged on a sofa under a gray cashmere shawl. A table in front of her was set for tea, with a plate of slices of bread and butter, a bowl of apricots, and blue and white cups and saucers, some painted with dragons and some with clouds.

"Hello, Aunt Willa!" Barbara said. "You're looking well." She bent over and kissed the old woman, her bulk suspended awkwardly over the small brittle figure resting on the hard, old-fashioned, pale green chesterfield.

"Hello, dear," came the answer. "So nice of you to come and visit. And I see you've brought someone." She peered up at me greedily through her pearl-gray cat's-eye glasses.

"This is the new curator," Barbara said. "Bernie asked me specially to bring her to meet you. He's sorry he can't come himself, but you know how Bernie is—always rushing around!" She gestured, and I stepped forward into the light so she could see me better.

"I'm so happy to meet you," I said. "Your garden is so beautiful."

The old woman stretched her neck, her mouth working as though chewing a tough bit of quahog. "*You're* not Alena!" she announced.

A hollow place in my chest dilated, filled with an icy sting.

Barbara sat down on the sofa and took the old lady's hand. "You know Alena's gone, Aunt Willa. This is her replacement. We've come to have tea with you."

"Tea, yes. I know. Everything's ready." She looked at me hard, as though daring me not to vanish. Then she looked pointedly away. The nurse sat on a low chair in a corner, the white of her uniform like a blank place in the crowded room in which a great number of glass cases and wooden shelves and little tables held any number of interesting objects: silver thimbles, faded cloth dolls, china egg cups, stone arrowheads, necklaces of sharks' teeth, necklaces of shells, and innumerable pieces of scrimshaw—oval panels and curved hair pieces, bracelets and knife handles and domino boxes. In the center of the mantelpiece, a filigreed clock on a footed wood-and-ivory platform was flanked by two large whale teeth inscribed with castles and waterfalls.

"Why don't I pour," Barbara said. She picked up the teapot. It was so quiet that the sound of the fragrant tea filling the cups seemed very loud, and I could hear our hostess's labored breathing as she reached for the plate of bread and butter to pass. "Have you had Portuguese sweet bread?" Barbara asked me. "Aunt Willa gets it from a bakery that's been there since I was a girl. She used to take me there and we would buy sugar cookies decorated with frosting stars. Remember, Aunt Willa?"

Our hostess didn't answer. Her face was a mass of wrinkles and brownish age spots, over which her spun-sugar hair floated like a cloud. I bit into the soft, buttery bread. "It's delicious," I said.

At the sound of my voice, the old lady turned to me, regarding me blankly as though she hadn't noticed me before. "Who are you?" she asked.

I put my plate down.

"Aunt Willa," Barbara said sternly. "This is the new curator. Bernie found her in Venice. She'll be organizing a new show so we can get the Nauk open again."

Found, I thought. Like a shell on the beach.

"I understand you donated the land for the Nauk," I said.

"New curator?" Her eyes clouded with confusion behind her sparkling lenses. "New? But what about Alena?" She glared at me, the ridge of her brow prominent beneath her sparse eyelashes. "Alena used to bring me things," she said. "That eighteenth-century snuff box on the mantel. The shadow puppet from Java. Hannah, where is it? I don't see it." Her gaze darted anxiously around the room until the nurse said loudly in her soothing Caribbean accent, "We moved it to the dining room, remember, Mrs. S?"

"That's right." She seemed to relax slightly. "The dining room, near the Mapplethorpe." Then she let out a little cry and exclaimed, "Flowers!" Her eyes, still looking at the nurse, were full of longing. "She brought me flowers when she came, didn't she, Hannah?"

"Yes, Mrs. S. Sometimes she did."

"Always! I told her it was coals to Newcastle, but she said you could never have too many flowers. I don't argue with that." I made a mental note to bring flowers the next time I came, though I hoped there might not be a next time. Still, she was on the board.

"The roses are beautiful," I said, nodding in the direction of a large vase on a table near the window, through which the ocean was visible in the distance, a shifting sliver of blue.

The old lady ignored my vacuous remark, but she stared at me for a long moment, her wrinkled face smoothing slightly like a pool when the wind dies down. "So, the Nauk will reopen," she said. "It's about time. We didn't work as hard as we did to see it languish up there on the cliff, waiting for the sea to take it. People said we were fools to build on that site. Storms, erosion, global warming. Every year the dunes recede, except, of course, for the years when they accrete. My family has lived here for two hundred years, and it's always been like that. The land comes and goes, the sea threatens. We decided to take our chances, Bernard and I. Why not? Nothing lasts forever." Her gaze bored into me, sharp and hawklike. "What kind of show are you thinking of? After all this time, you'll want to make a splash."

I told her I wasn't sure yet, but that I had thought of Celia Cowry.

"Celia Cowry!" She set her cup down, clattering it dangerously into its gold-rimmed saucer. "Celia Cowry wouldn't make a splash if you dropped her out of a helicopter into the bay!"

I set my own teacup down too, very carefully, not making a sound or a ripple, then sat up straight on the edge of my velvet chair. "I think her work is quite interesting," I said. "How she instrumentalizes local forms—seashells—to address political and social issues. The way she explores replication, figuration—how art mimics and does not mimic life. And of course, it's quite beautiful."

"Beautiful!" she cried. "You'd be better off with ugly!"

I blinked at that—at the old toad on the sofa advocating ugliness. I gestured around the room at the lovely objects dazzling from every surface. "You have an eye for beauty," I said.

She tipped her squat, quivering body in my direction. "A head for business, that's what I suggest *you* cultivate!" she said. "For the museum business. That's what Alena had, even when she was fresh from the egg." Her face went as gray as her shawl as she made this speech and she coughed, a low choking cough deep in her chest.

"Aunt Willa," Barbara cried, moving toward her as she shut her eyes, bracing herself with her hand on the tea table. "Are you all right?"

The nurse bustled over, flourishing an inhaler. "You sit back now, Mrs. S," she said. "You just sit still a moment." She slipped the plastic mouthpiece between the thin painted lips and depressed the canister.

The old lady gasped and sat back, blinking and wheezing.

"She'll be all right in a minute," the nurse said. "No matter what I say, she goes and gets herself worked up."

"Well, we'll be on our way," Barbara said, gathering her purse. "It was good to see you Aunt Willa."

The old lady sat passively as Barbara kissed her cheek, leaving a pink mark on the gray skin. Then she put out her hand with its ballast of rings and clutched Barbara's arm, holding her there. "I thought you were bringing Alena," she said.

Barbara glanced at the nurse, who shook her head, disowning responsibility. "Not today," she said.

"I always feel better when I see Alena," the old lady said plaintively. "So full of life, that one! It cheers an old lady up." Her eyes, trailing across the room, landed on me, and she started. "Who are you?" she asked.

There was a silence as the room waited for my answer. I felt lightheaded, all the glittering surfaces—teacups and polished tables and letter knives and glass doorknobs—like little suns that would blind me if I looked too long.

"Nobody," I said.

We went through the heavy door. The dogs waiting with their noses to the cracked car windows barked ecstatically.

"I'm so sorry," Barbara said, whether to them or me I couldn't tell.

"That's all right," I said stiffly. "I know I'm not Alena."

"That's not such a bad thing, you know." She stroked Dolly's silky muzzle. "I think it's lovely you're considering Celia Cowry. I've always liked those pretty shells."

Back at the Nauk, Barbara dropped me at the bottom of the lane. As I watched the station wagon disappear over the hill, a numb, uneasy feeling swamped me. It felt like homesickness, but homesickness for what? Not for LaFreniere with its long straight roads through the silent corn, its fish boil Fridays, its gravel parking lots behind taverns littered with empty Old Style cans. Not for my New York student days, sharing a smelly one-bedroom facing the airshaft. Not for working for Louise.

The gates were shut but not locked, and as always my heart lifted at the sight of them: the wood silvered by time and weather, the neat rows of living creatures lovingly carved, so many of them that each time I looked at the gate I noticed one I hadn't noticed before. Today my eye caught a fox, its pointed nose raised as though catching a scent, its bushy tail electric with the joy of being a fox. It seemed to look up at me, steady and bright-eyed and sly. I ran my hand along the smooth wood, wondering as I had so often wondered before at the way a dead substance like wood or clay, cardboard or steel or stone, having been touched by the artist's hand, became vital, animated, quick. It was the opposite of what King Midas did, the reverse of the Gorgon's gaze. I'd never understood the idea one heard so often that art—as opposed to life—was eternal. Didn't paint fade, wood crack, canvas buckle, photographic negatives turn brittle and decay? Ask any conservator and they'd tell you just how fragile a work of art was. Ask the exhibition installers in their white archival gloves, the insurers with their checkbooks, the watchful uniformed guards. Already time was working on this gate, splintering the edges. The whiskers of the rabbit and the smallest tentacles of the jellyfish were beginning to wear away. No, it wasn't art that was eternal, but nature, ever resourceful, always rising out of the ashes. The implacable ocean, the tireless wind. The shifting, gritty, penetrating sand.

Poison ivy gleamed on the side of the road as I pushed through the fence and walked up the lane past the wild roses and the ripening beach plums and the heather teeming with field mice and ticks. In the mown grassy space where the museum staff parked, an unfamiliar car was pulled in next to Agnes's big Dodge sedan. As I climbed the stairs to the offices, rather than the usual sepulchral quiet, I heard voices, laughter, something being poured. A man's voice was speaking loudly, women's voices chiming in. My first thought was that Bernard had come back early, but even as I hurried up the steps, I knew that wasn't it. The voice, though clearly male, was pitched too high. It was bright and unfamiliar, its words tumbling into the air like fizzy liquid into a glass.

In the moment before they saw me, I took in the scene. Agnes and Sloan and Jake sat on the low couches, glasses in their hands, their faces tilted toward a man who sat in a low chair with two big wheels like a Roman chariot: a tanned, handsome, crooked man with black hair and blue eyes and a big silver watch glinting on the strong wrist of the hand that held his glass. He had no left arm, and in another moment I saw that he didn't have a right leg either—at least not beyond a short stump around which his trousers were sewn shut. Despite this, he seemed physically very at ease as he leaned toward Agnes, saying something that obviously pleased her. Her pale face was a shade less pale than usual. She sank back against the cushions, smiling, balancing her glass on her chest with her crimson claws. On his other side, Sloan wore an intent expression on her little pointed face, reminding me of the carved fox on the gate at the bottom of the lane. Her hand rested on the shiny wheel of the chair, close to the stump, and as I watched, I saw her finger stretch toward it, possibly grazing the cloth of his pants, though her eyes were directed at Jake, who was examining the bottle they were pouring from. Squat and heavy, it held a pale greenish liquid that might have been chartreuse or absinthe, both drinks I only knew of from reading. Papers were spread on the coffee table. Frozen in the doorway, I thought perhaps I could disappear back downstairs before anyone noticed me. But as I began to turn, the quick, restless eyes of the stranger found me, and he smiled. He had strong teeth, like a movie star or a shark. "Don't run away," he said. "I bet I know who you are: Bernard's new pet."

As the others turned, the mood turned too, dimming and cooling, although out the window the noon sky remained as bright as a robin's egg. Agnes sat up, straightened her splayed legs in their black fishnets, neatened the papers and turned them upside down. "I thought you were visiting Mrs. Somerset."

"I was," I said. "I did." It occurred to me that when Alena had made such pilgrimages, they had lasted much longer. All day, perhaps. No need for the staff to hurry back to their desks, then. Sloan set her glass down, and Jake nodded an embarrassed greeting, not meeting my eye. But it was hard to look anywhere but at the man in the chair: his wide torso in its pressed gray and purple shirt, a weird, off-kilter symmetry in the missing arm and the opposite missing leg. The broad, tanned, handsome face that seemed almost to belong to some other body.

"This is Morgan McManus," Agnes said. "He just stopped in."

McManus—to whom Alena had made a promise.

"Oh," I said. "Don't let me . . . I have some work." I blushed. It was so obvious I was lying.

"Not yet," McManus protested. "Sit down at least for a minute." He had to put his glass down on the table to shake my hand. His grip was cool. His fingers curled, eel-like, around mine. "So you're the new boss," he said. "Agnes, pour the new boss a drink, she looks skittish. Don't look that way, I'm an old friend of the Nauk. I love the place! A little dream museum out on the rim of the world. Bernard's dream, of course, but here we are all living in it."

Jake moved over to make room on the couch. Sloan tossed her head so that her hair fluttered in the light. Agnes poured, handed me a glass.

Despite his disfigurement, Morgan McManus held himself as though he wanted to be looked at—as though he knew what a sight he was with his handsome face, his crooked smile, and his differently crooked body, attractive and repulsive at once, like both poles of a magnet. Electricity seemed to pulse from him, filling the room with its crackling scent. My eyes were drawn toward the parts of him that weren't there, unable to absorb the wrongness of a shoulder with no arm, a few inches of thigh that stopped short like a bridge no one had bothered to finish building. He raised his glass toward mine. "So," he said, "how did you find the old toad?"

I blushed again, because hadn't I too thought of her as a toad? Somehow he had unzipped my mind and seen inside. "A little confused, but fine."

"Alena used to say she was like that person in Greek mythology who asked for eternal life and ended up shriveled into a grasshopper. Better off dead, but forgot how to die!" He laughed, showing those teeth. "Of course, some people would say the same about me."

Agnes made a noise in her throat like a suppressed giggle. "Stop it. You're shocking the new boss."

"She's not shocked. Are you?" McManus shifted in his chair, leaning forward so far I was afraid he would topple out. His bright eyes probed me.

I sat up straighter, tossed my hair over my shoulder. "I thought she looked very well for someone so old."

"Well said! And what about the cowlike sister? Have you seen her cow palace with its daisies and clover, where she chews her cud?"

I looked away. I didn't like him talking about Barbara like that, but I found that his words rang a bell in me: a small, clear, silver bell. I wondered what they had said about me before I came in. "Yes. I've had the opportunity of enjoying every category and variation of floral upholstery. Not to mention wallpaper, rugs, tea services." I lifted my glass to my lips and took the cool viscous liquid into my mouth. It tasted bitter, vegetal, like the husks of walnuts. Sloan giggled, whether at what I'd said or at something else I couldn't tell. From where I was sitting, I couldn't see if her fingers touched the stump or just hovered near it. What would it be like to be touched on a place that wasn't supposed to exist?

"It's hard to think of them coming from the same parents," McManus said. "He's the cuckoo. The changeling." He nodded at my glass. "Drink up."

I took another gulp. It burned, like something a medieval herbalist might prescribe to flush out demons. "They seem very attached to each other," I said. "Despite their differences. Of course, I didn't know them before." Before this month, I meant; before I came to Nauquasset. But I thought they must all be thinking that I meant before Alena—before Alena drowned—as though her death were the one still center around which everything turned.

"Alena was the changeling," Agnes said. "Alena was the one the fairies left."

"To drive the humans wild," McManus said.

I lifted my glass and let my tongue lick up the last drops. Alena was a changeling. Alena drove the humans wild. Her name ran through my head as though on a droning loop. To make it go away I said to McManus, "Do you mean you? Did she drive you wild?"

When he smiled, the crookedness of his face grew more apparent, one half lifting higher than the other like an animist mask, which had the disconcerting effect of making him look handsomer. He gestured to his body. "I'm only half human," he said.

"Half wild, then." I stared at him openly, the warmth of the alcohol rippling through me in pleasant wavelets.

"Morgan is half wild all the time," Sloan said, and leaned into him, her hair falling across his chest.

"Jake," McManus said, "pour the new boss another drink."

Jake refilled my glass and topped off the others as well.

"Not for me," Agnes said. "I have work." She stood and strode with superb dignity to her office, impersonating in her stiffness the matron of a boarding school, or an old-fashioned English housekeeper, her back straight, her torpedo breasts leading the way.

McManus said, "Agnes says you're reopening Labor Day weekend."

"I hope so. Nothing's settled yet."

"You know Alena promised me a show."

The alcohol burned less now when I drank. I supposed I must be getting used to it, the way one got used to anything new: the taxidermied goat wearing a tire around its middle, portraits of dollar bills and electric chairs, painting on the body with sunburn or with scars. "I heard it had been discussed."

He picked the papers up and rattled them. "We were looking at the plans," he said. "Of course, things are different now. I understand that. My work has changed too." He shuffled the papers in his one hand, looking for the ones he wanted. I could see mock-ups of the galleries, xeroxed blueprints, printouts of what looked like photographs of human limbs. "I'd love to show you what I'm working on." He wheeled closer to the table and fanned the papers out, forcing Sloan to sit back. I pulled my own chair up and glanced reluctantly through the pixelated images. They weren't, though, like the photos Sloan had shown me on her phone, which came as a relief. There was a waxy yellow arm, a foot mottled red and blue, a cocoa-brown torso from the navel to neck, and another arm, this one shark-skin black. Still, there was something about them. They looked dead, but at the same time they seemed to vibrate darkly, as though something living throbbed, trapped inside their deadness. Perhaps it was the alcohol.

"These are casts," he said. "Usually they lie on the floor of an installation, though occasionally I've shown them on their own."

"Interesting." I blinked, trying to see more clearly. They were ugly pieces, bland and cold and smooth. They made my stomach flutter. I didn't want to look at them. "What are they made of?"

"A lot of them are plastic. I have a fabricator I work with. Some, though, I make myself out of wood, or wax. Styrofoam that I coat and paint."

"I like the wax ones best," Sloan said. "They look like they want you to squeeze them."

McManus leaned forward. "You really have to see them in context," he said lightly, touching my leg.

Startled, I jolted back, banging my knee on the table. "Sorry," I said.

McManus smiled, the one side of his face rising, the other remaining still. "Maybe you could come by my studio sometime."

I pulled the shards of my dignity together. "I'm afraid my mobility is limited at the moment. I don't have a car."

He leaned back in the chair, his hips slipping forward so that the end of his stump slid over the edge of the seat, the sewn seam twitching. "I'll pick you up," he said.

Alone in my office, the door shut, I stood by the enormous window and dialed Bernard. The sky, so blue an hour earlier, was pale with haze.

"*Cara,*" he said. "How are you? How are things in that dimple on the sea nymph's elbow?" He sounded relaxed, ebullient, his voice projecting a brightness I hadn't seen in person. Through the phone I could hear voices, rumblings, chinkings. Ice rattling, laughter. "Wait," he said, "I'll just go outside." I listened to the sounds shift, the roar of voices exchanged for the roar of cars. "That's better," he said. "Now, how are you? What have you been doing?"

"Barbara took me to see Willa Somerset today," I said. Standing wasn't easy. I steadied myself against the glass, then took a careful step toward my chair and dropped into it, clutching the hard leather arm.

"Wonderful! Willa is the Nauk's guardian angel. She's sharp. She sees things clearly."

I thought of the old lady's flickering confusion, her plaintive desire for Alena, her unconscious chewing. I wondered when Bernard had last been to visit her. "Yes. Barbara said. Only, Bernard?"

"What, *cara*?"

"*I'm* the curator. Right? *I* choose the shows."

Through the phone, I could hear footsteps approach, heels clattering. The squeal of a bus, the slam of a door, a snatch of music from a radio. Out the window I watched the wind ripple the grass, the gray-green waves churning glassily in the afternoon glare. A barely visible airplane droned overhead, a silver flaw in the hazy sky. Why was Bernard still there—wherever there was—when he claimed to love it so much here? "Of course," he said.

"Good. I just wanted to make sure. I want to be clear about my role." I opened my mouth again to tell him about McManus, but instead I found myself saying, "It's all so new, and everything's so undefined."

Faintly through the phone came a man's voice, musical and unfamiliar: "You almost done?"

"We'll work together, of course," Bernard said. "Consider, discuss."

"But ultimately it's my job?" Out over the water a black cormorant flapped heavily by, flying low over the churning bay. A motorboat drew a seething line of dirty white through the gray-green water. The sky, nearly drained of blue, was the color of skimmed milk.

"Yes," he said. "Your job."

15.

I WAS MAKING AN OMELET for dinner when someone knocked on the door. Chris Passoa stood on the step in the cooling air, tall as an August cornstalk, the blue scrub casting bulging shadows across the grass behind him. "I thought I'd see how you were doing," he said. "I know Bernard has been away."

"Oh!" I said. "Thanks! I'm doing fine."

He stood patiently, holding a bottle of wine, his eyes even bluer than I remembered, until it occurred to me to invite him in.

The cramped kitchen smelled of scorching egg even with the windows open. Yesterday's dishes cluttered the counter and the floor was sticky. "I'm just making dinner," I said.

"Do you like to cook?"

"Not much. When I was in New York, I lived on takeout."

He looked without comment at the faded curtains and sagging cabinets. "I spent a summer in New York once, as a bicycle messenger. Makes police work look safe." In his faded jeans, short-sleeved shirt, and close-cropped hair, he looked almost like someone I might have known if I'd stayed in Wisconsin, but there was a brighter edge to him: an expansive tang of sea and salt half concealed by his loose-limbed way of moving, the way a plainclothes cop might, under certain circumstances, half conceal his gun. He was Bernard's age, but he didn't look it. Barbara had mentioned that he was divorced, that his wife had run off with a contractor to Florida years before, taking the kids. Had he ended up in a fading suburban ranch with empty bedrooms haunted by the past? Or had he moved somewhere else, to a white-painted condo with a little deck overlooking the bay, or a weathered barn in a salt meadow with the bed in a loft? I couldn't guess. He was relaxed, alert, opaque. He gave off a faint mineral scent, astringent and clean.

"Did you like New York?" I asked.

"It served its purpose. It confirmed that I'm not a city person." He handed me the wine.

What did he want from me? Was the chilled bottle a courtesy, a pretext, a cue? Was he just being neighborly? Whatever his motive, I wasn't sorry to see him: a human face in my lonely cottage under the dune. "Should I open it?"

"Why not?"

The sun slanted in through the west-facing window. I moved self-consciously around the room, finding glasses and a corkscrew, folding over the omelet. I held the pan up. "Hungry?" I didn't expect him to accept, but he did. I got out a second plate, beige with a brick-red border. The one already on the table was yellow with a design of poppies. Both of them were ugly, though the yellow one seemed to be trying not to be, while the other didn't seem to care. Which was worse?

We touched glasses. "To the Nauk," Chris Passoa said. "What's the new show going to be?"

"Oh—nothing's settled yet."

Out the window, the sky was a sentimental abstract, pink and orange and reddish gold. Chris Passoa ate his omelet. His benign, quizzical gaze settled over me. His big wristwatch caught the sun and sent a disk of light fluttering around the room, while his long legs bumped the underside of the table. "You have an idea, don't you?" he said.

Despite myself I felt, at his words, a spark of pleasure. A glow. "Yes. I have an idea."

"Does it involve dead things?"

I thought of McManus's dismembered bodies, his bereft orphaned ears and smooth lonely limbs, separated from their familiar sockets. I looked at Chris Passoa—his clean, whole, wholesome self. "No," I said. I sipped my wine. "No dissections. No dead fish."

"Living things? People or, I don't know, sheep? Bats? Beetles in jars, maybe?"

"Ah," I said, "you're a traditionalist."

"I like paintings. I like Gauguin and Salvador Dalí. And that guy who painted the diner at night."

"Edward Hopper."

"Him."

"I like them too," I said.

He cut what was left of his omelet into thirds, rearranged them on the plate. "I guess people don't paint like that anymore." His eyes, watching me, were like patches of noon sky. I understood that this was a question.

"Some people do. But you have to remember, part of what makes those artists great is that what they were doing seemed new and strange to people in their time—a hundred years ago! Just as strange as some of the things people are doing today seem to you."

"As strange as a lot of dead fish nailed to the wall?"

"I heard they made beautiful patterns."

"They stank," he said. "Literally stank." He stabbed the pieces and finished his omelet in three quick bites, gulping like a pelican.

"Maybe part of the idea of the installation was the contrast—the tension—between the beauty of the form and the ugliness of the smell."

He thought about that. He seemed to think with every part of himself, waiting for new ideas to light up his mind. "Can I ask a stupid question?"

"Go ahead."

"It seems like art these days is mostly about ideas. Is that right? Not about things?"

"That's not a stupid question," I said. "You'll have to try harder." The golden coolness of the wine slipped through me as I thought about how to answer him. "Art has always had ideas," I said. "It's always been about something. It's not always clear, of course—even to the artist—what those ideas are. But think about it. Take the cave paintings in France from fifteen thousand years ago. They weren't about decorating cave walls. They were about the idea of hunting—about effectuating a buffalo. Helping the gods to provide one. Or the early Renaissance paintings of the Madonna that made Jesus look like a real baby for the first time. They're not in any absolute way an improvement on the flat pictures that came before, but they're about the idea that the Son of God is truly, actually human. And Gauguin—isn't painting an orange horse partly about the idea of color in painting—how color can evoke reality without mimicking it?"

The blue of his eyes edged slowly toward gray as he concentrated. "That's still different from fish on a wall," he said. "Isn't it? Or a canvas with nothing but a couple of a words? Or a big pile of candy?"

"Yes," I agreed. "It is different. But it's more useful to focus on the ways they're all the same."

"Which is how?"

"They all engage your visual sense in a new and powerful way. They all provoke you to feel something." I listened to my words fall slowly through the room, rippling outward. I believed them to a point, but it wasn't so simple either. You couldn't nail art down like a fish to a wall.

"And what if I feel nothing?"

"Then maybe the artist has failed," I said carefully. "Or maybe the failure is yours."

His eyes edged grayer. "How do you know which it is?"

"Sometimes you don't."

"But isn't that important?" He sounded frustrated for the first time. "Shouldn't you be able to tell the difference?"

"That's why you need to see a lot of art," I said. "Look and think and talk to other people and look some more. You get better at it."

"The pile of candies," he said. "Bernard has those in his living room."

"Félix Gonzáles-Torres. That work is about AIDS, among other things. About depletion and loss, and about consumption. It involves you pretty directly, right? You eat a candy, you deplete the work, you take it literally into yourself."

He shook his head. "I hear your words," he said. "But they're just words to me."

I thought about getting up, clearing the table, signaling that it was time for him to go. Instead I poured more wine into the glasses. "How long have you known Bernard?" I asked.

"Since we were kids. They summered here, his family, and we lived across the road. In a small house with no view. Like this one." He grinned, resting both arms squarely on the oilcloth, and for half a moment I thought how strange it was—how arbitrary—that humans had two arms. His watch was plain, heavy, silver, with a black leather band, and his hand was large and calloused. A capable hand. "Bernard and I used to wade around the marsh together. Get wet. Catch frogs. Sometimes we'd paddle around in an old canoe. And then, when he moved here year-round, we were in school together."

"What was he like? When he was younger."

"He was always artsy, I guess. He drew, and he sang in the chorus. But basically he just seemed like one of us. Only richer, of course." His fingers played silent arpeggios on the table, all ten of them, a mute sound track. "He loved the water. Sailing, fishing. He was into archery, which I guess was kind of unusual. He went to tournaments and won medals. He said he wanted to be a professional archer, but that was a joke. He was hardly going to say he wanted to run an art museum, was he? Even if he knew."

"How about you? Did you always want to be a policeman?"

The sun had moved and the room was growing dark. Chris Passoa stretched his legs across the floor, taking up more and more space in the little room. "I wanted to sail around the world," he said. "Go to Tahiti. Isn't that where Gauguin went? Drink coconut milk for a while. Get back on the boat, continue on to New Zealand. Madagascar. Keep going till I fell off the edge of the world! Just imagine it: Alone on the ocean at night. A warm breeze, a million stars. Silence." The electric pulse of his interest hummed at me through the briny air. In the dusk it was easy to forget how much older he was. And anyway, I liked it that he was older. Seasoned, and clear about what he wanted. Accustomed to himself. "Silence," he repeated, "and darkness. The world the way it was before electricity. Before outboard motors. Before Jet Skis, machine guns, televisions, tourism. Alone with your thoughts, reliant on your wits and your own two hands. And then, when you got tired, another green island waiting." In the near dark, his pale hair glowed faintly, the way moon jellies glow in the waves at night.

I leaned across the table. "It wasn't ever really like that, you know. There was violence, syphilis, hurricanes. People have always longed for Arcadia. But you could only ever get it in art."

"Not even in art, I'd say," he said, "these days."

And then we were kissing, very gently, with the plates disarrayed across the table, the glasses and forks and salt shakers splayed out. I stretched toward him over the Formica like a figurehead on a ship, and I shut my eyes, wanting him to press his mouth hard into mine, to lift me across the table onto his lap. To draw my breast from my blouse like a prize. But he just kept kissing, softly, tirelessly, his lips caressing my open mouth, his breath steady. He tasted familiar—well, like omelet and wine—and I thrust my tongue deeper to see what other flavors lurked in the dark. I touched his face, ran my palm along his cheek, ear, neck, arm, thigh, noting their textures, their particular sizes and shapes. As though a man were merely a collection of parts, each one capable of giving and receiving pleasure without reference or connection to the whole. With my eyes shut I seemed to be sinking through the floor into some dark buoyant space between the house and the dune.

"Open your eyes," Chris Passoa whispered.

The dim room spun into view. His face looked younger than I remembered, unclouded and innocent.

"You all right?" he asked.

"I'm fine," I said politely, as though we had just met.

16.

THE NEXT MORNING, up early as usual, I walked out of my little house to find no bright blue dome—no sky at all—but rather wispy swaths of gray-white fog that had settled low and damp over everything. It was like an installation piece I had once seen in which a long room was filled with gauzy scarves and big balls of cotton and heaps of feathers and linen streamers, all in shades of white, with the sounds of fountains splashing and doors squeaking and children calling piped in. *Life on Venus*, I remember it was called—though I have forgotten the name of the artist—but it could easily have been called *Nauquasset Morning with Fog*. Standing on the crest of the dune, I couldn't see the ocean at all, though I could hear it: the low roll of the gathering wave, the tumbling as it spilled itself onto the shore, the heavy water sighing and hissing as it dissipated into the sand.

I walked down to the beach swaddled in fog, breathing in the wet, heavy air, then turned parallel, I hoped, to the shore. The ocean was still mostly hidden, only the lacy foam of the occasional wave reaching, like a tongue, far enough up the sand for me to see. Now and then I heard a voice, but sounds carried oddly, and I was never sure if the person speaking was down on the beach or up on the dune, and the long lamenting note of the foghorn sounded its warning over the invisible world. Once I heard the jangle of dog tags, and an old Labrador trotted out of the white billows and then back into them, paying me no attention at all.

I didn't see the old man until I was almost on top of him. There, easel set up in the middle of the fog, was the wild-looking painter I had seen before. His white hair floated around his head like the fog itself, a faded bandanna tied tightly around his brow as though it were the only thing keeping his brains from spilling out. His jaw was stubbled a paler gray than his grayish skin, his paint-stained jeans were more hole than denim, and his ropy arms were awash in faded tattoos. He was painting quickly, so intent on what he was doing that he didn't seem to notice me. He gazed straight ahead into the fog as though—despite the beach and the sea being invisible—he could see the scene he was painting in front of him. The mute otherworldliness of the surroundings and thepainter's unconsciousness of my presence began to make me feel disembodied, as though I were peering through an invisible mirror. I stepped farther around behind him to get a view of his canvas.

He was painting a jungle scene. Bright garish greens from acid lime to bluish olive pulsed and shimmered in the sinuous forms of leaves, vines, muck, grass, snakes, rivers. There was even a greenish tinge to the skin of the men wearing camouflage in shades of sage and pea, carrying guns—who weaved across the picture plane. And then, in the middle of the canvas, a dark blot: black smoke and red flame and redder blood that dripped and spurted from broken bits of bodies. A hole ripped in the middle of the world. The black and the red flowed into the green, and, on either side of the blot, men screamed, their stained faces painted in incredible detail, miniature portraits of agony. Across the top of the frame, in a margin of lurid sky, ghostly skeletons drifted weightlessly: finely articulated constructions of smoke. Every few moments the painter would look up and stare into the fog, his face a blind mask. Then he would look quickly back at the canvas and make a mark. It wasn't like watching someone paint out of their imagination. He really seemed to be seeing the scene before him, as though that terrible carnage were happening *now*—as though he had access to a crack in time, a peephole to a place where men had never stopped dying in the steamy jungle heat.

Suddenly he sensed something behind him. He whirled around. "Get down!" he cried.

"What is it?" I stood frozen in the billowing fog, beyond which, I suddenly half believed, men were crouching with machine guns as bombs hissed from lurid skies.

"Don't you see?" He gestured frantically into the fog. "It's a massacre! How did you get here? They've been blasting and burning for days!"

Somewhere above us, a gull squawked. The ocean thumped and sighed, steady as breath, and the warm air smelled of decay and salt. "There's no one here," I said, struggling to hold this fact steady in my own mind.

He stared at me, his pale eyes laced with red. Then, cautiously, he turned his head, first one way and then the other. Blinking, he seemed for the first time to take in the fog, the quiet, the white empty world. Slowly, he took his hands out of his hair.

"Is it heaven?" he asked tentatively.

"No. It's just the fog."

"You're not an angel, then?"

I smiled. "I'm from the museum." I pointed back in the direction of the Nauk.

He squinted. "I don't recognize you," he said. "You're not the fat one, and you're not the thin one, and the other one is . . . gone. Hush, though, don't tell."

"I'm new," I said. The fat one would be Agnes, I supposed, and the thin one would be Sloan, and Alena would be the one who was gone. But what was I not supposed to tell—that Alena was dead? Did he think people didn't know? "I've seen you painting here before," I said. "It must be hard with the wind and the damp."

"Hard?" he repeated. "No. Do you know what's hard?"

"What?"

"Dying. And it doesn't even matter how—whether you're shot or blown up or drowned or set on fire—it doesn't make any difference!" He moved toward me, his white bushy eyebrows rising as though in surprise, his eyes as blue as fire.

"Oh," I said. "Yes. I'm sure that's true."

"I don't want to die," he said. "And I don't want to go back to Brockton!" Taking another step, his foot sinking deep into the soft sand, he aimed his brush at me, the red paint on the bristles wavering. "I won't tell anyone," he said. "I didn't see, I really didn't."

"I'm sure," I said, not knowing what I wanted him to think I was sure of: that he didn't see, that he wouldn't tell, that he didn't want to go back to Brockton, wherever that was.

"I keep my promises!" he said. "You can ask Denise, she'll tell you."

"Who's Denise?"

"My sister. She takes good care of me. Don't move!"

He lunged, his hand coming down hard on the side of my head. "Don't touch me!" I yelled. Something dropped to the sand.

"I didn't hurt you! I didn't hurt you! I told you not to move!" He pointed wildly with his paintbrush at something on the ground.

I looked down. At my feet lay a big dead horsefly. Its green eye bulged, iridescent and strangely beautiful, among the empty shells.

Sporting an artificial arm and leg, Morgan McManus picked me up at ten in his black Jeep. He wore faded cut-off jeans and a ribbed wife beater in desert camouflage, a leather boot on his real foot. Even though they had been mostly hidden by a button-down shirt and dark trousers the first time we had met, it had been the gaps in his body that had held my eye, the absences, the place flesh became air. Today, with so much more of him exposed, I could see raised scars around his collarbone, the pink ridges where his prostheses attached to his limbs, and, when the wind blew back his thick black hair, the delicate remains of what had been an ear. As I got in, he laid his hand on my thigh. "I'm looking forward to this," he said.

I didn't jerk away this time but sat awkwardly as his broad palm burned through my skirt. "Me too." I cleared my throat, and he smiled his handsome, crooked smile and took his hand away to turn the Jeep around, but I could still feel the imprint on my skin.

I had wondered how he managed driving, but it didn't look so hard. He had his good leg for the pedals and his good arm for the steering wheel. His prosthesis—the arm one—worked fine for manipulating the turn signal and, presumably, the wiper blades when he needed them, and for punching the buttons on the radio. I had never seen anything like McManus's prostheses. There had been a girl in my chemistry class in college with a stiff plastic arm several shades tanner than the rest of her, and I'd seen a piece on the TV news about a famous skier with a shiny steel-footed rod that attached below the knee. But McManus's were different. The arm was a bright jade green, a straight tube from where it attached near the shoulder tapering to a kind of flat paddle, like the end of an oar, where the hand would have been. An assortment of appendages stuck out from the paddle like the attachments on a pocketknife—one shaped more or less like an index finger, one with a flat ring on the tip like a bottle opener, and one with a sharp skewer. The arm itself was carved—or, more likely, fabricated to look carved—in the manner of a totem pole, with strange squat figures in raspberry pink and turquoise stacked on top of one another. These figures had big staring eyes and peculiar limbs that, looking closer, I saw were depictions of the very limbs McManus was wearing—self-referential self-portraits, then, in a primitivist style, of a new race of prosthetic men. Each figure had a fat red quill slashed across its middle that I took at first to be a knife. But then it came to me that it wasn't a knife at all but an erect phallus—a priapic animus—a defiant symbol of potency engraved into the inanimate limb. The leg, harder to see from where I sat, was made out of something dark and shiny.

As we reached the bottom of the lane where the gates were, he put the car in neutral, set the parking brake, and leaned over me to fumble something out of the glove compartment, coming up smiling with a joint and a book of matches. "Give me a hand?" He tossed the matches into my lap and slipped the joint between his lips.

I lit a match and turned toward him, holding it to the tip of the joint till it glowed. There was nobody around. A warm breeze blew through the open windows as he pulled in the smoke. After a long moment, he let it out with a groan of pleasure, and the air filled with the smell of it. Then he offered the joint to me.

"I'm working," I said.

"Might make you see more clearly."

I shook my head.

"Well, let me know if you change your mind." He put the car back in drive and turned onto the main road. I put the matchbook and the spent match back in the glove compartment, wondering if the joint would look like a cigarette to other drivers.

"Wouldn't a lighter be easier? You could do it yourself."

"I can generally find someone to help me out," he said as we sped between the green rippling dunes. "It's medical," he added. "Helps with the pain."

"They don't have that in this state."

"Medicinal, then. A case of taking the law into your own hands."

"Hand," I said.

He smiled. "Very good."

After a few minutes the road widened, the old bleached asphalt giving way to a new blue-black ribbon, the dunes beside us changing to scrub. "I like your arm," I said.

"So, the studio visit begins before we even get to the studio." He looked at me sideways, his mirrored sunglasses reflecting me back to myself: an insubstantial figure with a wild nest of blowing hair. I scrounged in my purse for an elastic, then remembered Bernard saying he liked me better with my hair blowing. I missed Bernard. I missed how it had been in Venice. I shut my purse again, letting my hair blow.

"Do you have different limbs?" I asked. "For different moods?"

"I do! I often wish I could wear six or eight at once, like those Indian gods. Do you notice how they're always smiling?"

"Are they?"

"Absolutely. And do you know why? Because they can feel up half a dozen milkmaids at once. Or, you know, stable boys."

Beach traffic was picking up. A surfboard protruded from the open window of the dusty car in front of us like an enormous tongue. Bicycles passed us on the sandy, treacherous shoulder. The fresh salty air was mingled with the stink of diesel. "Do you know that man who paints on the beach?" I asked.

"Ben?"

"Is that his name?"

"That crazy old vet who talks to himself?"

I hadn't seen him talk to himself, but I could imagine it. "Who is he?"

"Why?" McManus asked, looking over. "You thinking of showing him? Outsider art?" His green arm twitched, all the wide-eyed heads bobbing mockingly.

"I've just seen him, that's all. So I wondered."

"He's nuts. Whacked. Crazy as a loon. PTSD, psychosis, God knows what. He was in the psych ward till the eighties, when they emptied those places out. Now he lives with his sister."

"In town?"

"When she can keep him there. A lot of the time he sleeps on the beach. Which is illegal."

"Even if it's your own property?"

"It's not his property. It belongs to the Nauk. Alena used to call the police sometimes, but they couldn't do much. Take him home, fine him. But it's not like he has any money. His sister would have to pay. And then a few days later he'd be back again. Shit."

The roach had slipped from his lips and fallen into his lap, and he couldn't pick it up without taking his hand off the wheel. "Sorry, but can you . . . ?"

Carefully I lifted the damp roach from a fold in the denim as the Jeep hummed along the road. I could feel the heat radiating from him as though he burned inside his body like the sun. I wondered if he had dropped it on purpose.

"It must be cold, sleeping on the beach," I said. "Even in summer."

"There's a kind of shack in the dunes. Sometimes he sleeps there."

"Oh!" I said. "Maria Hallett's shack?"

McManus barked a laugh. "Women love that story. It has everything. Forbidden love, the fair-minded outlaw, a hint of the supernatural, and a tragic ending." Awkwardly, I raised the stub to his lips, but he shook his head. We were through the town now, the Jeep purring smoothly. Not sure what to do with the roach, I just held it, moist from his mouth. Still hot. Then I thought, What the hell, and I raised it to my own lips to see if it would draw.

"Did Alena like it?" I asked, trying not to choke on the harsh smoke. "The story, I mean."

"Alena? Alena ate it up," he said. "Who would have thought. She wasn't usually sentimental. She liked to say she saw Maria's ghost walking on the shore at midnight, when she went for a swim." I waited for more, and after a moment or two he added, "I could never tell if she was making it up on purpose or if she believed it."

"So it's true?" I asked, looking at him sideways, feeling how tight my muscles had been as they began to relax. "She liked to swim at night? Alone?"

"It's true."

"She must have known it was dangerous."

"That's why she liked it. Sometimes I went with her, and then she would show off, swimming out till she was just a glimmer on the horizon. I'm awkward in the water, if she got into trouble there wouldn't be much I could do. Then after a while she'd swim back, make circles around me. Oh, she was beautiful in the ocean! White and silver, her hair like black seaweed, her breasts floating on the surface, salty and silken as oysters, glowing like moons." He looked to see what effect he was having on me.

"I guess she was a strong swimmer," I said.

"She used to say she couldn't drown if she wanted to. Not that she would want to."

"But she did," I said. "Drown, I mean." I paused. "Anyway, that's what I heard."

He said nothing.

"You don't believe it?" I looked at him: the handsome crooked face and the thick black hair; the flesh arm and the totem arm; the threadbare denim cutoffs hiding the seam between skin and shine. And what about the rest of what that denim might hide? Was that intact, or blasted away like his ear? My eyes slid down, but it was impossible to say.

"I have a different idea," he said, and it took me a moment to remember what we were talking about. Oh, Alena.

"What?"

He shook his head. "Can't prove it," he said. "No point spreading rumors." For a while he was quiet, but then he said, "It wasn't as though there was a storm that night. Big waves or strong currents. And oh, she could swim! She was a *rusalka*. Do you know what that is?"

"No. What?"

"A Russian water sprite. A spirit of the water. The ocean was her element. She might swim for an hour or more, and I mean *swim*, not just float. And then, when she was done swimming, she would get out and stand on the beach, water streaming down her body, and dance herself dry, naked under the stars. You could almost hear Old Ben in the dunes rubbing his paintbrush! She was more alive than anyone I've ever known. She relished everything—art, sex, clothes, pain. Beautiful things, ugly things. She would try anything. She was always waiting for the next thing, the new thing. The thing she'd never seen or done before." He turned and looked at me for longer than I liked, given that he was driving. Driving under the influence, even. Then he said, "She called me the night it happened, but I was out. She couldn't reach me. She left me a message saying she wanted to show me something, but she didn't say what. I'll never forgive myself for not being home." Then he jerked the wheel, hardly slowing as he swerved into a driveway where a mailbox, shaped like the head of some kind of beast, was nailed to a weathered fencepost, and roared to a stop near a dusty clump of rose of Sharon bushes, white flowers with blood-red throats. Using the little hook on one of the paddle appendages, he removed the key, tossed it in the air, and caught it with his hand. "Here we are."

McManus's studio was a long, ugly, flat-roofed building made of cinderblock and aluminum siding. The concrete floor was spotless, the ranks of low metal shelves along the wall filled with cans and tubes, jars and bottles, rolls of tape and boxes of tools. There was a big table saw and a lathe, and a lot of other equipment, only some of which I recognized. A heavy curtain of clear plastic divided the room in two, and on the far end I could see a rank of computers and tape recorders, monitors and projectors.

McManus had walked from the Jeep to the studio—he could walk quite well on his prosthesis—but once inside, he dropped into a low wheelchair in which he zipped around the room with the speed and agility of a big cat. "I thought we'd look at some slides first," he said. "Older work. All right with you?"

"Whatever you like."

We went into a kind of office off the main room. An old metal desk held a laptop, a telephone, a metal basket of papers, a cluster of pill bottles, a big bottle of whiskey, and an out-of-date calendar with photographs of buxom surfing amputees. "Pull up a chair," he said.

It was a mistake to have smoked, even just the one toke. My mind didn't seem quite tethered inside my skull, as though it might go floating away at any moment, like a balloon clutched by a child.

"This is some of the work from my last show," McManus said, powering up the laptop. On the screen, images like the one Sloan had shown me clicked by: brightly colored bits of things that seemed at first abstract—patterns, smears, blobs—or like extreme close-ups of life under a microscope. Except that, as you looked more closely, you began to find yourself identifying some of the parts. A fingertip. A bit of hair clinging to a bit of scalp. Those were clear. Also, more mysteriously, names drifted up from my brain and attached themselves to things I knew I'd never seen: ligament, kidney, kneecap. Or who knew? Maybe I'd seen pictures—illustrations—in some high school biology textbook. Not that there was anything illustrative here. These images demonstrated nothing useful about the kneecap except that it was better to keep it, if possible, inside the knee.

"Of course, you can't really get a sense of the scale," McManus said. "But this is an installation image, and you can see the person standing in front—there. So that gives you some idea."

My God—the pictures had to be ten feet high! Better not to imagine it. I cast about for something to say. "How did you make these?"

"Different ways. I used Photoshop to collage a lot of the individual images together, and to manipulate the elements in various ways. To make them brighter, or change the color, or to make the outlines sharper. The raw material, I got some of it from the internet, and some from guys I know. Combat photographers, but also just guys who are over there with phones. They save things for me. They know what I like." He wheeled closer in the dimness, the little laptop wheezing. He was like an air mass, I could feel the pressure of his closeness in a tightening band around my head. "You see that?" He pointed to a ragged pink thing on the screen with something round and whitish protruding from it. "You see what that is?" I shook my head. He tapped the keyboard to enlarge it, and then I saw. It was an eyeball, swimming in a ragged sea of flesh. "Sometimes you get a gift like that," McManus said.

"A *gift*?"

"The man it belonged to is dead. It doesn't matter to him whether I use it or not. The eye is a miraculous organ. You, more than most people, should know that." He reached out and touched my eye, the tip of his finger coolly tracing the brow, the lid, the hard ocular bone. I felt sure, had I not closed it, he would have touched the jellied eyeball itself. "I bet you'll never look at an eye the same way again," he said softly.

I pulled away, blinking. But I knew it was true, what he had said. "That's not enough. It's not enough to make someone say they'll never look at something the same way again. You have to do more."

"More, like what?" His breath made currents in the air I could almost see, as though he were blowing smoke through water.

"Transform it. Make it yours. It can't just be the material, it has to also be you."

He took my hand from my lap and pulled it toward him. Gently, he placed it on his left arm and closed it around the border where flesh met prosthesis. "What about that?" he said. "Would you say that's the material and also me?"

I ran my fingers lightly across his arm, the soft and the hard. What had Celia Cowry said? If you could make a sculpture the texture of skin . . . But you couldn't, it wasn't possible, not if you tried for a million years.

Now he leaned forward again. His hair grazed my ear as he reached across me for my other hand, then took it and laid this one on his thigh, again straddling the flesh and the nonflesh. It was as though we had invented a new form of dancing. "Feel it," he said, pressing my hand into his leg. "Sculpture is made to be touched."

I pressed my palm into the seam, feeling the give on one side, the resistance on the other. I stared down at our hands, mine touching the cloth, rubbing it, the broad oblong of his covering mine, and I thought: This is the place where life and art meet! Literally!

And then I thought, I've got to get ahold of myself.

I let go of his body and stood shakily up. I folded my two reclaimed hands in front of me. "What else did you want me to see?" I said.

He looked up from the chair, grinning. His totem arm rested in his lap at such an angle that all the wide-eyed faces seemed to gape at me. "It's an installation," he said. "It's called *Battlefield III, with Screams*."

"Where is it?"

"You sure you're ready?"

"Just show me it," I said.

Back in the main room, he pulled the dividing curtain open like an impresario. A section of the space was marked off with black electrical tape, forming a sort of stage. At the back of the stage, on the wall, was a photograph, eight feet high and perhaps twice as wide.

My first thought, as my mind scrabbled to postpone recognition, was to wonder how he had mounted it. And then the picture careened into focus, the images slamming into my mind.

The photograph showed a battlefield: a wide dusty-beige expanse of ground under a dusty blue-white sky. It was like a hundred of the works I'd just been looking at stitched together into a single coherent scene. Bodies, mangled or burned, lay in impossible positions, ripped open, missing vital parts, visible in stunning detail. A shattered and bloody arm hung in a bush. A foot with part of a leg was propped on some rubble. There was blood—raw streams and dark lurid puddles of it—crimson and rusty, a study in red—and what I took to be guts, though I'd never knowingly seen human guts. Some of it, thankfully, was concealed by oily smoke that billowed and ballooned across the brown dirt and the flat sky like charcoal scribbles in a Cy Twombly.

And then there were the faces. The parts of the faces.

The objects lying on the studio floor were easier to look at only because you knew they were false—made by hand or machine from plastic or foam, paint and glue and God knew what else. At least, despite the real forays into flesh by Joseph Beuys, Damien Hirst, and others, I presumed they were fake. Even so, they were revolting—pink and oozing, blackened and bilious green with specks of yellow and white. A bloated, blasted torso extruding slimy strings of viscera. A leg split open from thigh to ankle, with the bone sticking through. A pink seashell-like ear. A white hand. My eyes skated across the surface, unwilling to settle. *Look,* I told myself. *Look!*

That was my job.

"Wait a sec," McManus said. He spun himself to the sound wall and hunched over it, pressing buttons, turning dials. From all corners of the room, like a sudden wind from hell, the sounds of human wailing and groaning swept through the space, increasing in volume, pain, number, and intensity like a vise tightening or a migraine blooming. Wanting to run, I stayed where I was, the sound clinging to me like an odor, abrading my skin, invading my synapses so that I couldn't think. McManus was watching me: his handsome mask, his totem arm, his shiny leg, and his leg of flesh. Here was a man who had lifted himself from the ashes and literally remade himself. I stood still, pretending attention. Was this art? Was it obscenity, propaganda?

Was it a hostile, manipulative scam?

"There you go," he called. "The full sensory experience! Every channel engaged, every receptor on the body enthralled. The pores on your skin blazing with sensation." He wheeled himself over to where I stood, drenched with sweat as if I were melting. It was true, it was a *full sensory experience*. My body was a drum, my heart a fist pounding on a locked door, my breath a ragged sheet flapping on a line. The noise was so loud it was hard to breathe—my pursed lips sipped air like a rabbit sipping water from a bottle—and like a rabbit, caught in an open meadow by the yellow eye of a hawk, I stayed very still and prayed to be invisible. This was lightning, this was acid. It was a single engulfing flame.

The cool metal of McManus's chair grazed my thigh. I could smell him—him and his work, indistinguishable: perspiration and burning plastic, hard steel and salt and pot. The pungent oceanic stink of whale's breath. "I doubt you saw anything like this at the Midwestern Museum of Art."

"Is all your work about war?" I asked, taking a step sideways.

"War is just an occasion," he replied, "not a subject. My work is about the human body. It's about abjection. You know. The gossamer line between beauty and decay."

17.

The moment I got back from his studio, a droning started up in my head—a steady buzz of narration refuting McManus's work point by point in favor of Celia Cowry's. Where he was bombastic, she was modest. Where his work was brutal and merciless, hers was characterized by restraint. His work literalized pain while hers transfigured it, opening to personal response, ambiguity, grace. If there was something else, something in what he did that stirred me, I pushed it away like a spiderweb or a dream. I kept my back to it as I sat at my desk researching Celia Cowry online, full of curatorial purpose. Busily I sketched the galleries on a pad and made notes. In my mind's eye, certain works materialized to fill certain spaces. When I looked up, Agnes was standing in the doorway dangling a key from a rabbit's foot, a silken oblong of fur fitted with a metal cap attached to a chain. I had won a similar trinket at the Vernon County Fair when I was ten by tossing a Ping-Pong ball into a goldfish bowl. "Here's your key." She crossed the room like a fat black chess piece gliding across a board. "I apologize for the delay." She dropped it onto my desk where it clanked against the metal surface. Four little leathery stubs lurked in the dull ivory-colored fur.

I reached out a finger and touched the severed foot. "It's real."

"Alena got it from a fortune-teller a long time ago."

The long lifeless fur was softer than skin, softer than silk. Faintly electric, it was warm to the touch in the cool room. I stroked it, thinking of the human hand in *Battlefield III*, paper-white. I imagined Alena's hand stroking this dead rabbit's paw in years gone by. Was it a rear paw or a front paw? In my mind's eye I saw a rabbit standing up, wearing a dress, like Peter Rabbit's mother. In my mind's eye, Alena's hand shimmered the same ivory color as this fur, her fingers long and sensitive as a puppeteer's. "Alena believed in fortune-tellers?"

"Only the real ones," Agnes said. "She could always tell." She peered around the edge of the computer screen. "What's that?"

"Just browsing."

Agnes leaned in. "That's Celia Cowry, isn't it?" On the screen, the ceramic shells looked lifeless, like real shells taken up from the beach and dried out.

"I had a studio visit with her. I'm following up."

She nodded, her hair, now maroon-inflected, bobbing forward and falling smoothly back into place as if it were a helmet of fine metal. "And today you had a studio visit with Morgan McManus. What did you think?" She stood over me like an iron Hofstra sculpture of a woman, and though the light from the window cast her shadow behind her across the rug, I seemed to feel a chill.

"He doesn't suffer from an excess of subtlety," I said.

She looked at me with her cold eyes. "War isn't a subtle subject."

"It's not. But maybe a shout isn't the best way to handle a subject that's already screaming."

"If Celia Cowry took war for a subject," Agnes said, "probably the only way to tell would be from the wall text."

"Thank you for the key," I said.

"Don't thank me. It's my job." She turned to go. On the bright expanse of the desk top, the rabbit's foot lay like a drowned thing washed up on a blazing shore.

"Agnes."

She paused.

"How did McManus lose his arm and his leg?"

"He fought in the first Gulf War."

I wanted a more detailed answer, but I nodded. "And is that all he ever makes art about?" I asked.

Her fleshy black shoulders stiffened. "Some things you don't get over," she said. I knew she was talking about herself as well as him, drawing a closed circle around them—and Bernard too—from which I was excluded. I longed to be old enough for something irrevocable to have happened to me.

When she was gone, I got up from the desk and went to the door, which she had left open. Sloan, staring into space in her sleeveless yellow dress, looked up, and we both startled. Her spine straightened and her fingers reached for the keyboard: the spine that had bent so her hair fell across McManus's chest. The fingers that had caressed his stump. I shut the door.

Crossing to the desk, I picked up the telephone and dialed Celia Cowry's number. In the long interval while the phone rang, I had plenty of time to arrange my words. Instead I sat numbly, listening to the regular buzzing that we call a ring even though there is nothing bell-like about it. Maybe she was out, or napping—maybe trying to nap, wishing she had unplugged the phone. Maybe she was working, her hands slippery with clay, the buzzing—ringing—phone driving her ideas out of her head, so that the very fact I was calling was detrimental to the art I wanted to support.

Then a click. Her clear voice leaped into my ear. "Hello?"

I grasped at my words, managed to mention my name, hers, the museum's, then blurted it out: I wanted to do a show.

Celia's voice was queenly and pleased. "I could tell you liked the work," she said.

I sat up straighter in my chair, tugged at my skirt. Was this what artists said when curators called offering shows? Surely not. But what did I know? "So you're agreeable?"

"It's appropriate. You're a museum by the sea, and I'm an artist of the sea. Of calms and currents and hidden depths."

"Good!" I said. "Wonderful!" I managed to tell her about the timeline, how short it was, how we would need to get started immediately.

"Come whenever," she said. "I'm here. Predictable as the tide."

A jolt of terror and delight went through me as I hung up the phone. I picked up my new key and rubbed my fingers through the rabbit fur, slipped it into my pocket. The room felt too small to contain me, so I went to the door and flung it open, to announce what I had done. *I'm organizing a show of Celia Cowry!* I would say. *Please prepare the contracts!* Or maybe, *I'll need the contact information for her gallery.*

Her gallery. Should I have called them first?

There Sloan sat, typing in her yellow dress, frowning slightly as though I were not there.

"Sloan," I said.

Slowly, making a show of her reluctance, she looked up, her nose twitching, her eyes bored. I couldn't see Agnes, but I imagined her in her office, listening.

I should tell Bernard first, I thought. Before I tell anybody else. "Is the newspaper here?" I asked.

"It didn't come," she said. "Do you want me to call?"

"That's all right. I can read it online."

"I can go check again if you want. Maybe it showed up late." Her cool tone gave the lie to her obliging words.

"That's all right," I said again. I shut the door. I looked out across the shark's-fin desk to the blue bay beyond the dunes. *An artist of the sea.* Did people really say things like that about themselves? It seemed they did. Could that, perhaps, be the title of the show?

Or maybe *Celia Cowry: Hidden Depths*—was that better?

I had to call Bernard. He would be glad, proud. His approval would sing in my ear. I picked up the phone.

Of course, I probably should have discussed Celia Cowry with him first—*before* I called and offered her the show.

Suddenly my arm was heavy. I should have called him. Of course I should have. The knowledge poured through me, cold and slow as vodka from the freezer. I put the phone down. I wanted to scuttle out of the building and disappear somewhere, but Sloan was sitting outside the door like a warder.

Slipping my hand into my pocket, I felt the rabbit's foot. Out the window, the ocean lay as placid as a quilt. I had to calm down. What, after all, had I done? Just my job! I hadn't killed anybody. Surely Alena hadn't checked all her decisions with Bernard.

And anyhow, what did he expect, disappearing like this when I was so new, leaving me to be juggled among Agnes and Sloan, Barbara and Willa Somerset? Between Chris Passoa and Morgan McManus? And it was true that the time was short, that we needed to act more or less immediately. I had acted. Bernard had hired me, and I was moving ahead. I touched the key, squeezed the silky paw, my new talisman. Now that I had begun, the only thing to do was to keep going. Bernard would be here tomorrow, I would talk to him then. In the meantime, I turned to the computer, careful to keep my back to the invisible shadows, and began to type.

For Immediate Release

The Nauquasset Contemporary Museum is pleased to announce its official reopening with the presentation of *Celia Cowry: Hidden Depths*, the first mid-career survey of the work of this acclaimed Cape Cod artist.

Cowry (b. Kansas City, Kansas, 1965; lives Falmouth, Massachusetts) works with the natural forms of the land she has made her own: the sea and shore of Cape Cod, which has been her home for two decades. Exquisitely rendered and deceptively simple, Cowry's work in ceramic sculpture uses the curved geometries of shells—their whorls, spirals, and concavities—together with mirror images—imperfect doublings—to suggest the liminality and exigencies of human relationships. Deeply sensual, alert to the particularities of texture as well as form, this art is also deeply and complexly political, suggesting the ways race informs identity, family life, Cape Cod history, and the American experience. Cowry's small, deceptively quiet sculptures demonstrate that politics in art can be both subtle and emotionally rich, and that beauty still functions as a generative value in the work of today's most passionate artistic producers.

When I checked the outer office again, Jake was sitting on the couch with his legs stretched out across the carpet, his cornrows bouncing, talking to Sloan, who slouched at her desk, and Agnes, who stood in her office doorway with one hand on her ample hip. "That's cold," he was saying. Press release in hand, I had been headed for the copy machine, but as the three faces turned to me at once—freezing a little as if I were the one who was cold, as if I had a chilling effect—I changed my mind.

"Hey," Jake said. "How was your studio visit with McManus?"

They were looking at me, Cerberus-like with their three heads. "He's obviously very talented," I said.

"So you're going to give him a show? I mean, the guy is a legit hero! And his art is totally radical. *Guernica* for the war on terror." Jake's knee, lightly furred with golden hair, jounced with conviction.

"You're comparing Morgan McManus to Picasso?" I said.

If my question took him aback, it was only for a second. "I'm just saying," he said.

"I'm not as enthusiastic as the rest of you," I said. My press release had grown damp in my hand. I took a step backward, shut the door. On the other side I could hear Jake say, "He's going to be pissed." I stayed very still, but I couldn't hear anything after that. Perhaps the women, understanding the office acoustics better than he did, had shushed him. Still, I was sure that they were scheming. I could feel their collective will like a weather system moving through the office, pressing against the door. On one side, me and my press release; on the other, the trio of them with their shared history and their local expertise and their clear sense of what they wanted. Their sense of what the Nauk owed McManus, of what Alena would have done.

I sat at my desk—at Alena's desk—with its dull gleaming surface. My flushed body buzzed, it was hard to sit still. The Arno prints on the walls and the Akari light sculpture on the floor and the shell arrangements by Andy Goldsworthy on the table pulsed, communicating silently among themselves. Alena had organized every detail here, her spectral presence hung in the air like a scent. I laid my press release on the surface and smoothed it with my palm. It wasn't much, but it was what I had.

~

It's painful, even now, to recall being young enough to think art that glimmered as quietly as a glowworm—no matter how good—was the right choice to relaunch a small museum that the world had already mostly forgotten. Poor Bernard, what a shock it must have been! From where I sit now, in our little office, I can hear him chatting up an energy-drink magnate in the next room. His voice rises and curls, a warm current of air in the bright gallery where we have mounted a show of work by a young painter: naked men crossing bridges and riding on the backs of helicopters, men turning into birds or angels, their muscles and arteries visible beneath the scrim of skin. The painter isn't gay, but his collectors mostly are, and Bernard allows them to make their own assumptions. It's just business. If someone offers you a $10,000 check in exchange for a two-by-three-foot piece of canvas marked with pigment—that is, for a literalized dream—wouldn't you do your best to keep them from waking up? It's our job to perpetuate the dream of art, not to go around sticking pins into balloons.

In Venice, that palimpsest of experience, Bernard chose me for my innocence. That fact should make it easier for me to forgive myself, but I don't. I might have been brought up in LaFreniere, Wisconsin, surrounded by new cornstalks pushing themselves out of the earth, but I had lived in New York City. I had a master's degree. I had revered Andy Warhol, but apparently I had learned nothing from him, nothing at all.

~

That evening I went home at the usual time, tried to settle down. I ate some dinner, swept the floor, watched the news—or rather, turned on the news but couldn't sit still to watch it. The day looped and relooped in my head: McManus slouched in his black Jeep. McManus pressing my hand into his thigh. The dizzying sensory turbulence roiling through his studio—roiling, still, through me. Celia's voice on the phone saying *I could tell you liked the work*, my press release damp in my hand. I put that hand in my pocket now and stroked the silken severed foot as the newscaster squawked on about an Amazonian bird sighted in a local marsh and the most popular summer ice cream flavors. When the phone rang, I was afraid to answer it. Who could it be that I would possibly want to talk to? Bernard telling me he was staying away another week? Celia Cowry saying she'd destroyed all her work and was starting over? My mother wanting to know how things were?

But I had to answer it. It was the way I had been raised.

"Hey," Chris Passoa said. "It's a beautiful night. I wondered if you might want to go for a walk?"

Twenty minutes later he was knocking on the door, dressed in khakis and a clean white T-shirt, his hands in his pockets, jingling change. "You look lovely," he said.

I hadn't had time to shower, but I'd changed my clothes, afraid the ones I'd been wearing reeked. I'd combed my hair. "So do you," I said. He did. He looked handsome and clean and limber, like an ad for the Marines.

He took my hand. "Shall we?" he said, and I wondered if he always spoke in received phrases and I just hadn't noticed before. Yet the touch of his hand was fresh wood tossed on a fire. When I stumbled going up through the dunes and he steadied me with his arm, I thought he must hear the crackle of flames along my smoldering nerves.

It *was* a beautiful night. We had missed the sunset, but the sky was still blue and gold in the west, though darkening quickly. We left our shoes and walked barefoot across the cooling sand, seeking the firmer, packed part of the shore.

"So," he said. "How was your day?"

I laughed. Impossible to explain—to anyone, even to Bernard! Even if I'd wanted to.

"Why are you laughing?" He squeezed my hand, and I shivered, and he asked me if I was cold.

"No. No, I'm fine. I'm not laughing, really. It was a fine day. It just . . . takes some getting used to."

"What does?"

"My new life."

I led him down to the water's edge. Waves washed over our feet and calves. The bay was cold, a shock every time a wave broke, and the water was hard, abrasive with sand. The tide was coming in, and inside me, too, a tide was rising. The things I had seen with McManus roiled nearly visibly: naked eyeballs and gaping livers and dilatory limbs left behind when their torsos scurried away. I was hot and light-headed as though I had caught a germ, as though I had been infected by something in that bunker masquerading as a studio, that dark rip in the fabric of summer.

"You're shaking," Chris Passoa said. "Let's go back."

"No," I said. "I'm fine."

We walked on in silence. What was there to say? My body overflowed with desire, my tongue felt too big for my mouth, and beside me Chris Passoa walked on as though walking were his great calling, as though he would be content to keep walking until he fell off the edge of the world. It was full dark now, the shy stars finally consenting to show their skin-white selves. I'd been holding his hand so long I could barely feel it anymore, it might as well have been my own hand. So I let go, stopped walking, and began unbuttoning my blouse.

"What are you doing?"

"Going for a swim."

I removed my blouse, slipped off my skirt, unhooked my bra, tossed my panties up onto the sand. I didn't look at Chris Passoa until I was completely naked. Then I did look. "You coming?" I asked. His expression was very solemn, but I could see his chest rising and falling faster than before, and as I waited, stippled with cold, he reached, at last, for his belt buckle.

Of course, I was thinking of her. Of Alena. How could I not? I dove under a wave and came up, gasping and scoured. After a moment Chris Passoa's broad, square shoulders surfaced, his head dripping, blinking water from his eyes. I smiled at him and stroked out beyond the breakers to where the swells rose and fell more gently. Then I turned onto my back and lay floating, my breasts streaming with water, thinking of McManus in the Jeep saying how Alena's breasts were as salty as oysters, how they glowed like moons. The silken fingers of the water caressed me, loosening my hair.

Chris Passoa swam well, much better than McManus ever would. He cut silently toward me, then stopped to tread water, taking the ocean into his mouth and spouting it out like a whale. "You're a good swimmer," he said. "Anyone would think you were a native."

"I grew up in lakes," I said. "I told you that. Weren't you listening?"

"I heard every word you said," he told me. *"Art engages your senses in new and powerful ways. Art provokes you to feeling something."*

"Shush." I dove, aiming myself at him, barreling into his body under the water. My head butted his stomach, my hands reached for his legs, air bubbled from my nose. Then I surfaced, staying close, pressing the length of myself against him. Our mouths came together, both of us spitting sea water, needing our hands to stay afloat but caressing each other—keenly, seriously—with our bright skins. My breasts bobbed up to find his tongue, and my legs wrapped around his hips like tentacles, holding him in place. But as he slid inside me, I let myself shut my eyes, and what I saw inscribed on the blackness there were the bits and pieces of the bodies of the dead. Or maybe—who knew?—of the living. A hand, a knee, a breast, a heart. There they lay, pulsing and shuddering, as I pulsed and shuddered.

We didn't stay out long. We swam to shore, struggled into our clothes, and he walked me back to the cottage with his arm over my shoulders as though he were protecting me. I didn't ask him in. We kissed good-bye on the step, and he said he'd see me soon. In a minute his car was rumbling away.

For the second time that day I changed my clothes, putting on this time jeans and a sweatshirt with a hood I could pull tight over my hair. Then I took my new key and went back out.

By now the stars glittered brightly, cheerfully. The Milky Way was a road in a fairy tale I might follow if I needed a quick escape. Instead, I took the sandy path up through the dunes, fireflies blinking in the dark bushes as I approached the museum entrance. I drew the rabbit's foot out of my pocket and fitted the key into the lock. It turned, smoothly and silently, and I went inside, feeling like a thief, expecting to feel my heart pounding. But in fact I was calm. It was the first time I had been in the Nauk alone. I liked it. I liked the cool air and the sense of space around me, the large smooth tiles under my feet and the glimmer and movement of the water beyond the glass wall, surging and ebbing. A silver path, cast by the moon, lay across the backs of the waves as the Milky Way arced across the sky, as though nature wanted to remind me that the world—my life—was full of possible directions, paths I might choose that would lead me—where? It was impossible to say.

I went upstairs, opened the door to Agnes's office, and switched on the light. I didn't want anyone to see me, but even less did I want to be someone who skulked and sneaked in the dark. I faced the row of file cabinets. They were neatly labeled: exhibitions, budgets, fundraising, and so on. I opened the first drawer in the public relations section, and it didn't take long to find the press distribution list. I turned on the copier, waited through the comforting mechanical buzz and clack as it warmed up, then ran my press release through. Despite my fears, the machine did not jam. It did not run out of paper. It took me till after midnight, but I stuffed, addressed, and stamped a couple of hundred envelopes, humming to myself, cheered by the neat tower rising into the air. It was boring, but no more than canning tomatoes or detasseling corn, and far less sweaty and exhausting. I had a moment of doubt as I finished and found myself with a bountiful harvest and no obvious way to get it to market. I couldn't just leave all this in the outbox by the elevators. I should have been able to, but I couldn't. And there certainly wasn't a public mailbox out here in the dunes. Then I thought of the rusty three-speed in the laundry yard that Roald had patched and oiled. I'd ridden it a couple of times down the road as far as the convenience store at the gas station, and once all the way to town.

Ten minutes later I was sailing down the two-lane highway, my cargo in a plastic garbage bag bungeed to my basket, my hair blowing everywhere. It was one a.m., and the road was empty. I pumped hard over the shallow hills. A million stars lit my way, and the gentle pulse of the surf kept me company, sighing, hushing itself, on my left hand all the way there and on my right as—cargo safely delivered into the sturdy belly of the mailbox on Ocean Street—I raced the setting moon home.

18.

THE NEXT MORNING Bernard phoned me from his car. "I'm on the bridge," he said. "The canal is the color of blueberries."

"Funny. In Europe the canals weren't blue."

"Listen to you," he said. "The voice of experience." His words in my ear were like water on a parched tongue. I felt myself open and settle, filling the space around me more convincingly.

"Remember the light on the Grand Canal?" I said. "So green and gold."

"I remember."

"And what about the canals on Mars!" I was thinking of the photographs my father had shown me, dry red arteries in the dust of a distant planet, and of the summer sky over the fields: the Great Bear and the Lesser Bear, the Summer Triangle and Cygnus the Swan. My father's shirt was soft, his face scratchy as he lifted me up in one arm and pointed with the other.

"I thought that was a translation error," Bernard said.

The rumble of a car in the lane floated toward me. I opened my eyes and carried the phone to the window, thinking maybe it was him—Bernard—that he was just teasing me with his talk of the canal.

Instead, Agnes's sedan nosed up the sandy track and pulled into the parking area. It was a windy day, the grass bent over almost flat, the bushes leaning. I watched Agnes get out, a black blot on the bright morning. Sloan climbed out the other side, slim as a nail paring, her pale hair blowing. They ambled up the path, bent against the wind, and disappeared behind the white trellis.

"I should go," I said.

"We'll need to talk about the fall show," Bernard said. "We don't have much time."

The dune grass fluttered in the yellow light. "Right," I said.

"I have some ideas. And of course I'm eager to hear yours."

I waited to hear myself tell him about Celia. Maybe it would be better to do it in person. Through the phone a seagull squawked mournfully, echoed a moment later by the call of a gull above my house. "See you soon!" I said brightly. Out the window, wings spread, the gull faced into the wind like a swimmer in a current, going nowhere.

Somewhere to the west, Bernard's car raced toward me down the Cape, while up on the Nauk's second floor Agnes perched in her black dress. The steady wind rushed over the building, nosing for loose shingles. Glancing in the mirror, I saw that I was wearing, once again, the yellow shirt with the floppy collar. I pulled it up over my head, catching my hair on a button. I yanked, the blouse came free, the button bounced across the room and rolled under the dusty dresser. I slipped on my black dress and faced the mirror again. I looked pale as an egg, but at least I didn't look fifteen. Scrounging a lipstick out of my purse, I painted my mouth with its oily cherry shine. I fluffed my hair. My hair would be all right, I thought, if it were only a different color. Maybe I should dye it! Or shave it off.

It was quiet on the second floor of the Nauk when I came in. Sloan wasn't at her desk across from the elevator. I directed my feet to Agnes's office, someplace I usually avoided. The two of them, Agnes and Sloan, were standing on either side of the desk leaning toward each other, almost as though they were about to kiss. I rapped on the door frame and they turned in unison, like two heads on a two-headed beast.

"Bernard's on his way!" I said.

They blinked their two pairs of eyes, one pair gray and the other green. "We know," Agnes said.

"Oh," I said. "Good."

Out Agnes's window I could see the ocean, gray with big foam-topped swells as though each wave wore a jaunty cap.

"I'm glad you're here," Agnes said. "I wanted to ask you—have you been going through my files?" Her face remained impassive, unreadable, but Sloan's was suddenly more alert.

"No," I said. "Why would I do that?" We eyed each other. My disavowal had been instinctive, like a child lying about the cookie jar.

"How should I know? Maybe you were looking for something. You know I'm always happy to get you anything you need."

It still wasn't too late to say, *Now that you mention it, I did go in there one day . . .* The files weren't private, after all. "Thank you," I said.

Crowlike, she tilted her head on her neck, first one way and then the other. "Someone was in here."

"How do you know?"

"One of the drawers wasn't closed all the way."

"Is anything missing?" I knew nothing was, but my heart galloped anyway.

"Not as far as I can tell."

"Well, then. Probably Don jostled it when he was cleaning." Don was the janitor. I turned away, grateful that I had copied and returned the list.

"Just a minute," she said.

Anxiety fizzed in my chest as though someone had opened a bottle of soda in there. I turned back. "I told you, I don't know anything about it!"

Agnes let me wait. Then she said, "I was only going to ask you about lunch."

"Lunch?"

"Alena always liked to make a little fuss when Bernard showed up after being away."

"Oh," I said. "Certainly."

"Of course, you might have other ideas."

"Not at all. Please go ahead."

"What do you want us to order?" She waited. Sloan solemnly picked up a pad and a pen.

"Whatever you think. I'm sure you know what he'd like better than I do," I said, then wished I hadn't said it.

As though hers was the face that registered emotion for the two of them, Sloan smiled.

I expected Bernard to sweep through the offices like sea spray, rinsing away the falseness, the awkward stage-show quality of the days. I sat waiting for him in my office like a child waiting for recess, and when I heard the car, I ran down, plunging through the door into the cloudy morning. He was standing on the grass, his hair blowing sideways across his face, looking up at the building. I couldn't tell what he was feeling: pride, perhaps, or uncertainty, or sadness. I knew he must think about Alena all the time when he was here, though he never mentioned her. I knew this must be why he always left almost as soon as he arrived (though, no doubt, he did really have business to see to). He seemed thinner than I remembered, thin as a shadow in his pressed gray slacks and black linen shirt and moccasins. His smile when he saw me burned through my chest like brandy. Still, I resisted the urge to fling myself at him and instead walked slowly down the path, the wind pushing me on. He took my hands and kissed me on both cheeks.

"Cara," he said. All around us the dune grass waved as if in greeting, and the gray sky lightened a shade or two. "Everything's going well?"

"Of course!" And then the door opened again, and I could feel them behind us, looming in front of the trembling roses: Agnes and Sloan. Bernard let go of my hands to wave, and we went to meet them. He didn't seem to mind at all.

Lunch was laid out in the boardroom, which didn't look out on the ocean but the other way onto the dunes and the lane. You could see my little house tucked under the swell of land, looking picturesque. Agnes had ordered lobster already out of the shell, and there was coleslaw and roasted corn salad, Portuguese rolls and petit fours iced in pink and green. There was Pellegrino and white wine, white china and fluted glasses. Bernard seemed to take all this for granted, filling his plate and pouring the wine, sitting back and stretching his long legs across the floor. I wondered what else he expected just to happen—things I couldn't begin to guess at—and whether Agnes would mention them to me, or ask me about them, or just go ahead and do them.

"How's the beach holding up?" Bernard asked, piling lobster onto a roll.

"Pretty well," Agnes said. "We haven't had a bad storm in a couple of years." They talked about storms, storm fencing, erosion, sand bars, jetties, tides. I thought of Willa Somerset saying people had said they were crazy for building the museum on a dune. I thought of the wind, and what it would be like here in a storm in the winter, about ships that wrecked, drowning all hands. The talk turned to money: donors and insurance costs, the alarm system. Payroll, interest rates, assessment, property taxes. I tried to pay attention, asking questions until Bernard said kindly, "You don't need to worry about the financial side yet. You can leave that to Agnes."

Agnes nibbled a petit four. Sloan, sipping Pellegrino, raised her chin and looked at me with her cool green eyes.

After lunch, Agnes and Sloan went back to their offices. Bernard opened a second bottle of wine. "I'm sure you've been thinking about a show," he said.

"Yes!" I set my empty glass down hard on the table. "Yes, I have."

"Good," he said, refilling my glass. "Me too."

The wine was buttery and bright. It cooled my throat and slowed my jumpy heart. I hadn't known wine could be like this until I met Bernard. There were a lot of things I hadn't known. "I've been reading," I said. "And thinking. I've made a couple of studio visits."

"Who with?" He leaned back farther in his chair like a parent getting comfortable before a child's recital.

I sat up straight, tugging at my black dress. I was glad I wasn't wearing the shirt with the floppy collar. "Celia Cowry, for one," I said. "That's who I want to show. Celia Cowry."

When Bernard smiled, he looked like a minor benevolent god. Leaning forward, he took my hand. "I can see why you'd think of Celia," he said. "She's done some beautiful work."

"And she's local but with a national reputation, which is perfect for us," I said. "We want to get the Cape Cod folks excited, to give them a feeling of ownership. We want to make a splash here, with ripples that spread out across the art community!" Splash, where had I heard that word before in connection with Celia? Oh—when Willa Somerset had said she wouldn't make one falling out of a helicopter. Luckily, Bernard had not been there.

"Not really much of a national reputation," he said.

"But enough!" I took my hand back. He tilted his head as if trying to see the idea, or perhaps me, from some new angle, and I resolved to stop speaking with exclamation points. "We don't want someone who's already famous," I said. "We want someone poised to move to the next level."

"Cara," he said, "you don't need to tell me what our mission is."

"Good! Then I'm sure you'll agree!"

But he didn't agree, not at all. He took my hand again, insistently, firmly. I could smell him, pressed linen and shaving cream and bitter orange. He turned my hand palm up and examined it like a fortune-teller looking for clues. At the V of his shirt, his chest was starting to freckle. I felt a great tenderness toward that constellation on his skin, which I imagined emerged every summer like a message in invisible ink revealed by sunlight. "I see what drew you to Celia," he said. "I do. Is she talented? Yes. Is she underrecognized? Certainly. Would her work look good in our galleries? Absolutely. But is she the right artist to re-launch the Nauk? That's a different question."

"Why? I don't see that. Her work is terrific. It looks simple, but there's so much going on. It's ideologically complex." I didn't say "political," it would have sounded too blatant and calculating. I didn't say she was black, though that was what I meant too. *Ideologically complex!*

Bernard sighed. He reached across to the plate on which he had left a mound of coleslaw and pressed it down with his fork. "It's not like she's underrecognized and thirty-five," he said. White liquid spread out in a pool, trickling across the dish. "Maybe she's past the point of going to that next level, if she hasn't done it by now."

I stared at him.

"I'm just being realistic."

"I don't understand! You say the Nauk prides itself on showing underrecognized art. On not showing the people everyone else is showing. How a show here can be the thing that finally nudges an artist into the broader sphere! And now you're saying that we won't show Celia because she's too *old*?"

I waited for him to look embarrassed, but instead he looked at me the way you look at the corner of a jigsaw puzzle that suddenly doesn't seem to fit together neatly after all. "In the first place, you can't turn your back on reality. We can only do what we can do. In the second place, I'm not saying we'll never show her. I'm saying that now is not the time. In the third place, Celia hates it when people try to place her work in any kind of ideological context. She won't go along with that."

"What's the point of bringing me here?" I cried. "What did you intend for me to *do*? Not the business part, not the fundraising part, and apparently not the curatorial part either. I thought you hired me because you trusted my judgment." He was beginning to see what Barbara, Agnes, and Willa Somerset—even Roald and Sloan—had seen the moment they met me: that he had made a fabulous mistake! Still, here I was.

"I do trust your judgment," Bernard said. He pushed the coleslaw apart with his fork, one shred at a time. "About art. But a decision like this has many dimensions."

"I've thought about it multidimensionally. Besides." I took a breath. "I've already told her."

"You *what*?"

"You said we were in a hurry! You said this was my decision!"

He shoved the plate and it spun off the edge of the table onto the floor, landing upside down. I jumped up and lifted it. On the beige carpet the slaw lay in its constituent parts: green cabbage, orange carrot, red pepper. Lunch deconstructed. "Agnes!" he yelled.

The door opened instantly.

"Clean this up!" He turned to me. "You'll just have to tell her you changed your mind."

"I can't do that!" I was shocked. "How can I do that?"

"You're the curator," he said. "Figure it out."

"Actually," I said, "I sent out the press release too." Bernard's head jerked toward me, and his body trembled in its black and gray like a Doberman that has been ordered to stay. For a moment, trying and failing to meet his gaze, I was afraid of him. "Two hundred copies."

Agnes looked at me, and then she looked away. "I'll just get the carpet sweeper," she said.

"You—" he said.

"What?" I said wildly. "What?" My mind clattered through the catalogue of names he might call me, and I saw myself storming back to the cottage, packing my things, catching a bus.

Bernard shut his eyes and lowered his hand. He sagged like a luffing sail when the wind dies. But he said nothing.

19.

The next day, a Saturday, I was up early, hanging my laundered clothes in the cramped laundry yard, its dry grass pocked with anthills, and thinking of my pioneer great-grandmother who homesteaded in Nebraska (what, if anything, had she hung on her whitewashed walls—embroidered samplers?) when Bernard rang the bell.

He looked thinner, perhaps because he was holding his spine so straight, as though he were a fragile vessel that might break if jounced or jostled. He wore a jacket over a dress shirt with an open collar, a lapel pin in the shape of a scallop shell, scuffed shoes. The shadows under his eyes were burnished to a bluish gloss. Perhaps he had been out walking in the scrub. Perhaps he hadn't slept. "May I come in?" he said.

"Of course. If you want to."

We sat at the kitchen table. I wished I had music playing, or the radio news, but the only sounds were the dull tock of the clock on the wall and the gurgling hum of the refrigerator and the buzz of insects in the long grass around the house.

At last he said, "I got a call last night from someone at the *Times*. He said he got a copy of the press release and would like to set up an interview with Celia."

"Oh, good! That's good, isn't it?" I didn't know whether he meant *The Cape Cod Times* or *The New York Times*, but for the moment I was thrilled with either one.

"It's good," he acknowledged. "If Celia is willing to be interviewed."

"Why wouldn't she be?" I asked. "Of course she will."

"Have you asked her?"

"No."

"Give her a call," he suggested. "See what she says." He held my gaze with bloodshot eyes. How differently he had looked at me across the breakfast table at the Gritti when he'd proposed that I come to work for him! That had been barely a month ago, but I felt I had both aged greatly since then and grown younger. There seemed to be so many things I didn't know.

"You mean now?"

"Unless you think we have time to spare." He spread his long hands on the table and examined them—clean oval nails, hairless knuckles, a thick gold ring with a black stone.

"So," I said, needing to hear him say it, "we're moving forward? With the show?"

"We have no choice."

"You mean I've left us no choice."

He reached out one of his hands—the one with the ring—and laid it gently over my own. "Look," he said. "What's done is done. The only thing to do is to move ahead. That's what we're going to do. My assumption is that the show is going to be fabulous."

At his touch, all the air seemed to go out of me. I looked at his striped shirt, his sober eyes. "It will be fabulous," I repeated, like someone under hypnosis.

His fingers traced gentle, soothing circles on the back of my hand. "But there's lots to do."

"I'll call Celia," I said.

"We should have dinner with her," he said. "See if she's free tonight."

But as I was looking up her number, the phone rang, and it was Celia calling me. "I was just going to call you!" I said. At the table Bernard looked like a dog that has caught a scent. His scallop-shell pin sent a spot of brightness jumping across the wall.

"I just got off the phone with a man from the *Times*," she said. "Calling people at home on a Saturday morning! Doesn't anyone have manners anymore?"

I didn't know where else the reporter would have called her, her home and studio being one. But I only said, "That's good news, Celia. Interest like that. That's very good for the show."

"It is *not* good for the show when people have the wrong ideas! This man. A show by a black artist has to be about race. The artist has to be making a political point, everything has to have a hidden meaning! I don't know where they get these ideas. But, oh." Her tone shifted, her generalized outrage becoming pointed. "*Hidden Depths*? I know you must have meant well, but you really should have *talked* to me. You should have *consulted* me before you went off giving my show some name that would give folks the wrong idea. I've never not been consulted about the title of a show before. I know you're young, honey, but surely you know that!"

All the time she spoke I felt hollower and less substantial—emptied out like the husk of a dead insect that the first breeze will blow away. I spun myself slowly toward the wall so Bernard couldn't see my face. Still, he had to smell the stink of abjection streaming from me. I had done everything wrong. "Celia," I said. "I'm so sorry. You're absolutely right, I should have called. But I got the title from you! From something you said to me! I should have asked you explicitly. But time was so short. And, as I said, the words were yours."

"That's a poor excuse," she said. "And I don't believe I did say that—*hidden depths*. I do my best not to speak in clichés. But even if I did! People say all kinds of things. They don't mean every single last one of them. I hate to say it, but this whole thing is starting to feel like a mistake."

Oh, how I agreed with her! A mistake from beginning to end, a sequence of little explosions running down the length of a string of Christmas lights, each bulb shattering, filling the air with shards of glass. If only I could go back to the day Bernard drove me up the lane to the Nauk, I would do everything differently!

Or perhaps it would be better to go back further still, as long as I was time traveling, to the moment Bernard asked me to come to Nauquasset, and shake my head sadly. I could be back at my old job right now, listening to Louise talking on the phone . . .

But no. No, I wouldn't do that. I was here; I was lucky beyond all reason to be here. I turned back toward Bernard, holding his weary gaze as I said, as soothingly as I could, "No, Celia—not a mistake. We are so thrilled to be doing this show. We're so enthusiastic about your work! It's truly luminous, and it's a travesty that the world hasn't given it its due recognition." I paused, wondering if *travesty* had been going too far, but the throaty, grudging, punctuating sounds that came through the phone suggested otherwise. "I apologize again about the title. You're absolutely right. But we can talk about changing it"—here Bernard winced a little and shook his head—"though I really think that doing that would be a mistake at this point. It's a good title. It refers both to your engagement with the ocean and to your complexity, and it will pique people's interest." This was a lie—by now I hated the title—but Bernard gave me a small encouraging nod.

"The work is what should interest people," Celia protested. But some of the anger had gone out of her voice.

"Of course! And it will. But they have to get into the galleries and see it first. You know that."

"Getting people out to the edge of the world and into a couple of rooms. That's a lot of work to expect some old title to do."

"The title is just part of it. Getting the press interested—that's huge. The reporter who called you this morning? That's good, that's just what we want. Now our job—yours and the Nauk's—is to make sure the reporters get something they can use. That they have something they can write about. Even if the art is what they care about, they have to have a story. That's their business."

"I can do that," Celia said, half scornfully. "Of course. As long as they don't go asking me about race."

I was glad Bernard couldn't hear her. His handsome face brightened slowly like a fluorescent tube warming up.

The silver lining of our absurdly short timeline ("compressed" was the word we used, no one ever said "insufficient") was that there was so little time to reflect on what a disaster the whole thing was. Not a total, unqualified disaster—a *qualified* disaster—but a disaster nonetheless. Celia had complete integrity, by which I mean she never compromised her unwillingness to talk about her art in relation to race—or, in fact, in relation to anything outside of itself. Neither did she tolerate anyone else doing so in her hearing. When she finally saw a copy of my press release, she was so angry she refused to speak to me for two days. Luckily we had done most of our work by then—chosen the pieces, transported them to the Nauk, tried them in various arrangements. There is nothing that lifts the heart like the absolute grace with which big tattooed art handlers lift and assemble a complicated piece of sculpture, shipped in parts and put together with the aid of a sketchy diagram. The show was mostly new work—there wasn't time to fuss with loans, except from people Bernard knew well, and of course there was the work she had destroyed—so it was flatter than the exhibition in my head, a little one-dimensional. Still, it was a good show, even given the circumstances. It was a very good show. And some of the work in it was extraordinary. The enormous glazed sculpture of the horseshoe crab sent shivers through me every time I caught sight of it unexpectedly. Celia had made, as well, a series of long, whitish, intricate sculptures that looked abstract, but were, in fact, representations of sea foam as a wave broke onto the shore. That series alone, with its rhythm and simplicity, its virtuoso craftsmanship, and its subtle variation in color (some of the whites were almost green, others verged on purple, all of them with a depth reminiscent of a Gerhard Richter squeegee painting) would have justified the show to me. Celia was, I believed, an exceptional artist. I still believe it. Like many exceptional artists, she had (she still has) iron ideas, but unfortunately she lacked the instinct of some artists for productive provocation. Call it the Warhol strategy—or the Duchamp strategy, if you prefer. Like a child at bedtime who insists she's not tired, Celia's provocation was all unproductive, almost self-negating. Sometimes I thought this was just her scorpion nature, but other times it seemed to me that she had settled on this pose purposefully, out of some dimly perceived, horribly misplaced idea that the job of an artist was to hide her light under the darkest bushel possible and wait for a dedicated acolyte to be drawn to it like a clairvoyant moth.

Roald was extraordinary during the short, brutish installation. I have since known many wonderful preparators, but Roald stands out in my mind for his tireless cheerful calm and his understated skill. Dressed in a striped jersey like something a sailor might wear in an old movie, he ambled through the galleries, loose limbed and sharp eyed. He had a gift for spotting a difficulty before it arose, then preparing the atmosphere to handle it with a quip or a useful suggestion, like a gynecologist making a joke while lubricating the speculum. Celia's shell pieces were simple enough to handle, though very delicate. But the crabs (there was a green crab, a fiddler crab, and a trio of lady crabs titled *Nefertiti's Handmaidens* in addition to the spectacular horseshoe crab) were each made of five or six finicky pieces that had to be fitted precisely together. The sea foam series required tweezers and museum wax to assemble, which Roald insisted on doing himself. When Celia was there, she hovered and swooped, admonishing, warning, sighing theatrically, and generally prophesying doom, like a plump and muumuued Cassandra. Meanwhile, invitations were designed, nixed by Celia (too bright), redesigned, and sent out without consulting her again. When a friend showed her one, she was furious. When she found out the brochure we were publishing wasn't in color, she threw a tantrum. When a reporter asked her about the titles of the works (her titling was, I suppose, productive provocation—or would have been if she hadn't regularly squashed people's interest the moment she provoked it), she hit the ceiling and stayed up there, bouncing and squeaking like a helium balloon, until the air finally went out of her.

I felt terrible, of course. I felt I could have found an artist to show whose work I liked and who wouldn't have made everyone's life so miserable if only I had asked for a little guidance. To his credit, after his initial outburst, Bernard never said another word about it. But for Agnes—and, following her example, Sloan and Jake—no opportunity to complain about Celia went unwasted. Unless, that is, the opportunity to criticize me superseded it, as when, the day before we opened, Celia sought me out in my office to complain about the shade of white the gallery walls were painted. I heard her out (everyone in the offices, I suppose, heard her out), then soothed, murmured, apologized, nodded, explaining that—regrettably—it just wasn't physically possible to repaint the walls in time. When she eventually stalked away down the stairs like a coral and blue dust devil, the following dialogue floated clearly through my open door:

Alena would never have stood for that.

She would have given her the stare. Rapier of ice, voice of honey!

Half a minute and she would have had her eating out of her hand. She had such a way with artists.

They were always grateful to her. And why not? What's an artist without a curator? Nothing. Alena understood that.

Even then, it pleases me to recall, I was more puzzled than wounded by the implication of this final remark. An artist without a curator was still an artist—that was clear. But a curator without an artist?

A conjurer in the void.

Looking back on that time, it seems to me that I was not unhappy. Anxious, tired, unsure, occasionally mortified—but never bored, never unengaged, always the thousand tiny cogs in my mind whirling like Ferris wheels, twinkling like stars. Even when exhausted I felt deeply awake, as though my senses had developed new subtleties of perception. I discovered in myself a new decisiveness—or, more likely, a decisiveness that had always been there but never had occasion to be employed—so that when Roald consulted me about the placement of the lights or the height of the vitrines or the typography of the wall labels, I found answers rising effortlessly to my lips, like bubbles in champagne.

And then there was Chris. I was so busy that there wasn't much time to see him, but once or twice a week he came by the cottage, usually late, and we walked on the beach or else stayed in, drinking wine, talking a little, going to bed. I can't say he had my whole attention—always a part of my mind was busily roaming the galleries, moving things around, worrying about wall text, and how I would ever finish my essay for the brochure. Still, I enjoyed having him in my bed: an older man, a handsome man whose sky-blue eyes blinked and lost focus when he moved on top of me on the lumpy mattress, between the sandy sheets I had no time to launder. After that first night, we slept together only indoors, only in the bed. I found if I kept my eyes wide open I could remember where I was at all times, and with whom. I could keep track of our wholeness. And if the pleasure was not as intense as it had been that first night, when the waves tumbled and the separate limbs and organs of the body floated like flotsam and jetsam through my mind—like something out of a surrealist painting—well, that was all right with me.

By mutual consent we told no one. It seemed simpler. Also, I worried what Bernard would think, and maybe Chris did too. He was, after all, twenty years older than I. Old enough, as the saying goes, to be my father, though happily my actual father was nearly sixty, and far away. Besides, there was pleasure in keeping a secret.

Despite my growing confidence, things could not be said to have gone well. Every installation has its surprises—delays, miscalculations, snags. Museums build time for them into the schedule, but in this case time would have been tight even if everything had gone smoothly. It did not go smoothly. We lost several members of the crew—one got mono, one had a car accident, and a third was offered a job on a fishing boat and couldn't turn down the money—and Roald had to scrape the barrel a little to find bodies to get the work done. The vinyl maker misspelled Celia's name ("Selia"!) and we had to rush order the eight-inch "C." A lot of people who should have didn't get their invitations, and the caterer backed out at the last minute, causing a scramble to find someone who could provide light hors d'oeuvres and pass glasses of prosecco on short notice. And then there was what happened up in the cherry picker, which we used for hanging lights and painting the twenty-foot-high ceilings.

One had to wonder at the number of mishaps. Was it just bad luck? The vinyl maker, the caterer, the invitations: these were all under Agnes's purview. Every glitch reflected badly on the Nauk—that is on me, the curator, and on Bernard. Was it possible Agnes had neglected to send out a hundred invitations—had intentionally, perhaps, provoked the caterer—in order to undermine the institution to which she'd devoted a decade of her life? Why? Just because she didn't like me?

Jake was certain we were being haunted. "It's Maria Hallett," he opined in a loud stage whisper to anyone who would listen.

To which Sloan replied, "That poor ghost's never done us any harm in all these years, why would she start now?"

I didn't hear Jake's answer to this question, but I did catch him looking at me from time to time with a thoughtful expression, as though weighing the effect I might have on an old restless ghost.

Or, possibly, a new ghost. Because when I thought about invisible hands working to obstruct me, it wasn't Maria Hallett's name in my mind but Alena's—her cold fingers licking against my spine, the clammy breeze of her ghostly breath against my cheek. Her inaudible footsteps hounding me from room to room, so that even when I was alone, I felt watched, judged, found wanting.

20.

As the opening drew nearer, nobody slept much. All through the bright blue days—already, in late August, noticeably shortening—a stream of cars and pickups, vans and bicycles, jounced through the yawning gates and rattled up the lane, serenaded by deafening choruses of cicadas, invisible in the low scrub. Day and night, men (and a few women) in paint-stained jeans and work boots buzzed from room to room with Makita drills and measuring tapes, leaving their empty coffee cups on ledges and benches the way the cicadas left their empty shells in sandy clearings. In town and on the beaches, the summer crowds swelled as Labor Day approached, and the weather remained perfect from morning to morning, even as the days themselves lost meaning—impossible to tell a Sunday from a Thursday in the syrupy current of August—so that time became an endlessly unfurling and silken bolt of blue.

Switch on the television, however, and the view was different: somber faces with teeth like blocks of snow jabbered, and chalky shapes swirled on green weather maps, while leaning palm trees undulated their fronds like hula dancers. A hurricane, gathering strength off Cuba, was predicted to make its way up the Eastern Seaboard: Florida, the

Carolinas, the Jersey Shore. Possibly Cape Cod. Of course, this early no one could say for sure. But Roald told me that the line at Mid-Cape Hardware, where he'd stopped for narrow-gauge wire and extra paint, was nearly as long as the one at Janie's Famous Cones just down the block, tourists and residents alike buying up batteries and flashlights, masking tape and Band-Aids and bottled water. We stood in the museum lobby with its view of the bay, resplendent as an Aivazovsky, the blue waves sailing in equable as sheep, the ghost of a quarter moon dozing in the flawless sky.

"What do you think?" I asked. "Will we get hit?"

"I've lived here too long to speculate about the weather," Roald said. *He-ah, whe-tha.* Two months in, I was less aware of the local accent, but every now and then its peculiar music pierced me, and I felt my own alienness like a loose bit of metal rattling in a fan.

I followed Roald into the second gallery where a row of blank black plinths waited like tilled fields. "What if we lose power?" I asked.

He flipped through some papers laid out on a folding table covered with packing blankets and open crates. "There's the generator."

"What about all the glass? Should we be boarding it up?"

He put the papers down. "Look," he said. "The weather industry is paid to be alarmist. We almost never get a big storm up here this time of year. November, December, sure. But I can almost guarantee this isn't going to be problem. We've got plenty of other things to worry about, if you feel like worrying."

"All right," I said. But again and again I caught myself checking the sea, trying to tell if the waves were higher, turning on the radio to hear the latest forecast, stepping outside to feel the wind. Standing still and listening, as though I might hear a whine in the air, or a faint rumble, signaling that something was coming. I listened for a sound like the tornado siren that would send us scurrying to the cellar several times a summer back in LaFreniere. Was that what you did during a hurricane too?

But there was nothing. The clear, bright weather held all week like a soap bubble, perfect and shimmering, while summer crowds fled seaside resorts from Miami Beach to Cape May. The days passed in irregular bursts, the hands of the clock spinning hours away so that it might be any time at all when you looked up. Nights I was too jangled to sleep. I lay in the lumpy bed, very still, breathing quietly, as though sleep would reward me for good behavior. Sometimes Chris's straight-limbed body dozed beside me—he never stayed the night—but mostly I was alone. When all this was over, I thought—when the show was open—I'd look for a place to live that was really mine. Maybe I could find a little house with an actual view of the bay rather than this absurdity: a cottage a stone's throw from the beach where you couldn't even hear the surf!

One night, still sleepless at two a.m., I left the house and walked up the path to the top of the dune. The sea was black with bits of froth glowing white, the lace of foam visible across the dark sand when the waves broke. The sky was awash with stars, the Big Dipper lowering toward the bay. I scrambled down the steep sandy stairs to the beach, the chill that rose from the slow waves washing over me. On nights like this, Maria Hallett must have watched, as I was watching now. The same fine dry sand would have spilled into her shoes, the same cold stars glittered overhead, the same roaring in her ears as she looked out over the restless water. A young woman, like me, who had taken a leap in the dark, steering her life abruptly off the prepared track. Here she had stood, waiting for her lover as the storm that would grind his drowned body into the seabed gathered strength beyond the horizon. On a night like this, Alena had dived, naked, under a wave and stroked out into the darkness, never to come back. Never mind how strong a swimmer she was.

Maria Hallett had come so close to redemption only to see her hopes dashed to pieces, quite literally, before her eyes. If she haunted this shore—or if Alena did—who could blame them? If they chose to call up a storm on the day of my opening, who could stop them? Not I. Not any human hand.

Looking out, I thought the swells seemed larger. The wind on my face blew chilly and damp, and the sand blew, stinging and gritty, against my calves. I walked up the beach, wary of shells, my ears full of the roar of the waves. Back toward the dunes, a light bobbed faintly. It was a small, clear light, like that I imagined a whale-oil lantern might cast. I kept walking. If it was a ghost, it would melt away as I got closer. Either that or I would meet it face-to-face.

The yellow light grew brighter as I approached, and I could make out a standing figure, busy with something there in the dark. I stopped, my heart leaping, but it wasn't a ghost. It was the painter, Old Ben, with his easel set up, working by the light of an old camping lantern.

"Hello," I called. I didn't want to startle him.

He looked up, saw me, then waved me away with an impatient motion and went back to work.

I came up to where he stood. He ignored me, painting steadily, his eyes moving between the black sea and his blackening canvas, his face taut as a bowstring. "Ben," I said, "what are you doing?"

"Painting."

I squinted at the canvas: dark mounds that might have been waves, a darker swath that might have been the sky. A gray boat was tipped up on the edge of a swell, and in the middle foreground a silver streak with a feathery tail arced toward a pale figure whose face was hidden by a wing of hair. I looked steadily, my eyes adjusting to the dark, and the more I looked, the better I liked it. It was a good painting—a surprisingly good painting. I admired it, as I had admired his war painting with its obsessive, delicate strokes, its eccentric composition and haunting atmosphere. Though who knew how this canvas would look in daytime under bright, steady light? Or maybe the painting wasn't meant for day but, like the horses and bison painted on cave walls in France, made to be seen only in the flickering half-light of ritual and dream.

I pointed to the silvery streak. "What's that?"

"Arrow."

"Arrow?" I wasn't sure I'd heard correctly, but it did look like an arrow, now that he had said it. I could see a sharp point, tiny feathers, the suggestion of motion.

"Shh!" His brush dug into the dark blob on his palette and he looked down the beach in both directions. "She wouldn't like me talking."

"Who wouldn't?"

He went back to work.

"What's that on the head?" I squinted at what might have been a bun of hair, except that the figure's hair was clearly blowing across the face.

"Nothing," he said. "I don't know." The tip of his brush found the shape, caressed it once, twice, three times with swirling strokes of crimson.

"I just paint out of my imagination," he said.

The next morning I slept late for the first time since coming to Nauquasset. When I opened my eyes to what I took to be the gray of dawn, I was startled to see the hands of the clock out of place, both of them angled in the general direction of the nine. Stumbling out of bed, I pulled back the damp curtains. Rain spattered the window and fell in heavy, hissing sheets over the grass and the bayberry and the arrowroot shrubs, dusty no more. The windows rattled in their swollen frames, and the sky over the sopping gray-green dunes was the color of stone. As I stood, marveling at the way the world had changed its palette overnight, a new sound swelled over the spitting rain. Or rather, not a new sound, but one I had never heard from this room before: the swelling roar and seething crash of the surf. The storm had hit, and at last the ocean had become audible from my bedroom. It was ominous and threatening, and I wished I could not hear it.

Half an hour later I struggled up the path to the Nauk, which lay low and silent under the assault of the squall. I leaned into the wind, my hair blowing, my wayward umbrella tugging hard against my grip, wanting to be let go, and then suddenly inverting itself, metal struts on the outside like an arthropod. I was soaked by the time I reached the entryway bower and saw that one of the trellises had been ripped away, and the battered roses were pink smudges scattered across the muddy grass. And all the time the ocean boomed and thundered, the surf hissing like a dragon, streaming in frothing runnels down the water-darkened breast of the sand.

Inside, as usual, the air was cool and dry. Not for the first time I thought what a folly it was—an art museum on a cliff overlooking the sea! What the cost in electricity must be to dry the air I hated to think, not to mention the insurance. I paused in the lobby, dripping onto the tile floor. On the other side of the wall of glass, the flattened dune grass, the sky, and the furious bay were nearly blotted out by the rain.

Noise on a human scale—a cheerful clattering and banging—came from the galleries. I threaded my way among folding tables and half-erected vitrines, skirting a paint-spattered tarp, stepping over a thick orange extension cord. Roald was up on the cherry picker, fifteen feet in the air, measuring something and talking into his phone. "Sixteen and three-eighths," he said. Behind him, also in the bucket, a young man more or less my age, with bright tattoos and thin blond hair pulled back in a ponytail, held a drill up to the ceiling and bored a hole.

Roald put a hand over the mouthpiece. "Not like that," he said. "Tim, stop a second." Then he was back to the phone. "I don't think it'll be a problem." *Prwah-blum.* "Nah, nothing to worry about." He snapped the phone shut as the kid beside him—Tim—moved over a few inches and raised the drill again. "Did you hear me?" Roald said. "I asked you to stop. Okay?"

"Hello!" I called up. "How are things going?"

"Great!" Roald said. It was what he always said, whether the crew was ahead of schedule or the wrong kind of lumber had been delivered or a crate was dropped instead of being set down gently as a feather on the gallery floor. "Lovely weather we're having!" he called. *Weh-thah.*

"Is the ark ready?" I asked. "Are the animals lined up?"

"Nah," he said. "It's not so bad as that."

The kid beside him started drilling again, making a frantic whining that rose above the banging of hammers and the clattering of the rain.

"Hey," Roald said sharply, "cut it out. We're just going to have to do it over." *O-vah.*

"It'll be fine," the boy said sullenly.

"I said stop." Roald touched the arm with the drill.

"I know what I'm doing!" The rebellious fierceness in the kid's voice surprised me—I'd never heard anyone on the crew talk back to Roald. He jerked away from the older man's hand and held up the drill. Gritty plaster dust snowed down over their heads, settling in the bucket and drifting to the gallery floor. I brushed some from my hair and stepped back, peering up, trying to see.

Again Roald reached for the kid's arm and said something I couldn't hear, and then the shriek of the drill was replaced by the boy's furious cry. "Why should I listen to you!" He waved the drill wildly in the air. "A crazy, pervy old man who cut off his own finger!"

A silence, except for the drumming of the rain. And then Roald said, "Give me the drill, Tim."

All work in the room had stopped. The four or five other members of the crew looked up, some of them shading their eyes to see better. A man I recognized—older, heavyset, with a heavy black beard going gray—stepped forward. "What's going on up there?" he called.

"I heard you did it to impress her!" the boy cried. "That's disgusting. And I guess it didn't do you any good!" He switched the drill back on, and Roald tried to grab it. They struggled. Then someone called out, and something tumbled down, thudding dully on the hard floor.

"Christ!" someone yelled, and the man with the beard shouted, "Call an ambulance!" The room whirled into motion. Only Roald's body lay like one of the figures in Morgan McManus's installation at the base of the cherry picker—face down, one leg splayed out at a terrible angle—while up by the ceiling Tim crouched in the cupped palm of the lift.

"Oh my God," he said. "Is he all right?"

Nobody answered him.

21.

Midafternoon. Roald had been taken by ambulance to Cape Cod Hospital in Hyannis. Installation had been halted and Bernard was in his office with the door shut. My own office door was open as I pretended to work, waiting for word about Roald and praying Celia didn't show up. The rain rattled and pounded against my window, and the huge breakers sailed in—black mountains of water caped with foam the way real mountains are caped with snow. Out at the edges of my vision I seemed to see, again and again, the shadow of a body falling through space, and my own body would brace, waiting for the thud. I covered my face with my hands, and when I removed them, there was Agnes, standing still as a statue in her low-necked, long-sleeved, bat-black dress and her pointy black lace-up shoes, witch's shoes, the streaks in her dark hair looking more crimson than maroon in the odd afternoon stormlight.

"I came to see if you were all right," she said. "I heard you were there when it happened. When Roald fell."

"I'm fine." I stood up as she moved closer, black and relentless as the waves out the window. "Have you heard anything?"

"Heard?"

"How he is." Whether he was going to die, I meant. But I couldn't say it.

"It must have been awful to see him fall," Agnes said.

"Yes. Awful."

"I once saw someone plunge from a hotel window. Eight floors up. She died instantly. Well, probably not instantly. I always imagine time bends at the end. Stretches. Like when a glass slides from your hand and you watch it drop, and it feels like it's happening in slow motion. The shattering. I think the last moments before you die must be like that, don't you?"

We looked at each other, both of us waiting to see if I would ask again about Roald, whose body had seemed to fall not in slow motion but so fast I could hardly see it, and silently. But I didn't ask. Agnes moved around the desk and went to the window, where pea-sized raindrops immolated themselves and slid down the thick glass in rivulets. "Look at the bay," she said. "This office has the best view of any room in the Nauk. Alena insisted on it. See where the dunes dip? It looks as though the waves will crash right through the gap when they're high like this. Alena loved storms."

"You must miss her enormously," I said. "I know you were close." I couldn't see her face, but the hem of her long black skirt swayed slightly, as though a breath of the gale had found its way into the room.

"Yes," she said. "I miss her."

"It must be hard. Having to look every day at the bay where she . . . swam."

Now, slowly, she turned toward me, tilting her head like a crow considering a shiny object or a bit of trash. "Where she died, you mean."

"Yes," I said. "Where she died."

"Alena wasn't afraid of dying. Just of dying tritely. 'Everyone dies, Aggie,' she used to say. 'You only get one shot at it. I don't intend to waste mine!' She had no patience with people who were afraid of risk. She drove fast with the top down, the wind in her hair."

I blinked, trying to keep up. "You mean," I said, "that she courted danger?"

Her face glowed palely. "No. It wasn't danger she courted. It was beauty. To live life as one continuous beautiful gesture, like a wave breaking!"

I knew my horror must be seeping from every pore. "You're saying she equated beauty with death," I said. Again I saw Roald's body falling through the gallery. Was that Alena's idea of beauty? Would it have lit the fuse of delight in her to see it?

"Not death. Risk. Dancing at the edge of the cliff in a storm."

"I think of beauty quite differently," I said.

"Alena's vision was always ahead of its time."

Out the window, the racing waves towered higher, hurling themselves onto the martyred shore. It was easy to imagine a wall of water rushing up through the soaked dunes, breaking over the roof. Washing the Nauk into the sea. Alena would be sorry, if that happened, that she had missed it.

But the Nauk did not wash away into the sea, not then, and Roald did not die. His death still waited for him, either more or less beautiful than being semi-accidentally shoved out of a mechanical lift during a gallery installation; there was no way of knowing. He had broken his left femur, three ribs, and his tailbone, that was all. Though surely it was enough. I found this out a few hours later when Chris Passoa came up to the offices. I heard his voice saying something to Sloan, and the next thing I knew I was standing in the doorway looking at him in his long black impervious policeman's raincoat that dripped copiously onto the rug as he unbuttoned it. "Hello," he said, in what might have been a perfectly neutral voice, but which seemed to me to contain the charged totality of what lay between us. Suddenly Bernard was standing in his office doorway too.

"Roald," I began.

"Roald is going to be all right," Chris said. "I went to see him at the hospital."

Thank God.

"What about Tim?" Bernard said.

Chris inclined his head toward Bernard's office. Bernard turned around, and Chris followed, and I hurried in after them before the door shut.

Chris took off his raincoat and draped it over a chair. He sat down, and Bernard and I sat down too. "We sent Tim home," Chris said. "Everyone seems willing to agree it was an accident."

Relief made Bernard spray his irritation around the room. "God knows how we're going to get everything done before the opening without Roald! Assuming there is an opening. If the storm keeps up like this, maybe there won't be."

"Does that happen?" I asked.

"I've never heard of it," Chris said cheerily when Bernard failed to answer. "Probably there's some ritual sacrifice involved."

"Alena would have taken care of that," Bernard said. "That was her kind of thing." It was strange to hear him say her name. He almost never spoke of her.

Chris raised his eyebrows, nearly transparent lines on the ridge of his forehead, velvet to the touch. I thought he might turn and look at me, but he didn't. "I remember those things she used to do on the beach," he said. "That first summer she came to visit. Dancing around the fire. Burning stuff. Wearing feathers. Do you remember that, Bernard?"

"I remember," Bernard said.

"I wouldn't waste time worrying about the storm," Chris said, as a gust hurled the rain against the window like fistfuls of pebbles, and the dark sky darkened another shade. "It'll blow itself out by tomorrow night. Wednesday at the latest. A good storm always stirs things up. This one's already washed up some interesting junk."

"Like what?" I asked.

"A boot." Chris looked brightly around the room. The wind whined higher, and a wretched seagull, careening through the feverish air, sent its lament spiraling down through the cascade.

"That's not unusual," Bernard said.

"Ah, but this is not your standard Carhartt. Some kind of shiny plastic. And inside, a surprise." He looked at Bernard, casually but with a lurking sharpness. "The remnants of a sock. Could be a stocking. And inside that, bones. Tibia and fibula." He reached down that broad, warm hand and touched his own lower leg.

Alena, I thought. I looked at the men to see if they were thinking it too. The circles under Bernard's eyes were darker than ever, as blue-black as newly poured asphalt. Chris's face remained bright and blank, a mask rather than a face. It was the first time I'd seen him when he was working, and it gave his body an alert tension, like a sheepdog sniffing the air. "The first thing," he said, "is to figure out who's gone missing over the last, I don't know, year. Two, three years, maybe." He paused, as though waiting for Bernard to say something, but Bernard remained silent. "Fishermen washed overboard," Chris went on. "Pleasure boat excursioners. Locals, tourists." Another pause. "The body would have had to be in the water a while. Hard to say how long. Or how far they might have traveled. The bones."

Finally Bernard spoke. "It couldn't be Alena," he said. "I mean, after all, if she was swimming, she wouldn't have been wearing boots." He stopped. The wind moaned and sighed.

"Unlikely to be a swimmer," Chris allowed.

But nobody knew for sure Alena had been swimming.

We listened to the wind, which seemed determined to tear the grass and trees and buildings out of the sand, and then Bernard asked absently, "Where was it found? The boot."

"Willet's Landing." Chris checked the sky. "Might be letting up a little. Think I'll make a dash for it." He picked up his raincoat. "Let's hope this is the end of your troubles," he said to Bernard. Then he turned to me. "I'm looking forward to the show. I hope it will engage my visual sense in a powerful way and provoke me to feel something."

"Thank you," I said.

"Have a minute to walk me out?"

I followed him down the stairs into the lobby. His body in its policeman's raincoat was confident, confidential. I wanted to touch him, but I wasn't sure it was allowed. There was a new hard energy around Chris, a bright shield that drew me toward him and at the same time kept me back, like a humming science fiction force field. He was newly compelling, and yet I didn't like the way he had spoken to Bernard. Did he think the boot might be Alena's, or not? We reached the empty lobby. The rain rattled against the glass and the vexed wind whined hungrily. The weather didn't look like it was letting up to me. Chris stopped. "I heard you were there when it happened," he said.

"Yes. I was right below the lift. I saw him fall."

He stepped closer, but not close. His boots were loud on the terracotta floor. "Are you all right? Because Roald's going to be fine, you know." I could feel the heat of him through his invisible force field, but he was behaving like someone professionally concerned for my welfare. Someone older and scrupulous. Which, of course, he was.

"Yes," I said. "I know."

"It was an accident. Just one of those things."

I wanted to tell him that I knew about accidents; I had grown up on a farm. Men being run over by tractors, men drowning trying to rescue cattle from floods. Instead, I leaned toward him as though inclined by the wind. "Before it happened," I said, "Tim said something to Roald. He said Roald had cut off his finger—his own finger—to impress a woman. I'd seen that he was missing one. Do you know anything about that?"

"Just the rumor. The one everyone knows."

"I don't. Tell me." I could see he didn't want to. "Please," I said. I plunged my hand through the force field and touched his arm.

Chris looked away from me out the windows. Perhaps he preferred the sight of the storm to the avidity I couldn't hide on my face. Yet he didn't pull away. "Roald was supposed to have been in love with Alena," he said. "She flirted with him, but she was never really going to be interested in someone like him. That was obvious. So, apparently—this is what people say—he got it into his head that doing something like that, cutting off his own finger, would mean something to her. Prove something. God knows what." He turned back from the window and looked at me, and he laid his own calloused hand over mine on his black-clad arm. Between our bodies, a radiant slice of air shivered. "Of course it's crazy, the whole story," he said, leaning closer. "I'm sure it happened in a moment of carelessness when he was working." Then he kissed me, a slow, hard kiss, right there in the gray light of the empty lobby. It was different from our other kisses. I could feel him on the other side of it in a new way, as though before it had been only his lips I was kissing.

I wanted to press myself against him, to unbutton his raincoat and slip inside it with him, but I didn't dare. Anyone could have come by and seen us. Bernard or Agnes. Anybody.

And so we lurched on toward the opening.

As Chris had predicted, the storm soon blew itself out. The weather cooled and the leaves on the rosebushes, from which every flower had been wrenched, turned frail, the browning flesh of the leaves shredding around the tenacious veins, the spotted rose hips showing autumnal colors. The bay was a crazy quilt of blues and greens and grays, alive with ripples and furrows. Inside the Nauk the show unfurled like a flower, the galleries in constant flux, the floors gritty with plaster dust and sawdust. The crew redoubled its efforts, and a collection was taken up for Roald, who had been released from the hospital and lay in bed at home, attended in shifts by his sister, who worked nights at the doughnut shop, and his teenaged niece. I supposed Bernard must have sent a big check too, but I didn't ask. Bernard had withdrawn, armadillo-like, inside the shell of himself, and although he always spoke to me pleasantly, politeness had taken the place of the warm, intuitive bond I had felt in Venice when thoughts and ideas seemed to wash between us as though we were two bathers immersed in the heat of the same mineral spring.

We did what we could to keep Celia happy and out of the crew's hair, but most of what needed to be done was to settle what should go where, which necessarily involved her, and which proved more contentious than I was prepared for. I felt the rooms should reflect the chronology of the work, so the viewer could see the way her vision unfolded, follow the thread of a kind of story. To Celia, however, that approach seemed pedantic. "Who cares when or what or how I made what!" she said. "What matters is the way they exist in the present moment." She wanted to group the pieces according to what she called *season*—spring, summer, and so on—though how she decided which pieces went with which season I could never figure out. It was intuitive, and therefore not susceptible to discussion.

Some artists have a powerful instinct for displaying their work to its best advantage, but Celia was not among them. Unable to distinguish her best work from the mediocre, she couldn't edit, wanting to crowd too many pieces together until they could barely breathe. I resisted as tactfully as I could.

Collaborating with the artist on the installation of her art was one of the parts of the job I had most looked forward to: the framing of a shared vision; the careful arrangement of a thousand details small and large like twigs and sticks and logs laid to make a bonfire; and then, on the night of the opening, the pleasure of holding two tandem sparks to the kindling and watching it blaze. But I had chosen Celia, and if I had chosen badly, well, I had no one to blame but myself.

A part of me was saddened by her transformation from an artist who claimed to have no interest in a career to someone determined to control every angle. But if she stridently and obstinately insisted on time-consuming, trivial, last-minute changes—well, wasn't this show the distillation of all the passion, the lonely days, the breakthroughs, the failures, the seared skin and sleepless nights and refusals and renunciations of her entire life? Who could blame her for her suspicious vigilance, her reluctance to cede control for an instant? Or even for her relentless testing of all of us—of me and Bernard and the crew—to discover whether we might, at some crucial moment, stand between her and the consummation of her vision?

Not I.

Bernard took her to lunch, to dinner, drove her out to Provincetown to see some galleries. I met with her in my office to talk about wall labels, installation photography, invitation lists. But of course we spent most of our time in the galleries, where she demanded the plinths be made an inch and a half higher and complained that the non-reflective plexi used for the vitrines was too reflective. She grumbled about the lack of advertising, demanded to see the list of the press we'd contacted, wondered why *Artforum* wasn't doing a feature. She was terrified that the show would come and go, as all her others had, and nothing would be changed. Well, of course she was.

I remember the opening as a whirl of tanned cleavage, hair every shade of artificial, complicated dresses in a hundred shades of black. Every now and then a familiar face floated into view—Barbara's, Willa Somerset's, one or two members of the crew. I had braced myself to see McManus, but he didn't show up. I supposed he was too angry; after all, in his mind this should have been his show. Bernard, wearing a tuxedo and looking very handsome in a slightly vampiric way, made a speech that seemed well received, though I was too nervous to take in anything he said, just as the names of the people he introduced me to over the course of the evening skipped off the surface of my brain like arrows off a castle wall. Celia, sea-queenly in shimmering green silk with many pleats, drifted from group to group, nodding and smiling, inclining her head to exchange a remark or throwing it back in mirth. She never looked my way, except for once, when I was standing by myself in a corner and she, also alone, came sailing like a great shining dragonfly through the arched doorway from the colonnade. For a moment I forgot all my frustration and all my regret, and I could only think how magnificent she was! Between us in the room, Celia's vivid and startling sculptures gleamed on their plinths, displaying their peculiar beauty to hundreds of pairs of eyes. She didn't notice me at first, but then—feeling my eyes on her, perhaps—she looked up. Just for a moment the diamond stare softened, and she ducked her head in a quick nod of recognition. And then someone came up to speak to her, and she turned away. It was Chris, taking Celia's adroit ceramicist's hand in his policeman's paw. It was the first time I'd seen him since we'd kissed in the lobby three days before. They exchanged a few words, then he noticed me, excused himself, and made his way to my corner. "Congratulations," he said.

"Thank you," I said. "What do you think of the show?"

"It looks like someone went down to the beach and picked up a bunch of shells," he said, smiling.

"There's a little more to it than that," I said.

He seemed to be standing very close to me, but he wasn't really. It was as though he extended beyond his body, the way you can feel the chill and damp of the ocean as you approach it over the warm sand. I put my hand lightly on his arm and guided him to the nearest vitrine, in which a pair of mussel-shell sculptures glistened, purplish black threaded with silver. One was open wide like a mouth, the other shut tight. *Arguing*, it was called. "You don't really think they just look like a couple of shells, do you?"

He stared down through the plexi. "Maybe not. They don't look cold, somehow. They look briny, but kind of . . . I don't know." He laughed and looked at me instead. "Not *human*, exactly."

"You're taught to see in a particular way, right? As a policeman. To—what—look for clues? Be open to possibilities? To turn things over in your mind, waiting for patterns to emerge."

"The life of a small-town policeman is hardly Sherlock Holmes," he said. But I could see he didn't really mean it.

"Try looking at the work like that."

He turned his gaze obediently down.

"Now tell me what you see."

"Curves."

"Good. That's a start."

He looked up. "Are the mussels meant to be women, then?"

"Try not to be so literal. Don't stop looking. You're just warming up."

"Actually," he said, "as much as I'm enjoying the art lesson, I'm looking for Bernard. Have you seen him?"

"Oh." I let go of his arm. "What for?"

"You mind if I check upstairs?"

"Is it about Roald and Tim?"

"No. Nothing like that."

I trailed half a step behind him through the humming galleries and across the crowded lobby and up the stairs. In the outer office, Sloan and Jake and a couple of other young people lounged on the sofa passing a bottle. They startled when they saw us—probably some of the kids were under twenty-one—but Chris just raised his hand peaceably. "Seen Bernard?" he asked.

No one had.

He knocked on Bernard's office door, waited, tried the knob. The door swung open onto shadows: the hulking shape of the desk, the spidery chairs, the black bottomless pool of oval rug in the middle. "Bernard?" Chris called, as though he might be hiding somewhere in there in the dark. But the only answer was the sea, gathering and breaking, gathering and breaking down on the shore. "Do you think he might have gone down to the beach?"

"I don't know. Why would he do that?"

"Breath of fresh air?"

First, though, we checked the other offices—mine, Agnes's—and the conference room, and the bathroom, even the storage closet, as the young faces on the sofa watched, only slightly curious, waiting for us to go.

Outside, the night was chilly. A few people stood around in clumps near the bare trellised rosebushes, slapping mosquitoes and smoking cigarettes. Crickets chanted frantically in the bushes, broadcasting the end of time, and the wind shivered the long blades of the dune grass, which tossed and settled like hair. Surely Bernard was here, I thought, relieved—doing his job, just out in the open air. But as we moved from group to group, my relief curdled, and I felt queasy, as though I were in a small boat among heaving seas.

We went through the sighing grass to the steps leading to the beach. Chris headed down the steep staircase in his polished shoes. Wiggling out of my sandals, I followed him.

The steps were cold, splintery, slippery with sifted sand. At the bottom, a small crowd stood in their dress clothes on the beach, cheering on a couple of pale figures splashing and whooping ten yards out in the water. The moon blazed a silver path across the humped backs of the waves. The stars glittered like mica. Every wave that neared the shore glittered too, with bioluminescence—tiny sea creatures, moon jellies most likely—carrying their own light wherever they went like tiny prophets. The smell of dried seaweed hung in the air, mixed with bonfire smoke. Chris approached one person after another, but no one had seen Bernard.

I rubbed my goosefleshed arms, following Chris's gaze as he stared out toward the horizon. "What are you looking for?" The splashing bathers had come in, dried off, were made much of by their friends, and I couldn't see anything out there, just the cold moonlight glittering on the cold waves.

"Bernard likes to sail at night."

"He doesn't sail anymore," I said. "He sold his boats." But I looked as hard as I could into the dark, searching for a gliding shadow, a glint of white hull on the water. "Anyway, wouldn't he have lights?"

"With the moon like this you can see okay."

"What about other people seeing you?" I pictured collisions, hulls split in two. Though who else would be out there, lightless themselves, to run into him?

He sighed, kicked the sand, turned to me. "There's nowhere else? Back offices or storage places or, I don't know, a secret passageway?"

And then I remembered Alena's rooms. "I'm sure he wouldn't be there," I said aloud.

"Wouldn't be where?"

22.

We climbed up from the beach and plunged back into the blazing galleries. The blaring chatter ricocheted off the white walls faster than ever, and no one seemed to be looking at the art, which posed patiently in its vitrines like statues in Midas's garden. We threaded our way among the shifting groups, the eccentrically cut dresses and colorful cummerbunds and glittering handbags and women's eyes painted to look like peacock feathers. No Bernard. As we approached the end of the colonnade, I began to worry, realizing that the door would certainly be locked; I didn't have a key, we would have to find Agnes and ask her for it. But the handle gave at once under my hand. A black gap yawned in the white surface of the wall, and we slid through, pulling the door shut behind us.

It was pitch-black in the hallway. The cascading lights were off. Pipes clanked in the walls, and my heart clapped like a muted bell in my chest as Chris switched on a flashlight, swinging the beam around to take the measure of the space. Aiming the light downward, he picked out the perforated metal wedges of the spiral staircase steps. "This way?"

There wasn't any other way to go.

Down and around he clattered, disappearing into the dark until I could see only the top of his head, the pale fuzz that I tried to keep in view as I picked my way down as fast as I dared, clutching the railing, the smell of damp earth filling my nostrils. I could hear Agnes's voice as though her words still echoed in the stairwell: *Careful. You don't want to fall.*

Below me, the footsteps stopped. There was no sound, only the yellow glow of the flashlight beam. Then Chris's voice rang out cheerily: "Hey—this is better than the stuff upstairs. You should charge people money and let them come down here!"

Another voice floated up toward me. "I thought you were a man of simple tastes," it said. It was Bernard's voice, though stretched and made echoey by the shape of the stairwell, giving it a ghostly sound.

"No. Just modest means."

"You could always start taking bribes."

"How much are you offering?"

"Me? Why—did I do something?"

I hurried down the remaining stairs and stepped into the long, low room with its carpets and carvings and fringed silk scarves, its heavy textured wallpaper and haunting smell of jasmine. "I don't know," Chris said lightly. "Did you?"

Bernard lay stretched out on one of the velvet sofas with a cigarette between his lips, the smoke catching the light from a single lamp burning on a polished side table. I had never seen him smoke before. In his tuxedo, with his full lips and his dark eyes and the elegant sweep of his wrist as he dangled the cigarette over the edge of the sofa, he looked like a movie star from the thirties, the kind who was most handsome when dissipated. One ankle was crossed over the other, and his shined and tasseled loafers winked in the light, the crimson tip of his cigarette reflected in the patent leather. A fluted glass sweated on an inlaid table within arm's reach. Seeing me, he struggled to sit up, then changed his mind and fell back again into the cushions. "*Cara!* I apologize. I'm not discharging my duties very well."

"We've been looking everywhere for you," I said. "What are you doing down here?"

"Drinking and smoking. As you see."

Chris fiddled with a cloisonné box. "That's what they're doing upstairs too."

"But without the same concentration," Bernard said.

Chris opened the lid, raised his pale eyebrows, and shut it again. I leaned against the wall, running my fingers over the seaweedlike ridges in the wallpaper. It was clear enough to me why Bernard was here: it was the closest he could get to being with Alena. I thought how they must have snuck down to this room together during the openings of the past, tossing back a quick drink before reemerging, fortified by intimacy and gin. How they must have laughed together, compared notes, shared triumph or exasperation—maybe shared a cigarette too, or a joint. I could see them passing it back and forth, her violent lipstick making its way, via that burning conduit, to his mouth.

Bernard exhaled streams of smoke through his nostrils. "You want some bourbon?" he asked Chris.

"Actually, I'm working." There was a pause, and something seemed to shift, the way the ocean floor shifts underwater after a storm. Then Chris said, "I wanted to let you know. The boot we found matches a description of one that belonged to Alena."

I want to say a silence descended over the room—that was what it felt like—but really the world clanged and clamored on as noisily as ever. The ocean crashed; the crickets trilled; the sounds of the party drifted toward us as though from another country. Still, there was that sensation: as though the volume on a film had been suddenly turned down.

"Who told you that?" Bernard's voice was like a shiny glaze on fired clay.

"She had distinctive things, didn't she? This boot, it's pink plastic. Translucent. Studded with stars. Some designer, apparently, I forget the name. Plastic holds up pretty well in seawater, as we know from those sad pictures of sea turtles crippled by six-pack rings."

Bernard stubbed his cigarette out in a green glass ashtray the size of a dinner plate. "I'm not sure what you're telling me." He directed his words at the primrose-yellow ceiling. "We agreed a few days ago, a swimmer wouldn't be wearing a boot."

"Well, maybe she wasn't swimming," Chris said.

"What would she have been doing, then?"

"I thought you might be able to tell me."

Bernard swung his legs around and sat up. He stared at Chris, his eyes pale and cold. "How would I know? I was in Venice." He pulled a cigarette case out of his pocket. It was gold, sleek, engraved with his initials: B.O.A. I realized I had no idea what the O stood for—what his middle name might be. I didn't know Bernard, not really. Not at all. Waiting for him to answer, I started running through possibilities in my mind: Oscar, Oliver, Owen, Oswald. The long blunt-tipped fingers dipped back into the tuxedo pocket and emerged with a lighter, also gold. He spun the wheel, producing a gold-colored flame. Even the cigarettes themselves, longer and slimmer than the Marlboros my father smoked, were goldish in hue—the color of sunflowers in autumn. Bernard lit one and let the case clatter onto the table. He drew a long pull of smoke into his lungs and it drifted out through his flared nostrils, diffusing the harsh, haunting smell of burning tobacco into the jasmine air.

Orlando, Omar, Otis.

"I just thought," Chris said, "you might have some idea. Who she gave things to. Or whose boat, say, she might have gone out on. I know she didn't have one of her own."

"If she'd disappeared from someone's boat, wouldn't they have reported it?" Bernard said.

"Or maybe she took a boat out by herself."

"Then where is it now?"

Otto? Obadiah? Or maybe it was a family name—Oakes or Ogilvy, Osmond or Olson—in which case I'd never guess it, not in a million years.

Chris leaned forward and picked up Bernard's cigarette case. "I don't know," he said. "Maybe it sank. I don't know anything, really, except that things were different than we thought before. Maybe Alena swam out alone and got caught in a current, and maybe she didn't. I came to ask if you could help me. I know it's difficult."

"I'd like to help," Bernard said. "I wish I could."

"Why don't you tell me about Venice," Chris said. "Let's start with that."

Bernard's cigarette had burned down and his glass was empty. His fingers toyed with the edge of his pocket in a way that made him look old, like an old man worrying his bathrobe. I didn't like it, seeing him like that. I crossed the thick Sarouk carpet and sat on the sofa next to him, and I took his hand. It was cold, as though he had been out gloveless in the snow. I thought of my grandparents' stories about carrying hot stones or baked potatoes in their pockets during the bitter Wisconsin winters. Bernard could have used some of those.

"We were supposed to meet at a party," he said at last. "A grand reception. But she never came." His voice sounded different now that I was sitting so close. Less hollow. It sounded flatter and scratchier, like an old record, like he had something unclearable caught in his throat.

"And?"

"And, nothing. I thought she must have missed her connection. Or that the flight had been delayed. When I got back to the hotel, I asked at the desk, and they said she hadn't checked in, so I figured it was that, a problem with a flight, and I put it out of my mind. And then the next day, I kept thinking she'd show up. Probably I called her cell and got no answer. Obviously. But I wasn't worried. Things come up. Alena was impulsive. The reason we weren't traveling together was that she'd decided to visit some friends in Paris first. She'd switched her flight. I thought she might have decided to stay on longer there and not bothered to tell me. It was the sort of thing she might do."

In my corner of the sofa, I held my breath. I'd thirsted for information about Alena the way a plowed field thirsts for rain, and now the first drops were scattering from the darkened skies.

"Did you call the friends?"

"I didn't have their number."

"Did you call Agnes? Or anyone at the Nauk?"

"No. Not for a few days."

"Why not?"

"Because Alena was in Paris."

Chris shrugged. "You thought she'd changed her plans and stayed in Paris, but you didn't think she might have changed her plans and never gone there at all?"

Bernard hesitated, thinking about that. "No," he said. "In my mind she was in Paris."

"Still, Agnes might have heard from her. They were so close."

"I think Agnes had gone away too," Bernard said. "I think her mother was dying."

Chris nodded. He didn't have a notebook, or if he did, he wasn't using it. I thought he must already know where Agnes had been when Alena disappeared. I remembered now that Agnes had told me she'd gone away when Alena went to Venice, that her mother had been ill. Dying, Bernard said. How terrible for Agnes to lose her mother and Alena at the same time. I found that I felt sorry for her.

"And then?"

"And then nothing. I called her phone a bunch of times. I believe I was annoyed. I thought she was being irresponsible, having fun in Paris, or, I don't know, maybe she had gone on somewhere else. I was angry that she wasn't returning my calls."

"But you did eventually call the Nauk, a few days later. Tell me about that."

"I called Sloan and asked her if anyone had happened to hear from Alena. She said no, but that Agnes had called asking the same thing. Agnes had emailed Alena, texted her, and hadn't heard back."

"Agnes was worried. Were you?"

"No." Bernard's scratchy tone hollowed, harshened. "I've never known anyone who could take care of herself better than Alena!"

"Well," Chris said mildly. "But apparently not so well, after all."

"Look," Bernard said. "After a certain point, I threw my hands up. I could picture her, sitting in Paris or wherever, seeing my name come up on her phone and not answering. Counting up my messages to see how many there were. One thing about Alena, she craved attention. She liked you to think about her before you thought about anyone else. I was getting tired of it."

"Of course," Chris said. "But I still don't really understand. It's hard to imagine she wouldn't have shown up in Venice—the Biennale is *the* art-world event, right?—and you wouldn't have been worried about her, even a little? Even if she could take care of herself. Even if you were annoyed at her. Unless maybe you'd had an argument?"

Bernard didn't answer right away. I waited, perched on the velvet sofa, my fist pulsing like a heart inside his hand. Then he said, "We had disagreed. That's true. About the direction the Nauk should take."

"Disagreed how?"

Yes, I thought, how?

"About what kind of art we should show. Alena was increasingly interested in more extreme art than I was."

I could almost hear Chris Passoa thinking: More extreme than piles of candies having something to do with AIDS?

"What, specifically?"

Bernard's voice was still flat, but an acid derision seemed to leak up around the edges, eating away at his impassivity. "Body art. Performative stuff. She had experimented with that—doing it, I mean—before she was a curator. You were talking about her masquerades the other day. But this was different."

"Performative?"

"Like Marina Abramović. Vito Acconci. Michel Journiac. Have you heard of any of them?"

"No."

Bernard looked at me.

I said, "Michel Journiac is best known for giving out pieces of blood sausage, made from his own blood, during a mock Mass. For Marina Abramović's most famous work, she lay down next to an array of seventy-two objects, including a feather, a gun, a rose, honey, scissors. The audience could use these things to do anything they wanted to her. And they did."

Policeman or not, Chris looked shocked. Which was, of course, the point. "Alena wanted to do things like that at the Nauk?"

"Not exactly like that," Bernard said.

I thought of Morgan McManus, his intricate prostheses and fabricated corpses and recorded screams. But that was more atrocity art than body art—more documentary than performance. It wasn't as though McManus was mutilating himself; the war had done that work for him.

"So you argued about that? And then you went off to Venice, and when she didn't show up, you thought, Just as well. Is that what you're saying?"

Bernard's hand grew heavier in mine as though somebody had turned gravity up. "Look," he said. "I don't understand why you're asking me all this. You don't even know if those are Alena's bones."

"That's true," Chris said. "I don't."

"Like you said, maybe she gave the boots away. Maybe she sold them on the internet!"

Chris ran a hand through the fuzz on his head. "Maybe," he said. But I don't think anybody in the room believed Alena would do that.

Upstairs, the opening was winding down, and down in Alena's room, the interrogation was too. Chris stood up.

"Great show," he said to me. "Great to see the Nauk open again." Halfway to the door he stopped and turned. "We should go fishing sometime, Bernard. You still fish, don't you? Even if you don't sail."

"It's been a while."

"Why did you sell your boats, by the way?"

Bernard sighed. "I was tired of sailing."

"That's what I don't understand. I mean, there was a time, Bernard. I remember a time when sailing was your life."

He left the door open when he went out. I thought I should follow him up the stairs, but I had entered that state beyond exhaustion when the mind empties and shimmers like a soap bubble, floating up seemingly outside one's body. And besides, Bernard kept hold of my hand. "Stay a moment," he said. "I meant to say—congratulations on your show, *cara*. Have I said that yet?"

"Thank you."

"I mean it. It's a beautiful exhibition. Thoughtful and compelling. And you did it so quickly, and with so unconscionably little help."

The soap bubble quivered and thrilled. "Thank you," I said again.

"You should be prepared, though," he went on gently, like a parent explaining to a child why she can't have a kitten. "I doubt it's going to get much attention. Don't let it upset you, it's just the nature of these things."

I looked at him, amazed. "There are three hundred people upstairs!"

"For the party. Free food and drink. And, of course, because they're curious. About you, and me, and about the Nauk." And about Alena, he didn't have to say; she was all around us, her body in the rich and opulent objects, her breath in the very air. "I just don't want you to be disappointed."

I heard him with my ears, but his words didn't touch me. I was too light, too high, drifting in the scented eddies up by the ceiling. "It doesn't matter," I said.

Bernard leaned back into the plush cushions, sighing, pulling me back too; pulling me toward him until my head rested on his shoulder. I shut my eyes, breathing in the smell of his jacket, his fine white shirt, his skin. "I've been— I haven't been . . ." he said. "Since we got back. I brought you here and then— You've deserved a better employer. I'm sorry." His voice clanged hollowly, like the hulk of a rusted ship hitting rock.

"It's fine," I said. "It doesn't matter."

I must have known then, dimly, or suspected; not what he had done exactly, which no one could have guessed, but that he had done something. Like a swimmer caught in a current, I flailed in the tide of my dawning knowledge, unwilling to acknowledge or even consider the implacable, indelible truth.

Upstairs, the party glittered and tintinnabulated on, though its ranks had thinned somewhat. It was undeniable that more sparkling, swaying guests were topping off their glasses than looking at Celia's work. I slid among them, inconspicuous enough in my black dress, and then, finding the heat and noise unbearable, I ducked out the door, thinking I would go home. Outside, Chris had stopped to chat with some people I didn't recognize. I tried to slip by, but he caught up to me as I started down the path. "Hey," he said. "Are you all right?"

"Of course. Why wouldn't I be?"

"Well," he said. "Things have changed."

I didn't answer. He walked with me down the slope in the dark, through the trilling of the crickets and the rocking of the waves. I kept my head down. I found I didn't want to look at him. At last he grasped my arm to stop me, the sudden warmth of his hand making me realize how cold I was: cold and wrung out, my ears ringing with voices and screeching laughter and wheezing evasions and half-truths.

"You're caught up in something," he said. "You stumbled into it. It has nothing to do with you."

I looked up, but instead of Chris's steady noontide face looking down at me, it was Bernard's face I saw—his grizzled head and his gentleness and the darkness in his eyes. I saw him crouching beside me on the floor in the Arsenale in Venice, his questions and the smell of bitter oranges and his beautiful socks. I heard his voice in my ear as we entered the Scrovegni Chapel, saw him sitting across the table in the breakfast room at the Gritti saying, *You could stay with me*. He had reached out his hand and pulled me up into this new life. Even with Chris Passoa's fingers tight on my arm, and warmth rooting through me from his hot skin, I knew, if I had to choose, whom I would choose. And it seemed to me, rightly or wrongly, that I did have to.

I pulled away. "I wish you'd leave Bernard alone!" I said. And then I stumbled down the path through the dark.

23.

The morning after the opening, I got to work early and walked through the silent galleries. In the first room the seashell sculptures lay coupled on their plinths—pairs of scallop shells and oyster shells, slipper and jingle shells—all in their distinct and slightly unsettling colors, while a wider vitrine held a grid of coiled snails. In the second room, crabs and crayfish, tiger shrimp and pink shrimp smoldered under plexi, while whorled and fluted barnacles fanned out around the huge relic of the horseshoe crab. In the room after that were shimmering jellyfish in reds and yellows, and in the final room the sea foam pieces glittered in staggered rows like sunlit waves caught at the moment of breaking. Every time I saw the sea foam pieces they stopped me, caught me weblike, as if I were a fly. That day I stood among them for a long while, feeling the old familiar spark leap to life inside me, traveling down to the core of me, my whole body thrumming in recognition. They were elegiac sculptures, fragile and glossy, the creamy glaze laid loosely over black and purple and oxidized green, so that the milky surface gradually revealed to the eye something richer, darker: a depthless submarine world of teeming color.

Upstairs, I answered email and waited for Bernard. Sloan, bright as a canary with her yellow dress and darting eyes, was at her desk in the outer office, and Agnes was in her own office with the door shut, talking on the phone. I could hear her voice rising and falling on the other side of the wall, and though I tried not to listen, once or twice I caught myself with my head cocked, trying to parse the stream of sound into words.

Did Agnes know about the boot? About the bones? Could it have been she who had identified the tattered pink plastic as belonging to Alena in the first place?

Sometime after ten, Celia showed up. I heard her talking to Sloan, asking for Bernard, expressing surprise he wasn't in yet. "Did you have an appointment?" Sloan asked.

"Do I need one?" The razor's edge in Celia's voice turned Sloan haughty.

"I'm just saying—you might not just expect him to be here, you know, whenever."

I got up and hurried into the outer office. "Celia!" I said. "I'm so glad you're here. Congratulations!"

Clad in a purple and gold tunic over black leggings, her eyes thickly outlined, her lids sparkling gold, Celia did not look placated. She looked like Cleopatra disembarking from her barge. "What for?" she wanted to know.

What for? "On the show, I mean! I was just downstairs walking through it again. It looks as spectacular this morning as it did last night."

"No news, then?"

For a moment I thought she was talking about the bones.

But of course she didn't mean that. She meant reviews, articles, an inquiry from a collector. "Come into my office," I said.

We sat on the sofa in front of the Goldsworthy coffee table. Moodily, she put a finger on a ribbed scallop and moved it to a different spot.

Together, haltingly, we recapitulated the night: who had come, what they had said, who had worn what. I was depressed by the awkwardness with which the conversation bumped along. The show had just opened, but in a real way the passion was already over. The exciting labor—hers and mine—was all behind us. We were like a poorly matched married couple who, having dropped a child off at college, find themselves trapped together in the car on the long drive home.

We were both relieved when Bernard showed up. Hearing him speaking with Sloan in the outer office, we bustled out to greet him. He looked stiff and gray, and there was a patch of bluish grizzle on his jaw that he had missed shaving; but his shirt was pressed and his mist-colored linen jacket was crisp, and his smile as he took Celia's hands and kissed her on both cheeks began to burn away the yellow fog that had been coiling around us.

"What a night!" he said. "What a way to relaunch the Nauk! Celia, I knew the show would be good, but I have to say—it exceeded even my expectations."

Celia glowed, a gold undertone shimmering under her skin, echoing her gilded eyelids. "But where did you disappear to?" she asked, more flirtatious than angry. "I looked and looked!"

Squeezing her hands, he notched his smile up. "Sometimes I have to put on my invisibility suit," he said. "But I'm always there."

"Oh!" Sloan said. "I'd rather fly than be invisible!" We all looked at her. In her bright, scant dress and teased, bleached hair, that she had no taste for invisibility was hardly a surprise.

"I knew a man who said he could fly," Bernard said. "He made himself a pair of quite beautiful wings."

"What of?" asked Celia, ever interested in materials.

"Tyvek and bamboo. Hello, Agnes."

Agnes stood in her open doorway, a pillar of coal in her habitual black. "There's that man who *grew* wings," she said. "That bio-artist in Australia. They make these synthetic frames, then use stem cells or something to train the flesh to grow over them. Alena knew him. She wanted to give him a show."

Alena's name made cold ripples in the air, and then Bernard and Celia spoke at once.

"Do they work, though?" Bernard asked.

"Can he grow feathers?" Celia asked.

"No," Agnes said. "They're more like bat wings."

"Ah," Celia said. "For night flying."

Then the door opened, and Chris Passoa came in wearing jeans and a mustard-colored button-down shirt and a brown woven tie. "Morning everyone," he said cheerfully. "I might have thought you'd take the day off after a night like last night. Glad to see it's not true." He didn't look at me.

"Good morning, Chris," Bernard said. "We do work hard in this business."

"Well," Chris said, "if you call standing around and yakking work." He turned to Celia. The pale fuzz on his head seemed as alert as buzzing antennae. "I'm full of admiration," he said. "I had no idea you could do things like that with pottery."

"Ceramics," she said.

"I'd be scared to touch them."

"I'm sure you deal with more frightening things in your profession every day. Good-bye, Bernard." Not bothering to take her leave of the rest of us, she sailed regally out the door.

Agnes's red and gold earrings threw off agitated shards of light. "Is it true?" she asked. "That boot you found—it was Alena's?"

Chris Passoa slouched against the wall, his pale blue eyes grazing each of us—Bernard, Agnes, Sloan, finally me—like a herding dog keeping tabs on its flock. I looked away. I couldn't help it. I could feel his bright tug, the way my body was pulled toward him like a daisy turning toward the sun, but I didn't want that now. "Yes," he said. "They're hers. And the bones as well. I'm sorry. We've all but confirmed it."

Bernard startled. "But you said— How do you know? Did you get a DNA sample or something?"

Chris sat down on the sofa. He pulled a handkerchief from his pants pocket, set it on the coffee table, and unfolded it. Inside were four small metal bands, two thicker and two narrower, glinting dully in the wan office light.

Slowly, her earrings trembling, Agnes crossed the room and knelt on the carpet in front of them. "Her toe rings."

"They were in the boot. Tangled in the nylon stocking."

Frozen in place, Bernard's eyes were fixed on the twists of metal. From her knees, Agnes looked up at Chris, then wrenched her gaze wildly around the room. Sloan crossed to her on her heron legs, sank to the ground, and enfolded her aunt's black-clad bulk in her bare bony arms.

Agnes's hands folded over the rings. Chris let her take them. She squeezed them in her fists, pressed her fists to her chest. There were no tears, no sound, but her white face blanched whiter still, like a bone bleached by the sun.

"It makes it real, doesn't it?" Chris said. "Alena's dead. We knew it before, but now we know it differently."

A faint mosquito-like whining seemed to start up in my head. My thoughts buzzed in confused alarm.

"But," Sloan said. "Wearing *boots*?" It seemed as if she wanted to say more but was unable to find the words.

Chris's eyes, animated by an electric alertness, kept moving, from Agnes's hunched form, to Bernard's stiff figure, to Sloan, to me. "Yes," he said. "So she wasn't swimming, as we originally guessed." His statement fell through the room like a stone. "Of course, it could have been a boating accident. Though we don't know of any missing boats." Another stone. "Except for Bernie's, of course." He smiled like someone making a joke. "But he sold those."

Still clutching the rings to her chest, Agnes stared at him. "I don't understand!" she cried. "What happened to her?"

"We don't know," Chris said. "That's what we have to find out." Again his eyes roamed, pausing at each one of us. When his gaze fell on me, I realized that I felt ill. My breathing was irregular and I was flushed and sweating.

"I looked through the files again this morning," he said. "Just to refresh my memory. Alena was seen last the evening of the day before the flight she was supposed to take to Paris, but which she didn't get on. She had dinner with Monica Halloran in Wellfleet." I knew Monica Halloran; she was the blond woman who looked like an opossum whom I had met at the dinner Bernard had given when I first arrived. Chris leaned back against the couch, crossing his legs. The room was completely silent now, except inside my head, where the whining, the buzzing, grew steadily louder. I remembered what Morgan McManus had told me—that Alena had tried to reach him by phone that night. She'd called to say she had something to show him, but he hadn't picked up his cell. Presumably that information was in Chris's file too. And in any case, it amounted to nothing. "Monica left her around eight-thirty," Chris said. "It was June, still practically broad daylight at that hour. She was packed, ready to go. What did she do then?" He couldn't really have expected an answer, and certainly he got none. He amended his question. "What did she usually do at such a time? The evening before she went on a trip." He paused. "Bernard?"

Bernard's head jerked up. "I didn't see her," he said.

Chris waited. "No," he said. "I know that. I was just going to ask, I know you traveled together a lot over the years. I thought you might be able to say what kinds of things she usually did on the night before she was going somewhere." The empty handkerchief in which he'd brought the rings still lay on the coffee table, and he picked it up now and stuffed it thoughtfully, bit by bit, into his fist.

"I don't know," Bernard said. "Different things, I guess."

"Different things like what?"

"Meet a friend for a drink, go to a movie, go for a swim. Sometimes she went up to Boston the night before, to see people."

"She didn't do that this time," Chris said. "Her car was still in her garage." His words were grains of sand poured through a funnel into my head, joining their brothers by the thousands. Soon there would be no room left in there.

"I should have been with her!" Agnes said. Her brittle voice rushed through the words so that she sounded like a tape played slightly too fast. "Usually I did her packing on the night before a trip! Alena was a terrible packer. She always traveled with far too much luggage, and she'd squash everything together so it was wrinkled when she got anywhere. But I had to visit my mother, so I did it a day early. I wasn't here that night to help her." She sat very still, black as a charred stump after a forest fire, though her earrings continued to tremble slightly, throwing red beads of light across the floor. The discovery of the bones had made Alena's death raw again, and now she had the anguish of thinking her absence might have contributed to that death. I remembered what she had said to me, the first time she took me down into Alena's room. *It was good fortune that our trips overlapped.*

"Bernard?" Chris prompted gently.

"I don't know what she did," Bernard said irritably. "I was busy getting ready to leave myself."

"Of course." Chris put the fist with the handkerchief inside it up to his ear, listened, then tapped the flesh near his thumb. The sound of my blood thundering through my veins was so loud I was having trouble making out anyone's words. "It must have taken a lot of time, getting ready for a trip like that. And you were alone? No friend to help you pack?" He glanced at Agnes, who was staring into space, looking at nothing. "No one to confirm where you were or jog your memory?" Bernard might have agreed—or disagreed—or snapped at Chris Passoa, or cried out—but I wouldn't have known. The wave of rushing blood overtook me, and everything went black. The next thing I knew, I was on the floor looking up into Bernard's haunted face. *"Cara?"* he said.

On the sofa, Chris Passoa opened his hand, releasing a fistful of air.

24.

News about the bones was on the internet that night. By the next morning, like a change in the weather, the Nauk offices were flooded with phone calls and emails, everyone wanting to know what we knew. As they had two years earlier, reporters made their way through the gates and up the winding drive. I was surprised at first that there was so much interest—after all, everyone already believed Alena had drowned. But I suppose no one likes to miss the opportunity to finger the bones of the dead. Besides, what else was there to report on out here on the edge of the earth, especially once summer was over? We put together a brief statement: *Complete surprise . . . deeply saddened . . . old wounds reopened . . . no idea how*. To his credit, Jake, who was the front line, urged all the reporters and gossip seekers who came through the door to see the show, which some of them did. In the absence of actual information, what else was there for them to do? One day, coming downstairs from my office, I found Bernard standing like a trapped animal among flashing cameras and bulging microphones in the lobby. I told him to go home. I would talk to the press. I would come and see him every day and give him a report. It would be easier for me, I said, since

I hadn't known Alena. I remember how strange it felt, saying that. *I didn't know Alena.* I felt so powerfully that I did know her.

It wasn't just the press. Ordinary people came too—from the town, locals mostly, who worked in tourist shops and real estate offices and restaurants, many of which closed up the Tuesday after Labor Day. Not a lot of people, but some. A couple of the news stories mentioned the name of the show if only in passing, at least once identifying it as the last exhibition Alena had organized. You could see the work in some of the TV segments, the grid of curled snails showing up in a pan of the galleries, or a quick collage of images from different rooms preceding a longer shot of the beach at Willet's Landing, where the boot had washed up. I wouldn't have expected the work to look as good on television as it did—rich and gleaming, the tension between the fidelity to realistic form and the idiosyncratic use of color catching the eye and holding it. Maybe I was the only one who noticed.

My relationship with Bernard had entered a new stage. He wanted me around him all the time. I would look up from my desk to see his tall shape hovering in my doorway, his shadow falling across my rug. Or the phone on my desk would ring, and there would be his voice in my ear asking if I'd seen some email, or if I'd spoken to Celia lately, or if I wanted lunch. Suddenly we were eating most of our meals together, at restaurants in Nauquasset and Wellfleet and Truro where Bernard was greeted by name, though neither of us ever seemed to be very hungry, and the waitstaff was constantly removing nearly full plates. Or in the evenings when the galleries closed—when Agnes slung her big black purse over her shoulder, and Sloan dangled her small black purse from her wrist, and they sauntered together out to where the cars were parked—Bernard would ask if I wanted to come by his place for a drink. I always said yes.

Bernard seemed to dislike the deck overlooking the bay, preferring to sit in the den on the other side of the house, each of us cupped in our own black Bertoia chair, drinking Lillet and Lagavulin. He'd light the gas fire, though the September nights were not particularly cold, and we'd sit watching the flames the way we had watched the artificial fire in the desk in Venice during the first day we'd ever spent together. Wasn't this what I had imagined, back when Bernard had asked me to come to the Nauk with him? What I had longed for all summer when he'd been away in New York or Provincetown or Boston, or even here in Nauquasset shut up alone, not wanting company? At least not my company. But despite the semblance of intimacy now, we spoke very little. Or if we did speak, it was of superficial things: Barbara's new puppy or the latest art-world gossip or the weather. These conversations petered out quickly, coughing and sputtering like a dying outboard motor until we were left drifting in an opaque and watery silence. Marooned.

In the evenings, after the Nauk closed for the day, I would bicycle over to Bernard's house in time for the local news. He couldn't stop himself from watching it, and I didn't want him to be alone. It was strange—truly surreal—to see the parade of faces, our colleagues' and our own, on television. I watched Bernard watch his on-screen simulacrum, hollow-eyed and grim, declining to comment; but also his older—or rather, younger—self, handsome in a pale gray suit. In those bright pictures of happier days he was smiling, touching flutes of golden liquid with a tall angular woman with dark wings of hair and a ruby pendant nestled between her breasts that matched her laughing scarlet mouth. Alena.

She wasn't beautiful. Her face was asymmetrical, as though she comprised two slightly different versions of herself, and her nose was sharp and bumpy, like a shard of rock. But there was something about her. Her black eyes glowed and her white neck stretched, lifting her pearly breasts slightly out of her black spangled dress. She moved with the self-conscious elasticity of a dancer, and her sharp mobile face drew the eye, as though she were a burning candle and the rest of the world were moths. There she shimmered on the other side of the gauzy screen, vibrant, glamorous, slipping her bare white arm around Bernard's waist, fitting perfectly, as though she were literally a part of him. Then, as the camera ogled, she reached up with her shiny lips and placed a kiss on the edge of his mouth, marking him with a fat red slash that remained after she had finished, like a wound.

That was the first night I stayed at Bernard's house, in the guest room down the hall from his bedroom with its Mapplethorpe photographs and its Paul Thek painting and the small treasured Brancusi. His bathroom with its marble tub on winged brass claws was the size of my parents' living room back in LaFreniere. I tried not to make comparisons like this—what did one world have to do with the other?—but sometimes they presented themselves with the force and persistence of a groundhog in the garden, burrowing under all fences, eluding all snares.

Even with the unexpected publicity, attendance was modest. On the first day after the opening—that Labor Day weekend Saturday—we had nine visitors. Sunday, the day the story broke, we had twenty-two, and after that, we averaged between about fifteen and thirty. Sometimes less. Chris Passoa stopped by several times over the holiday weekend, before I sent Bernard home. I'm sure Jake counted him in the attendance figures to make them look a little better, but he wasn't there for the art. He wanted to talk to Bernard. He kept asking him the same questions, or similar questions, over and over, as though Bernard had some useful perspective he would offer up if Chris found the right way of approaching him. And maybe that's all it was. But it seemed to me that there was a trick hidden somewhere, like the one with the disappearing handkerchief. He was fixated on Bernard's loss of interest in sailing, and he asked to see the bills of sale for his two boats, which Bernard obligingly dug up. He had sold the big sloop to a man on Martha's Vineyard and the catamaran he kept on the beach to a couple up in Maine, both through ads on the internet.

One night I was at Bernard's house when Chris rang the bell. When he came into the room and saw me, his face lit with an unpleasant light like a fluorescent bulb in a plastic lamp. "Hello!" he said. "Seems like I never see you anymore. How's the show going?"

"Fine, thanks. How are you, Chris?"

"Oh, fine. Busy, as I'm sure you can imagine." He accepted the whiskey Bernard offered, and the chair, then sat for an hour going over all the local friends of Alena's he had talked to who hadn't seen her that night, and all the out-of-town friends who hadn't heard from her, and the restaurants she hadn't eaten at, and the owners of the boats she sometimes borrowed whose vessels had been safely docked. "What am I missing, Bernie?" he asked. "Who am I overlooking?"

"It sounds like a pretty complete list to me, Chris."

Then he told us that the last number Alena had ever called, according to phone company records, belonged to Morgan McManus. "He's an artist," Chris Passoa said. "Do you know him?"

"Yes," Bernard said.

"Any good?"

"Alena thought so."

"I guess somebody interviewed him two years ago, but it wasn't me. So I went out there this afternoon. To his studio." His mouth went thin and his eyes got small. It was as though just thinking about McManus's work could make a person uglier. "I've never seen anything like it," he said. "I thought it was sort of the art equivalent of a slasher movie."

Bernard made a noncommittal sound through his nose.

"He says he didn't talk to Alena," Chris reported. "He says his phone was off, she left a message. Nothing in particular. No information there, just another dead end."

Which wasn't what McManus had told me, quite. He'd said Alena wanted to show him something. But maybe he didn't believe in cooperating with police, or maybe he didn't like Chris. Why, after all, would he?

Oh, I was tired of the whole thing! Of Chris's nosing about and studiously unstudied glances, and the so-called news stories that contained no news, and the way Alena continued to occupy the center of everyone's attention despite having been dead two years! "Can I ask a question?" I said.

"What?" Chris said.

"The investigation of Alena, of how she died, has reached this whole new pitch since the boot washed up. But I don't see how anything is really different. Before, she had mysteriously disappeared, no one knew what had happened to her, and she was presumed dead. Now, she mysteriously disappeared, no one knows what happened to her, and we know for sure that she's dead. Isn't the situation basically the same? She drowned in the bay, one way or another, even if we don't know exactly how. Why can't you just leave it at that?" I could feel Bernard listening beside me like a schoolboy listening for the recess bell.

"There are two reasons," Chris said. "First, now we have a body. That necessarily sets certain procedures in motion."

"No, you don't," I said. "You have a handful of bones."

"Second, before this, I could see in my head what might have happened. Alena goes for a midnight swim, which we know she likes to do. She gets a cramp or hits a current, or maybe she just overestimates herself, and that's it. But this, with the boot, doesn't make sense to me. I can't picture what the accident would have been."

"Maybe she committed suicide!" I said. "Maybe she went for a swim wearing all her clothes, including the boots, the way Virginia Woolf put stones in her pockets!"

But Chris had already dismissed that theory. "No one says she showed any signs of being suicidal. Also, it's hard to believe she would have got far enough, laden down like that. The tide was running in all night. Her body should have washed right up."

~

And then, the next day, there was Morgan McManus in the frame of Bernard's television, standing on a beach—our beach, the beach at the Nauk—gesturing with a sleek black prosthesis at the dunes. It was cloudy, the sky low and white, the yellow sand crisscrossed with bird tracks and tire tracks and the manic, galloping tracks of dogs. "Over there," he was saying. "She left me a voicemail saying to come, and to bring my video camera. She told me she had something. Something I wouldn't want to miss."

Out of the frame a voice asked, "But when you arrived, she wasn't here?"

"No. I was late."

"But you saw something?"

The screen switched to a dark wobbly scene, a different view of the same beach. In the green glow of what seemed to be a night-vision camera, you could see a boat running out of the water onto the shore, a tall figure splashing out. "I did," McManus said. "I saw this man, Bernard Augustin. Getting out of his boat."

I stared. It was almost impossible to make out what was going on in the shaky video. The tall figure had its back to the camera. With its long legs and broad shoulders, wet hair plastered to its head, it might have been Bernard. But then again, it might not. The sail fluttered down and the man—I could tell it was a man now, I could see the bathing trunks—bent over it, folding, bunching. He seized the bow of the catamaran and dragged it across the sand onto a two-wheel dolly, then bungeed it in place and heaved it up toward the dune. Everything seemed to be happening very fast. Then the screen went blank, and a sound came from where Bernard sat in his chair—a strangled sound like water gurgling in a drain. He slumped, the remote dangling from his hand.

"Bernard," I said. My voice sounded tinny, swallowed up by the resonant silence of the dark room. But he didn't seem to hear me. "Bernard, listen to me! So he taped you coming back from a sail. So what?" I got up and squeezed beside him in his chair. "You used to sail a lot. Who could keep track of every time? It's perfectly plausible that you forgot."

"I shouldn't have brought you here," he said.

"No," I said. "This is where I belong. I wouldn't want to be anywhere else." I touched his cold face, caressing his jaw, the skin near his lips where Alena had kissed him. The doorbell rang.

Bernard got up. I followed him into the foyer, where he flipped switches to turn on lights and opened the door to the black windy night. A few brown leaves swept into the hall. Morgan McManus stood on the stoop in camouflage pants and a T-shirt. His arm prosthesis was shaped like a real arm as far down as the wrist, but instead of a hand a sort of red rubbery flower, spiky and bright like a cactus blossom, bloomed uselessly. "Hello," he said to Bernard. Then his eyes found me. He took his time looking. I was wearing a new dress I'd bought at an end-of-summer sale in town—emerald green, sleeveless, with a pattern of whorls and spirals in midnight blue—and I could feel his gaze traveling from my face to my chest to my hips and on down to the silver polish on the nails of my bare toes. I stood up a little straighter. If he wanted to look, let him go ahead and look.

"I could sue you for invasion of privacy!" Bernard said. "Not to mention trespassing."

McManus smiled. "How could I be trespassing when I was invited? Alena asked me to come. I was a guest."

"Whose guest?" Bernard said. "Alena wasn't there."

"No. But you were."

"I was there," Bernard said. "Alone. Alone with my boat. If you don't believe me, watch your own video!"

"That was on the way back," McManus said. "Not going out."

The light was attracting a swarm of night insects. A brown moth fluttered into the house, and a large June bug, out of season, collided with the doorframe and fell, buzzing frantically, to the ground. "What do you want?" Bernard said.

"Can I come in? You could offer me a drink. I wouldn't say no to a drink."

It looked as though he had been drinking already. His face was flushed and he swayed slightly on the stoop, though I suppose that might have been the false leg.

We sat in the formal living room, with its Félix Gonzáles-Torres candies and its pale sofas and its row of Cindy Sherman film stills over the fireplace. Bernard poured something clear into small glasses and handed them to us. He said, "What kind of person sneaks around with a night-vision camera taking secret pictures in the dark?"

McManus took his glass with his real hand, nestled it in among the spiky rubberized petals of his false hand, lifted it to his mouth, and sipped. "An artist," he said.

"A snoop," Bernard said. "A spy."

McManus held out the glass in his flower for a refill. "Alena wanted me to see something. What was it?"

"You tell me," Bernard said. "What's on your tape?"

"What do you think is on it?"

They stared at each other, waiting and assessing. These two men who had loved Alena.

McManus said, "She died, in the bay, with her boots on, and you were out at the same time in your boat."

Bernard said, "If you have something to say, say it." Slowly, deliberately, he raised his glass to his lips. Like a mirror, McManus raised his. The pure spectacle of McManus's gesture struck me—the red rubbery petals or sepals, comical and obscene, contrasting with the delicate faceted glass. The way McManus maneuvered the artificial arm, which was permanently bent at the elbow, in a motion not quite mechanical and not quite human. Bernard was drinking, but what McManus was doing was something else.

"I'm saying you killed her," McManus said.

The room seemed to sag and droop like a clock in a Dalí painting. The lines in the Sol LeWitt quivered dizzyingly, and the faces in the Cindy Sherman photographs looked shocked.

"If that were true," Bernard said, "you'd have it on your video."

"You're afraid I do have it," McManus said. "You should be afraid."

"You're crazy," Bernard said.

"You don't know what I have. You can't guess. But I'll tell you what. I'll make you an offer." He watched Bernard wait. Then, after time had oozed and jerked along a while more, he said, "I can give the tape to the police, or I can give it to you."

Bernard laughed. "Why would you give it to me?"

He reached into his pocket with his flesh hand and pulled out a video card. He laid it, flat and black as a shard of night, on the table. "I want a show," McManus said. "Alena promised me a show, and I want that promise kept." We all stared at the dull piece of matchbook-sized plastic as though, if we looked hard enough, we could read its secrets, translate its digital code. Then, with a jerk, Bernard pulled his phone out of his own pocket and started pushing buttons.

"Who are you calling?" McManus said.

"If you want to accuse me of something, you can do it in front of the police."

"Bernard," I said, "you're not calling Chris."

He didn't look up.

"I'm not sure," I began, and then there was a click, and we could hear a tiny voice through Bernard's phone saying *Yes?* I finished my drink. The vodka burned through me with a blue electric sizzling. The world was a dinner plate spinning through space. Bernard said, "Could you come over? Now. Morgan McManus is here. Did you see him on the news?" Chris Passoa's voice scrambled and squawked through the speaker. Bernard hung up and dropped the phone on the table. He flicked the plastic video card across the polished surface as though it were a bug. The black square spun sideways and skittered onto the carpet.

McManus smirked. "Is that what you did to Alena? Pushed her over and watched her go down?"

"Alena could swim like a shark," Bernard said.

"Not if you drugged her," McManus said. "Not if you killed her first."

"I loved Alena," Bernard whispered, and my heart shriveled and toughened like a piece of overcooked meat.

"You hated her," McManus said. "You were jealous of her."

"She was Artemis," Bernard said. "I was Orion."

"She was brave. You're a coward." Plucking his glass from his sculptured hand and setting it on the table, McManus leaned over to retrieve his video card, but he lost his balance. Down he went to the floor with a crash, the plywood chair flying away behind him, his limbs splayed across the rug like a spider. Bernard and I stared down at him, doing nothing. He grunted and slowly began to gather himself back up, like a boxer in the ring, or a newborn foal in a corral. Why I didn't move to help him I can't say. Maybe it was the vodka, or the shock, or my shriveled meat heart. Maybe I was afraid of what I would feel if I touched him. Or maybe it was because it was so interesting to watch him, flailing and gyroscoping on the floor, trying to rise.

By the time Chris Passoa's car pulled up, McManus was back in his chair, but his false arm had slipped out of position. It sagged from his bicep at an odd angle, the way my brother Mark's arm had sagged after he fell out of a tree and broke it during a hunting trip when he was thirteen. I had to keep reminding myself that McManus's arm couldn't be broken—not like that. Not in a way that would cause him current pain. He had crossed the frontier into a foreign country of injury, had climbed the mountain and slalomed down the black diamond trail of bodily harm. When the bell rang I jumped up and said I'd answer it.

Chris was dressed casually in faded jeans and a gray sweatshirt, but his expression was rigid, formal, stern, as though it constituted his uniform. "What's going on here?" he said.

I took a step closer and laid my hand on his wrist, pretended I didn't notice his flinch. "Morgan McManus has a video he claims he took the night Alena died," I said, looking up into his square set face. "He's drunk. Probably high too. I think when you went to see him it must have opened the whole thing up again. He hates Bernard because he's never had a show at the Nauk, and now he's throwing around these crazy accusations. Making threats. It's as though he's lost his mind." I was standing very close to Chris, my fingers pressing lightly into his arm, and as I spoke, I could see him, reluctantly, taking me in, me in my new dress standing barefoot in the airy foyer of Bernard's house.

"And what a mind," he said.

"You saw his work," I said. "You've seen how he sees the world." I said, "Didn't he tell you Alena's message was nothing in particular? And now this story about summoning him to the beach, about video cameras! If it's true, why didn't he tell you yesterday?" Then I led him into the living room.

"Hello, Bernard," Chris said. He looked at McManus. "Hello."

"Hello," McManus said.

All three of them ignored me. It was as though I had become invisible.

Chris took a seat, crossed his legs. I wondered if he would accept a drink—if he considered himself on duty or off—but Bernard didn't offer him one. Maybe he didn't want to find out. "Catch me up," Chris said.

"Morgan is trying to blackmail me," Bernard said. "He claims I killed Alena. He offered to trade me a recording of the killing for a show at the Nauk." He nodded at the video card on the table.

Chris Passoa picked the card up, looked at it, weighed it in his hand. "This the tape they ran on Channel Seven?" he asked McManus.

"They ran part of it," McManus said.

"And you're saying the other part shows Bernard drowning Alena? Two years ago? And you've kept it lying around all this time?"

"No," McManus said. "I'm not saying that."

"What, then?"

McManus rearranged himself in his chair. A few inches of his shiny leg prosthesis showed between his sock and the hem of his camouflage pants, and his neck bulged, the architecture of the tendons straining against the scarred skin. "Bernard went out in his boat," he said. "The night Alena died. He launched from the beach where Alena told me to meet her. But Alena wasn't there. Where was she? She went into the water that night, and he—Bernard—was out on the water. Is that a coincidence? Is that what I'm supposed to believe?"

"So nothing's on the video," Bernard said. "Nothing at all!"

"You're on it," McManus said stubbornly. "You're getting out of the boat just around the time Alena was dying!" His face was as crimson as his hand.

"Why on earth would I kill Alena? For what possible reason?"

"She told me to meet her," McManus repeated. "She had something she wanted me to document. She said she'd be there, but she wasn't there."

"She died!" Bernard's voice was like hot oil sizzling in a pan. "She had some kind of accident and *died*! That's why she wasn't there!"

Chris Passoa had let the conversation, like fishing line, play out this far, but now he flipped the pickup and began to reel it in. "This video," he said to McManus. "You didn't mention it to me when we talked yesterday."

McManus turned his big head toward Chris, then his torso with its one real arm and its one false arm, hanging crookedly now like a gutter that has come loose after a storm. "I didn't," he admitted. "I should have. Truthfully, I didn't remember exactly what was on it. Two years, after all! But after we talked, I started thinking. And I started remembering more and more. So I went and dug up the video, and things came back."

"But you didn't call me," Chris pursued. "You didn't bring the tape to me. You brought it to Channel Seven."

McManus smiled wryly, half his face rising, the other half staying where it was. Chris's own face tightened in response, his disgust visible. "Why are you interrogating me?" McManus said. "Bernard's the one you should be questioning. Ask him what he was doing on the beach that night."

Chris slipped the video card into his pocket. "Is that much true, Bernie?" he asked. "Were you on the beach?"

"For God's sake! It was two years ago!"

"Yes," Chris said. "So stop a minute and think."

A hot silence fell over the room, broken only by the sound of the surf beyond the deck. Alena had died out there in the cold water in her toe rings and her boots. For two years the water had held her in its dark arms, sucked her down to bone, dissolved the essence of her through Cape Cod Bay. I wondered, as I had wondered before, why it mattered exactly how.

"I may have gone down to the beach," Bernard said at last. "I may even have gone for a sail. I've forgotten. I often sailed at dusk. Maybe I did."

"So you weren't tired of sailing then."

Bernard looked at him for a long moment, his eyes dark, the shadows under them darker. "No," he said. "Not then."

"And was Alena with you? Did you see her on the beach?"

"I didn't see her," Bernard said. "I didn't see anyone."

In my mind I could see McManus's grainy video—the man dragging the boat out of the water. The man rolling it across the sand. The sail, loosely bunched around the boom, flapping its ghostly hand in the dark. Could you guess from that what had happened in the hour before the tape was made? Impossible. From McManus's angle, hidden in the tick-infested dunes, you couldn't even make out the man's face.

"She told me to come to the beach," McManus said. "She told me to bring my camera. Something would happen, she said. Something I shouldn't miss. What was it?"

"Nothing!" Bernard cried. "Nothing! Nothing! She could have been anywhere up and down Cape Cod! She didn't have to be in Nauquasset at all."

It was true: Alena could have been anywhere. But I didn't believe it. None of us did.

Maybe Maria Hallett had lured her out to sea. Maybe she'd gone swimming with her boots on, racing a ghost. What a picture that would have made: a woman, naked except for her bubble-gum boots, plowing through the surf, swimming down the moonlit path straight out to the horizon! I thought of what Agnes had said Alena had told her: *You only get one shot at death, I don't intend to waste mine.* Was she looking down now, rejoicing in the drama she could make happen even in her absence? "Maybe she committed suicide," I said. "Maybe that was what she wanted you to *document*!" Despite what Chris thought, it still seemed plausible to me. Who knew how far a determined woman could swim with her boots on?

The men's heads swiveled toward me with the suddenness of guns. The room thrummed.

"She wouldn't do that," McManus said. "We were working on a project!"

I almost laughed! Not, She wasn't depressed. Not, She was full of life, she wanted to live. *We were working on a project!*

"What was the project?" I asked.

McManus raised his chin and looked down over his canny nose. "It was going to be fantastic," he said. "A major reenactment. We were going to restage the sinking of the *Whydah* with an exact replica of the ship, all made by hand! We were going to rig it and train local volunteers to sail it. Everyone in eighteenth-century clothing! Pirate garb for those on board, spatterdashes and buckled shoes for the ones on shore. Bonnets and corsets for the women. And then we were going to capsize it and the participants would go floating into the bay! Not during an actual storm, of course. And then those watching from the shore would try and rescue them. The bodies would lie on the beach for an afternoon, simulating death."

Bernard guffawed.

Chris's face shut up like an anemone.

I said, "Alena would have been Maria Hallett, of course."

McManus smiled at me, and for a moment, as our gazes caught, we might have been alone in the room. "Of course," he said. And then a thought came to him, I could see it flicker to life on his face. "Maria Hallett's hut," he said. "That bum who sleeps in it."

"Old Ben?" Chris said. "What about him?"

"He was there that night. I heard him moving around the way he does. Maybe he saw something."

25.

McManus couldn't walk well on sand, so Chris Passoa suggested we drive his Jeep out to Willet's Landing, where four-wheel-drive vehicles could cut through to the beach. The night had grown cold. Bernard and I sat in the back as we bumped along the driveway, then headed up the shore road. I reached out and took his hand. It lay limply in mine, like a dead hand, and he turned his head away, watching the dark shapes of the scrub rise and fall in the salty dark. At Willet's Landing, Chris turned down the track between the dunes, the long grass sighing against the metal body of the Jeep. And then we were through onto the beach, with the waves breaking and the white foam gleaming on the cold sand. I rolled my window down and let the chilly air wash over me. Stars were bright and thick. McManus tapped his rubbery flower against the dashboard. It made a flaccid, squelchy noise. This was the stretch of beach where the boot had been found—a bit of plastic detritus spat out by the sea. Where was the rest of her, the hundred-odd lost and lonely bones? In the front seat, McManus started whistling. Chris Passoa stopped the Jeep. "It's just over there," he said.

I opened my door and stepped out into the soft sand. We were the only people on the beach, but up on the dune you could see the lights of a few houses, though the summer was over. A little way down, a long low building crouched on the crest of the bluff, a prism of darkness against the stars. "That's the Nauk," I said in surprise, and suddenly the shape of the shadowed beach around me became familiar. Chris Passoa got out from behind the wheel, and McManus got out too, holding on to the side mirror. Bernard stayed where he was.

"I'll go see if he's there," the police chief said. "If he is, I'll bring him."

We waited. The surf roared dully, monotonously, as though nothing could ever surprise it. The cold beach was littered with broken shells and egg cases and hard dark stones. A shadow slipped across the sand, and looking up, I saw a large bird—an owl, possibly—gliding by in silence. McManus said, "Whatever you did to her, it must have been here."

Bernard said nothing. He had closed his eyes and leaned back in the seat. He might have been asleep.

"Did you tie her up?" McManus said. "Did you hit her with a rock? Didn't she scream? Or did you gag her first?"

"Stop it," I said.

McManus looked at me and said, "If you think he's ever going to sleep with you, you're kidding yourself."

"He's my boss," I said.

"Even Alena couldn't convert him. Though of course they slept together once or twice when they were in college. She could always tell he was queer, though. She told me she knew before he did. She always saw things clearly, Alena. Her inner eye was as sharp as a scalpel."

"Alena's dead," I said.

"I know," he said. "But it doesn't feel that way, does it? It feels like she's gone for a swim and will be back any minute. She loved swimming at night, didn't she, Bernard?"

Bernard opened his eyes as though his lids were made of lead. "Yes," he said. "She did."

In Wisconsin too we had swum at night: in depthless quarries and silty ponds, in wide shallow rivers and black indifferent lakes. But this was different—the hungry waves grumbling and churning at the edge of the earth, the doorway to the kingdom of krakens and sharks. It was a miracle anyone ever made it out.

Chris Passoa materialized from the dunes, leading a thin, windblown figure with a wild white cloud of hair and beard. "I didn't do anything," the old man said. "Don't send me back."

"Nobody's sending you anywhere," Chris said. "We want to talk to you."

"No one uses that place," the painter said. "Just ghosts."

"We want your help. We're hoping you can help us."

"I can't help anyone. All I can do is paint."

"Bernard?" Chris said. "Can you please come out here?" Bernard got out of the car and stood, tall and pale in the wind, his jacket blowing. "Do you know this man, Ben?" Chris asked.

The painter stared at Bernard. We waited.

"He can't tell what's real from what's not," Bernard said.

The old man gestured in the direction of the Nauk. "He runs that place up there," he said.

"Have you seen him on this beach before?"

"Lots of times."

"Have you seen him with the woman who used to work there? Alena? You know who that is, don't you?"

The old painter turned toward the policeman. The wind was cold, and freezing spray drifted up from the black, hissing waves, but he wore only a vagrant's threadbare shirt, and his feet were bare. "She's gone, isn't she?" he said. "She went into the sea."

"That's right."

"She used to swim, lots of nights. Without her clothes on," the painter said. "I didn't watch."

McManus laughed. "Do you think she cared if you watched or not? If you jerked off, crouching in the dunes? Why should she care about that?"

"McManus," Chris said.

"I only see her in dreams now," the painter said.

"I'll bet you see her in your dreams," McManus said. "The question is did you see her the night she died?"

The old man blinked. His face was wrinkled and creased like an old tortoise, but his white hair and beard shone in the moonlight like the pure breath of cows on an autumn morning.

"Ben," Bernard said. "These men want to know if you saw Alena and me together, here on this beach, two summers ago. The night she disappeared. June, it would have been. Near the solstice. This man thinks I killed her. He thinks I put her body in my boat and sailed away and dumped it in the ocean. They want to know if you saw that."

The painter looked out to sea as if he were struggling to remember. The waves rolled in, as they did every night. How many nights had he seen them? How could he be expected to tell one night from the rest? Then he said, "I saw the arrow."

"What arrow?" McManus said.

"A streak in the air."

"A streak?"

"Like a tracer. They would start the tracers first, and then the shooting. Green light everywhere! Flares exploding red and yellow, mortar rounds dazzling, color everywhere, light painting the sky, the jungle going up in flames, orange on black."

"What jungle?" Chris Passoa asked, a tic of impatience in his voice. "What are you talking about?"

"He's talking about the war, I think," I said. "Vietnam."

"How to paint that?" Ben was growing agitated. "All that horror—how to capture it?"

"Surely they didn't have arrows in Vietnam," Chris said.

"Streaks in the burning air the color of snakes," the painter said. "Snakes in the jungle the size of culverts. An arrow streaking like a white snake through the air. A body falling. Bodies floating down the river, surrounded by leaves and old rubber."

"Stop it," McManus said. "Stop acting crazy!"

"It sounds like he's describing one of your installations," Bernard said.

"Ray Donovan died," the painter said. "Charlie Claymont died. Rusty Bigelow died." He swiveled his head in small jerks like a bird, as though he were seeing them out there in the dark. "Ghosts don't sleep. They blow across oceans, carrying their deaths in their hands like melons."

"Ben," Chris said. "Listen. Do you remember the last time you saw Alena?"

The painter didn't seem to hear. He rubbed his long fingers down the sides of his jeans, his shoulders twitching.

"He can be perfectly lucid if he wants to be!" McManus said. "Ben, remember Alena? She used to give you a pint of bourbon sometimes, and cigarettes. I'll give you a whole gallon of Old Grand-Dad if you can tell us about the last time you saw her!"

"Why not cash?" Bernard said, but Chris put up a hand.

The old man blinked rapidly as though trying to clear his vision. "I'll tell you," he said. "The last time. She swam out of the bay and crawled up onto the sand. She was exhausted, poor thing. She'd been in the water too long." He stared out at the dark waves. Behind us, up on the dune, a light went on.

"When was this?" Chris said.

"Last night. No—the night before. She crawled out of the sea and walked along the shore. The waves lapped at her white feet. You say she's gone, but she's not gone." He was trembling all over now, tugging at his beard.

"Ben!" McManus cried. "You know she's dead. You know they found her bones! When was the last time you saw her *alive*?"

Chris Passoa put his hand on the old man's shoulder. "Let's go," he said. "I'll take you back to the hut." The stars, which see everything, glittered coldly in the deathless sky.

"You'd better get him his bourbon, McManus," Bernard said. "He's answered your question."

Up on the dune, a second light went on. This time Bernard saw it too. "That's coming from the Nauk," he said. "Who's up there?" He moved through the dark across the soft blowing sand toward the stairway. McManus lurched after him, placing his fake leg carefully, though once he reached the weathered staircase with its sturdy railing, he was fine. I followed them, wondering what they expected to find. Did they think the ghost Old Ben claimed to have seen had climbed the stairs and slipped into the Nauk? That they would get a last look at Alena? That a ghost would need lights?

The museum doors were unlocked. The lobby was dark and empty, and no light shone in the galleries or along the colonnade. We climbed the stairs, Bernard still leading. Lights blazed in the deserted outer office, illuminating Sloan's cluttered desk and the pristine sofa area and the black rank of filing cabinets. The door to Agnes's office was ajar, but no one was in there, no one we could see. "Agnes?" Bernard called. "Sloan?" He opened the door to his own office and peered in, then shut it again and moved to mine, where he hesitated, hand on the knob. If Alena had come back—if her ghost had come back—this was where she would be, wasn't it? Despite the months I had spent in it, it wasn't really my office at all.

Bernard opened the door and went in. McManus followed, limping into the dark space, his flesh hand brushing the walls, the Robert Arno prints, the coffee table shells, the cold fin of the desk. Except for them, the room was empty. McManus stood by the big window and looked out at the bay surging restlessly under the cold stars. "Alena loved this view," he said. "She said she could see whales."

"There aren't any whales in the bay," Bernard said. "The water is far too shallow."

"She said she could see them."

"Let's go," Bernard said. "There's nothing here." But in the lobby, he yawed around the empty front desk, turning away from the doors, driven on as though before an insistent wind into the darkened galleries. Still in single file, we tacked through them, watched by the shadow sculptures waiting for daylight on their plinths.

The door at the end of the colonnade was unlocked. The cascade of LEDs was illuminated, plunging into the cavity in the floor through which the iron staircase helixed. Down we went in a clanging stampede, no one saying a word. The door to Alena's room was ajar. Bernard laid his palm on its surface and swung it wider, peering in as McManus huffed behind him, pawing the floor like a restless horse.

There was no one in the first room, that lush chamber of rugs and velvet sofas and jade figurines, though a brass lamp in the shape of a mermaid cast a pinkish glow through the patchoulied air. Bernard strode to the far end, then ducked behind a Japanese paper screen etched with cranes and chrysanthemums.

There was another, smaller room behind the screen, also carpeted with red and pink and blue carpets. This one was dominated by a high square bed that looked like something Queen Elizabeth might have slept in: canopied and curtained in lapis and silver, bolstered with silk pillows the size of Saint Bernards. A large wooden cabinet inlaid with dark stars crouched opposite, along with a carved bench with a velvet seat and a big oak writing table with pigeon holes and narrow drawers at which Agnes was perched like a fat black ibis, turning over the pages of a book. She looked up slowly, her pale face shining in the light of an oil lamp of the kind that would have burned whale oil in another century, a faceted goblet topped with a glass globe. Dried tears had left salty tracks on her face. When she spoke, it was to McManus, and it was as though they had picked up in the middle of a conversation they were already having. "What were you doing when she called?" Agnes said. "What was so important you couldn't be bothered to pick up your phone? Was it whores? Were you in an OxyContin stupor?"

McManus sagged. He sat down on a velvet ottoman at the foot of the bed. "You think it doesn't make me feel like shit every day?" His hollow tone matched hers. They were like people calling to each other from the bottom of separate wells. "You think I don't replay that night in my mind, over and over? Leaving my phone on this time, picking it up, hearing her voice? I was working."

"Laying out your fake bodies," Agnes said. "Steeping in your false death while Alena was actually, truly dying! And where were you?" she asked Bernard. "Cavorting in the dark with some boy you picked up on the beach? Counting your treasure? You know you never paid her what she was worth!"

Bernard's voice was a faint scratch on the surface of the air. "Alena was very well compensated," he said, but his words were swept away by the gale of Agnes's fury and grief as they left his lips.

"The Nauk couldn't have existed without Alena. She made it what it was." Agnes caressed the book on the desk. It was folio-sized, its leather covers etched with the shapes of leaves. Her hair lifted electrically, as though she were amber rubbed on silk. "This is her notebook," she said. "Her last one."

Bernard stood by the door, holding on to the fluted jamb. McManus's eyes were flares in the darkness of his face. Agnes opened the book. "This is the last page she wrote."

We converged, moving across the rug with its pattern of curling vines and pomegranates. At the top of the heavy paper, Alena had written what seemed to be a title:

Dying Is an Art, 1, and two lines from Sylvia Plath:

"Dying / Is an art, like everything else."

Next came a line from Duchamp: "In fact, the whole world is based on chance . . ."

Below that was a diagram, a graph with two axes. The x-axis was labeled "Trajectory" and the y-axis was labeled "Outcome." On the graph she had drawn a standard bell curve tailing away toward "1 / White" at the left and "10 / Gold" at the right. The top of the curve was marked by a skull and crossbones.

"'Dying is an art,'" McManus read aloud, slowly, as though each word were a needle in his mouth.

Agnes seemed to be growing bigger, her dress blacker, her face haughtier, her hair more electric. It rose from her head like the feathers of a furious bird. "Have you even heard of Sylvia Plath? She's that poet who stuck her head in the oven." The words spread out in ripples through the room, liquid and cold.

"Alena wouldn't kill herself," McManus said, as he had said before.

"There was nothing she wouldn't do," Agnes said. "You thought you pushed things so far! Alena was willing to go farther than anyone."

Even in the midst of all that horror, which prickled my skin like snow falling in summer, and the despair that bubbled up through the soupy room, I found the circuits of my skepticism lighting up. Was that what art was about—who was willing to go the farthest? Were risk and chance more valuable than form and feeling? Had abasement utterly displaced transcendence? And if so, had I made a terrible blunder in choosing the direction of my life? But I leaned in even as I was wondering this, my eyes catching in the diagram's web. There was something undeniably magnetic about the puzzle aspect of art, teasing meaning from marks and clues, the mind ticking away in tandem with the eye like the right- and left-hand parts on a piano. What was *1 / White*? What was *10 / Gold*? What was the meaning of that Jolly Roger, hoisted high and speared on the top of the y-axis like a head on a pike?

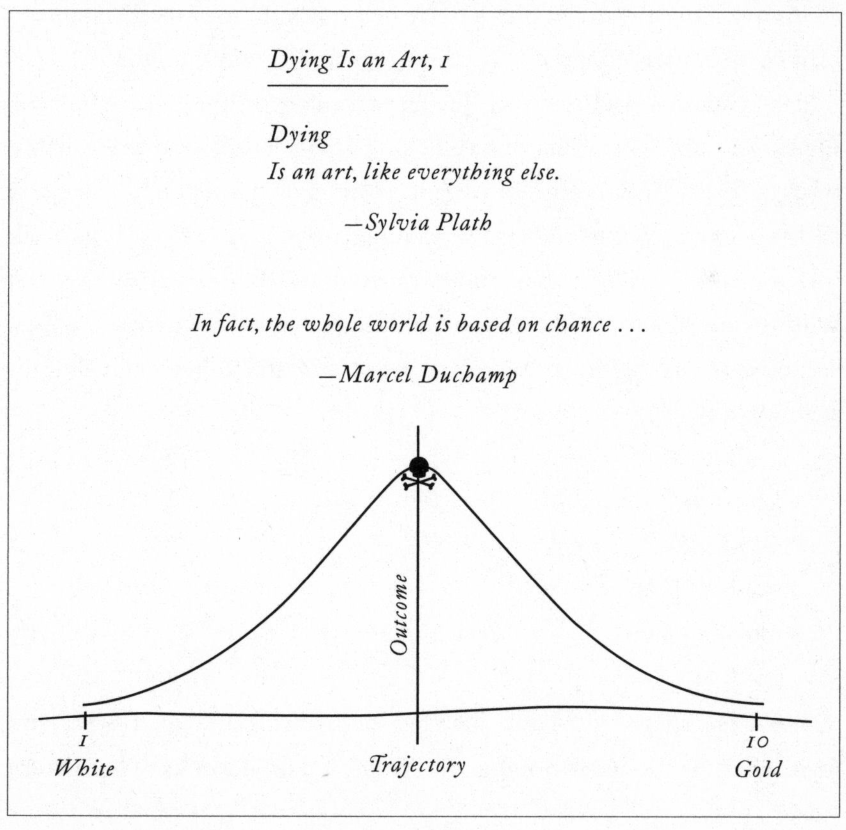

Dying Is an Art, 1
Dying
Is an art, like everything else.
—Sylvia Plath
In fact, the whole world is based on chance . . .
—Marcel Duchamp
Outcome
1
White
Trajectory
10
Gold

"What does she mean by the quote about chance?" I asked. "She wasn't sure if she was going to die or not?"

"She died," Agnes said. "She died and the crabs ate her body."

I leaned in closer to the bone-white page. "Trajectory of what?"

Footsteps rang on the iron steps, and Bernard reached out and slammed the book shut. Agnes squawked, and McManus wheeled around, his flower hand a streak of red in the air. Chris Passoa stood in the doorway of the room, which seemed to tilt toward him as though we were on a raft and he had weighted down one end. His eyes slid to the nut-brown cover of the book with its stamped pattern of leaves that looked like they were gusting in the wind. "What's that?" he asked.

Agnes's voice clanged like a buoy bell marking the rusted iron caverns of a submerged wreck. "A message from beyond the grave."

He made his way forward, his feet treading on the pomegranates. He looked tired. Fine bits of sand clung to his jacket, and there was a wisp of dried salty eel grass caught in his hair. He opened the book and turned the pages covered in writing, rows of words in fine black ink, the letters calligraphic, runic, crossed and flourished so that the writing looked almost like Cyrillic, although it wasn't. There were lists, some of things to do, others of names, and still others of random-seeming objects:

1. cat's eye
2. eggshell
3. rabbit's foot
4. burning leaves

There were sharp, vivid ink sketches of seabirds and of oysters and of jeweled necklaces drooping from long headless necks. There were weather reports: *clear sky with SW winds, gusty, seas three feet*. There were menus:

mint soup
rabbit stew
frisée with pears and pistachios
meringues

and lines of poetry: "The blood-dimmed tide is loosed, and everywhere / the ceremony of innocence is drowned." If she wrote down private thoughts or recorded events of her life, she didn't do it here. At last Chris reached the final page, the one we had been looking at. He studied it a long while. Then he raised his head and studied us.

"What does it mean?" he asked. "Dying is an art?"

No one answered him. At last, seeing that none of the three of them would speak, I said, "It's a line from a poem by Sylvia Plath."

His pale eyebrows lowered and his jaw braced as though to squeeze the name's identification out of his memory. "That poet who killed herself?"

I nodded.

He thought about that, then looked at the page again. "What about the graph? What are *trajectory* and *outcome*?"

Again his question was met by silence. I looked at the triumvirate of dumb figures: administrator, collector, artist. They seemed to stand together on one side with their biases and intuitions and practical skills, while here on the other side stood I, the lone art historian. "It looks as though she was working on a new work of art," I said. "Some artists use chance as an element in their work. Marcel Duchamp was one of the first. You can see the other quote is from him. The idea was to trick yourself out of your own subjectivity, to free yourself from only doing the sort of thing you yourself would think of to do."

Chris Passoa shook his head. "You're speaking in riddles again." He sounded fed up with puzzles and enigmas, with art and artists and their tranced oracles. Maybe with women. He wanted things to be what they seemed. Well, that was his problem.

"It looks as though she was planning some activity—something risky—without knowing how it would turn out. For example, if she swam off the beach in the dark for a certain amount of time—or maybe at a certain angle, a trajectory from the shore—maybe she would be able to swim back, and maybe she wouldn't."

He stared at me. "And that would be a work of art?"

"Ideas, processes. Contemporary art often deals in things like that."

"You think that's what happened?"

"I have no idea," I said.

He touched the page, tracing the bell curve with a blunt finger. "Death is in the middle," he said. "The trajectory goes both ways. Presumably she'd live at either end."

"Maybe the trajectory at either end is swimming parallel to the shore, and the one in the middle is going straight out."

"And how would she decide? You're saying by chance?"

"Maybe she would—I don't know—pick an angle out of a hat. Or find a sign in nature. If the wind is blowing southeast, I'll swim southeast. Or if I see a gold bird . . ." If she saw a gold bird, what? The colors were clues, I could see that, but I couldn't make sense of them. How were gold and white opposites, for instance? And, if the angle from the shore was the issue, wouldn't the numbers go from 0 to 180?

"Forget the details for a minute," Chris said. "You're saying Alena committed suicide—she drowned herself—as a work of art?" His stark words scorched through the room. Agnes made a drowning sound in her throat, and McManus waved his flower hand like a torch. Bernard seemed to recede into himself, his face metallic, his body attenuating like a blade. From the beach, the liquid heartbeat of the blind waves toiled and sighed.

"Maybe," I said.

"It seems crazy," he said. "But it fits with the other things you've told me. That Alena was interested in extreme forms. People lying down with feathers and knives."

"What does she know?" McManus said. "She didn't even know Alena!"

The roiling air of the room seemed to shift, settling here and churning there.

By the desk, Agnes began to cry. She sat up straight and tall in her black dress, earrings sparkling like constellations of bloody stars.

Chris Passoa took the book and tucked it under his arm.

26.

Rather than be driven home by Chris Passoa, Bernard came back with me to the little house under the dune. We walked together down the sloping path, and when Bernard stumbled I took his arm to steady him, and we went on like that under the brilliant stars. Something felt different—odd—and after a minute I realized that the crickets were gone. There was no urgent chirping to counterpoint the monotonous dirge of the sea.

We went into the kitchen with its Formica table and warped cabinets, its wallpaper decorated with teacups and roosters. I got the gin out of the pantry. We drank it, iced, out of juice glasses, the only light coming from the flickering fluorescent tube over the stove. "It's over," I said. "It's been awful, especially tonight, with McManus, and the video, and Old Ben, and the notebook. But now it's over." My voice shrilled like a teakettle in the damp kitchen. Bernard drank his gin as though it were water. "Stop," he said.

"I'm sorry," I said. "I know there's nothing I can say that helps. I know—I know even though you disagreed . . . How you felt about her."

He banged his hand on the table. "I said *stop*! You don't know how I felt about her. How could you?"

My face grew hot, my eyes stupidly wet. "You're right," I said. "I couldn't."

"Oh, God," he said. "Don't cry."

"I'm sorry." I wiped my eyes. "I just feel so bad for you." It was true that I felt bad for him, but mostly I just felt bad. I almost wished Alena wasn't dead. How much worse competing with a ghost than with a living woman!

"Bad for me!" Bernard laughed. "Bad for *me*! I'm the luckiest man in the world." His face began to color, blood rushing to it until it was dark red like a polluted moon. He said, "Do you want to know why?"

I stared at him—at his cooked lobster face and his sunken bloodshot eyes and his big bony hands tented around his glass. "Why?"

"You don't want to know."

"Tell me."

He finished his gin and poured himself a refill. Then he scraped his chair back across the linoleum and got up and began walking around the room, crossing from the stove to the door that led to the laundry yard and back. As he walked, he began to speak, not looking at me, holding his glass in front of him like a candle through a dark hall.

"When I was a kid," he said, "I hated sports. I was that quintessential skinny, faggy boy who couldn't hit a baseball or shoot a basket, and I didn't care. I didn't want to do any of that. I loved music and drawing and dressing up. My grandmother used to sew costumes for me. My favorite was an Indian brave, a fringed leather tunic and beaded moccasins and feathers. I used to change into it the minute I got home from school and run all over the house, whooping.

"And then, when I was nine, my parents sent me to summer camp for a month in Maine. It was a primitive place, up near Moosehead Lake, with no electricity or hot water. There were sports every afternoon, and so, in order to avoid baseball, I signed up for archery." He stopped. The only sound in the room was the buzzing of the fluorescent bulb over the stove. "You can't hear the ocean from here," he said in surprise.

"No."

"So restful. Sometimes I think if I hear one more wave breaking . . ." He started walking again. "Right away I loved archery. I was good at it. Have you heard of instinctive shooting? Our instructor, a young man with a little beard—his name was actually Robin, if you can believe that, or he said it was—taught it to us. Instinctive shooting is about being in harmony with the bow, feeling the flight of the arrow in your blood. It's about breathing and stillness and not-thinking. He used to come around and place his palm on your chest as you drew to make sure you were breathing correctly. There would be his hand on my bare skin, and I would pull the bow back, aiming not with my eye and brain but with my whole being. And he would make me hold it, drawn like that, the arrow cocked on the taut string, saying, 'Breathe, Bernard, breathe!' And then, at last, he would say, 'Now!' And I would let my arrow fly. My very first time I hit the gold." He stopped again, and this time he turned to me with a hard, dark look. "Do you know what gold is?"

I shook my head.

"It's the color of the bull's-eye in target archery. The center of the target. If you're scoring points, that's a ten." He waited, letting the buzzing silence fill my ears like water. Then he said, "And the outer circle of the target. Do you know what color that is?"

"No."

"But if you had to guess?"

"White?" I whispered.

"Very good. Excellent. And how many points do you think white might be worth?"

"One?" My lips shaped the word, but my breath could barely push it out.

"One," he repeated. Then he began to walk again, up and down the room, which felt to me like a sealed capsule, cut off from the world, hurtling through the darkness of a starless universe.

"After that summer," he said, "I started to compete in tournaments. My mother would drive me to archery competitions all over New England and down into New York and Pennsylvania. For a couple of years I dreamed of being an Olympic archer. But then I hurt my wrist falling off my bike, and by the time it healed, I had lost so much practice." He drank again, the glass nearly empty so that he had to tilt his head back, exposing the pale skin of his throat. He was right behind my chair, and I could smell him: salt and bitter orange and alcohol. He put out his hand to steady himself, placed it on my shoulder for the barest instant as he regained his balance. Then he sat down across from me again. "And then, when I was in seventh grade, we moved to the Cape year-round. I had always been happier here than in Boston, and even though we moved because my father was sick, I was thrilled. I had always liked sailing, but now I was obsessed with it. I was always out, in almost every weather, from April to October. I had my own boat, named after my dog who had died, the *Caspar*. My first boat.

"My father died my senior year in high school. I went to Middlebury for college, where he had gone, mostly because my mother wanted me to. They didn't have a real sailing team, though, so I joined the archery team and started shooting again.

"I met Alena during freshman orientation. We were in line for something or other, me and all these other nervous kids, and there she was. She was standing right in front of me in a white dress and a Cleopatra wig and gold lamé sandals. We started talking. She had seen an exhibition of Joseph Cornell boxes that summer at MoMA, and as it turned out, I had seen it too. That was enough. We became inseparable. Everyone at school was in love with her—or else they scorned and despised her—but she didn't care about that. As long as they noticed her, as long as they talked about her, that was what she wanted. She turned out to know quite a lot about art, mostly through reading. A lot for an eighteen-year-old, anyway. I did too. My mother had taken me to the MFA and the Gardner when I was younger, and we went to New York frequently—my parents kept an apartment there—so I had spent a lot of time in museums. But I can't say art was my passion before I met Alena. For her it was a mystery, in the sense of a religious mystery. She knew about all kinds of artists I'd never heard of—Donald Judd, Eva Hesse, Louise Bourgeois, Allan Kaprow. Joseph Beuys. People who were pushing art in new directions. It was thrilling to me, and learning about it through and with Alena made it twice as thrilling. Sometimes on weekends we would take the bus to New York and go to openings and performances she knew about. I had the key to our apartment, which made it easy.

"When summer came, I invited her to Nauquasset with me. My mother was thrilled I was bringing home a girl. I didn't tell her Alena was just a friend. Well, of course, she wasn't—she was much more than that.

"That summer I taught Alena to sail. She was good at it immediately. She had a natural sense for the wind, and she was strong, and nothing scared her. She had studied ballet, so she had balance and agility. But ballet was too old-fashioned for her. Too rigid. She had started making up her own dances, and then she decided she should have props—scarves and umbrellas and papier-mâché masks. She would take things from the beach to drape over herself—seaweed, and strings of shells that she would spend hours tying onto fishing line. She started doing these performances on the beach. I invited my high school friends.

She would make her entrance from the water, which meant she had to basically lie down in the shallows with only her face up, trying to look inconspicuous while the audience arrived. And then, when it was time, she would come out of the ocean and dance, leaping and crawling across the sand, draped in dead man's fingers and jingle shells.

"I had to keep up my archery, for the team. Alena wanted to learn that too, and I tried to teach her, but either I was a bad teacher or she didn't have a talent for it. Either way, she gave up, but she would hang around when I was practicing in the meadow behind our house, where I had set up a course with bales of straw and a target. I had gotten pretty good again. One day I hit five bull's-eyes in a row. Alena took the apple she'd been eating and balanced it on her head, and she said, *Let's play William Tell.* She said it would make a wonderful finale to one of her shows.

"Of course, I said no. It was crazy, no one was that accurate, certainly not me. But she wouldn't stop talking about it. She kept bringing it up. She teased me, saying I was a coward. Why should I be afraid if she wasn't? She said it didn't have to be a real apple. To make her point, she made a big model of an apple out of papier-mâché. It was about two feet high, and she made a kind of stand for it that fit like a crown on her head. She put it on and ran down to the end of the course. *Fraidy cat,* she called, when I wouldn't shoot. As though we were children. Which, of course, we were."

The level in the bottle had dropped alarmingly. This time Bernard poured, his hand steady as a hand of ice despite everything he had drunk. He filled both our glasses up to the rim so the viscous liquid curved up over the lip. I bent my head to drink, but he sat down and lifted his to his mouth, not spilling a drop.

"There was something else too," he said. "A boy. A surfer. I'd met him at the beach, and he'd offered to teach me to surf. He was older than me. He had done a year of community college, then dropped out and gotten a job somewhere and rented a room over the paint store. I said no at first, but then I wished I hadn't, and when he asked me again, I said yes. He took me surfing, and then we went back to his room, and he taught me about sex." That was all Bernard said, but I felt I could see it: the crooked room with its stained shag carpet; the lumpy bed, its striped sheets wrinkled and gritty; the yellowed window shade always pulled down to hide the view of the alley; the boom box on the floor with a pile of cassette tapes overflowing a cardboard box. On the bed, one boy arched over the other—Bernard's slim body braced yet pliant, fierce and alive, his amazed face buried in the musty pillow, his hair a mane for the surfer to grapple in his calloused hands.

"After that, I refused to go to the beach," Bernard said. "I wouldn't go into town. I was afraid of running into him, even though of course I was desperate to run into him too. Alena could see something had happened, but I wouldn't tell her what. I couldn't talk about it. And then one night, when my mother was out, she got a bottle of vodka and we went up to my room and drank it, and she made me tell her what had happened. She was like that—she was relentless, and seductive, and she placed her hand on my chest and stared into my eyes and said, *Tell me*. And so I told her. How she laughed! I don't know what I thought would happen—I guess that she would be appalled—but of course she didn't care. She just couldn't believe that this beautiful surfer boy wanted me and I was hiding in my room. She tried to make me go see him right then—she wanted us to go into town and find him. She said I was a coward—a *fraidy cat* again—a sissy. I'd been called that before, of course. I said I wasn't a sissy, and she said I was, I was afraid of my own desires, and I wouldn't even shoot a two-foot-high papier-mâché apple off her head! She was back to that again. *You have to do at least one,* she said. And so I got my equipment, and we walked down to the beach.

"It was a chilly night, but thank God the wind wasn't blowing. The flags were limp on their poles. She put the apple on her head, and I paced out thirty steps along the beach, and then I turned back and drew the bow. It felt effortless, the way Robin had taught us, though probably it was the vodka. And the rage, of course. I was so angry at Alena, and at the surfer, and, of course, at myself, that I didn't care what happened. I didn't care if I killed her, it would serve her right. I could almost see it—the arrow flying, burying itself in Alena's heart, and the stupid apple falling off as her body dropped to the sand with the arrow sticking up, quivering, like a stake in a vampire at the end of a movie.

"But if that happened, what would I do with her body? I decided I would get a tarp from the boat shed and wrap her up tight with some rocks, and take her out in the little boat we kept on the beach, out to the Plunge. That's a place we used to fish. A kettle. A kind of well in the bottom of the ocean floor."

"I know what the Plunge is," I said.

"I would dump her overboard," Bernard said. "And no one would ever know. So you see, it was all planned out a long time ago." All the time he was speaking, Bernard had one hand clenched loosely around his glass of gin and the other hand on the Formica surface of the table, moving it slowly, so slowly I couldn't see it move, but every time I looked, it was closer to mine until at last the tip of his middle finger nudged up against my own. For a moment we sat without speaking, connected like that. Even with just that tiny bit of him touching me, I seemed to feel his whole heavy weight, as though he were a drowning, flailing body I was trying to rescue in deep water.

"Go on," I said.

"I didn't miss. I drew the bow, and I loosed the arrow, and it shot right through the center of the apple and split it clean in two.

"Alena and I were closer than ever after that. I had passed her test,

I suppose. And she had freed me, because it was true, I stopped being afraid. After the surfer, there was another boy, the son of some friends of my parents. And after him, there were always boys, or men.

"Alena kept doing her performances. They got stranger, and more complicated, and she started inviting more people to watch. Grown-ups too, not just kids. Everywhere she went she met people. In coffee shops, on the beach, or just walking around town. She was practicing her charm, starting conversations with strangers. And now she was using all kinds of props—dead birds she found, and little paper cups that she would fill with paint or Kool-Aid and pour over herself. She started using the ocean not just as a backdrop. She would run in and out of the water, catching the surf in glass jars and setting them out in patterns, making little fires out of driftwood and burning origami fish that she had folded out of silver paper that made green sparks when it burned. Sometimes she burned real fish too, or dead birds, which made a terrible smell. These performances—*masquerades*, she called them—were part dance, part witchcraft, part burlesque. And they were utterly hypnotic.

"And then she got another idea. She would get into the water and ask someone to call out a number, and then she would have the group count to that number while she went under and waited for them to finish counting. We had to count very loud so she could hear us and know when to come back up. And after a while, people started yelling out higher and higher numbers, and once someone yelled out a hundred and fifty, and I tried to make the counting go faster, but I couldn't, and she made it all the way to the end, but then she just lay on the sand, half dead, and couldn't finish the masquerade.

"I made everybody go away.

"In the fall we went back to school. Both of us were studying art history. Alena claimed to be bored with the Roman architecture and the Italian Madonnas and the Dutch still lifes, but I loved all of it. Still, she kept bugging me to go away more and more often. One weekend we went to Philadelphia, where she had some friends in art school. We went to the art museum and stumbled on the Duchamps. And then one of the art students told us about the ICA, where they were having a show of Paul Thek, and we went to see that. We both got obsessed with Paul Thek: the casts of body parts, but also the complex small sculptures with lights and shells, and the paintings, and of course the meat. The work was so raw, and also so beautiful. It got Alena interested in objects again, which was a relief to me, after the masquerades. We started to fantasize about having our own gallery—or better yet, our own little museum, only not an ordinary museum. It would be small, intimate, devoted to the work of one artist at a time. Neither of us knew the word *Kunsthalle* then, but that was basically what we were dreaming up.

"And eventually, a long time later—I'm skipping over many things, of course—we opened the Nauk. I paid. Well, I could afford it. My mother had died, and Barbara and I had inherited everything. After college I worked at Christie's in New York for a while, and Alena worked for a couple of galleries, Janis Saunders and later Gagosian.

"In almost every important way, the Nauk was hers—Alena's. She chose the land, she worked closely with the architect, she designed the interior herself. She picked the artists she wanted to work with. We talked about all these things together, of course, but for the most part I followed her lead. She had an extraordinary eye—an instinct for what was interesting, a sense of which artists were about to take enormous leaps in their work. I was happy to be a part of it, and to see her happy." He paused, letting the word—*happy*—ring out. His eyes blazed with darkness, and the quiet of the room seethed.

"Go on," I said.

"I can't." Panic fluttered in his voice like a bat caught in a drape. "I can't. I shouldn't have told you any of this."

"You were happy . . ."

"Yes. We were happy! We lived happily ever after. The end!"

"Bernard." I pressed the tip of my finger against the tip of his. "Finish the story."

His tanned skin was chalky and his eye sockets looked too big for his face: dark pools someone might fall into and drown. He got up from the table and began opening all the cabinets. "Don't you have anything else to drink?"

"There's rum above the broom cupboard." The rum had come with the house, a sticky, half-empty gallon of Captain Morgan.

"I hate rum," he said, pulling it down.

I tried to smile. "And I thought you were a sailor."

"Sailors only drank rum because it was all they had."

"I think you really missed sailing these last two years," I said. "Chris told me how much you loved to sail." It felt strange saying his name, and I stumbled over it. I wondered if Bernard noticed. I wanted him to. I couldn't remember, anymore, why I had wanted to keep any secrets from him.

"Chris believes Alena committed suicide," he said. He stood drawn up in the corner where the broom cupboard was, the jug of rum hugged to his chest, his limp hair as gray as dust in the pulsing light.

"Yes."

"Do you think he really does? Really believes that? Maybe he'll wake up tomorrow and believe something else."

"Sit down," I said.

"I should go home."

"Bernard," I said. "Sit down."

He looked at me doubtfully, like a dog eyeing a newspaper. Then he crossed the frayed linoleum and sat, pouring an inch of rum into both our glasses. It smelled like cough syrup and rancid butter. We drank.

Then he laid his hand back on the table where it had been, where mine still was. Again our fingers touched. And he went on.

"It wasn't until we had been open for maybe a decade that things began to change. Alena began to be more and more interested in working with a different kind of artist. People who were doing things that were darker, more violent, more extreme than artists we had shown before. More to do with the body. Of course, the art world has always had room for that strain of work. But the new generation—people like Galindo working with blood, or Ron Athey's S&M spectacle, or Daria Angel's knife dances—it started to seem to me that it was the extremity alone that interested them. And what interested Alena. Maybe it had to do with getting old. She was approaching fifty. Well, we both were. Alena had always enjoyed showing off her body as though it were a valuable possession, but suddenly the value of that possession had plummeted. That was intriguing to her, even as it was dismaying, and I think that was part of what rekindled her interest in the body, her own and other people's. She wanted to do a show of Iris Vertigo, and I didn't want to, and we argued, but in the end we did it. And then she wanted to do a show of Kira O'Reilly, and we argued again. And then we were arguing about every show. It seemed to her, she said, that I was smothering her creative impulses. And it seemed to me that all she wanted to do was to push me, to propose shows I didn't want to do because she knew I wouldn't want to do them.

"And then we seemed to be back where we had been so long ago, with her calling me a coward. *You've lost your edge,* she said. *You just want to play it safe. You want to live in your comfortable house and keep everything clean like all the other rich people!*

"It was around this time that Alena met Morgan McManus. I was relieved at first. Before that, I had noticed that Roald, who'd worked for us for years, had started looking at her differently—as though he were cold and she were a fire. Well, lots of men have looked at her like that. But Roald! I was angry at her. I could see the way she kept touching him, whispering to him. I told her to leave him alone, but she just laughed. And then one day he called and said he wouldn't be at work, he'd had an accident." Bernard shut his eyes, his long lashes stiff and bristly as straw.

"So I was glad at first when McManus showed up to occupy her. He started stopping by the Nauk, hanging around. You couldn't help noticing him. Alena was intrigued by him—how he could have a different body, basically, every time he showed up. I didn't see it that way. I used to say he was just changing his clothes.

"Alena did a studio visit with him and encouraged his work. She saw him emerging from the tradition of Paul Thek—which superficially he was, I guess, but without, in my opinion, the depth or vision Thek had. We argued about that. About McManus. By then, after so many years, it was established between us that she was the one with the eye, and I was the money guy. She had the daring sensibility. I was amenable. That had been our shtick for a long time, and when it was a shtick, it was fine. But somewhere along the line, it had hardened. It had become, for all intents and purposes, our reality.

"And then there were the drugs. We'd both done a lot of experimenting, of course. LSD, Ecstasy, mushrooms. And then cocaine, increasingly, as the eighties wore on. At a certain point we both cut way back. We had seen too many people, artists especially, disappear down that dark hole. Alcohol was good enough for us, we agreed, or grass. I didn't even smoke pot for years, though Alena liked to, she had a steady supply. But McManus was into all kinds of drugs. He was in tremendous pain all the time, Alena said—real pain and phantom pain, though I guess phantom pain is real enough. He took Vicodin and OxyContin and phenobarbital. He liked cocaine, and he dabbled in meth, and he did heroin sometimes—just now and then, Alena said, when the pain was unendurable. But how many people take heroin just now and then?

"And then Alena started showing up for work high on one thing or another. Agnes would cover for her, saying she had called and was running late, or that she was sick, but half the time she had no more idea where Alena was than I did. If she was downstairs in her rooms, Agnes could go wake her up and try to get her dressed. After a while, she was doing that almost every day—going down there and dragging Alena out of bed, pouring coffee down her throat, running the shower. But if Alena wasn't there—if she was at McManus's, or somewhere else—well, there wasn't anything to do.

"One night Alena showed up at my house and said she was giving McManus a show. That's what she said—*she* was giving him one. I said no, she wasn't. We weren't. I had never said that quite so baldly before. I had tried to argue her out of doing certain exhibitions, but if she insisted, I always acquiesced. But not McManus. Not those recorded agonies and fake bits of gore and derivative corpses. No.

"And so, again, we had the old argument. That dull, exhausting, endless wrangle about risk and edginess, bravery and cowardice, and about, always, *the next thing*. What it would be.

"We were in the living room, I remember, and the doors were open, and we could hear the waves rolling in. We were leaving for Venice the next day, for the Biennale. I had been looking forward to that—to getting away from the Nauk for a week or so. Getting Alena away. We always had a good time at the Biennale, and I thought it would be good for us. But now she told me that she had changed her ticket so we weren't traveling together. She had a friend she wanted to see in Paris, she said, and there were a couple of shows. A couple of performance pieces. She said—I hardly noticed that she said this, she slipped it into the conversation when I was already angry, but I've thought about it often enough since—she was thinking about going back to performance herself. She had an idea that had been going around in her head, and she thought if she saw these particular pieces, it would help her think it through. She would stay a day or two, then get a flight to Venice. Or, if she couldn't get a flight on such short notice, she would take the train.

"I told her I was disappointed. I said I hoped she'd come to Venice soon. And she said, why should she come when I wasn't going to want to have any fun. She meant drugs, parties. She was taunting me, telling me again that I had gotten old, that I'd lost whatever daring I'd once had. She took out the little silver vial where she kept her coke, and a silver tray, and she laid out a couple of lines. *You won't even do a little coke, will you?* she said.

"Well, I did the coke. Why not? It was an easy enough gesture to make, and I missed the energy it gave me. The sense that everything was within reach. I used to feel that way a lot, even without coke, but it seemed to me that night that I couldn't remember the last time I'd felt it. And of course, we'd had a lot to drink. I thought—it was stupid of me—but I thought once I did the lines she'd shut up about the rest, about edginess, and cowardice, but that wasn't what happened. That was just the beginning.

"She started to go on about McManus. She said what a great artist he was, and how the Nauk show would make him an art-world star, and how anyone who couldn't see it had scales on his eyes! Maybe she was just trying to work me up. I told her she was wrong, that she was the one who was blind, that McManus had her fooled. He was a charlatan, she was in love with his ruined flesh, his freakishness. I wish I hadn't said that, but I did.

"And she said—Alena said—*You're not the man I knew!* You're not the man who shot the apple from my head. The brave archer. I've always remembered that, she said. That beautiful night. That grand gesture!

I have never felt so alive, she said, *as standing on the beach that night as you drew your bow.*

"And, after a while, I gave in.

"The night was overcast, no stars, but the clouds formed a milky dome over the beach that seemed to cast its own eerie glow. *A good night for ghosts,* Alena said. *Maybe we'll see Maria Hallett,* she said. Alena had always wanted to see Maria Hallett's ghost.

"*There's no such thing as ghosts,* I said.

"There was no papier-mâché apple that night, just a real apple Alena had taken from the kitchen when I went to get my bow. It had been a long time since I had drawn it, but it felt good in my hands. It felt right as I strung it, like an old friend I was meeting again after a long absence. I felt—it's terrible to say it—young again, and I thought maybe Alena was right. Maybe, I thought, we could go back to the beginning—that this could fix things between us. This act. This one bow shot.

"From thirty paces, standing in the cloudy dark, Alena was beautiful. She wore a white dress embroidered with tiny red beads, and those pink plastic go-go boots she loved, that she had bought on eBay, and that were good for the beach because you could hose the sand off them. She was smiling, though I remember that I thought even then that it wasn't the smile I had expected. It wasn't joyful but rather a smile of calculated satisfaction, the smile not of the bride but of the mother of the bride, watching the wedding go like clockwork.

"And then I drew. I was picturing already how we would walk back to the house together, and maybe open a bottle of something, and talk. I remembered that she had said she was thinking about a performance, about creating a piece, and I thought I would ask her about it, not realizing we were already in the middle of it.

"I lined up the shot. It felt effortless, intuitive, just the way it was supposed to feel. But as I let the arrow fly a noise startled me, a sort of cry. Something white disappeared into the dunes—a cloud of hair, maybe. And when I looked back, Alena was on the ground with the arrow in her throat.

"I ran down the beach. Already the sand was dark with blood, and a terrible sound came from the hole in Alena's throat. Almost anywhere else I could have hit her would have been better than that. In what seemed like a few moments, though I don't know, really, how long it was, she was dead.

"Of course—I should have called for help. Of course! She might have been saved somehow. But I doubt it. And anyway, I panicked. The boat was right there, on the beach where it always was, and the tarp was in the boat shed, and there were rocks scattered on the sand. The plan was already in place. It had waited in my head all those years for its moment, and now that moment had come."

Bernard shut his eyes. He put his head down on the table. I sat, unable to speak, as if I too had an arrow buried in my throat. My finger was numb where, unfeelingly, it still touched his. I wanted urgently to take my hand away, but I didn't. It seemed to me that if I moved it, if I took myself away from him, Bernard would collapse right there in the kitchen, a man of ash.

I covered his hand with my own. "It wasn't your fault," I said. "It was what she meant to happen."

He head was still on the table, but he moved it back and forth, indicating no.

"It was," I said. "It was her last grand gesture! Her great performance. And if McManus had gotten her message in time, if he had come earlier, the world would have seen it. A terrible stunt, or a great work of contingency art—who knows? But he wasn't there. You did what you did, and no one saw. No one but Old Ben, who can't tell the present from the past, fact from imagination. Chris Passoa thinks she killed herself. In a way, she did kill herself. You were just the instrument she chose."

His voice was muffled by the table. "No."

"Yes. It's over. You can get up tomorrow, and come to work, and start again."

He sat up slowly. His eyes were black stones in his gray face. Vacancies. "It's too late," he said. "Alena was right. I've lost whatever courage I once had. I can't start over. I tried. Finding you, bringing you here. I thought it could be done. I felt all right in Venice, showing you the Scrovegni Chapel, seeing the light in your eyes. The dawning of something.

"But once we got back here, I could see it was a mistake. She was everywhere. Alena. In every room, in every view, in the sound of the waves. I even thought, not for the first time, of turning myself in, but I couldn't do it. I couldn't stand it, I had to leave. That's why I ran off almost as soon as we arrived. I kept thinking about her out there in the Plunge, her body devoured, her bones caught in their plastic shroud, maybe drifting free. Assuming I even had the place right in the dark. Assuming no storm stirred up the ocean floor, changed the geography. But that's what happened."

"It doesn't matter," I said. "Yes, the storm came up. The bones washed up. None of it matters. It was an accident! It was suicide by proxy. You might as well have been driving a bus she jumped in front of!"

"She didn't know she was going to die."

"She left it to chance. That was how she wanted it. You read the quotation. She died as part of a piece of art."

We were quiet, thinking about that. And then Bernard said, "It's so strange how you can't hear the ocean from here. I wouldn't have thought it was possible."

"I hate it," I said. "I've hated it all summer."

"Why didn't you say anything?"

"Oh, what does it matter?"

"We could have exchanged houses. Every time I hear the ocean, it's like hearing her voice. It's as though she's been diffused into Cape Cod Bay, so that every time a wave washes up, she's back again."

"No," I said. "It's not like that at all. She's gone! For two years you've held her inside you, she's been burning through you like acid, destroying you. But now that you've told me, it won't be like that anymore." I took his hand and tugged at it, that cold shred of flesh. "Come on," I said. "I'll show you. It will be all right. Let's go down to the beach right now. There are no ghosts. I'll show you."

He let me pull him heavily to his feet, let me drag him across the linoleum to the door, steady him over the threshold and down the crooked steps.

The night was cold, clear, still, like a night in a paperweight. A million stars pricked the blackness with their icy tongues. As we came around the side of the house, the sound of the bay rose up out of the darkness, and Bernard stopped where he was as if frozen, a man not of ash but of frost and rime, arctic-hearted, snow-blind. A glacial prince.

Off to the east, where the Nauk hulked on its dune, an orange glow spread across the low horizon. "Is the Nauk burning?" Bernard asked. Hope rasped in his voice like a wasp in winter. Every instant the color of the sky shifted, lightening from shade to shade like a clarinet rising through shimmering octaves.

But it wasn't fire, or music, or any other human fabulation stippling the world with beauty.

"No," I said. "It's just morning."

Acknowledgments

I am grateful to Ingrid Schaffner and Rob Tuchmann for their attentive reading of this manuscript and their astute recommendations. Susie Merrell read an early draft and saw what was missing; Ira Pastan offered advice on birds, boats, and underwater geography; Linda Pastan reviewed every revision. Special gratitude to Harvey Pastan, who suggested a solution to a difficult plot point. And many thanks to everyone at the Institute of Contemporary Art at the University of Pennsylvania, who gave me an education in an unknown world; any mistakes or misapprehensions about contemporary art are entirely my own.